A WOMAN WORTH TEN COPPERS

MORGAN HOWELL

BALLANTINE BOOKS • NEW YORK

A Woman Worth Ten Coppers is a work of fiction. Names, characters, places, and incidents are the products of the author's imagination or are used fictitiously. Any resemblance to actual events, locales, or persons, living or dead, is entirely coincidental.

A Del Rey Books Mass Market Original

Copyright © 2008 by William H. Hubbell

Published in the United States by Del Rey Books, an imprint of The Random House Publishing Group, a division of Random House, Inc., New York.

DEL REY is a registered trademark and the Del Rey colophon is a trademark of Random House, Inc.

ISBN 978-0-345-50396-1

Printed in the United States of America

www.delreybooks.com

OPM 9 8 7 6 5 4 3 2 1

This book is dedicated to
Kaaren Anderson
and
Scott Tayler,
who serve as Bearers
in the everyday world

Praise for The Queen of the Orcs: King's Property by Morgan Howell

"Howell has created a fascinating, believable world and a compassionate, kick-ass heroine who helps the weak and uses wit and agility to survive and triumph."
—*Booklist*

"Every once in a while, a novel comes along with a character that I absolutely love. [Dar] is such a character. She is fierce, protective, passionate, scarred, loyal, and wise. . . . I truly loved *King's Property* and I highly recommend it."
—Fantasy Debut

"Author Morgan Howell has created an outstanding foundation for the next two books to build upon. . . . Be warned, you will NOT want to put down this story."
—huntressreviews.com

"An unusual tale . . . Howell's depiction of orc culture is fascinating—these orcs are as big, strong, and dangerous as any in fantasy, but they also have moral and ethical issues of importance. This is not a book to read for fun on a rainy night—it's a book to think about."
—ELIZABETH MOON, Nebula Award–winning author of *The Deed of Paksenarrion*

"Dar never loses our admiration and compassion—qualities at the heart of any struggling hero. *King's Property* tests your own presumptions of 'the other' and brings to mind the cultural prejudices and wars born from betrayal that are so sadly evident throughout our own history."
—KARIN LOWACHEE, author of *Warchild*

"In a crowded field, Howell has succeeded in creating an original and vivid fantasy. [The] characters display unexpected depths of humanity—even when they're not human. I was captivated by Dar. Highly recommended."
—NANCY KRESS, Nebula Award–winning author of *Beggars in Spain*

By Morgan Howell

A Woman Worth Ten Coppers

THE QUEEN OF THE ORCS TRILOGY
King's Property
Clan Daughter
Royal Destiny

Oh Goddess, cup your hands about me!
Tumult fills this world,
and I am but a candle in the storm.
—*The Scroll of Karm*

NAMELESS
LANDS

Turgen River

GREY FENS

Midge River

Serpent River

THE EMPTY LANDS

WESTERN REACH

■ IRON PALACE

BAHLAND

✕ TOR'S
GATE

▦ CARA'S HALL

AVEREN

YIM'S JOURNEY---

ONE

THE WAGON resembled a tiny house on wheels. Pots and other wares dangled from its eaves and clanked against the rig's wooden sides as it slowly ascended the mountain road. By dusk, the driver reached his destination, a lonely hut perched near the edge of a cliff. A circle of half-buried stones surrounded the structure, marking it as a Wise Woman's home. After halting the horses, the driver remained seated and chanted under his breath. The verses were supposed to bring tranquillity. They failed, for the man was convinced that the hut didn't mark the end of a long and arduous journey, but rather the beginning of a far more perilous one.

The man stopped chanting when he heard a door close and footsteps on the frozen ground. He turned to see a white-haired woman approach. She halted and scrutinized him. "The wagon looks right," she said at last, "but you don't look the peddler."

The man bowed his head respectfully. "I'm a Seer, Mother."

"Aye, you have that temple softness to you." The woman sighed. "So, no skill with arms?"

"None at all. The goddess will protect her."

The woman shook her head. "Nothing's certain. As a Seer, you should know that better than I."

"I'll do my utmost," said the Seer. "I was told I'm to play her father."

"Aye, so show her no deference. That could betray her.

And you should leave the morrow. When spring comes, the roads will turn to mud."

"Where shall I take her?"

"South."

"Toward trouble?"

"Aye, indeed. But that's what's been revealed."

"And nothing more?"

"Not yet. Until then, best you pick the road. When she makes choices, her heart sways her overmuch."

The man turned his gaze southward before descending from his seat. The ground dropped just a few paces away, and from his perch, the ridges of the highlands looked like crumpled garments cast from the peaks above. Below, a small village nestled in one fold, its homes already shuttered for the night. The plains beyond were obscured as the world turned dark.

The hut's door opened, spilling light and catching the man's attention. Someone peered from the doorway. "Is that her?" he whispered.

"Aye," replied the Wise Woman. She raised her voice. "Yim! Come here."

The Seer studied the advancing figure. *She's only a girl!* he thought, judging her age as eighteen winters. He feared her appearance would draw attention, for she was lithe and comely, with large dark eyes and flowing hair. She wore a shift of gray wool, a matching cloak, and sturdy boots. In peddler fashion, her cloak was festooned with ribbons, each lightly stitched in place to permit quick removal and sale. They fluttered as she walked.

"Yim, tend the horses," said the Wise Woman. "This man will show you how." Then the elderly woman sought the warmth of the hut, leaving the two alone.

"Have you ever fed a horse?" asked the Seer.

"Only goats and sheep," replied Yim, regarding the animals warily.

"I'll show you what to do. Follow me." The Seer walked

to the back of the wagon, opened its door, and retrieved two cloth sacks with straps attached. "These are nose bags," he said. "They fit on the horses' heads so they can feed in harness." He uncovered a large barrel affixed to the wagon's rear. It contained oats and a scoop. "Put two full scoops in each bag."

After Yim did that, the Seer demonstrated how to attach a bag. Then he observed Yim carefully as she affixed the other one. While she appeared intimidated by the horse, she didn't shrink from it. That was all he could observe, despite his heightened powers of perception. Realizing that Yim's inner qualities were veiled against his gaze, he sought to probe her through conversation. "Your guardian said we should leave tomorrow. Are you familiar with the roads?"

"I've never been more than a day's journey from here." Yim turned her eyes toward the plains, which were black beneath the fading sky. Her gaze lingered there as though she saw something within the shadows. The Seer noticed that Yim froze as a fawn does at the scent of wolves. After a moment, she stirred and said, "So, you spoke with my guardian. What did she say about me?"

"Very little."

"Did she tell you I lack sense?"

"No."

A wry smile passed over Yim's lips. "She will, ere we depart."

They headed out at first light after receiving a terse farewell from the Wise Woman, who retreated to the hut before the wagon reached the road. The Seer drove the team from the broad seat at the wagon's front. Yim sat next to him, bundled against the cold in her cloak and gazing at familiar scenery that she would never see again. It was a long while before she spoke.

"I know that I must call you 'Father,' but is your true name Theodus?"

"No. Why do you ask?"

"That name was revealed to me. I'm supposed to follow his footsteps. Since you're my guide, I thought my vision referred to you."

"The goddess is your guide. I merely drive the wagon."

"My guardian said you're a Seer. Doesn't Karm speak to you?"

"I find children for service in the temple. I've never had a vision."

"So how do you know where to take me?"

"I don't. Karm will tell you what path to take."

"But my vision only said to head southward. I thought that you would . . ." Yim's face reddened. "If you don't know where to take me, why did you bother to come?"

"The Wise Woman sent for me. She said you were ready."

"Well I'm not, if I'm supposed to know the way. You're a Seer. Why didn't you foresee that?"

"The future's not ordained. The most a Seer can hope to foretell is what's likely. I can't even do that."

Yim sighed. "Then what's likely is that we'll wander for moons. I haven't had a vision since autumn, and my visions often make little sense. Sometimes I'm shown things I don't understand. Even when Karm appears to me or I hear her voice, her guidance isn't always useful. How can I follow Theodus if I've never met him?"

"Time often reveals a vision's meaning," replied the Seer. "Time and contemplation."

"That's not much use nigh sunset when the road forks and you must choose which way to take."

Yim resumed gazing at the landscape. Though it remained in winter's grip, patches of bare earth had appeared beneath the barren trees. The palette of gray, brown, and dirty white matched Yim's pessimistic mood, and it was a while before she made another attempt at conversation. Turning to the Seer, she asked. "Have you done this often?"

"What?"

"Delivered girls to their destinies."

"There have been no other girls. There will be no others."

"But the Wise Woman said I'm no one special."

"You're Karm's servant, as are we all, and humility befits a servant," replied the Seer. "Yet the goddess chose you alone for this task. You mustn't fail."

"If the goddess wants me to succeed, how can I fail?"

"Karm's benevolent, but the world is not. If men are to be free, then they must be free to choose evil, and many have. It's always a struggle to fulfill the goddess's will."

Yim sighed. "I've heard that talk all my life. I thought I was leaving it behind."

The Seer gave Yim a sympathetic look. "Was it hard living with the Wise Woman?"

"Hard enough."

Yim's thoughts turned to her upbringing. It had been not only hard, but also unusual. She knew the name and virtue of every herb, where each grew, and when to harvest it, but she had never played a game or had a single friend. Yim had been a small child when she was given to the Wise Woman, and for a long while, she had believed her life was normal. True, she had never known her mother, and her father vanished after the Wise Woman took charge, but being young and living in isolation, she took her circumstances for the way of things. Thus she thought all girls were taught to read and learned secret arts that they must never mention. She even assumed that everyone had visions.

Over time, Yim shed those illusions. As she grew older, Yim accompanied her guardian not only when she gathered herbs, but also when she practiced healing or midwifery. Through those excursions to nearby farms and to the village, Yim made contact with girls her age. They had some things in common: Like them, Yim had been taught to cook, mend clothes, and tend animals. She also knew how to make cheese, a common accomplishment in the highlands. However, none of the girls could read, and Yim doubted they had late-night lessons in even more arcane arts. But the girls differed most from Yim in that they would spend their lives in the highlands and Yim knew that wasn't to be her fate.

"You've been singled out," said the Wise Woman when Yim reached her twelfth winter, "and all your life has been preparation for one task."

"And what's that?" asked Yim.

"It's your duty to bear a child."

Yim knew better than to laugh, but she had witnessed too many births to see any uniqueness in that. The Wise Woman seemed to read Yim's thoughts, for she added, "The goddess will choose the father, and you will go to him."

Since parents arranged marriages, the Wise Woman's revelation seemed only a twist to the common custom. Yim imagined that she would be matched to some holy man and saw her secret lessons as preparation for her role as his spouse. At twelve, the prospect of marriage didn't enthuse Yim, and it still didn't when she grew to womanhood. Having received no love from her stern and taciturn guardian, Yim had little expectation of receiving it from a man. She felt that only the goddess loved her. Karm seemed like the mother for whom Yim had always yearned. It was for the goddess's sake that Yim acquiesced to her duty.

Yet after her conversation with the Seer, it was starkly apparent that she had embarked on a journey with no concrete destination to find someone unknown to her. It was a distressing prospect, and duty seemed a poor reason for doing something so rash. *I never chose this path,* she thought. *I was raised to follow it without question.* Yet Yim did question what she was doing. She knew she couldn't go back, but she didn't have to go forward. Wavering, Yim considered her alternatives.

Women without kin had no standing, which was why she was masquerading as the Seer's daughter. A lone woman might become a servant, but being in no position to bargain, she'd end up little better than a slave. *At least I'd be safe*. When Yim imagined such a life, she thought it wouldn't be any harder than her former one. But by choosing it, she would be thinking only of herself, and Yim found that hard to do. She had pined for human contact throughout her lonely childhood and had tasted it only when she began assisting the Wise Woman with healing. Yim's role had been to comfort the sick or injured through simple acts of caring— preparing a meal, cooling a feverish brow, or holding a trembling hand. She soon discovered that such deeds sustained her as much as they did those she comforted, for compassion created bonds with others.

That compassion made Yim consider the Seer beside her. He had a drawn look, with skin that hung loosely on his stubble-covered face and eyes that possessed the vacant gaze of the weary. Yim surmised that he was unaccustomed to hardship and the road to the highlands had worn him down. *He's ill suited for this journey, but he undertook it*. In envisioning his disappointment if she abandoned her quest, Yim found a reason to continue it. She could make the Seer's sacrifice worthwhile by striving to fulfill its purpose. Additionally, she could ease his hardship on the road by gathering wood, tending the horses, and cooking. It was a meager rationale, but since it involved giving comfort, it seemed more compelling than mere duty. In the end, it helped Yim decide to go on.

Having made up her mind, Yim felt she should speak to the Seer and say something that assured him that she appreciated his efforts. As she tried to find the words, he began chanting softly in some archaic tongue that was mostly nonsense to her. Yim waited for him to stop, but he kept at it. Eventually, she tired of waiting and retreated inside the wagon. There, she wrapped herself in a blanket and slept to escape her boredom.

When Yim awoke, she rejoined the Seer. He was still

chanting. Yim gazed about and found the countryside unfamiliar. Having entered strange territory made her decision seem irrevocable. Yim's apprehensions heightened, and she wanted to know what she faced. To that end, Yim studied the chanting man who was taking her onward. She sensed he was hiding things from her. *Just like my guardian,* she thought. But Yim had the skill to see beneath surfaces and discerned that the Seer had some inkling of what lay ahead. Underneath his calm exterior, she glimpsed fear.

TWO

DESPITE YIM'S misgivings, the journey was easy at first. Her apprehensions eased as the horses pulled the wagon at a steady pace over the frozen road and the novelty of travel replaced her dreary life in the Wise Woman's hut. Whenever she gazed northward toward her former home, she saw the Cloud Mountains that rose high above it. Even when she could no longer see the highlands, the mountains stood out, white with snow against a gray sky.

The Seer continued heading southward through a rolling plain that was often wooded but seldom cultivated. Yim knew nothing about this country until the Seer told her a little of its history. The sparsely settled lands south of the highlands were called the Northern Reach. In former times, they comprised the northernmost extent of the Empire. Farther south were realms that still belonged to the Empire, but in name only. The emperor's authority had so faded that folk looked elsewhere for strength. They found it in warlords, petty nobles, their kin, or not at all, depending on where they lived. The Seer recited the names of realms and towns—the duchies of Lurwic, Walstur, and Basthem; the province of Argenor; the towns of Larresh, Kambul, and Durkin; the county of Falsten; the Eastern and Western Reaches; the empty province of Luvein; and others—until Yim learned them. Still, they remained only names to her with no sense of place about them.

Yim fell into her role of a peddler's daughter, and as such she made the Seer's journey easier. He drove the wagon, but she did nearly everything else. After she learned how to hitch up the horses, that became her job as well as caring for them. Yim gathered wood for the campfire, lit it, and cooked upon its flames. On the few occasions when strangers approached them, she usually did the talking. This role became hers by default, for the Seer was a reticent man, while she had a knack for fabricating stories.

The Seer proved an odd traveling companion. He was unworldly for a man of over fifty winters, but he knew how to handle a team and wagon. He wouldn't reveal his name, insisting that "Father" sufficed. He spoke little and spent much of his time chanting so softly that Yim couldn't make out his words. Usually the chants sounded like a quiet drone, which Yim found easy to ignore. But when they took on a fervent, pleading tone, she found them troubling. Yim seldom spoke to anyone other than the Seer, for he chose those roads that avoided settlements. He claimed he did this because what wares he had were purely for display and a peddler who turned away customers would arouse suspicion.

The items dangling from the wagon's eaves and the ribbons stitched on Yim's cloak were the only "wares" they carried. The wagon's interior was piled with provisions for a long journey. There were sacks containing oats for the horses and grain to make porridge. A large barrel held salt mutton. Additionally, there were several crates of brandy. Yim and the Seer slept wedged between those supplies within the wagon. It made for cramped quarters, and Yim looked forward to warmer weather, when she could sleep outdoors.

Yim never touched the brandy, but she made good use of it. Like a dutiful daughter, she brought a bowl of it for the Seer to drink while she gathered wood and prepared the evening meal. She also refilled his bowl throughout the evening. Drink cheered the Seer up. Moreover, it loosened his tongue so that he sometimes answered Yim's questions. Over successive evenings, she teased out bits of information. She learned that the Wise Woman had corresponded with the temple for years; that visions were extremely rare and it was rarer still to have more than one; that the worship of Karm had been on a long decline; that the new emperor had forsaken the goddess; and that war raged in the west.

By the twelfth day of the journey, the Cloud Mountains were no longer visible on the horizon and damp winds blew from the south. They whipped about the ribbons on Yim's cloak so vigorously that she shed it and wrapped herself with a blanket. By evening, Yim was thoroughly chilled, and she gathered extra wood for a large fire. The Seer gulped his brandy to warm himself, and was glassy-eyed even before Yim started cooking.

As Yim prepared dinner, she noticed the Seer's bleary gaze and began posing questions. "What's Karm's temple like?"

"What did the Wise Woman tell you?"

"That it's far away. That Seers and Sarfs and other holy folk train there. That Karm used to have other temples, but now it's the only one."

"That's all?"

"Yes."

"Then that's all you should know," said the Seer, taking another gulp of brandy.

Though the porridge was done, Yim kept on stirring it and watching the Seer drink. After she refilled his bowl a second time, she said, "So I'm to know nothing about the temple, while those at the temple know everything about me."

"Not so," mumbled the Seer. "Only Seers know of you, and only a few of them."

"So you're one of the select?" asked Yim, making sure that she sounded impressed.

The Seer puffed up a bit. "I am. I've known of you since I was trained."

"And when was that?"

"Over forty winters ago."

Before I was born! thought Yim. When she spoke again, she had to struggle to keep her voice even. "And who told you?"

"My master. He learned it from his master. It's an old secret."

"How old?"

The Seer shrugged. "Old."

Yim felt stunned, and when she ladled out the porridge, her hand shook. The Seer didn't notice, being more than a little drunk. While he wolfed down his food, Yim served herself. Despite her empty belly, the Seer's revelation so occupied her thoughts that her porridge was cold before she tasted it. Nothing had changed, but Yim saw her situation in an entirely different light. It was as if she had been blithely walking down a narrow path at night when a lightning flash revealed abysses on either side. Every step thereafter felt different. While her new knowledge couldn't aid her, it made Yim feel burdened by fate and the expectations of strangers. She understood at last why the Wise Woman had been so closemouthed. Yim wished with all her heart that the Seer had been the same.

The next morning, Yim warmed leftover porridge for herself and the Seer, then hitched up the horses after cleaning the pot. The sky was clear for the first time since she left the highlands, and a mild breeze was melting the last patches of snow. But this first taste of spring did little to ease Yim's brooding. *I'm only an ant on a leaf in a river.* She felt helpless and ignorant. All she could hope for was that Karm would send her a vision that would make sense of things. Riding down the thawing road, she silently prayed for one.

In the late afternoon, the road took them through a tiny village. They were nearly past it when a man called out. "Hey, birdie, how much are your ribbons?"

"A copper apiece," Yim called back. It was a price that discouraged buyers.

"That's dear," said the man as he ambled toward the wagon. His weather-beaten face had a prominent scar running down one cheek, and a long dagger hung from his leather jerkin. He grinned. "Sure they're worth it?"

"Finest in the Empire," replied Yim.

"Well, hop down and let me take a look."

The Seer reined the wagon to a halt, and Yim climbed down to the muddy road. There, the man glanced at the ribbons tacked to Yim's cloak, but he seemed mostly to gaze at her. His look made Yim uneasy. After a while, he grabbed a wide red-and-yellow ribbon tacked near Yim's collar. "My woman would fancy this one."

"Let go, and I'll have my father remove it."

"No need," said the man. He drew his dagger, and passing its blade close to Yim's throat, cut the ribbon, leaving its stub still stitched to Yim's cloak. Then he sheathed the blade, opened the purse that dangled from his belt, and took out a single coin. "Here's yer copper."

Yim palmed it and quickly climbed back on the wagon.

"Where ye headed, old man?"

"South," replied the Seer.

"Then ye should know the road's washed out nigh here. Ye'll need to take another way."

"What way is that?" asked the Seer.

"After ye reach the woods, there's a lane that forks left. There's only one, so ye can't miss it. 'Tis tight, but a wagon can pass. It heads east, afore turning south and west to join the road beyond the washout."

The Seer nodded his head. "Thank you for that advice." Then he shook the reins, and the team headed out. After passing a series of fields, the travelers entered the woods and reached the fork. Yim peered down the narrow lane as the Seer guided the team toward it. "This way looks little used," she said.

"The ground's newly thawed," replied the Seer. "That explains the lack of wheel marks."

"I didn't trust that man. Nor his advice."

"His face was unsightly, but he dealt with you honestly. Don't be swayed by appearances," said the Seer. Still, he briefly hesitated before he shook the reins to make the horses advance. "It'll be dark soon. We'll want to be through this wood by then."

The dirt lane seemed little more than a footpath, and trees grew so close to it that the Seer had to take care not to wedge the wagon between them. The way was also muddy, and Yim often had to climb down and push the wagon while the Seer urged the horses forward. She kept expecting the lane to turn, but it continued running straight and eastward. It wasn't until dusk approached that Yim could see where the woods ended in the distance and the lane entered a grassy field. Yet until they reached that open space, the way was so hemmed by thick, tangled brush that it resembled a tunnel. In the fading light, it was nearly as dark as one.

Neither the Seer nor Yim saw the tree until they were quite close to it. Its trunk was no thicker than a man's arm, but it spanned the lane at waist height, effectively blocking the horses. The Seer drove the horses on, halting them just before they reached the barrier. Then he climbed down to examine it.

From her perch on the wagon's seat, Yim watched the Seer walk toward the tree. As he did, she spied movement in the brush and saw three dark shapes pushing through it. The shapes resolved into cloaked and hooded men. "Grab the trunk, old man," said one. "We'll help ye heave it."

"I'm obliged for your help," replied the Seer, seizing hold of the barrier.

As the strangers clustered around the Seer, something caught Yim's eye. Poking out from one of the hoods was a bit of ribbon. It was red and yellow. Recognizing it, Yim cried out, "Father!"

The Seer began to turn. Before he could face Yim, he gasped and jerked slightly to the rear. Then he moaned and his hands slipped from the tree trunk. Afterward, he stood still for a long moment, wobbling slightly, before his body twisted in Yim's direction. Then Yim could see the Seer's belly. The man who had bought the ribbon was pulling a dagger from it. The long blade was bloody to the hilt. The Seer moaned again and gazed at Yim with a face filled with surprise and anguish. Then he silently mouthed the words "I'm sorry" and collapsed.

Yim reacted instinctively. She leapt from the seat to the side of the lane farthest from the men and dashed into the surrounding brush. Twigs and branches clawed at her, scraping her face and hands. Each stride met resistance. The ribbons sewn on her cloak entangled in the brush before tearing free, so that Yim left a rainbow trail as she struggled forward. Yim could see that the brush was thinner ahead of her. With the strength born of panic, she pushed onward. *Soon I'll be able to run!*

Yim heard the thud of heavy footsteps and noise of large bodies crashing through twigs and branches. As she fled, Yim glanced about for something to use as a weapon and spied a fallen limb that might serve as a club. She rushed toward it as her pursuers sounded ever closer.

A hand gripped Yim's shoulder. Then she felt a sharp pain at the back of her skull. It seemed that lightning flashed inside her head, white hot and brilliant. The light quickly faded to red and then black. The world faded with it. When Yim crumpled to the ground, she was senseless.

THREE

WHEN YIM became conscious, her first sensation was of pain. Her head ached with dull throbs that pulsed from the back of her skull. They made her queasy, and she feared that she might throw up. When Yim attempted to move, she discovered that she was bound. Her cloak was gone and so were her boots and socks. For a moment, she was confused. Then, with a surge of terror, Yim recalled that they had been attacked. The memory of the Seer's murder came to her with the visceral impact of the actual moment: The blood-covered blade. His anguished parting look.

It was night and Yim was lying on her side in the wagon. She couldn't see her bonds, but she could feel them. Her wrists were tied behind her back with what felt like thick, coarse rope. Her ankles were bound also and roped to her wrists so that her body was bowed backward and her hands touched her cold, bare feet. It was an uncomfortable position, and it rendered her completely helpless.

Despair threatened to overwhelm Yim. After a lifetime of preparation, everything had gone awry in an instant. *How could Karm desert me so quickly?* she wondered with a mixture of resentment and disillusionment. *I was doing her will.* Yim felt the urge to scream or sob, but she stifled it. If she surrendered to fear, it would own her. Furthermore, the last thing she wanted to do was draw attention to herself. The robbers had taken her boots and cloak and tied her up, but they hadn't molested her. *Not yet,* Yim thought, fighting another wave of panic.

The wagon was moving. Yim worried about the horses, for they had been driven all day and were surely at their limit. It made her wonder if the robbers were ignorant about horses or spurred by desperation. *But what could they be fleeing from? No one will know or care that I've disappeared.*

All her captors were apparently sitting on the driver's bench, for Yim could hear their voices through the wall at the wagon's front. She couldn't make out what they were saying, but they seemed to be arguing. Their loud and slurred voices had a drunken tone, which made her guess that they had found the brandy.

Yim lay shivering for what seemed a very long time before the wagon halted. A few moments later, its rear door opened and moonlight spilled in on the wagon's ransacked interior. Sacks lay strewn about. Several had been slashed open. Yim saw a man's silhouette as he climbed into the wagon. In his hand was a bottle, which he put to his lips, upended, and drained. After tossing the bottle away, he reached into a crate and took out another. Yim made no sound and lay absolutely still, hoping that brandy was all the man wanted. The robber staggered back to the door and handed the bottle to another who stood outside. "Don' get so stinkin' ye get lost," said the man. Yim recognized his voice; he was the scar-faced man who had bought the ribbon.

"I know the way," replied the man on the ground, "drunk or sober."

"Then don' bother me till we're there. Got me some business."

Yim heard a laugh. "I'd like a bit o' that, too. Let me know when yer done."

"Stick to yer drivin'. This birdie's mine."

The door shut and it was dark again. Soon the wagon began to move. Yim heard boots crunching spilled grain and then a drunken voice softly calling as one might to a frightened cat. "Ribbon Girl. Purr-ty Ribbon Girl."

Yim remained silent as the man stumbled about in the

dark. She heard him trip and curse. Then a boot struck her knee. "Ah! There ye are."

Yim forced herself to be still and silent, then watched terror-stricken while the man moved so he straddled her. His shadowy form swayed unsteadily as he drew his long-bladed dagger and squatted to touch its cold blade against her neck. "Well, birdie, yer father walks the Dark Path. Wanna join 'im?"

"No," whispered Yim.

The man pressed the flat of the blade more firmly against her throat. "What?"

"I don't want to die."

The man pulled the blade away. "Then don' make me mad, 'cause it's no great loss if I slit yer throat." He used his dagger to cut the rope that bound Yim's wrists to her ankles. "Get on yer back."

The man stood aside so Yim could roll on her back and extend her cramped legs. She remained as helpless as before, for her wrists and ankles were still securely tied. Afterward, her captor dropped his dagger so he could use both hands to tug at her shift. He jerked its skirt upward to expose her shins and then her thighs. He didn't stop tugging until the fabric was bunched around her midsection and she was naked from the waist down. Then he clawed between her legs in a rough travesty of a caress. His touch made Yim shudder, and she clenched her teeth so as not to cry out.

When the man finished with his pawing, he untied the cord about the waist of his trousers, lowered them part-way, and flopped upon Yim as if he were falling into bed. He did nothing to soften the impact, which knocked the wind from her. When Yim gasped for air, she smelled the thick, sweet stench of drink on her assailant's breath. His face was so close to hers that she felt warmth each time he exhaled. "Girly, Girly, Ribbon Girly," he sang tunelessly as his heavy body pressed against hers. He felt as inert as a corpse. "Spread yer legs, Ribbon Girl."

"I can't," said Yim, her voice constricted by fright. "They're tied together."

"I said spread them!"

"I will! I will! Just cut my bonds."

The man began groping for his dagger and Yim had no idea if it was to cut her bonds or her throat. His hand struck the wagon's floor, feeling for the blade without finding it. The beat gradually slowed, then stopped altogether. By then, the man's stubbly cheek rested against Yim's. It remained there as he became dead weight. Yim held herself absolutely still—except for a tremor that she was unable to control—although the mere touch of the man's bare thighs against hers was repellent. After a while, her abuser's breathing became regular. Soon, he was snoring loudly and wetting her face with his drool. Meanwhile, the wagon rolled onward.

Throughout the remainder of the night, Yim lay beneath the unconscious man. Lying still was agonizing, but she didn't dare move for fear of reviving her attacker and causing him to finish what he had begun. Yim couldn't sleep or even rest. Every moment, she expected her nightmare to begin anew.

Eventually the sun rose and the wagon halted. Someone pounded on its door. The pounding continued until the man atop Yim moaned. Then he shouted, "Stop yer noise!" He moaned again. "Oh my head!" He rose, pulled up his pants, found his dagger, and sheathed it. Then he gazed down at Yim with bloodshot eyes. She was still half naked. "Well Ribbon Girl, did I tup ye proper?"

Yim faked a smile. "Yes."

"Good," replied the man. "Wish I remembered it."

The pounding resumed, though more softly than before. "I found a buyer for the oats and grain."

As Yim wiggled in an attempt to pull down her shift, her abuser swung open the wagon's door. Outside were one of his accomplices and a man who was missing an eye. "What's yer offer?"

"Afore I say, I want to see the goods."

The man in the wagon extended his hand. "Then climb up and take a look."

By the time the one-eyed man entered the wagon, Yim had managed to get her shift over her legs and was looking out the open door. She saw low, squalid buildings packed tightly together. They were built of timber and wattle and flanked both sides of a dirt lane that reeked of sewage. At the lane's edges, men and women seemed gathering for an open-air market where all of the goods for sale were used.

Yim glanced at the buyer and saw that he regarded her indifferently, as if he were accustomed to viewing bound women. Soon he turned his attention to the goods for sale, kneeling to examine the grain spilled on the wagon's floor and fingering the contents of a slashed oat bag. Having done that, he gave Yim's captor a disinterested look. "A copper a sack fer the oats, two coppers fer a sack of grain. Half that fer any sack that's slashed."

"That's robbery!"

The buyer grinned. "Aye, no doubt 'tis. But I didn't do the robbin'. If ye don't like my price, take this lot to Lurwic and see what it fetches."

"Bahl's headed for Lurwic."

"They say his army's already there," replied the buyer. "War ruins the market fer bulky goods. Yer lucky I'm buyin' at all."

Yim's captor sighed. "Sold. Count the sacks."

The buyer called out to the street. "Nabs! Tomby! Move quick and empty this lot."

Two ragged boys came over and the buyer tossed the sacks to them as Yim's captor counted each one. Since the robbers had sold the provisions, Yim doubted that she would be journeying farther. Otherwise, she had no inkling of her fate. Once the sacks were emptied, her captors left the wagon's door open and drove up the lane, stopping periodically as men and women appeared to haggle for the remaining goods.

The wares dangling from the wagon's eaves were sold, along with the pot that Yim had cooked in. The brandy went next, with the robbers keeping a few bottles for themselves. After much dickering, two ragged men purchased the barrel of salt mutton for eleven coppers, and then chortled as they rolled it away. It made Yim surmise that either her captors were poor bargainers or very anxious to leave town.

When the wagon was nearly emptied out, Yim discovered that the robbers had taken the Seer's boots. She spotted them, along with his bloodstained cloak, among a small pile of her and the Seer's clothing. A pinched-faced woman arrived and began rummaging through the garments. As she held up Yim's cloak to inspect it in the light, Yim's captor said, "Twenty coppers for the lot."

"Twenty! Do ye think I shit money?"

"'Tis a bargain, lovey. Ye know it."

"Ten coppers."

"Pah! There's two pair o' boots here and a cloak what's nearly new."

"Twelve."

"Fifteen and I'll throw in these ribbons."

As the woman made a show of deliberating, she glanced at Yim, who had retreated to a corner. "And the lot includes her shift? It goes with the cloak."

"Aye, lovey, ye can have it."

"And the undershift if she's wearing one."

Yim's captor reacted with mock horror. "'Twill leave her naked!"

The woman laughed. "So what? 'Twon't affect her price."

Yim, who had been listening to the conversation with growing alarm, shrank against the wagon's wall as her captor advanced. "Don't give me trouble," he said as he pulled Yim to her feet. He spun her around and untied her wrists. "Take off yer shift. Are ye wearin' an undershift?"

"Yes."

"I want that, too."

"Please . . ."

"Please won't get you nothin'. Now be quick. Most like, yer clothes have fetched more than ye will."

Yim obeyed because she had no choice. After she shed her clothes, her wrists were bound again. Yim slumped to the floor and huddled in the corner, drawing up her knees in an attempt to cover herself. The woman departed with her purchases and the wagon moved on. When it halted again, Yim was dragged from it to stand upon the muddy street before a small stone building with an iron door. Near the door was a knee-high stone cube, marking the building as a place where slaves were bought and sold.

Yim stood shivering in the chill morning air, unable to hide her nakedness while one of her captors pounded on the iron door. She was painfully aware that when the door opened someone would emerge to exchange a few coins for her. Yim had never felt more miserable or so utterly forsaken. Soon someone else would claim her body, and only her soul would be wholly hers.

FOUR

TO THE north in Lurwic, the duke's castle was burning. The duke didn't care; he was dead. So were his family, his servants, his soldiers, and everyone within the surrounding town. Lord Bahl's men had been thorough. After the battle ended, Honus had walked through its aftermath. Although a veteran of many engagements, he was appalled by the wantonness of the destruction. Whatever wasn't looted had been destroyed. Every house was burning. Not a single crock or chair or bit of cloth remained intact. But the owners of these things fared worse. They had been slain with such ferocity that Honus often had to avert his eyes. None of the dead were completely whole, as if their attackers had been unsatisfied with merely killing them. No one had been spared indignity, not even tiny babes. As far as Honus could determine, he was the sole survivor.

After performing his reconnaissance, Honus returned to the castle. By then, it was late afternoon. He removed his chain mail, sharpened his sword, and washed the gore from his clothes and body. Then he sat cross-legged in the center of the castle's cobbled courtyard. There, surrounded by the slain and drifts of ever-thickening smoke, he meditated. Gradually, the disciplines that he had learned during his childhood in the temple permitted him to master his turbulent mind. He conquered his fear, cooled his rage, and struggled to shut away his grief. The latter proved the most difficult, and dusk arrived before he was calm.

While Honus was meditating, Yaun cautiously pushed up the cover of the latrine, poked his head out, and listened. The castle was eerily quiet. Yaun decided it was safe to emerge from hiding. He climbed from his foul refuge, shed his ruined clothing, and washed the filth from his body in a bathing pool. Its water was cold and also pink with the blood from a floating corpse, so Yaun scrubbed as quickly as possible. Emerging from his hasty bath, he lifted an over-turned stone basin and was pleased to find his things untouched. Yaun smiled at his cleverness.

Yaun dressed himself, something he had seldom done before he became a squire. Out of habit, he sometimes snapped his fingers to summon the servants he had left behind when he joined Alaric's band of mercenaries. Yaun regretted his decision to become a soldier, but at least he had survived it.

When he was dressed, Yaun made his way through the castle, skirting the burning portions and ignoring the carnage all around him. Eventually, he reached the entrance to the wine cellar. Using a burning brand as a torch, he descended to the subterranean vault. He found its floor littered with broken glass and awash in wine and blood. Yaun stepped over a mutilated woman who still clutched half of an infant to reach the wine casks. The casks had been hacked open to spill their contents, but a few weren't completely shattered. Yaun drew his sword for the first time since the battle had begun and swung at one of the more intact casks, chopping through oak to reveal what wine remained. The cask was large and had been resting on its side, so a sizable pool was trapped within its curve. Lacking a drinking vessel or the patience to look for one, Yaun poked his head and shoulders into the newly made opening. Then he drank. The wine was new and harsh-tasting, but Yaun didn't mind. There was enough to get him drunk. For the moment, that was all that mattered.

A hand gripped Yaun's shoulder and shook him awake. Yaun cried out in terror, before he realized that the face gazing down at him wasn't that of a foe. It was tattooed, marking its owner as a Sarf. Yaun recalled that the Sarf's name was Honus, and that he served a holy man whose name Yaun couldn't remember.

"Aren't you Alaric's squire?" asked Honus.

"Yes. How fares he?"

"I'd think you'd know."

"We were separated."

Honus gave no sign as to whether he believed the lie or not. He simply replied, "Alaric's dead, as is everyone else. I've found naught alive but crows, rats, and you." Honus rose. "Are you done celebrating your good fortune?"

Yaun got unsteadily to his feet. "It's been a trying day."

"I think you speak of yesterday," said Honus. "The battle's long over."

"So it's morning already?"

"Well past then. But there's still daylight. Come see for yourself."

Yaun was affronted by Honus's manner, but he took care not to show it. He needed protection, and Honus was renowned for his deadly skill. Yaun's difficulty was that Sarfs served holy men and were aloof to those things that bought the loyalty of worldlier folk. In fact, Yaun was surprised that Honus had spoken to him, for he had never done so when they supped at the duke's table. In light of that, Yaun was encouraged that Honus had bothered to rouse him. It seemed evidence that the Sarf had some need of him, a need that Yaun might turn to his advantage.

The two men who emerged from the cellar were a mismatched pair. Yaun was scarcely out of his teens, and his face bore the softness arising from a life of privilege. His apparel reflected a noble birth. He wore a helm engraved with battle scenes. Fur trimmed his cloak. His fine leather boots were elaborately tooled. The sword that hung at his waist was expensively, if gaudily, decorated.

In contrast, Honus had an ascetic air. His dark blue clothes were plain and threadbare. His feet bore sandals, the straps of which wound about his leggings. Loose pants covered the leggings to below the knee. He wore no helm and his long, jet-black hair was pulled back and tied with a bit of cord. A simple long-sleeved shirt and a long woolen cloak, both without ornament, completed his austere apparel. His sword was undecorated and forged in the style of his order—slightly curved, with a hilt long enough for two hands, yet a blade sufficiently light to wield with one.

The midnight hue of Honus's clothes extended into his face. The lines tattooed there made it look older than his nearly thirty winters and also fierce, as if frozen in an expression of rage. Blue lightning slashed down his brow. His pale blue eyes peered from pools of permanent shadow. Scowl lines had been needled into his cheeks along with ancient charms. His dark blue clothing proclaimed him as one chosen to serve Karm, the Goddess of the Balance, and his face marked him as a Sarf, a master of the martial disciplines.

Yaun spoke first. "If all are slain, does that mean your master has perished?"

Grief briefly visited Honus's eyes. "He's gone."

"So what will you do now?"

"Return to the temple and receive a new master. But first, I must find someone."

"Who?"

Honus gazed at Yaun, seemingly mulling over some distasteful choice. After a prolonged silence, he spoke. "On the night before the battle, my master studied portents. Afterward, he said that I must never carry my own burden."

"Why?"

"It was not my place to ask, nor his role to explain. All I know is that I cannot leave until I find someone to bear my pack."

Yaun smiled. "And Karm's temple lies to the south?"

"It does."

"Then I'll carry your pack."

"Don't make that promise lightly. The temple lies far from here and the way is hard."

"I'll bear your pack. I so swear by Karm. Does that satisfy you?"

"It must," replied Honus. "We should head out now. Bahl's gone north to ravish the duke's lands. But when he's done, I think he'll turn his army south."

The Turmgeist Forest lay south of Lurwic, a dense tract of trees that took three days to traverse on foot. It was densest toward its southern edge, where the onset of spring was barely perceptible. In the gloom beneath the pines, the undergrowth remained brown and crowded the path. Honus led the way through this maze, with Yaun lagging behind. The two seldom walked close enough to converse, an arrangement that seemed to suit them both. The pair plodded onward in this manner until the sky darkened. By then, pines had given way to oaks that were in first leaf, and the forest pathway had become a road. Honus halted. "We'll camp here," he stated.

Yaun put down the pack with relief and rubbed his sore shoulders. The Sarf removed his sandals, sat cross-legged on the ground, and closed his eyes. Yaun had seen Honus assume this position before, and it always made him uneasy. He knew that although the Sarf was perfectly motionless, he was roaming the realm of the dead. Yaun shuddered at the thought of it and set off to gather firewood. When he returned, he was disappointed to find Honus still trancing, for only the Sarf had the skill to strike a fire. Yaun wrapped himself in his cloak to ward off the evening's chill and impatiently waited for the trance to end. Eventually, Honus's eyes opened.

"What did you see?" asked Yaun in a hushed voice.

"Many crowd the Dark Path. There's much confusion."

"What of our comrades?"

"Some of their shades still journey with us, but not the one I seek," replied Honus. He gazed at Yaun and added, "Alaric is nearby."

The blood drained from Yaun's face, and he glanced anxiously about the twilit forest. "Did . . . did he speak with you?"

"I cannot speak with the dead. I can only sense their memories."

"What's on his mind?" asked Yaun.

"He's troubled by regret; the newly slain usually are."

"Anything else? Does he think of the battle?"

"He yearns for a child with golden hair, nothing more."

"That's all?" asked Yaun, sounding relieved.

"The girl was dear to him."

"I would have thought he'd dwell upon his glory."

"Glory?" said Honus, his voice hard with incredulity. "The dead care not for glory. The Dark Path doesn't ring with song." He took up the iron and flint. Soon, he had a fire blazing.

Yaun watched as Honus poured some water and a handful of grain into a brass pot to make porridge. After Honus set it on the fire to cook, Yaun gathered his nerve and spoke. "When Alaric died, I was released from my vows."

"You don't wish to remain a squire?" asked Honus without surprise.

"I rode forth on a charger, seeking renown."

"Renown?" Honus seemed amused. "I thought you were seeking your fortune."

"Yes, that, too," replied Yaun. "And now I return bearing another man's burden."

"Then you've found your fortune after all."

"I wasn't born to carry a pack."

"You seemed eager enough to carry it earlier."

"But now we approach my father's lands. I'm a count's son. I mean no disrespect . . ."

"I won't travel encumbered," said Honus. "You pledged an oath."

"Yet I need not bear your burden to fulfill it," Yaun replied. He drew a purse from his pocket and emptied its coins into his palm. "We're close to Durkin."

"And its thieves' market," said Honus. "So?"

"We could go there tomorrow," said Yaun, seemingly unaware of the disdain in Honus's voice. "This is enough to buy a slave."

Honus glanced at the coppers in Yaun's hand. "But not enough for a horse."

"It's all I have."

"What times are these," mused Honus, "when people are cheaper than horses?"

"It's been that way for a long time."

"That doesn't mean it should be so."

"Such sentiments remind me of your master," replied Yaun. "Yet his holiness couldn't save him."

A shadow crossed Honus's face. "The Balance is indeed askew."

Yaun noisily dropped the coins back into the purse. "So . . . What say you, Honus?"

"You're likely to discover your father's lands are no safer than Lurwic was." Honus shook his head. "But then, perhaps nowhere's safe."

"I'll take my chances. I'll get by."

Honus shot Yaun a penetrating look, and the young man grew tense under the scrutiny. Honus saw more than ordinary men, and in Yaun, he disliked what he saw. It was what he didn't see that bothered him most. *How can he be untroubled by what we've witnessed?* Yet Honus found only self-concern in Yaun's face. The Sarf released him from his gaze. "All right," he said. "We'll go to Durkin. A slave will do."

The tenseness left Yaun's face. He bowed his head. "Thank you, Karmamatus."

The term meant "Karm's beloved," and Honus had often used it to address his master. Thus it sounded wrong coming from Yaun's lips. "Don't mock me with flattery," replied Honus. "I'm not worthy of Karm's love."

FIVE

HONUS AND Yaun left the forest the next morning to travel through abandoned farmlands that were rank with weeds and tangled scrub. It was a melancholy landscape, even in springtime. Well before noon, the smoke of Durkin was visible in the distance. Yaun halted by a copse of trees to remove his helm and his boots. Then he hid them in the pack. Afterward, he wrapped a rag around his sword hilt to cover its jewels.

The marks on Honus's face exaggerated his look of contempt. "I see you're no stranger to Durkin."

"It's a lawless place," replied Yaun, "but goods are cheap there."

"If you don't mind their source."

"Few men wish to live as you do. A good price matters to them."

"Other things should matter also. The Balance, for example."

"Oh yes, Karm's holy Balance," said Yaun. "What does that mean? What does she weigh on her divine scales?"

"Everything," replied Honus. "What a man gives and what he takes. Both sides of a dispute. The worth of a soul."

"And to what end?"

"Harmony. Peace. Justice."

"After what we've seen, how can you say that?" asked Yaun. "Small wonder men look elsewhere for strength. What has your faith gained you?"

Honus didn't immediately reply. "That's my concern," he said at last. "Durkin is corrupt, regardless."

"That's because it's not in some divine realm, but in the living world, where folks weigh contentment by the heft of their purses and the fullness of their bellies."

"You grow bold, now that we approach your father's domain," said Honus. "Shoulder my pack one last time. I'm eager to finish this business."

When the travelers reached the crest of a rise, they saw Durkin for the first time. Even from a distance, the place's appearance reflected its reputation. The surrounding fields were haphazardly marked and rank with last year's weeds. The town's neglected walls seemed to signal that there were as many dangers within as without. When Honus and Yaun passed through the sagging and unguarded gate, the smell of sewage assaulted their noses. The rude buildings inside the walls were shoddily built and blackened by smoke from foundries that stood ready to melt down gold or silver at a moment's notice. Most were marred by graffiti, and none looked caringly maintained. Despite the warmth, only the taverns had open doors and unshuttered windows.

The narrow streets seemed remarkably crowded, considering the town's isolation. Most of the pedestrians were inspecting items laid upon the ground; some were haggling with vendors; and the remainder were drinking or brawling. Everyone seemed edgy, causing Honus to speculate that they'd heard news of the battle. More than a few he spied seemed preparing to flee.

Yaun was obviously familiar with the tangled lanes, for he led Honus without hesitation to a small stone building near the town's center. A knee-high stone cube stood in front to display the establishment's human wares. Yaun pounded on its iron door, and eyes appeared behind the slot near the door's top. "We wish to purchase a slave," Yaun said.

The eyes traveled from Yaun to Honus. "Is the Sarf with you?" asked the voice behind the door.

"Yes."

"He must leave first."

"The slave's for me," stated Honus.

"For you, Karmamatus?" asked the voice in oily tones. "Times are indeed strange."

"You know me, Peshnell," said Yaun. "This is no trick."

"Karmamatus," said the man in the dark, "do you pledge your word to preserve me and mine?"

Honus arched his thumb across his chest, making the Sign of the Balance. "I so pledge."

The eyes disappeared. Then came the sound of a bolt being drawn. The door opened, spilling sunlight onto a stone floor covered with soiled straw. A smell like that of a filthy stall issued forth and overpowered the stench of the street. Several ragged figures sat huddled against the far wall. A sharp-faced man with a scraggly black beard stepped into the light. His long, brightly colored robe contrasted with his dismal place of business. He smiled, revealing missing teeth. "You're fortunate indeed. I've acquired fresh stock."

"From where?" asked Honus.

Peshnell shrugged. "Who knows? But I was told the children are bred slaves."

A harsh voice echoed from deeper inside the dim room. "Outside!" The figures rose and there was the clink of chains. A large man with a thick switch in his hand and a club dangling from his leather tunic approached the slaves. The switch whistled, and a sharp snap mingled with a cry of pain, "Move!"

The slaves stumbled out the door in single file, for an iron ring locked their right ankles to a heavy chain. They were barefoot and wore identical gray garments—loose, sleeveless tunics made of cheap, flimsy cloth. All the tunics were the same size, so that upon the children they nearly dragged the ground, while upon the adults they didn't reach the knees. Three men, one woman, and two children stood blinking in the sunlight.

"The old man can figure sums and . . ."

Honus cut Peshnell short. "I'm interested in the two young men."

The leather-clad guard, a burly version of Peshnell, unlocked a pale-faced man from the chain. Honus watched him mount the stone block. "This man has a wound," he said. He lifted up the man's tunic to reveal a sword cut on his upper thigh. Pus oozed from the gash and the skin around it had already turned black.

"It'll heal," said Peshnell, "but, for you, I'll reduce his price."

"I'm not interested," replied Honus. "It's a marvel he could even mount the block. Let me see the blond fellow."

The slave stepped down from the block, this time not attempting to hide his pain. The guard made a move to lock him to the chain again, but Honus's hand gripped his shoulder. "There's no need for that," he said. "That man's going nowhere. Let him die unshackled."

The guard glanced toward Peshnell, who nodded. "Inside," barked the guard. The wounded man limped back into the darkness.

As the guard moved to unlock the blond man, Peshnell said, "There's a reserve on that one."

Honus shot Peshnell a menacing look. "If this is a slaver's trick . . ."

"No, Karmamatus! Remember your pledge!"

"I expect you to deal fairly."

"I am, I am," said Peshnell in a nervous voice. "He can be yours, if you but match the miller's offer. His treadmill goes through many slaves, so we have a standing agreement. Ask anyone, Karmamatus. I speak truth."

"What's the price?"

"Thirty coppers."

"Count the money, Yaun."

Yaun emptied the coins into his palm. "I've sixteen coppers, Karmamatus."

"That's not enough!" cried Peshnell. "I paid twenty for him. You pledged to preserve what's mine."

"What about the girl?" asked Yaun.

"Her?" said Honus, glancing at the chained woman.

"She's fully grown," said Yaun. "She could bear your pack."

Honus turned his attention to the young woman for the first time. Her dark eyes widened when she returned his gaze. "Perhaps she'd do," said Honus.

Peshnell turned to the guard. "Put her on the block."

When the woman was unchained, she hesitated before mounting the block. Only when the guard raised his switch did she hop onto the stone. Yaun grinned. "Show her naked," he said. The guard reached up with one hand and whisked the tunic over the slave's head. For an instant, she stood in stunned humiliation; then she tried to cover herself. The guard's switch whistled and struck her backside. She dropped her hands and became rigid, staring off into the distance, as if forcing her mind elsewhere. Passersby slowed to eye the nude woman on the stone. Yaun gawked openly. "Peshnell," he said, "you should sell this one to the pleasure gardens in Larresh."

"Larresh is far away. Could you reach there with one such as her? Up here, men don't pay for what they can take." The slaver leered. "I don't."

Emboldened by Peshnell's words, Yaun reached to fondle the slave girl, but his hand was stopped by Honus's iron grip. "That's a person there," he said, "not a horse." Despite his words, Honus looked upon the naked woman as he might a horse and judged her fitness. She was slender, but not skinny, and her muscles were sleek. Although she was dirty and had welts from the switch, she appeared not to have suffered overlong in Peshnell's "care." Honus judged that she had seen but eighteen winters and was probably a maiden before she was captured. *She's not as strong as a man.* He glanced scornfully at Yaun, who still quivered in his grip, and realized he could abide him no longer. *She'll have to do.* "Ten coppers," said Honus.

"Ten coppers!" wailed Peshnell. "Look at this beauty. Such delicate hands and feet. Long hair, like polished walnut. Firm, perfect breasts. A curvaceous a . . ."

"Ten coppers," said Honus with finality.

"I'm being robbed. You made a pledge."

"Perhaps I should visit the miller," said Honus in an ominous tone. "I made no pledge to him." Then, to make his threat perfectly clear, he added, "Dead men buy no slaves."

"Did I refuse you, Karmamatus?" said Peshnell quickly. "I merely hope you appreciate my openhandedness."

"I understand it well enough," replied Honus. "Yaun, pay him."

While Yaun counted out the coins, Honus lifted the shabby tunic from the ground and handed it to his slave. "You should dress now."

Throughout the sale, the woman had appeared oblivious of her surroundings, but she quickly seized the tunic. Slipping it over her head, she jumped down from the block.

Honus turned his attention to Yaun, who had finished paying Peshnell. "Don't put those coins away. She'll need a cloak."

"Please, Honus," said Yaun, glancing longingly at a nearby tavern. "I've already bought you a slave."

"So you wish to give her *your* cloak?"

Yaun sighed and handed Honus the remaining coppers.

"Now, take off my pack," said Honus, not disguising his contempt. Yaun slipped it from his shoulders and set it on the street. Honus opened it and began tossing Yaun's possessions on the dirt. Yaun's face reddened, but he said nothing as he scurried to collect his things. The last item Honus removed was a boot. The scowl lines needled on his cheeks fought with a grin. He shook the boot and things jingled in its toe. "Why, Yaun," Honus said with a voice dripping with concern, "such stones will bruise your delicate foot." He walked over to the sewage ditch that ran along the center of the dirt lane and upended the boot. Three coins tumbled out, flashing gold before they disappeared into the flowing filth. Honus tossed the boot at Yaun's feet. Yaun glared at him as a dog might regard a wolf—with a look that mingled hostility and fear. After donning his fancy helm and boots, Yaun walked over to the ditch. Without a word, he rolled up his sleeves and began groping in the sewage for his money.

"Slave," said Honus to the woman. "Take up my burden. We'll leave this swine to root for the price of a horse."

SIX

As HONUS walked through the streets of Durkin, he paused occasionally to examine the used clothing for sale. Whenever he glanced at his new slave, he found her watching him with apprehensive eyes. "Have you never seen a Sarf before?" he asked.

"No, Karmamatus."

"Don't imitate those swine when you address me!"

The woman paled but met his gaze. "I thought I was being respectful," she replied. "What should I call you?"

"Master. And you, what's your name?"

"Yim." There was a brief pause before she added, "Master."

"A strange name."

"It's common where I come from."

"Where's that?"

"North. The Cloud Mountains."

"And do folk still honor Karm there?"

"Yes, Master."

"Do you?'

"Yes, Master."

"Good." Honus threw down the tattered cloak he had been inspecting. "Come, Yim. I'm eager to finish my business here." He wandered down the lane until he spotted a man's cloak spread out before an old woman with a withered arm. Honus held it up. The garment was well made and fairly new. Its thick gray wool was tightly woven and felt of lanolin. "How much, Mother?" he asked.

"For ye, Karmamatus, ten coppers."

"I just bought this slave for that sum!"

"Then ye shan't need a cloak to warm ye at night." The woman laughed, causing Yim to blush.

Honus pointed to a slit that had been repaired in the back of the cloak. A large bloodstain surrounded it. "This garment is ill omened," countered Honus. "A man was slain in it. Four coppers."

"Six."

"I wish to buy her sandals also."

"It's summer soon. Her feet will toughen."

Honus held the cloak against Yim. It nearly reached her ankles. He thought of chill nights and spring rains, then tossed the woman his remaining coins. She quickly whisked them out of sight and rose to leave. As Honus stuffed the cloak into the pack, he heard the departing woman call out, "If ye're concerned about her feet, keep her on her back!" Cackling, the crone disappeared down an alley.

With his business finished, Yim's new master strode out of the squalid town, his grim face causing the crowds to part. Yim had to struggle to keep up with his rapid pace, which he didn't slacken. Soon she was sweating and panting from her effort not to fall behind. She feared that if she did, her owner would prove as wrathful as he looked.

They continued that way until they crested a hill and the town was hidden from view. "We'll walk more slowly," Honus said, "now that the stench is behind us."

Yim sighed with relief. They hiked until noon with Honus in front and her trailing. The pack she carried was large and even heavier than it looked, for it contained chain mail. Occasionally, Honus peered back to see how she was holding up. Each time, he seemed pleased to find that she wasn't lagging behind.

"We'll stop here," he said, when they reached a broad tree with pale, new leaves. "You may rest awhile."

Yim removed the pack from her shoulders and untied its water skin. She raised it to her lips, hesitated, and handed the skin to Honus. He drank his fill before returning it. Yim quenched her thirst and slumped down in the thin shade. "I'm not used to this," she said. Then, in an effort to bolster her standing, she added, "I was a princess in my land."

The lightning on Honus's brow moved as an eyebrow arched upward. "A princess?" There was amusement in his voice.

"Yes. And I didn't have slaves, only servants. Faithful servants."

"The market for princesses must be poor if I can get one for ten coppers."

Yim looked away, feeling stupid.

Honus was glad when his slave grew quiet. He turned his attention to the ruin across the road. It was roofless and overgrown with tangled vines, but its crumbling stone walls still retained a vestige of grace. Honus realized that the old tree under which they rested was the remnant of a double line that once had shaded a lane leading to the manor. He gazed at the fire-blackened house before him, closed his eyes, and tranced.

The ruin's inhabitants had long ago traveled the Dark Path, and the echoes of their memories were faint. Except for the very last, they were mostly glad ones. Honus sought out the pleasant remembrances, trying to find some solace in the happiness of others. His mind discovered a moment of lovers' passion, as fragile and faded as a wildflower pressed in a book. He wistfully lingered with their bliss until his heart could stand it no longer. Then he let his mind fall back into the living world. The transition was always a quick one, and when Honus's eyes shot open, he caught Yim studying him.

Her inspection felt intrusive, and it annoyed Honus. Rising abruptly, he glared at her and gave his voice a hard

edge. "You've rested long enough if you've time for imper-
tinence." He didn't wait for Yim to shoulder the pack before he set off at a pace as fast as when he first left Durkin.
Honus didn't turn around either, but listened for Yim's
panting. Only when her breath came in gasps did he slow
to a walk.

Yim followed her capricious master upon a road that
wound through a countryside that no longer even had a
name. Most of the farmsteads they passed were abandoned, their humble buildings succumbing to the ravages
of weather and man. The few that weren't derelict seemed
nearly as neglected. The rare travelers they met were
headed in the opposite direction. Yim thought they might
be refugees, for they were burdened with household goods.
Honus didn't speak, so Yim knew neither where he was
headed nor why. All she could determine was that no one
else was going there. The longer Honus and Yim walked, the
fewer travelers they encountered. By late afternoon, they
had the road to themselves.

As Yim trudged along, she pondered her changed fortune.
She had been anxious to leave the dark, fetid slave pen, but
she was uncertain whether her lot had improved or wors-
ened. The attack and what followed still seemed like a nightmare terminating in her complete humiliation. Her captors
hadn't even bothered to haggle over the pittance Peshnell offered. *They sold me for the same price as a few sacks of oats.
And now I belong to this Sarf,* thought Yim.

She had heard of Sarfs. Tales said they were deadly, but
virtuous. Honus seemed the former, but not the latter. Since
he walked in front, Yim couldn't study his face, but his silence and his punishing pace felt harsh. Yim feared Honus's
harshness was evidence of cruelty, and she worried how he
might use her.

The sun was low in the sky when they came upon a
creek. Honus halted and sat upon a rock next to where

clear water gurgled among rounded stones. Yim took his action as a sign that she could rest. She removed the pack, drank her fill from the cold stream, and refilled the water skin. Before she could sit down, Honus broke his silence. "Wash your filthy rag and clean yourself also."

Yim blushed. "Right here?"

"Yes, here. Now be quick about it." As Yim began to hop from stone to stone, Honus added, "Stay close by."

The water deepened to form a shallow pool about ten paces from where Honus sat. Yim halted there and glanced to see if her master was looking away. He was not. Feeling as she had upon the slave seller's block, Yim turned her back to Honus, removed her tunic, and washed it as best she could. Afterward, she wrung it out and placed it on a rock. Having finished with the tunic, she squatted down to clean herself in the calf-deep water. It was icy and she bathed as quickly as possible, scrubbing her goose-pimpled skin with sand until it was rosy pink. All the while, she felt Honus's eyes on her nakedness. It filled her with dread as she thought of the approaching night. Yim rose from the water and dressed in her tunic before facing Honus. He was gazing at her breasts, which were clearly visible through the wet, clinging fabric.

As Yim returned to the bank, Honus rose to resume their journey. Without a word, Yim hiked the pack upon her wet garment and waited for her master to move on. Honus crossed the stream by leaping from stone to stone, then continued up the lonely road.

Dusk was falling when Honus drew his sword and handed it to Yim. "Carry this and keep walking. There's something I must do."

Yim obeyed. She listened for Honus's footsteps behind her, but there were none. When she turned around, he was gone without a trace, leaving her alone. His action was as terrifying as it was inexplicable. Yim briefly wondered if she was being punished, but she couldn't imagine her transgression. She clutched the sword, but it provided little comfort on the darkening and desolate road. Thick brush hemmed in the narrow lane, so it resembled a twisting alleyway. *The Seer lost his life and I my freedom in just such a place.*

The only thing Yim could do was to keep moving. Her bare feet made no noise, and after a while, she could detect rustling sounds to her rear. "Master?" The sounds stopped. Yim looked behind her. The road was empty. As Yim stood listening, the sun sank below the trees.

Yim started walking again. The sound returned and became louder. This time, she turned to see two dark shapes step onto the lane. In the stillness of the gathering gloom, she could hear men's low voices.

"Are you crazy? The Sarf!"

"He's gone. And the fool left his sword behind."

"He might return."

"Then we'll be quick."

Yim grasped Honus's sword with both hands and waved it at the two silhouettes. They advanced with the confidence of dangerous men. Soon Yim could see them plainly. They wore heavy leather tunics, sewn with iron plates. Their coarse, scarred faces matched their crude armor. One man held an unsheathed sword; the other brandished an iron-headed mace.

"Throw that thing away, pretty," said the man with the sword. "You'll hurt yourself."

"I'll hurt *you*," said Yim, trying to sound confident, "if you come closer."

The man with the mace snickered and began swinging his weapon with swift, random movements. The studded iron became a blur that whistled through the air. Yim swung wildly with her blade, trying to fend it off. The mace wielder grinned and Yim sensed he was toying with her. Several times, the iron passed so closely to her face, she felt its breeze. With a sudden clank, the sword was jarred from her grasp. Yim's assailant stepped forward and pinned the blade to the dirt. "Enough of that," he said. "Now it's time to really play." He grinned and, with the end of his mace, began to lift the hem of Yim's tunic.

Yim heard Honus's voice. "The girl's mine."

The man pivoted, keeping his foot on the sword. "What use has a holy man for a woman?"

"You need only know that she's mine."

The man with the mace forced a smile on his face. "Of course," he said. "It's not my business." Then, he turned toward his companion and winked.

A sword flashed, reflecting the last of the sky's light. It passed through where Honus had stood an instant before. The Sarf rolled on the ground and sprang up so that he and the swordsman were chest-to-chest. At such close quarters, the sword was useless. Honus jabbed with his fist. There was the crunch of gristle, and the swordsman fell backward. Honus caught his opponent's sword before it hit the ground. Then he whirled, and the mace dropped with a hand still grasping it. A wail arose. It was cut short as Honus whirled again. The second man dropped to the road in two pieces. Honus turned and plunged the sword into the other man gurgling on the ground. There was a grunt, and the gurgling stopped. Honus withdrew the sword and stepped on its blade to snap it. Afterward, he hurled it and the mace into the bushes flanking the road. Then he picked up and sheathed his weapon.

Yim had stood paralyzed throughout the encounter. As she stared at the two dead men, she felt sickened by their violent end. Her stomach churned, and if it weren't empty, she would have thrown up. For a long while, she trembled as horror fought with relief. Then she subdued her emotions and asked Honus in a shaky voice, "Are we safe now?"

A grim smile came to Honus's fierce face. "Safe?" He glanced down at the pair of corpses. "These were but fleas. There are wolves abroad. Didn't you know?"

"No. My home's far away and isolated."

"Then you were ill-advised to leave it." Honus dragged the bodies from the road. "Don't worry, we'll be safe enough tonight. Come. We'll walk until the moon rises. Then you'll find firewood more easily."

By the time Yim returned to camp with a second load of wood, Honus had a fire blazing and porridge cooked. He tasted it before passing the pot to Yim. The porridge was burnt, but she ate ravenously. "Don't eat so quickly," Honus warned her. "You'll get sick." Yim slowed her pace, but she still cleaned the pot with her fingers, licking them noisily. Honus's teeth showed in the moonlight. "Such royal manners."

Withdrawn and tense, Yim didn't react to the jest. After eating, she sat near the dying fire, wrapped in her blood-stained cloak and shivering, though the night was not yet cold.

Honus spread his cloak over leaves and removed his sandals and outer pants. Yim looked away as he began to remove his leggings. "Take off that damp tunic," she heard him say, "and come to me."

Yim remained put, but turned to look at Honus. He was reclining on his cloak, his manhood covered by his long shirt. In a voice that trembled slightly, Yim responded. "You're a Sarf, a holy man."

"A Sarf is but a holy man's servant. I'm no purer than other men, probably less."

"If you had purchased the blond slave, would you have wished to tup him also?"

"No," said Honus, his voice betraying irritation.

"Then why must I do what he need not?"

"Come. There's pleasure in this."

"I've already suffered as a bound captive, so don't speak of pleasure. What pleases the man degrades the woman."

"This is my right," replied Honus. "I own you."

"You own your sword. Would you use it to hew rocks?"

"Stop speaking riddles."

"Only a fool destroys his possessions."

Honus sat up and glared at Yim. "Are you calling me a fool?"

"No, Master." Yim recalled the night with the scar-faced man in the wagon, and when she spoke again there was resolve in her voice. "You can have me by force, but you cannot force me to live. If you tup me, I'll kill myself. Then, the only burdens I'll bear will be memories upon the Dark Path."

"You're bluffing."

"Look me in the eye and see truth. I've experienced degradation once. I'd rather walk the Dark Path than endure it again."

Honus stared at Yim for a long time, and she sensed it was no ordinary gaze but one that saw beneath appearances. Yim met his eyes forthrightly and loosened her guard. Thus, though she couldn't fathom his tattooed face in the moonlight, she felt that she had communicated her determination. Finally, Honus looked away and pulled on his pants. "I'll not force you," he said. "I so swear." Honus made the Sign of the Balance. Then he took off his shirt and tossed it toward Yim. "Replace that damp tunic with this and lie beside me. We'll share warmth, nothing more."

Yim felt a wave of relief. She let out a long, shuddering sigh as Honus lay down and rolled on his side to face away from her. After she had put on the shirt and hung her tunic to dry, she noticed Honus's back was covered with little marks. She hesitantly crept over to his cloak, carrying hers to cover them both. Closer up, Yim saw that the marks were tattooed runes. The writing began at Honus's shoulders and extended to the small of his back, forming an extensive text. Some of the marks roused Yim's curiosity. She reached out and lightly touched them. "Your runes are old-fashioned," she whispered, "but I can make some words out."

"Don't!" cried Honus.

Yim jerked her hand away.

"Those runes concern deep matters, portents that only a Sarf's master should read," said Honus. "A Sarf may not know them. That's why they're needled on his back."

"Pardon me, Master. I didn't know." Yim drew up her cloak. As she pulled it over Honus, she thought of the runes and wondered why some spelled her name.

SEVEN

HONUS LAY awake, looking toward the stars and listening to Yim's breathing. Asleep, she didn't shrink from him. Instead, she lay curled on her side, her back and feet pressed against him for warmth. *When was I last this close to a woman?* It felt like ages. Yet Yim's closeness only heightened his loneliness. *How pathetic, to turn to a slave for . . . what? Pleasure from a frightened girl? What a shallow, futile thing.* Honus felt ashamed of his weakness.

He also reproached himself for letting Yim glimpse his back. If he had known she could read, he would have never removed his shirt. Honus wondered what signs she had discerned. *It probably doesn't matter. She wouldn't understand their import.* Still, he couldn't forget how Yim had softly brushed his tattoos with her fingers. Honus's wise and gentle master had touched the runes similarly when he puzzled over them. Honus reflected on the irony that Yim had deciphered words that he, who had borne them since childhood, had seldom seen and never read. All he knew of them was that the inscription was extensive. Occasionally, his master had teased Honus about it, telling of a Sarf whose back bore but a single word. He never revealed what it was.

Honus had often speculated on what his master learned from his back. When he was young, he believed his entire life was inscribed there, exposed to anyone who could make out the letters. Later, he learned that the Seer who tattooed them wrote riddles and hints. "Their meaning is revealed through time," Honus's master had said. "Life provides the missing puzzle pieces." Honus wondered if Yaun or even the slave beside him were pieces to that puzzle, and who would fit those pieces now that the one he revered was dead.

Honus's master had last touched the runes on the eve before the battle. If he foresaw his death, he didn't reveal it to Honus. He had only enjoined Honus to never carry his own burden, saying, "The will of Karm is strong in this." Honus had obeyed that command, and everything that followed had been a consequence.

Honus had no idea why he mustn't bear his pack. *Perhaps my master knew*. But he was gone, slain by forces that seemed as unstoppable as nightfall. *How can I oppose them, if even he had no answer? Seeking it doomed him.* Honus gazed toward the stars, but saw only the darkness between them.

Yim dreamed she was a girl again and relived the dreariness of her childhood. She was seated on the dirt floor of her guardian's hut. It was night and a small fire cast the only light. The warm air smelled of wood smoke and herbs. Yim hugged her legs close to her chest and peered over her knees at the Wise Woman. Her guardian stared back sternly. "Are you afraid?" she asked.

"Yes," said Yim.

"You should be," the woman replied. "This knowledge is perilous, even for you. You must never speak of it. Never! Is that understood?"

"Yes, Wise One."

"Then watch and learn." The woman sat on her heels, folded her hands in her lap, and became absolutely still. Yim scrutinized her guardian's face in the dim firelight. She appeared to be watching something in the dark, something Yim couldn't see. The air turned cold, and Yim was astonished to see frost forming on the floor. The white crystals advanced toward Yim's bare feet. Her toes began to sting.

The dream faded, but the cold remained. Yim awoke alone beneath the cloak in the dim blue light of predawn. The damp air was chilly and Yim drew her legs tighter to her body. They felt stiff; indeed, her whole body ached. Another day of drudgery loomed ahead, and she wasn't anxious for it to start. The hardships of travel, daunting as they were, seemed less oppressive than the prospect of serving a strange and unpredictable man. *My master,* Yim thought. The very word galled her. She remembered that his former companion had called him "Honus" and resolved to think of him by that name. It would help distance her from the demeaning idea that she was his property.

Nevertheless, Yim was already adjusting to that concept. She lay still to avoid being given a command, even after she began to feel restless. Passivity was an age-old slave's strategy, and Yim took to it instinctively. She knew retaining her inner freedom would require all her will. She viewed the previous day as a lopsided struggle between her and Honus where she suffered one rout after another. Yet, last night, she had won a major victory. Yim was still amazed by her success. When it happened, she had been steeling herself for suicide. Through that victory, she sensed that Honus needed her. Yim wasn't sure why, but it seemed to go beyond wanting a woman to lie with. *Otherwise, he wouldn't have made that oath. Something else is at work here.* She hoped to discover what it was and use that knowledge to her advantage.

Birds commenced their morning songs, but Yim remained beneath the cloak. She assumed that Honus was close by, despite hearing no indication of his presence. *Is he toying with me?* Yim grew restless and her thoughts turned toward a fire and hot food. Finally, Yim's hunger and chill drove her to pull off the cloak.

Yim looked about. Honus sat only a pace away. His perfect stillness and the markings on his face gave him the aspect of a malevolent statue. Yim jerked back with a small, startled cry. Honus, his eyes closed, didn't react. Regaining her composure, Yim regarded her master. He was dressed in his leggings and pants and wore her tunic like a cloak to cover the runes on his back. She would have requested its return, but he seemed beyond reach. His stillness reminded Yim of yesterday, when they rested by the tree. Then, he had seemed oblivious of everything. Fearful to disturb him and chilled by the raw morning air, Yim wandered off to look for firewood.

She returned as dawn tinted the clouds, carrying an armload of twigs and branches and a handful of herbs. Honus remained in the same position she had left him. *He can't object to a fire,* Yim thought. She arranged the twigs and branches over the ashes of last night's campfire, then opened the pack to search for a flint and iron. She found them and also a sheath knife. She removed the knife, intending to use it to shave tinder from a branch, for the grass was wet with dew. Testing the knife's keen blade, Yim thought how easily she might slit Honus's throat. She moved closer to him, knife in hand, and weighed her chances for success. *He seems in another world. He hasn't noticed me at all.* Yim studied his face for signs of awareness and noticed subtle, fleeting changes, like those of a sleeper caught in a dream, a dream from which Honus might never waken if she were quick.

And where would that leave me? So far, her quest had been a journey without a destination. When capture and slavery interrupted it, Yim had been expecting further guidance. Until it came, safety must be her primary concern. If she killed her master, she'd be alone where a woman without kin had no security. With no father, brother, or uncle to protect her and no husband to claim her, she was as vulnerable as a coin lying in the street. Anyone could take her, and anyone might. *Am I any safer with Honus?* Yim didn't know him well enough to answer. For the time being, it seemed wisest to remain his property and hope that he believed that only a fool destroyed his own possessions.

Yim made some shavings, placed them next to the twigs, and hit the flint with the iron. When sparks landed in the tinder, she blew on it until a flame appeared. Further blowing spread the flame to the twigs, then the branches. Soon she had a fire blazing. Yim was warming herself before it when Honus opened his eyes. "A princess who can make a fire?" he said with mock surprise. "Your kingdom must be a land of marvels."

"Would you like me to prepare some food?" asked Yim, adding "Master" as an afterthought.

"Why? Are you hungry?"

"Yes, Master."

"Then I'm most eager to view this second wonder, royalty that can cook."

Yim ignored his waggery. She took the brass pot from the pack, measured in grain and water, and shredded the herbs that she had collected, sprinkling them over the mixture. Honus watched what she did with interest. "What were those plants you added?"

"Lemon balm and faerie heart for savor. Bee's cup and springfoot for health. These are good things, Master. I swear."

"Since you declined to slit my throat, I doubt you'd poison me."

Yim looked up quickly and saw Honus watching her intently. "When I trance," he said, "I still see with an inner eye."

Yim paled. "I thought you were asleep or something like it."

"I was roaming the Dark Path."

Yim's eyes widened. "You were dead?"

Honus's blue lips bowed upward. "No. One need not die to go there. I was merely visiting, a skill that can be learned if you have the gift."

"Gift? Who'd want such a gift?"

"It's not altogether as you think," replied Honus. "The dead carry much to the Sunless Way. Though sorrow and worse are there, treasures can be found also. I look for those."

"You make it sound like robbing a graveyard."

"I take only memories," replied Honus.

"Only memories?" said Yim. "Except for the present, all of life is memory."

"You talk like my Bearer."

"I am your bearer."

Honus frowned. "You mistake the word," he said. "You bear my pack. In the Karmish Order, a Bearer is a holy person. My Bearer was my master."

"So, you've replaced your master with a slave?"

Honus flushed beneath his tattoos. "I won't tolerate blasphemy!"

"Pardon me, Master," said Yim. "I meant none. I'm ignorant of your ways."

"Bearers carry their Sarf's pack to practice humility and to insure their servant is ever ready to do their bidding. You're merely my porter. You haven't replaced my Bearer. You could never replace Theodus."

Yim started at the word. "Theodus?"

"Yes, that was my master's name. Why do you look so strangely?"

Yim glanced away, hiding her eyes from Honus. "Only because . . . because it's an unusual name."

"Like Yim?"

"Yes. Like Yim."

Yim busied herself with preparing breakfast. She stirred the pot to mix in the herbs and set it among the embers. "So you have no master now," she said. "Does that mean you're free?"

"Free?" said Honus. "I don't know what that means."

"Then you should ask me," said Yim. "No one sold *you* for ten coppers."

"We're all the goddess's slaves. She's the mistress who rules our fate. When Karm's Seers chose me as an infant for a life of service, my parents were paid in honors, not coppers. But what difference did that make?"

"They forced you to become a Sarf?"

"Oh, I wanted it badly enough. The temple was all I knew, so I labored long and hard to earn this face. Yet, I ask you—how can I be free if Karm wrote my fate upon my back?"

"Fate's but a word," replied Yim, "that we drape on mysteries beyond our understanding."

"And freedom's a word for something that doesn't exist."

"I was free once," said Yim. "It felt different from this."

"Then I've freed you from delusion."

Yim fell silent and turned her attention to the pot. She stirred the porridge with a stick to keep it from burning and tasted it occasionally to see if it was done. After a while, she said, "It's ready, Master." Using the stick, she removed the pot from the fire and placed it before Honus.

"Get me my spoon," said Honus. Yim found a wooden spoon in the pack and handed it to him. "I'd also like my shirt back."

Yim stiffened. "Will you look away while I remove it?"

"Yes," said Honus, handing Yim her tunic. "I'll close my eyes and not see you naked."

Yim relaxed and animation returned to her face. "Not even with your inner eye?"

Honus responded to her light answer in kind. "*All* are naked to my inner eye."

When Honus shut his eyes to let Yim dress, he realized how close his quip came to the truth. Those who could trance had a bit of the Seer in them. Honus found most people easy to lay bare. He knew he would find coins in Yaun's boot and that Peshnell would protect the miller by selling Yim. Yet some, like his late Bearer, were impenetrable. *This girl's like Theodus*, he thought, *a misty landscape where only the nearest things are clear*. It seemed strange that Yim should baffle his powers. Honus reflected on this until he heard her say, "I'm clothed, Master."

Honus opened his eyes. Yim handed him his shirt and sat on the ground. As she waited to eat, her face bore the faintest hint of a smile. It made Honus curious about its cause and more than a little suspicious.

EIGHT

HONUS TASTED the porridge and pronounced it "good." That was the last word he spoke. Afterward, he brooded silently. The transformation was so abrupt that it caught Yim off guard. Honus wordlessly handed her the pot and spoon when he was done, and she ate silently also. All the while, Yim wondered what she had said or done to so quickly change his mood. *It could have been anything—or nothing at all*. After some consideration, she supposed Honus's silence was a retreat on his part, an indication that he regretted having revealed anything about himself.

While Yim ate, Honus shaved using his sword blade, then put on his sandals and sword belt. After brushing the leaves from his cloak, he tied it about his shoulders. Yim read this as a sign that he wanted to resume their journey. Taking a cue from his silence, she didn't speak, but quickly broke camp and hefted the pack. Then Honus led them back to the road and set a pace that quickly drove away the morning chill. They walked wordlessly until Yim could stand the silence no longer. "Master, where are we going?"

"Bremven."

"Where's that? Is it far?"

Honus looked at Yim with surprise. "Are folk so ignorant in the Cloud Mountains they know not where the capital lies?"

"It's the Empire's capital, not ours. What know you of Taiben?"

Honus said nothing, but he picked up the pace. As Yim struggled to keep up, she sensed he was punishing her for impudence. She waited awhile before putting on her most humble and pitiful demeanor. "*Please,* Master, tell your slave girl about the way she must travel."

"It'll seem a long journey, if I must endure such whining."

"I didn't mean to annoy you, Master."

"I'm not used to slave ways."

"Was your former companion more to your liking?"

Honus shot Yim a hard glance, and she feared she had misspoken again. "He annoyed me in different ways."

"Master, I beg you. Please speak of our journey."

Honus sighed, but he rewarded Yim's persistence. "The way's not short nor easy. We've entered Luvein and must travel through it. It was once a fair and prosperous place, but not in living memory." He gestured at the road. "Though it's hard to believe, this was once a bustling highway."

"Yesterday, it seemed folk were fleeing here. Does an army wait ahead?"

"No. The invaders are to the north."

"Then why would folk rush toward harm?" Yim gazed about the wild and empty landscape, then guessed the answer. "Is the rest of Luvein this desolate?"

"Worse," said Honus. "I chose our route only because the enemy will shun it. There's naught to plunder."

"So it's safe?"

"The way's less perilous than some."

"Yet you seem to dread it."

"Is it so obvious?" Honus shook his head. "Luvein is full of memories, and few of them are fair."

"I feel it also," said Yim in a quiet voice. She walked awhile before asking, "How long till we reach Bremven?"

"A moon, perhaps less."

"And what will we do there?"

"Karm's temple lies on the city's mount. There, I'll seek a new Bearer. You'll get a new master also."

"Will you . . ." Yim paused, as if loath to say the word. "Will you sell me?"

"You're a slave," said Honus. "It's the custom."

"Perhaps you could find a family, Master. One with children to be tended."

"Perhaps. Or perhaps a master with a treadmill, if you displease me."

Yim fell silent again. She trailed behind Honus and took in the countryside. The road had shrunken to a weedy lane. With few feet and even fewer wagons to clear the way, the trees and brambles that had overwhelmed the fields and orchards were advancing on the road. The original pavement was exposed only in spots. It was ancient work, but the stones had been fitted with such skill that they endured. Their surfaces bore grooves from long-departed traffic.

Likewise, the landscape held traces of once-prosperous times. The high places were often crowned with impressive ruins. Many were razed fortifications. Others seemed built for peaceful purposes. These appeared to be the most ancient structures and were the most devastated. Yim spied humbler abodes, too. These were also neglected, but not all appeared abandoned. Occasionally, Yim caught fearful eyes watching her from dark windows.

Even nature seemed in decline. Spring was late in reaching the country, so grays and browns dominated. The tangled vines that strangled the trees were bare. Dead weeds choked the open places. The infrequent fields they encountered were littered with the rotted remnants of last year's plantings. Even the sky had turned somber. Thickening clouds vanquished the sun and the air chilled. As Yim walked through the bleak land, thorns raked her legs and stabbed her feet.

In sympathy with the scene about her, Yim's thoughts turned melancholy. She was heading south, and though an army threatened in the north, she felt danger lay ahead. Yim was certain that the Seer had believed the same. *I think he worried about more than robbers,* she thought. With insight that sometimes came to her, Yim perceived that something evil lurked ahead, something far more dangerous than lawless men.

Honus's thoughts were as dark as Yim's. They kept returning to Lurwic and what he had witnessed there. He wondered if those horrific deeds would transform that place into another Luvein. That dismal question troubled him, so he was relieved when Yim spoke and interrupted his musings.

"What happened here, Master?"

"The Balance went askew. Men came to love good things and not goodness itself. Fairness and charity were forgotten, and vast fortunes were born of greed. Justice was neglected, and great power arose from savagery. Then warfare raged for generations. Foul deeds inspired even fouler ones. The very land was abused. Now all is waste."

"How could such a thing come to pass?"

"When a man casts a shadow, who can tell if the darkness comes from him or goes to him?" said Honus. "All one can say is that evil arose here and lingers yet. Only now, folk murder for pigs, not palaces."

"You talk as if evil is a thing in itself and not the sum of ill deeds."

"Theodus used to say that it's a little of each. One feeds the other. Thus evil flourishes."

"How can that be so, if the goddess is good?"

"Why does a slave bother with such questions?"

"Men took my body and sold it. A mind is more difficult to snare. Do you think only Karm's Bearers ponder such things?"

"Apparently not."

"I see such cruelty in the world and wonder why Karm allows it."

"I'm unfit to answer such a question," said Honus. "But Theodus thought much upon it."

"And what did he conclude?"

"He believed something struggles against the goddess."

"The evil you spoke of?"

"Perhaps."

"But how can anything fight the goddess?"

"By corrupting the human heart."

"A thoughtful answer," said Yim. "Theodus sounds wise."

"He was."

"What happened to him?"

There was something in the tone of Yim's voice that made Honus glance at her. She walked bent under the weight of his pack, sweating despite the day's chill. Her eyes gazed into the distance, avoiding his. "Evil defeated him," said Honus.

When he uttered those words, Honus imagined a change in Yim. He felt he saw a different person—one who struggled under a terrible burden. Then the impression left him, and Yim was only a slave wearied by a heavy pack.

NINE

THE FARTHER Yim and Honus traveled, more silent the land became. Birds ceased calling, the air stilled, and the only voices were their own. Speech seemed out of place, as though they were disturbing a funeral. Nor was the quiet peaceful, for it was the result of tragedy. It oppressed Yim like the echoes of a thunderclap and felt as equally real. The day dragged on, and by afternoon, even Honus seemed fatigued. Yim trudged in senseless exhaustion.

"We must rest," said Honus at last. "Luvein is a wearisome place."

Yim slumped by the roadside without removing the pack. Honus drank from the water skin and held it out for Yim. She only stared blankly at the road, too tired to react. Honus began to put the skin away, halted, and knelt before Yim to bring the water skin to her lips. Yim drank, then looked at Honus with mute gratitude. Afterward, she closed her eyes.

When Yim awoke, it was early afternoon. She was surprised to discover that she was wrapped in her cloak and lying on the ground with the pack beside her. Honus was in the middle of the roadway, moving in what seemed to be a graceful yet savage dance. He kicked, swirled, and sliced the air with his feet and fists. There were moments of stillness followed by dazzling quickness that reminded Yim of the previous night's deadly encounter. Honus spun, and suddenly his sword was in his hand. It flashed to sever a leaf from a bough. The leaf fluttered toward the ground.

The sword sliced; then two parts fell. The blade whispered again, and the leaf was three, then four, then five pieces before it touched the earth. As suddenly as the sword appeared, it was sheathed and the dance continued. Yim was so mesmerized by the elegance of Honus's movements that she nearly forgot their lethal application.

Honus continued his exercises long after Yim tired of watching them. She was rubbing her sore feet when he came over, dripping with sweat, to drink from the water skin. "We must resume our journey," he said, "if we're to reach the foothills by nightfall."

Yim gazed down the road. Ahead, the land seemed to ripple, forming a succession of earthen waves that rose ever higher until they reached mountains. The peaks were hazy, but the nearer landscape was equally monochrome. It was merely a darker shade of gray. "What's in the foothills, Master?"

"A few poor farmers. Some may hold yet to the old customs."

"What customs?"

"Once, a Bearer or a Sarf could expect hospitality wherever they traveled. Now it is less so, especially in Luvein."

Yim saw that the sky threatened rain. "It'd be good to sleep under a roof." She put on the pack and felt as if it had never left her shoulders. Honus set out immediately. After a while, cold drizzle began to fall. Yim donned her cloak and was glad for its warmth. The drizzle changed to rain. As Yim trudged on, she looked for a homestead, but the empty land grew wilder and the hills still looked distant. When daylight faded, Yim began to despair of finding shelter.

"If we reach a farm, surely they'll take us in," said Yim. "Who would dare to defy a Sarf?"

"Food and shelter must be given freely," said Honus. "Otherwise, Karm's dishonored. Even if we find a farm, it's not unlikely we'll spend the night outside."

As if to further discourage Yim, the rain began to fall

harder. Soon she was treading through cold, viscous mud. Night arrived without any sign of habitation.

"It's too wet for a fire," said Honus, "and walking will keep us warm. We'll travel as long as we can."

Yim said nothing, but her thoughts dwelt upon how it was she, not Honus, who carried the pack. She trudged quietly through the gloomy rain until she spotted a faint glimmer in the darkness. "Master! A light!"

Away from the road was the ruin of a large stone house, black against a dark hillside. It appeared roofless, but from one of the lowest windows came the pale light of a fire reflected off stone walls. "Don't get your hopes up," said Honus as he headed toward the light. Yim followed him through a small, muddy field. The entrance to the house was doorless and the steps leading up to it had rotted away, stranding the doorway high on the wall. At the base of this wall, a man-sized hole had been smashed through the stones. It also lacked a door. Out of this cavity stepped a man bearing an ax.

"Ya stop thar!" he called out in a voice that mingled anger with fear. "What be ya wantin'?"

In the dim light, it was hard to make out the man's age, but he appeared ill-treated by life. His large frame looked gaunt and his face was lined and worn. Yet his tangled hair and beard were black, and he moved with wiry strength.

Honus bowed his head politely. "We're servants of Karm, Father."

The man spit. "Father, my arse! So it be Karmish beggars. Do ya na come in pairs? Ah see just one . . . an' his slut."

Honus replied in a calm voice, "We request shelter and food in respect for the goddess."

"Aye, an' if she ever respected *me*, maybe thar'd be some ta give." The man eyed Honus suspiciously and tensely held his ax at the ready.

"I'll take nothing you don't give freely, be it only a corner in your stable."

"Then take yar whore an' go rut in the woods," replied the man.

"Come, Yim," said Honus. "The goddess is not honored here."

Honus had turned to walk back to the road when a ragged woman with wild, white hair hobbled out of the doorway. "Karmamatus!" she called in a thin, quavering voice. "Karmamatus, do na leave us."

"Mam, go inside," said the man. "It be too cold an' wet fer ya."

The old woman ignored her son and struggled through the mud until she reached Honus. She grasped his cloak with dirty, gnarled fingers. "Please, Karmamatus, please . . ."

"Mam," said the man more gently than Yim expected, "they just be beggars."

The woman looked about in confusion and saw Yim for the first time. Her eyes widened, and she let out a long wail that seemed to combine both deep sorrow and joy. She sank to her knees, buried her face in Honus's cloak, and wept. The man dropped his ax and came over to lift his mother from the mud.

"Thank ya, Karmamatus," she said between sobs. "Thank ya." She turned to the man and said triumphantly, "Ah told ya, Gan! Ah told ya they'd bring her back!" She broke free from her son and embraced Yim with more strength than her frail frame seemed capable of mustering. Yim felt hot tears against her cold cheek as the woman sobbed softly into her ear. Gradually, the sobs changed to a whispered name. "Mirien . . . Mirien . . . Mirien . . ."

Gan sighed, his breath steaming in the damp air. "Come inside," he said to Honus and Yim, not bothering to hide his irritation. "She will na abide ta see ya go."

Yim walked through the opening with the old woman still clutching her. Inside the shell of the derelict house, an abode had been constructed by roofing over its basement. The stone walls were rough, but, unlike the chambers above them, they had withstood the assaults of time and man. The low, uneven ceiling was made of branches covered with slabs of bark and thatch. Rain leaked from it onto the dirty stone floor.

Gan's mother led them through three dark rooms to one lit by a meager fire. The room smelled of the smoke that drifted out of a hole in the ceiling and of the pig kept in an adjacent chamber. The sow watched them from behind a barricade of thorny woven branches. The room was furnished with a crude table, a single bench, and a chest. The rest of the household's few possessions were piled near one of the walls. Despite its rudeness, the room was mostly dry and the fire gave a bit of warmth.

As the old woman stroked Yim's cheek and kissed it occasionally, Yim gave Gan a puzzled look.

"She be havin' one o' her fits," said Gan in answer to Yim's unspoken question. "She thinks ya be my older sister, stolen as a child."

In the firelight, it was clear that Gan was at least forty and that his mother's eyes shone with madness. At the moment, they also shone with love.

"Mirien," said the old woman with a breath that smelled of rotted teeth, "ya have been gone overlong. Tell me," she whispered, glancing toward Honus, "be he yar husband?"

"Tell her what she wants ta hear," said Gan heavily. "It will make na difference."

"Yes, Mommy," replied Yim, "he is."

The old woman beamed, displaying a single yellow tooth. "A Sarf, too. What a fine husband, though Ah do na like his face."

"There's a tender face beneath the fierce one."

Mam squinted at Honus. "Aye, Ah think Ah ken see it." Her face grew sad and her mouth began to quiver. "Why? Why did ya na invite us ta the wedding feast?"

"We wed in Bremven, Mommy. You were there. Don't you remember?"

"Ah . . . Ah think . . ." replied Mam, growing confused. "It be hard ta recall. Aye. Ah remember now."

"I wore flowers in my hair and Honus frightened you before you learned how gentle he was."

A gleam came to Mam's wet eyes. "Aye . . . flowers."

"White roses."

Mam breathed in deeply. "Oh, the smell o' them. Did . . . did Ah dance?"

"Dance? You danced all night! You wore me out."

"Ah did! Ah did! Ah beed strong then. An' young!"

Gan, who had been watching this exchange with a melancholy expression, started to leave the room. "Ah'll get some more roots fer the pot," he said.

"An' ale," called out his mother. "Ale fer yar sister an' her fine new husband."

Gan scowled, but returned with an earthenware jug along with two roots. He threw the latter, unwashed, into a pot sitting on the fire. Then he took four rough wooden bowls from the floor near the wall and poured ale into them. The flat brew was sour and skunky, but Yim drank it all in hopes of a bit of warmth. Honus took one polite sip, then pushed his bowl away. Gan grabbed Honus's bowl and drained it before refilling his own. Mam raised her bowl in a silent toast and slurped down its contents. Afterward, she turned quiet and smiled blankly as she swayed to music only she could hear.

Gan downed the third bowl of ale and some color came to his face. "Yar woman," he said to Honus with a sneer, "be full o' tricks."

"Yes. She's surprising," said Honus. He fixed his eyes on Yim. "How did you know to call her 'Mommy'?"

Yim looked away to avoid his gaze. "That's what I called my own mother."

"Then it was a clever guess," said Honus.

" 'Twill make na difference," said Gan, glancing at his swaying mother. "She'll ferget all this by morning. Then, maybe, she'll have a new fit . . ." He grinned at Yim with jagged teeth. ". . . an' slit yar throat."

Yim didn't react to Gan's remark, but quietly asked, "What happened to Mirien?"

"Ah beed young, but Ah ken na ferget," said Gan. "It be like yesterday. Mam an' me came back from gatherin' mushrooms. My da be slain an' Mirien be gone."

"Was your sister young?" asked Yim.

"Aye," replied Gan, "but old enough fer some men. We found her in the road . . ." He poured and gulped down another bowl. "Mam went daft. Day after day, she prayed ta the goddess!" he said. "The goddess that took her child, then took her mind! Honor Karm? Ah'd sooner honor a whore! Ah'll tell ya 'bout yar Balance. A strong man pushes down on it, till the scale favors him!"

"Like the strong men who took your sister?" asked Honus.

"Ya ken na fool me with yar Karmish talk. Ah found a true god! A strong god, na some sluttish woman." He pulled at a cord around his neck to reveal an iron pendant in the form of a circle. "The Eater!"

Honus coldly eyed the rusty symbol. "The Devourer of Souls."

"Ta become one with his strength! My hate becomes his hate!"

TEN

GAN'S SHOUTING broke his mother's reverie, and she looked about in confusion. If she noticed Yim or Honus, she made no sign of it. "Gan," she said in a whiny voice, "Ah'm hungry."

Gan gathered up the bowls and went over to the pot. With a wooden spoon, he fished out one root for each bowl and poured in some of the cooking water for broth. He brought Mam's and his bowls over to the table, leaving Honus and Yim to get theirs. Taking out a knife, he peeled Mam's root and mashed it into mush with the spoon. He placed the bowl and spoon before her, then picked up his own dinner and began to eat.

Yim served Honus and herself. The roots in the muddy broth were small and partly rotted. She placed the largest one in front of Honus and sat at the end of the bench to eat. Before she could do so, Honus wordlessly switched their bowls. "Thank you, Master," said Yim. Honus didn't reply.

The meager meal was eaten in silence. The only sounds were Mam's slurping and the falling rain. Yim was so hungry she ate the root unpeeled and drank all the gritty broth. As she ate, the fire died down to embers and the room grew darker. When the meal was consumed, Gan rose. "There be some hay in the room closest ta the outer door," he said. He went over to the wall and dragged two large, lumpy sacks that served as beds closer to the dying embers. Mam hobbled over to one and lay down. Gan took the ale jug and a bowl over to the other sack and sat upon it.

"We'll find our way," said Honus in an amiable tone. He rose and left the room. Yim followed. She went slowly through the dark chambers. When she stepped in a puddle, she paused to wash her muddy feet in the shallow water. By the time she entered the outermost chamber, Honus was already wrapped in his cloak and lying on some hay piled near the wall. Yim could barely make out his dark form in the dim light. He didn't call for her to lie beside him and though Yim would have liked the warmth, she was relieved that he didn't. Yim groped for a dry spot in the moldy hay and wrapped herself in her cloak. She was exhausted and wished to sleep, but couldn't. Instead, she considered what to do.

Don't be foolish, Yim told herself, recalling all her guardian's warnings. Yet the Wise Woman was far away, and Yim couldn't shake Mam from her thoughts. The old woman's grief and madness tugged at her heart. In her mind's eye, Yim envisioned Mam weeping over her murdered child and the image overwhelmed caution. Yim abandoned prudence. Compelled to act, she listened to Honus's breathing for signs that he slept.

Yim waited a long while before she rose from the hay. By then, the rain had ceased and the moon glowed behind thin clouds. Cautiously, she made her way to the room where Mam and Gan slept. Moonlight shining through high windows revealed them lying on their sacks near the ashes of the dead fire. Gan snored noisily, an ale bowl still in his hand. Yim knelt on the stone floor a few feet from Mam, then sat on her heels and folded her hands in her lap.

Staring straight ahead, Yim took a deep breath and began the meditations she had learned as a child. As the world emptied from her mind, her surroundings seemed to fade while the invisible became apparent. Without moving her eyes, Yim glanced about until she spied a vaporous form. Wordlessly, she beckoned it.

Yim remained rigid, and for a while, the only motion

in the room was Mam's tossing and turning as she slept. Then, the moonlight wavered as if clouds were streaking across the sky. Vaporous patches of shadow began to move over the floor. They grew darker until they became absolutely black. The room turned icy, and as Yim sat in perfect stillness, her breath came out as a foggy mist. The blackness gathered before her, forming a pool. The surface of that pool began to move upward like a person rising beneath a velvet cloth.

Frost formed on the stones of the room, but sweat dripped down Yim's brow. The blackness stopped rising and a pale glow appeared within it. A translucent figure of a child could be discerned, her form illuminated by some unseen source of light. The dark dissipated, leaving the girl standing before Yim. She was unclothed, as are all spirits of the dead.

"Mirien?" whispered Yim.

The child's lips moved, mouthing words that only Yim could hear. Yim rose to her knees and held out her arms to embrace the ghost. The child stepped forward, and as Yim's arms enfolded her, she dissolved. Yim began to shiver violently as she peered about the room. Everything about her wavered, being one thing and then another. Gan was a drunken man, and then he was a tiny boy. The filthy clutter came and went. Mam's ratty white hair turned black and her wrinkled skin became smooth. Eventually, Yim's vision settled, and she saw everything through long-dead eyes.

She reached out and gently touched the cheek of the young woman asleep before her. The woman stirred. "Mommy," said Yim in a child's voice that was not her own.

The woman's eyes opened, then widened as she saw her daughter's spirit within Yim. "Mirien," she said, "Ah thought ya beed . . ."

"Ah'm embraced by the goddess now."

The woman's face crumpled beneath the weight of her grief, and Yim moved to cradle her in her arms. She held

Mam and let her cry. When the sobbing diminished, Yim spoke again. "Great was my sorrow, but now great is my joy. Ya must believe that, Mommy."

"Mirien . . . Mirien, Ah miss ya so!"

"Ah know, Ah know," said Yim.

"Did ya suffer much?"

"My life seems but a dream with the sad parts over quick. Think on this instead—we'll be together an' we'll be happy."

"Ah want ta die," sobbed Mam. "Die an' be with ya."

"Only ya ken take care o' baby brother," said Yim. "He's so sad and angry. Please help him. Do this fer me."

"Aye, Mirien. Ah promise."

Yim kissed the young woman who smiled and grew peaceful, then fell asleep in her arms. Yim continued to hold Mam while Mirien's spirit departed for the Dark Path. Then Yim's own vision returned. The woman in her arms grew old and the room turned dirty and cluttered. Yim lowered Mirien's mother down on the sack and covered her with a filthy blanket. The frost upon the stones began to melt, but effects of the spirit's visit lingered with Yim. She was chilled to the bone. Her hands and feet stung. Rising unsteadily, she cautiously made her way back to the outer chamber.

When Yim entered the room, she heard Honus's harsh voice in the dark. "Where were you?"

"I . . . I was cold, Master. I looked to see if there was any ale left."

"Such thievery dishonors Karm," said Honus. "I should beat you."

"Please, Master, I took none."

"No doubt, because there was none to take."

Honus jumped up and seized Yim's forearm. She gasped at his painful grip and flinched, expecting a blow. None came. Honus relaxed his hand. "Am I that fearful?" he asked. "You're trembling all over."

"I'm cold, Master."

"Gan is an ungracious host, yet he has little to give. It's not for you to betray his generosity."

"I won't do it again."

"See that you don't. Otherwise, you'll feel my hand."

"Yes, Master."

Honus released Yim. "Now go to sleep."

Yim went over to the hay, glad that Honus couldn't see her tears. She ached from the cold and her arm throbbed where Honus had seized it. Wrapped in her damp cloak, she was too cold and miserable to sleep, despite her exhaustion. Honus sounded like he was awake also, and swallowing her pride, Yim called to him. "Pl . . . pl . . . please, Ma . . . Master, may I lie beside you? I'm so c . . . cold."

"I think it best," said Honus, "that you lie alone and contemplate how you disgraced the goddess."

Gan awoke to the warmth of a fire. As much as that surprised him, he was even more surprised to see his mother sweeping. He couldn't imagine where she had found a broom. "Mam! Ya'll choke me with that dust."

"Ah be sorry, Son, but Ah could abide it na longer."

"It never bothered ya afore."

"That be true, but it should have."

Gan rubbed his bleary eyes and tried to ignore the throbbing in his head. Then, he noticed the pot was on the fire. "What be ya cooking?"

"Breakfast. We have guests."

Gan's expression turned sour. "Beggars," he said contemptuously. "A Sarf an' his whore."

Mam walked over to him and grabbed his shoulders. Her strength astonished him, but not as much as the look in her eyes. Her gaze was lucid and intense. "Do na speak o' what ya do na understand."

"Aye, Mam," said Gan meekly.

"Ya be a good son," said Mam, "but hate be poor medicine fer sorrow."

Mam went over to the pot and gave it a stir. "Ya ken tell our guests that thar be food fer them."

Gan rose to waken Honus and Yim. By the time the three returned, there were four bowls of porridge on the table. The steam that rose from them smelled of fresh spring herbs. Mam walked over to Yim, who looked pale and drawn, and hugged her. "Ah do na remember yar name."

"It's Yim, Mother."

"Yim," said the old woman so lovingly that Honus looked at her intently. "Thank ya fer yar visit."

"Ah told ya she'd be like ta have a fit," said Gan.

Honus nodded, but seemed not to agree. They all sat down to a meal that, despite its humbleness, was as savory as the last one had been loathsome. Mam put down her bowl and smiled at the way her son was enjoying his breakfast. "Gan, do ya recall the old gardens behind the ruins north o' the bend?" Her son nodded as he ate. "Roses used ta grow thar. White ones. Ah think they might still."

"So?" replied her son.

"Ah be thinkin' ya could dig one up ta put by our door."

"Why?"

"It would help me ta recall Mirien. She liked roses."

Gan studied his mother's face. "Aye," he said after a few moments. "White roses would be good."

Whatever was going on puzzled Honus and made him reluctant to leave. Nevertheless, he stood up. "Come, Yim," he said. "We should depart."

"Yes, Master."

"Wait!" said Mam. She rose from the bench, went over to the chest, and opened it. After rummaging about, she found what she was seeking and pulled out some cloth. It was yellowed and moth-eaten, but it appeared to have been white once. Mam gave the cloth to Yim and asked her to unfold it. It was a dress, embroidered with white roses.

"Ah've been saving this fer . . . fer . . ." Mam fought to control her tears. "Ah want ya ta have it."

"Shouldn't you keep it?" asked Yim.

"Nay, Mirien has na need fer it."

"Then I'd be honored by your gift."

"Put it on," said Mam, "an' wear it as ya leave."

"Yes, Mother." Yim left the room and returned a short while later in the dress. She turned around slowly so Mam could see the wedding gown. Honus and Gan watched silently as Mam's eyes welled with tears. She walked over to Yim and softly kissed her cheek. "Thank ya," she whispered. "Thank ya, Karmamatus."

Gan's lips were quivering as he turned to Honus. In a husky voice he said, "Pah! She has na cause ta call her that."

ELEVEN

YIM WALKED gracefully from Mam's home despite carrying the pack in her arms. Before she was halfway across the muddy field, the dress began to disintegrate. Bits of fabric fell like flower petals thrown after a departing bride. By the time she turned a bend and was out of Mam's sight, Yim was nearly naked. She stepped behind a tree and emerged wearing her slave's tunic and cloak. All that remained of the dress was a piece of embroidery, which Yim placed in the pack before shouldering it.

Yim's stately air had vanished with the dress. When she

resumed walking, she looked sullen and moved as though already weary. Honus started to say something, but thought better of it. Instead, he scrutinized Yim's face, trying to understand what had transpired. As before, his powers of perception were frustrated. All he could detect was resentment. Thinking upon it, Honus briefly regretted his harshness. Then he grew annoyed that Yim's mood affected him. He thought it was weakness on his part and a distraction from his obligations. *Stop fretting over her. She's only a slave.*

Honus picked up the pace, but Yim made no effort to keep up. Soon, she lagged far behind, and he was forced to wait for her. When Yim shambled wearily to where he stood, Honus didn't hide his irritation. "Are you doing this to provoke me?"

Yim tensed, as if expecting a blow. "No, Master. I'm doing the best I can. I'm not used to this, and I slept ill."

"Oh yes, I forgot. You're a *princess.*"

"Just a peddler's daughter, Master," said Yim, gazing at her feet, "but I rode in a wagon."

"So finally, a bit of truth. What did you think to gain from that silly tale?"

"I hoped you'd think better of me."

"Then you haven't been around royalty. Princesses incline toward vanity and indolence."

"I'm sorry I lied, Master."

Honus merely grunted and began walking again. He set a slower pace, and though Yim followed at a distance, she kept up with him. Every time he glanced back at her, she was glaring at him in a way he found annoying. At last, he halted and waited for Yim to catch up. "Will you mope all the way to Bremven?"

"If you wanted a cheerful companion, you shouldn't have bought a slave."

"I had my reasons."

"I obey your commands, yet I seem to vex you."

"That's because you do!"

"Then buying me was a bad idea, but that's not my fault."

Honus advanced toward Yim, and again she tensed. Honus scowled, saying, "I'm as displeased by that purchase as you." He started walking, then turned to see if Yim was following. When he saw that she was, he said, "Put away that sour face and I'll let you rest soon."

Yim flashed him a broad and patently insincere smile. "Thank you, Master."

"Soon" turned out to be not soon at all, for Honus walked half the morning without stopping. The road he followed, though paved, was devoid of traffic. It wound through hills, climbing ever higher. Trees hemmed its sides, but the surrounding forest didn't appear old. None of the tree trunks were thicker than the span of two hands, and most were smaller. They grew among the stones of tumbled walls and poked through the shells of roofless buildings like giant weeds. Throughout the entire morning, neither Honus nor Yim said a further word. They remained silent as Honus led the way up an embankment and entered a ruined house that consisted of three partial walls. Thorny vines shrouded the stones they were slowly prying apart. Then Honus spoke. "You can set down the pack. I'm going hunting."

Yim slipped the pack from her shoulders. Wordlessly, she spread her cloak over the dead weeds inside the ruin and lay upon it to rest. Closing her eyes, she heard Honus leave. She lay still, not resting but thinking. *If I'm going to escape, this is the time to do it.* Honus was taking her into desolate territory on a journey that suited only his purposes. *And at its end, I'll be sold again.* Yim's resentment grew as she recalled Honus's self-righteousness the previous night and his impatience during the day's march. *He's not carrying a pack! I am.* Even Honus's protection was suspect. Although he had saved her from rape or worse by the two brigands, he had also used her as bait to lure them out. The more Yim thought about her situation, the more freedom seemed less risky than remaining with such a man.

Yim rose and put on her cloak. Her apparent weariness had been partly a show to conserve her energy. With Honus gone, she was determined to use that energy to flee. She searched the pack for the knife and water skin, but Honus had taken both. Though disappointed, Yim didn't change her mind. She slipped out of the building and headed for the road. Yim assumed that Honus wouldn't hunt near the roadway, so it would be the safest route to take. Additionally, she'd be less likely to leave a trail, since the road was paved. Yim planned to head deeper into Luvein, for she thought Honus would be less likely to suspect her going that way. There, she would hide until she thought it was safe to return to more settled parts.

Yim ran down the road after she reached it. Without a heavy pack on her shoulders, running felt almost effortless and the exuberance of freedom invigorated her stride. Before long, Yim slowed to a more sustainable pace as she planned her next move. For the moment, she focused on evading Honus. She assumed he would search about the ruin and find her trail to the road. She hoped he'd head in the wrong direction, but she couldn't count on it. *Even if he does, he'll eventually come this way.* Yim envisioned the enraged Sarf tracking her, and she quickened her steps.

A short while later, Yim encountered a stream that crossed the road. Water had eroded the pavement, depositing it along a rock-strewn course that ran down the hillside. Yim saw that by stepping from rock to rock she could exit the road without leaving any footprints. She decided to take that route and began to carefully pick her way. With painstaking effort, she made her way down the hill. When the road was no longer visible, she relaxed and traveled along the stream bank.

Yim kept walking and the way grew less steep. By noon, she was traveling in a valley, and the stream flowed broader and more sluggishly. Thick bushes crowded its sides and they were often thorny, forcing her to wade in the water to avoid them. Thus Yim was relieved when she encountered a pathway that crossed the stream. It was only a dirt track, but it was used enough to be weed-free.

Yim looked up and down the path. Assuming that it would lead to people, she wondered if she should follow it. As she weighed the option, she regretted her hasty departure. *I should have stolen the grain, the pot, and the flint and iron.* The Wise Woman had taught her how to recognize edible wild plants, but Yim didn't relish the thought of eating them raw. Moreover, she had yet to see anything edible. Her growing hunger argued for seeking hospitality. Yim thought there should be folk who would welcome another pair of hands to share the work. *I could approach them carefully and size them up before I reveal myself.* Yim decided that if she used caution, the risk would be reasonable.

Listening for the slightest sounds and glancing all around her, Yim made her way along the path. For a long while, she saw only woodland and deserted ruins. She was passing another empty-looking building, a roofless hulk that clawed the sky with broken fingers, when she noted a plot of overturned earth. It lay just beyond a crude opening in the ruin's base. Assuming the tilled ground was a sign of habitation, Yim crept through tangled weeds for a closer look.

Except for the beginnings of a garden, the building looked deserted. Yim watched it awhile, and when she saw no sign of life, she moved closer. Upon reaching the edge of the plot, she heard the soft sound of a stick tapping against stone. Next she heard a woman's voice. "Fossa? Fossa? Be it ya?"

Yim froze, prepared to run at any instant. The tapping grew louder, and then a form became visible inside the dark opening. Yim could make out a ragged woman using a cane to find her way. When the woman reached the sunlight, Yim saw that she had a worn face, graying hair, and eyes the color of bluish milk. The woman halted and moved her head about as the blind do, not to look around but to listen. "Fossa?" The woman began to swing her cane in an agitated manner. "Someone be thar. Ah heared ya in the weeds."

"It's only me, Mother. A lone traveler. I mean no harm."

"Ya be a girl!" said the woman, clearly surprised. "It be na safe ta go 'bout 'lone."

"I have no choice."

"Come here, dear. Ah ken na see ya. Let me touch yar face."

After a moment's hesitation, Yim advanced to the woman, who held out her hand. Yim gently guided it to her face. The woman's fingers glided over Yim's features. "Ya be young." Then the woman brushed her hand down Yim's arm, pausing to squeeze it. The woman smiled. "Yar na starvin'."

"No."

"But ya be hungry an' tired, Ah suppose," said the woman. "Come inside."

Yim eyed the building's dark interior warily. "Do you live alone?"

"Nay, dear. Ah have a daughter. Fossa. She be out gatherin' herbs. Ah thought ya be her."

Like Honus, Yim could discern much about people by gazing into their eyes. However, the woman's milky orbs were curtained windows. They were set in a deeply lined and dirty face. Though the woman looked old, Yim guessed she was not, for she moved with no sign of frailty and her intact teeth looked strong. After a moment's indecision, Yim accepted the woman's offer. "Thank you, Mother. I'm indeed tired and hungry."

The woman smiled. "Call me Auntie, dear. Auntie Flora. Come."

Auntie Flora turned and entered the opening that served as a doorway. Like Gan and his mother's home, her abode was in a former basement. The chambers in this one had ceilings of vaulted stone that were intact except where an occasional block had been removed to admit daylight. These openings provided the only illumination, and it was dim. Yim could see little until her eyes adjusted. She followed Auntie Flora, for whom the lack of light presented no problem, through a series of small, empty rooms. At last they reached a sparsely furnished chamber. "Ya ken rest here," said Yim's host.

There were two sleeping sacks close to the ashes of a fire, a rude wooden table with a pair of equally rude benches, and a surprisingly large pile of clothing in a corner. Yim felt it would be rude to lie down, so she sat on one of the benches. Her host took the other one. "So dear, wha' be yar name?"

"Yim, Auntie Flora."

"An' wha' be ya runnin' from? A cruel husband or mayhap a da who beat ya overmuch?"

"I've escaped my master," replied Yim. "I was a slave."

Distraction was the cause for Yim's unguarded reply, for her attention was on the adjoining room. It appeared to be a kitchen. From her vantage point, Yim could see a large iron kettle set in an enormous fireplace. From that room came tantalizing smells that made Yim's mouth water and her stomach rumble. She inhaled deeply and took in the rich aromas of spice and smoked meat. Yim heard Auntie Flora ask a question, but it didn't register until it was repeated. "Have ya been runnin' long?"

"Just this morning. What's that delicious smell?"

Auntie Flora smiled. "Sausages. Fossa an' Ah make them fer folk. They bring us pigs, an' we turn them inta sausage. We keep some links as pay."

"You must be very skilled." Then Yim added shamelessly, "The smell's making me hungry."

"Aye, Ah be skilled," replied Auntie Flora, ignoring Yim's hint. "Ya do na need eyes to make good sausage, jus' a keen nose an' a clever tongue. An' good meat, o' course. It be hard work though. Mayhap ya'll stay an' help Fossa an' me."

Yim was glad for the offer. "I'd be happy to help."

Auntie Flora grinned. "Good! Good! It'll be pleasin' ta have a young one 'bout."

Yim still hoped that her host would offer her a taste, but Auntie Flora disappointed her. Instead, she began a rambling discourse on her craft. She was claiming that she wasted nothing " 'cept the oink" when she suddenly stopped talking. "Ah hear somethin'!"

Yim strained her ears, but heard nothing. "What?"

"Footsteps. Someone's comin'. Na Fossa. A man."

Yim immediately thought of Honus. She whispered, "It could be my master!"

TWELVE

AUNTIE FLORA rose immediately. "Quick. Ah'll hide ya." Using her cane like a groping appendage, she led Yim into the adjoining room. It was filled with the implements of her trade. In addition to the kettle, there were several wooden tables. One was long and particularly massive. Its bloodstained surface was thoroughly hacked and scored by the knives and cleavers that lay about. A heavy chain with a massive hook at its end dangled from a pulley set in the stone ceiling. Beneath it was a large crockery pot, its inside darkened by dried blood. A wide assortment of herbs hung on pegs set in the walls. Several ropes were strung across the dimly lit room, and the sausages that had so tantalized Yim hung from them. The links had a variety of shapes and shades. Close up, their aroma was even more intense and inviting. Beneath the strings of sausages, a chest sat against the wall. Auntie Flora went over to it and opened its lid. The chest was empty. "Quick! Hide inside."

Yim stepped into the open chest and folded her body so it fit into the space. Then Auntie Flora shut the lid. Immediately afterward, Yim was disconcerted to hear the metallic sound of a latch being closed. Though wedged into the close space, she was able to maneuver her hand upward to press against the lid. It wouldn't budge. The panic she felt about Honus catching her was replaced by the more primal one of being trapped in a dark, cramped place.

Stay calm, Yim thought. *I'll be here just awhile.* Yet even that prospect was unpleasant. Not only was the chest cramped, its wooden floor was damp and smelled of urine. Yim couldn't imagine why. At least the chest's interior wasn't entirely dark; there was a hole the size of a walnut in its side. The opening admitted some light and was close to Yim's eye. When she examined the hole, she discovered that it had been gouged out from the inside of the chest. Something was embedded in the wood about its edge. Yim pulled it out and discovered it was a torn fingernail. Then she noticed that the hole's edges were bloodstained, and she imagined it had been clawed in desperation.

The thought chilled Yim. *Others have been trapped in here before!* The dangling sausages took on sinister implications. Frantic, Yim pushed against the chest's lid. Her cramped position afforded little leverage. She began pounding on the chest's side, but it was stoutly made. Soon she heard a muffled voice. Yim placed her ear against the hole and heard Auntie. She was shouting. "Stop yar racket! Stop

yar racket! Thar be na one ta hear it 'cept me. Ya wanted ta
help make sausage an' help ya will. Meat be needed, an'
ya'll provide it."

Yim thought it would be best to keep pounding and
give the impression that she hadn't heard. She continued
awhile before tapering off. Then she placed her ear against
the hole and listened. Yim could hear Auntie Flora moving
about the room. Yim peered out the hole and occasionally
glimpsed Flora's skirt as she brought items to the table. It
seemed to Yim that her captor was preparing to go to work.

She's probably waiting for her daughter to come back,
thought Yim. She knew nothing about making sausages,
but she had seen sheep and goats slaughtered. The usual
method was to stun them with a blow to the head, quickly
hoist them up by the hind legs, and cut their throats. That
way the blood would drain quickly, helped by a still beating heart. *Most like, they'll do the same to me.* Yim assumed Auntie Flora needed her sighted daughter to deliver
the blow.

Yim envisioned her final moments. Flora would quickly
open the lid. Fossa would be standing beside her with a
cudgel. Yim would be exposed in a bent-over position, her
head an easy target. Before she could stand or even raise
her arms, the blow would fall. With luck, she'd be unconscious when her throat was slit.

Yim tried to imagine how she could avoid that blow. The
cramped chest would hamper her movements, and Fossa
was surely practiced. Yim's chin touched her knees, a position that would preclude springing up quickly. She could
cover her head with her hands, but fingers made a poor
shield against a heavy cudgel. Then Yim had another chill-
ing thought. *Perhaps she'll use a cleaver, not a cudgel!* Yim
wondered if she could land a punch before she died, but
even that seemed unlikely. *She'll be expecting it.*

Then Yim thought of something her attacker wouldn't
expect. *A kick!* Though the chest was cramped, Yim thought

she might be able to roll over on her back. Then her head wouldn't be exposed and her legs would be positioned to deliver a powerful kick, albeit only in one direction. Her ploy would require more than a little luck to succeed, but Yim could think of no other.

Turning over inside the chest proved difficult, but after a struggle, Yim managed. She lay on her back, her legs folded above her. Then all she could do was wait and listen. Flora continued puttering about the kitchen before eventually leaving. For a long while, Yim heard nothing. Then at last, she heard the tapping of Flora's cane accompanied by two voices. At first, Yim couldn't make them out, but they gradually grew louder.

". . . mahself," said Flora's voice. "Na sharin' with nabody."

"All fer us. How sweet," said another woman's voice. Yim assumed it was Fossa's. "Be she good stock?"

"Aye, choice. Young, firm, an' meaty. Ah squeezed her mahself."

"Good. Good. Then let's do it."

Yim tensed as she heard approaching footsteps, then the sound of the latch being unfastened. The lid opened quickly, and Yim saw two forms. One was Flora, who grasped the lid. She stood to one side. A younger woman leaned over the chest. She gripped a stout club. Yim's heels pointed straight at her. Yim thrust her legs with all her force and caught the woman in the stomach. Fossa flew backward, doubled over.

Yim tried to climb out of the chest, but her position impeded her. She was on her back with her legs dangling out. She grabbed the edge of the chest to pull herself up. Meanwhile, Flora was aware something had gone wrong. "Fossa, wha' be happenin'?"

For a moment, Fossa could only gasp for breath. "Cl . . . Cl . . . Close it!"

By then, Yim was partway out, so when Flora slammed

down the lid, it struck Yim's legs and shoulder. Flora instinctively groped for the obstruction. When she did, Yim seized her wrist. Flora pulled away and Yim used that momentum to raise herself enough to cause the chest to tip on its side. Then she rolled free from it just as Fossa, her breath recovered, charged with her club raised. Yim kicked again, but this time her assailant wasn't caught surprised. She swung at Yim's shin and struck a glancing blow.

The pain in Yim's leg was so intense that she momentarily thought her bone had been broken. But terror gripped and energized her. Despite her pain, she rolled and sprang to her feet beside the dangling chain. She grabbed it and pulled it loose, then spun so the heavy hook swung in her attacker's direction. The chain struck Fossa's neck and the momentum of the massive hook caused the links to wrap around her throat. Yim yanked hard. Fossa fell sprawling on the floor and lay still. When her assailant didn't rise, Yim half ran and half limped from the room. Behind her, Flora began to wail.

Yim made her way through the outer chambers into the sunlight. Then she sped back down the path as quickly as she could. Terror spurred her more than fear of pursuit; she craved to be far from the horrors in the dark building. When Yim encountered the stream, she followed it toward the road. The brambles that crowded the waterway's bank scratched her arms and legs, but she was mindless of her hurts. Her only concern was to reach the place Honus had left her before he returned from his hunt. She was approaching the road when she spied him following tracks that she thought she had skillfully hidden. Knowing that she had no other option, Yim stepped into the stream, feeling apprehensive. Then she called out, "Master!"

Honus bounded up to her. The rage tattooed on his face seemed to mirror his true feelings. Yim steeled herself for his blows, but he halted without striking her. "Is this how you rest? By betraying my kindness?"

"Master . . ."

"Take care how you answer. A lie will serve you ill."

"I . . . I ran away, Master."

"I thought as much."

"But I was coming back."

Honus took in the darkening bruise on Yim's shin, her bloody scratches, and the lingering look of terror in her eyes. "Why? Didn't you enjoy your freedom?"

"I've had a change of heart. I truly have."

"What inspired this miracle?" asked Honus, giving the impression that he had some idea.

Yim chose an answer that was vague but honest "I didn't value your protection until I was without it. Now I know I'm safer with you."

"And I've learned you're nothing but aggravation."

It suddenly occurred to Yim that Honus might abandon her. That seemed far worse than any beating, and the prospect panicked her. "But you still need me!"

"Perhaps. Theodus said I should never carry my own burden, so I believed I needed you to bear my pack."

"Surely that hasn't changed."

"Bearers often speak in obscure ways. Perhaps I mistook his meaning."

Yim felt a chill at the pit of her stomach. "Please don't leave me here!"

"I'm only a Sarf. It's not my place to gainsay my Bearer."

"I'll be less aggravating, Master. I swear!"

Honus made a show of deliberating before he replied. "See that you are," he said at last. Then he turned and began striding toward the road. "Come and get my pack."

Relieved, Yim limped behind him as fast as she could.

THIRTEEN

HONUS AND Yim returned to the ruined house. After Yim shouldered the pack, they resumed their journey. Yim was shaken by her experience and in far worse shape than before. Nevertheless, she struggled gamely to keep up. Pleased by her show of effort, Honus slowed his pace until they walked abreast. After a while, he decided to test Yim's newfound docility. "Tell me," he said, "what happened between you and Gan's mother?"

"I merely tried to humor her."

"I think you did more than that," said Honus, watching Yim carefully.

"Who can fathom a mind such as hers?" replied Yim. "Perhaps it helped her to think I was her daughter."

"What *really* happened that night?"

"I tried to steal some ale. That's all."

Honus continued to look Yim in the eye. She met his gaze until he looked away, shaking his head. "I don't understand you."

"There's nothing to understand," replied Yim. "I'm only a girl who carries your pack."

Honus grunted.

"You've never had a slave before, have you?"

"No. But already I find it tiresome."

"That's because it's unnatural to own someone. You should stop trying."

"Unnatural or not, I expect you to obey me."

"I will, Master," said Yim with meekness Honus didn't find entirely convincing.

"We need endure each other for only a short while," said Honus, as much for his benefit as Yim's. "Then our ways will part forever."

For a while, Honus and Yim passed isolated farms that were usually crude hovels surrounded by stony fields. What folk they spied fled at the sight of Honus. After the road climbed to higher ground, they encountered no one. The sole signs of habitation were ancient ones and long abandoned. Honus left the road well before sunset to camp. Yim gathered wood, built a fire, and cooked porridge. Honus had caught no game, so the boiled grain comprised their dinner. Exhausted, Yim cooked and ate in silence, then fell asleep while it was still light.

When the two resumed their journey, Yim played a willing servant. Although she fell short of being cheerful, her demeanor gave Honus hope that she'd be less grating in the future. *She seems to have accepted her lot,* he thought.

Despite Yim's improved attitude, Honus dreaded the journey ahead. He was familiar with Luvein, for he and Theodus had trekked up and down it. The way was hard, for the roadways were abandoned. There were perils as well. Luvein's tragic history had left a legacy of evil. The malevolent found refuge in the empty countryside, and there were haunted spots as well, malign places where travelers were prone to misfortune. But it wasn't hardship or danger that disheartened Honus; as a Sarf, he was used to both. What discouraged him was the prospect of a journey without Theodus.

Honus's late master not only had provided companionship, but had given meaning to Honus's life. Through obeying Theodus, Honus believed he was serving Karm. Since infancy, he had been taught that was the highest good. His role didn't require him to understand his master's ends, only to help fulfill them. Sometimes Honus fought for causes that Theodus deemed worthy. Sometimes he merely gathered firewood. Whatever Honus did served a purpose. Without Theodus, the trek through Luvein would be nothing more than a long and arduous hike.

Moreover, Honus dreaded the journey's conclusion. He had served only one master, and the idea of getting a new one daunted him. Honus couldn't imagine anyone taking the place of one he so loved and revered. Yet he was a Sarf, and a Sarf's function was to serve a Bearer. When he reached the temple, both he and Yim would get new masters. Honus glanced at his slave as she trudged uphill, bent beneath the pack. She gazed ahead with eyes already dulled by weariness. *What hope has she for the future?* It seemed to Honus that in the bleakness of her prospects, Yim and he were kindred.

As noon approached, they descended into a valley. There, Yim was surprised when Honus led her away from the road and up a wooded rise. Upon it was the ruin of a delicate stone building that provided more a semblance of shelter than its substance. Some of the many windows that perforated its partial walls retained stone mullions so finely carved that they blended with the vines entwining them.

"Set down your burden," said Honus. "I intend to seek what game's about." After Yim unshouldered the pack, he asked, "Need I bind you for my absence?"

"No, Master. I'll never run away again. I swear by Karm." Yim arched her thumb in the Sign of the Balance.

Honus seemed satisfied. He removed his cloak and handed it to Yim. "Find a spot to rest. You'll be safe here." Then Honus took a sling from the pack, gathered stones, and slipped noiselessly into the woods.

In one corner of the ruin, a portion of a vaulted roof remained, and the leaves beneath it were dry. Yim laid Honus's tattered, bloodstained cloak upon them. As she did so, she reflected that his garment was not as fine as hers. *With so many wares to choose from, why would he purchase me a cloak that was better than his own? Why is he so contradictory—sometimes harsh and sometimes gentle?* Yim lay upon Honus's cloak and curled up beneath her own. Soon her master was forgotten as sleep overwhelmed her.

Yim woke to view the light of afternoon glowing on the ruined walls. Honus sat nearby. "Have I slept overlong?" she asked.

"Don't concern yourself with that. We'll travel faster with you rested."

Yim rose, brushed off Honus's cloak and handed it to him. "Thank you for letting me sleep."

"Let's leave this place," said Honus. "It's less tranquil than it seems."

The remark caused Yim to guess that Honus had tranced. She went to get the pack and discovered two slain hares tied to it. Her mouth watered at the prospect of a hearty meal. As they started out, she said, "I'll look for wild onions and thyme as we walk. They add a fine flavor to roast hare."

"That sounds good," replied Honus. "We'll camp again in the open. There's no chance of finding hospitality."

"The last place we lodged was certainly ill-favored," said Yim, thinking of her brush with Auntie Flora. "Are all the folk here as poor as Gan and his mother?"

"Most are even more desperate." Honus gave Yim a knowing look. "As perhaps you've discovered."

Anxious to deflect Honus's line of thought, Yim replied, "No wonder Gan was so grudging."

"It goes deeper than that. The servants of Karm are seldom welcome here."

"It has something to do with that pendant, doesn't it?"

"Yes, many in Luvein have turned to the Devourer."

"Why's that?" asked Yim. "Gan's creed sounds hate-filled."

"Haven't you heard of the cult?"

"Only rumors. At home, all worship the goddess."

"Just as folk oft seek the protection of violent men, they've turned to a bloodthirsty god. Hate can be empowering, especially to a mob. I've seen it firsthand—men and women shorn of their humanity and capable of any cruelty. There's madness abroad. It's spreading."

"Why?"

"That's what Theodus sought to discover, and it cost him his life." Honus looked at Yim. "You're trembling."

"Just a chill," she replied quickly. "It'll pass when we walk a bit."

"I think my Bearer's fate touches you more than you pretend."

"It concerns me only because Theodus's counsel resulted in my purchase."

"That was happenstance," said Honus. "Don't look for omens in his death."

"What happened to him?"

"That tale isn't good to hear," replied Honus. "It would only trouble you as it troubles me."

Honus grew withdrawn, and Yim didn't question him further.

The road began to ascend again, and its winding way took Yim and Honus to a high ridgeline that headed toward a range of peaks. The ridge resembled a rocky spine, its lichen-encrusted rock softened only by stands of wind-stunted firs and pines. Yim marveled how the ancient roadway had been carved through solid rock in places. By late afternoon, the mountains ahead dominated the skyline. They looked dark and barren. Honus pointed to a notch in them. "That's Karvakken Pass. A great fortress once stood there."

"Is that where we'll spend the night?"

"No," replied Honus. "The ruin's a fell place, even in daylight. We'll camp near here, where it's more wholesome." Soon afterward, he left the road and followed a tiny stream until he found a sheltered spot. "This will do," said Honus.

"I'll gather wood," said Yim.

"Gather a lot. The night will be cold."

By the time Yim returned with her third load of wood, Honus had a blaze going. The hares, skinned and dressed, lay on a rock. Yim shredded the herbs she had gathered and rubbed them on the raw meat. "Your sword would make a good spit," she said.

"I'd sooner use my hands."

"Men and their weapons!"

"You think we prize them overmuch?"

"What kind of sword could you buy for ten coppers?"

Honus smiled. "I can see where this is going. Yes, the Balance is askew. There once were times when a Sarf might be a builder or an artist. Now, the only art we learn is that of killing."

"Killing an *art*?"

"Call it a trade, if it makes you feel better." Honus picked up the knife with which he had skinned the hares. "I've seen men do terrible things with these—cruel, inhuman things. Still, a knife can be used to prepare a meal or whittle a child's toy."

"Yet, you're not a knife," said Yim. "You're a sword."

Honus saw that Yim was watching him intently, and he became aware that she was probing him much as he had attempted to probe her. Despite that gaze, or perhaps because of it, he felt compelled to answer truthfully. "Yes," he said at last. "I'm a sword, best fit for killing. I take no pride in that. I don't believe Karm delights in death, but I think she's sometimes served by it."

"How can killing serve the goddess?"

"In the same way a great fire may be stopped by a small

one in its path. Good people may be protected. Good laws may be upheld."

"And what has all that killing done to *you*?"

Honus looked away so suddenly it appeared that Yim had struck him. Yet when he gazed at her again, his features were composed. Speaking in a voice that was calm but cold, he said, "It's not your place to ask."

FOURTEEN

IT WAS a frigid morning, and when Yim awoke, her back was against Honus's chest. His arm rested on her waist and his hand gently pressed her belly. The position felt far too intimate and Yim wondered if Honus was awake. The thought alarmed her. When she tried to slip away, Honus gripped her more firmly. In the effort to get up quickly, Yim threw her elbow back and struck Honus in the chest. "I'm sorry, Master," she said as she scurried from his reach on hands and knees.

Yim glanced nervously at Honus. His face bore the same aloof expression it had the previous evening. Like then, Yim was certain that it was a facade to hide his feelings. Beneath it, she sensed irritation. "Shall I light a fire?" she asked, hoping to defuse the situation.

Honus rose, put on his sandals, and strapped on his sword. "Break camp and shoulder the pack. We'll warm ourselves through walking."

"Won't we eat first?"

"No. Now hurry up. I'm eager to depart."

"I *said* I was sorry."

"What does that have to do with it?"

"Apparently nothing," replied Yim. Then she set about breaking camp. Soon, they were back on the road. Dark clouds hung in the sky, and the mountains ahead looked bleak. Karvakken Pass seemed particularly somber. Even from a distance, it was foreboding. Yim was dispirited, and that mood was exacerbated by her predicament with Honus. *We can never be friends,* she thought, *but must we be at odds?* She feared that might be the natural state between slave and master, but she wasn't certain. Hoping to ease the tension, Yim tried to make conversation about something they had in common—their journey. "Master, will it take long to reach the pass?"

Honus also seemed inclined to ease their relations, for he responded benignly. "It's not as close as it seems. We must walk quickly to reach it by afternoon."

"Last night, you talked as though it was an unwholesome place."

"It is. We'll want it far behind us when night falls. Karvakken has a grim history and many believe evil lingers in those ruins."

"Do you, Master?"

"I don't know if all the tales are true, but I certainly wouldn't tarry there."

Honus's reply reinforced Yim's disquiet. "Need we go that way?"

"It should be safe enough in daytime. Besides, it's the shortest route to Bremven."

Yim gazed apprehensively at the pass. "How could a place become so fell?"

"It's a long tale, but I'll tell it if you'd like."

"Please."

"Long ago, Luvein was rich and fair," said Honus, "but its lords were locked in conflict. Greed and power hardened their hearts, and they cared not that their struggles caused misery. Battles raged back and forth without any clear victor. Only scribes remember the combatants now. They're all forgotten—except the one named Bahl."

"I know that name. It's infamous," said Yim. Then she looked puzzled. "But Lord Bahl's alive today."

"Many men have borne that name. It's the legacy of his line. That, and a fearful reputation. But the first Bahl was no lord in the beginning. Where he came from is a mystery. Some say he was a wanderer from the north, others claim he was the bastard of a local lord. Wherever his origin, he possessed the dark power that makes his name so feared."

"I've heard of it," said Yim. "They say Lord Bahl sways men easily."

" 'Sway' is too gentle a word," said Honus. "Men become fanatics who fight heedless of their persons. I've seen it firsthand."

"And Luvein's where it all began?"

"Yes," said Honus. "Bahl was a common soldier in some lord's household troop. Even then, he had uncanny power over others. It caused him to rise quickly. Soon, he commanded an army. His patron became the most powerful lord in Luvein, but he had kenneled a rabid dog. Bahl destroyed what he conquered. When his master objected, Bahl slew him to seize his lands and title.

"The other nobles allied to fight Lord Bahl. The more destruction Bahl wrought, the stronger grew his hold over men. Reason forsook his soldiers, and they fell upon Luvein like ravening beasts, leaving only corpses and ruins in their wake. And the carnage reached its climax at Karvakken, where the nobility of Luvein made its last stand.

"Karvakken was called invincible, but Bahl overcame it. No one could say how, for no defender lived to tell. Peace came in the guise of death, for all Luvein was desolated."

"What was the purpose of such slaughter?" asked Yim.

"That's the mystery," said Honus. "Bahl's savagery

earned him naught but a wasteland. Tales speak no more of him, but he must have sired a son, for a new Lord Bahl appeared. And he possessed his father's power."

"What became of him?"

"He departed Luvein. In the west, he conquered a tiny realm. There, he erected an iron fortress."

"The Iron Palace?"

"The same."

"Even in the North, that name strikes fear," said Yim. "But Bahl's realm isn't tiny."

"Not now," said Honus. "Under each successive lord, it's grown larger. And the current Lord Bahl threatens to outdo the original." Honus gazed at the surrounding desolation. "Perhaps someday every land will look like this."

"And you've fought against him?"

"Only a skirmish in the scheme of things." A tormented look came to Honus's face that even his tattoos couldn't hide.

"Yet I see the memory pains you."

"It was hard to see my Bearer fall. And the way he fell . . ." Honus lapsed into silence.

"I grieve for your loss."

Honus nodded, but didn't speak again.

Yim had grown accustomed to Honus's sudden silences. *He hoards his words, and then spends them all at once.* It seemed the mark of a conflicted man. For the most part, Honus's silence suited Yim. She had no desire to become more involved with her master; her slavery involved her far too much already. The Wise Woman had warned Yim that she would face trials, and she feared Honus was one of them.

Karvakken Pass promised to be another. Yim perceived its malevolent aura as coldness that was of otherworldly origin. *If I can feel it from this distance, how strong will it be at the pass?* Already, her hands and feet were icy. She looked at Honus to see if he was affected also, but could detect no signs. Yim clutched her cloak about her and was glad for Honus's brisk pace.

As Yim and Honus neared the pass, the woods thinned out and the landscape grew more barren. The desolation of the lowlands paled against the starkness of the mountain road. The few remaining trees were stunted, bare, and twisted into grotesque forms. Nothing delicate survived. It was a hurtful landscape of rocks and thorns that offered no prospect of rest. Yet, these were only outward signs of the land's afflictions.

Yim began to perceive distant voices. At first, they were faint and easy to ignore. As the pass loomed ever closer, they became louder and more insistent. Yim began to distinguish individual sounds within the cacophony. Sometimes it was a wail of pain or a cry of rage.

"Master, what are those voices?"

Honus looked at her strangely. "What voices? I hear only wind."

Yim winced and said, "Don't say you didn't hear *that*!"

"What are you talking about? Is this some jest?"

Yim didn't reply, but her frightened look caused Honus to look about. They were nearly at the ruined fortress, a dark, ugly structure constructed from black basalt quarried from the surrounding cliffs. It nearly filled the inside of the pass, pressing against a sheer wall of rock that towered above it. No living thing was visible around the site, only bare stone. The crude and massive masonry fitted its stark location so perfectly that the ruins more resembled a malignant growth than the work of human hands. High crenellated stone walls, still mostly intact, encircled an enormous ruined keep. As Honus surveyed the grim structure, the wind died down and the scene was wrapped in deathlike stillness.

Yim saw far more than a ruined fortress. The sounds that terrified her were voiced by ghostly visions. An army was besieging the walls. While she watched, the wraiths became more solid. The noise of combat reverberated within her head. Screams and shouts combined into a roar, yet Yim could also distinguish sounds unique to war's butchery—the thud of blows, the hacking of flesh, the crunching of bone. Yim felt something sticky beneath her feet and saw blood. The road was covered with it.

All the while, Honus strode forward as if the road were not flowing red. Yim felt rising panic and the urge to run away. Still, part of her realized the horrors were illusions. Thus, she staggered behind Honus, knowing he was her sole guide through the terrifying vision. They reached the fortress. Yim saw a writhing mound of living and dead soldiers piled beneath its walls. They seemed as real as the black stones above them. As Yim approached, the pile grew and became a stairway of flesh. An immense human wave slowly mounted it. It crested the ramparts and overflowed them. The air was filled with the sounds of slaughter. Yim became nearly oblivious of Honus. She thought he might be shaking her, but she couldn't tell. The ghosts commanded her attention.

The blood seemed real. The blood *was* real. It flowed thick and hot over her bare feet. It steamed in the cold air, turning it heavy with its sharp, metallic smell. Soon it was above her ankles. It splashed her legs with every step. All around her were madness, agony, and gore. The sensation was so powerful that Yim shared the combatants' pain. She felt wounded in a thousand places and in a thousand ways. Then, in the midst of the chaos, she sensed something new. It was the malevolent center of the battle, a thing that was both its cause and effect. Yim knew it for a denizen of the Dark Path, where time and place were relative. For it, this ancient battle was perpetual. In some unknown way, it was aware of her and was attempting to draw her into eternal terror.

Yim struggled to remember that the horrors she saw and felt were not real, but only echoes from the distant past. That realization was her only defense against her unseen adversary. Still, it was hard to grasp when pain shot through every nerve and blood seemed to rise around her. It reached her waist and clawed at her legs like a swollen river. Yim feared that, at any moment, she would be swept away. The source of this torrent was right before her—the vast pile of groaning men that blocked her path. Crimson poured from countless wounds in their broken bodies. Convulsing with terror, Yim slipped and sank beneath the flowing gore. As blood filled her screaming mouth, the swirling crimson darkened to black.

FIFTEEN

HONUS WAS sitting on the ground, watching over Yim, when her eyes flew open. They seemed blinded by terror. Honus grasped her hand. "So you've returned," he said.

Yim clutched him and pressed her face into his chest. "I can't do it!" she cried. "It's impossible! Karm asks too much!"

"What's this talk?" asked Honus in a gentle voice.

Instead of replying, Yim began sobbing.

Honus wrapped his arms around Yim, and in her trauma-tized state, she accepted his embrace. Honus didn't speak again until she ceased crying and her trembling subsided. "The goddess asks only that we do what we can," he said, his voice still gentle.

"You don't understand."

"I understand this," said Honus. "Karm wants you to bear my pack."

"But she . . ." Yim cut herself short and became silent.

"It's within your power," said Honus.

Yim let out a deep sigh. "Yes. I can carry your pack." Honus felt her tense, and when she spoke again, her voice was vehement. "I can do that, but *only* that."

Honus started to rise, but Yim clung to him. "Hold me a while longer. I need to touch a living person."

"What did you see at the pass?"

"A battle, the one you described."

"It was a vision," said Honus, feeling awed. "I thought as much."

"It was horrible, just horrible." Yim looked at her legs and feet, as if fearful of what she'd see. "I thought I drowned in blood."

"War is indeed terrible," said Honus. "I'm sorry you witnessed it, even as an apparition."

"And you saw and heard nothing?"

"No, but after you collapsed, I sensed a presence," said Honus. "I dared not trance to seek it out."

"I remember nothing after I fell. I don't even recall walking here."

"You didn't. I carried you."

"How far?"

"Far enough."

Yim peered about and seemed aware of her surroundings for the first time. They were on the roadside, beneath a stunted tree. The mountains and Karvakken Pass were not close, but they still loomed against the darkening sky.

"If you're capable of walking," said Honus, "we should put more distance between us and the pass before nightfall."

The terror-stricken look in Yim's eyes returned. She released Honus and rose shakily to her feet. "Let's hurry, Master."

When Honus moved to shoulder the pack, Yim stopped him. "That's mine to carry."

Though Honus doubted Yim had the strength to bear the pack, he gave it to her. He was still trying to make sense of her initial outburst. *Perhaps she was confused by her ordeal.*

He suspected, however, that explanation fell short of the mark. Yim's despair troubled him, especially since it followed a vision. Honus had been taught that visions were significant portents. That Yim was so traumatized by hers seemed a cause for concern.

They headed down the road, and walking seemed to do Yim good. Her gait became steady, but she was wrapped in a brooding silence that Honus was loath to disturb. They walked until the sun approached the horizon. "We'll find no farmhouse this close to the pass," said Honus. "We should look for a campsite soon." Seeing Yim's haunted expression, he added, "You'll be all right. The vision has passed."

"It seemed so real. I even felt and smelled the blood. Is it really like that?"

"What?"

"A battle."

"I don't know what you saw," replied Honus.

"There was screaming and shouting and cruelty. I felt surrounded by pain. And the blood! It reached my waist!"

"I've never been waist-high in blood. I don't know if such a thing is possible."

"So a battle's not like that?"

"The rest rings true enough."

Yim turned quiet, but her face reflected inner struggle. She walked that way awhile before uttering, "There was . . ." Yim stopped speaking, and the struggle resumed. A moment later she spoke again. "There was something else in my vision. The most frightening part—a being that thrived on the slaughter. It cared not who won or lost, as long as men perished."

"What kind of being?"

"I don't know. Not a man or his spirit. Something powerful and malicious."

"It sounds horrific," said Honus, "but Theodus told me that visions are often metaphors. That being may have been one."

"It felt real enough."

"Whatever it was, it deserves contemplation," said Honus. "Your vision was divinely inspired. As terrible as it seemed, it was a gift."

"A gift! Visions are afflictions!"

"You mustn't say that."

"Why? Have you had visions?"

"No," admitted Honus.

"Then don't speak of things you don't know! Visions have ruined my life!"

Honus stared at Yim, dumbfounded.

"Look at me!" she cried. "I'm a slave! I'm dressed in a rag and a dead man's cloak. This is what my visions did to me! Gifts, indeed! Pray that you never receive such gifts."

Yim slumped down on the roadside. Before she covered her face with her hands, it reflected a mixture of despair and rage. Honus knelt down beside her. "You've had more than one vision?" Yim didn't answer. "Perhaps I can help you understand them."

"Would you take off your shirt so I could understand your runes?"

"That's different."

"My visions are no less private. I shouldn't have mentioned them. I regret that I did. They're my misfortune, but they're mine alone."

"Yim . . ."

"I'll bear your pack. That must satisfy you. I pray it satisfies Karm."

Honus was about to reply, but Yim's expression convinced him it would be futile. Instead, he stood up. "There's a brook we can reach by sundown," he said. "It'd be a good place to camp."

Yim rose and mutely followed Honus, who respected her silence. They left the road when they reached the brook, then walked upstream until they found an open, sandy bank. Yim set down the pack and went to gather firewood. While she was away, Honus tried to catch a fish. Upon her return, he was still bent over in a stretch of quiet water with his arms submerged to the elbows. He remained perfectly still while she watched curiously. Then with a sudden movement, he scooped his arms downward and then flung a large fish at Yim's feet.

She jumped back from the flopping trout. "Merciful Karm!" she cried.

"It's good to know you can still talk."

Yim didn't seem to hear him, but a moment later she spoke. "Master, about those things I said . . ."

"Yes?"

"I was out of my head. Don't pay attention to them."

"Are you speaking of your visions?"

"I don't have visions. Not really."

Honus was unconvinced. "Such things are matters for Bearers and Seers. I'm only a Sarf, but I think you may have a special talent."

"No, Master, I'm no one special. I'm only the slave who bears your pack."

"I don't believe you."

"That's all I've become," said Yim. "That's all I can be."

Honus thought he should be pleased by Yim's resignation, but it depressed him. "I'm sorry you were so frightened."

"I don't want to talk about it."

"All right," said Honus. He left the brook and walked over to examine the fish. "Do you know how to cook this? I'm unskilled at such things."

Yim appeared glad for the change of subject. "Hot stones work well." She went to the brook and searched for flat rocks of suitable size and shape. When she found some, she lit a fire and placed the stones in the flames to heat. While they did, she scaled and gutted the fish. By the time it was dark, the fish was baking in its makeshift oven.

"Theodus used to cook fish like that," said Honus.

"Your master cooked for you?"

"It's custom for a Bearer to cook." Honus stared wistfully into the flames. "But custom or no, he would've done it. He was a caring man, and he liked to cook."

Eventually, the fish was done and they ate it with some porridge. Afterward, Yim stared into the dying embers. She looked forlorn and in need of comfort. Honus spread his cloak upon the sand near the embers and Yim moved next to him. She leaned against his shoulder as might a weary child. "I think it'll be cold tonight," she said.

Honus put his arm around Yim. After they sat awhile, he moved his fingers up to her neck, softly caressing it. She didn't evade his touch, but surrendered to it. The feel of her kindled Honus's desire. He tenderly brushed Yim's cheek, and she turned to face him. Honus gazed into her eyes. The veil that obscured her thoughts was partly asunder. He could see her despair, her loneliness, and most of all, her vulnerability. At that moment, she seemed as frail as a blossom and as beautiful. He recalled the sight of her bathing and his ardor grew.

Honus slowly moved his hand to Yim's breast and cupped it through the thin fabric of her tunic. She didn't pull away. His fingertips found her nipple and gently caressed it. Yim's reaction was an almost imperceptible gasp. Honus was no stranger to lovemaking and knew how to arouse a woman. But his touch provoked only stillness. He detected neither resistance nor desire. *I can have her and not violate my pledge.* No force would be required. All he need do was assert his passion. In her fragile state, Yim would acquiesce.

But as soon as Honus realized he could fulfill his desire, he knew it would be a callous act. Four nights ago, he wouldn't have cared. But after the day's revelations, he saw Yim in a different light. *It's not what she deserves.* Yet touching Yim's body and the promise of her compliance tested Honus's resolve. Her eyes still met his. Her parted lips were so close he could feel her breath. Yim seemed nervously expecting more intimate caresses. Only a lifetime of self-discipline allowed Honus to overcome his desire. He moved his hand away. "You must be exhausted," he said.

Yim went limp against his shoulder. "I am, Master."

"Then lie down and sleep, knowing you'll be safe."

In Durkin, an old woman peeled roots for a late supper, though her withered arm made the task a struggle. A knock on the door interrupted her. A low voice spoke from behind the barrier. "Open up, Ma, it's Curdac."

The woman unbolted the door to admit her son. He slipped in quickly and secured the door behind him. "Ale!" said Curdac. "I must have ale!"

"Ale's dear," replied his mother.

"So? That cloak I brought ye last should have paid for plenty."

"I only got three coppers for it."

"Pah! Don't lie. 'Twas worth twice that. After what I've seen, I need drink!"

From a corner of the dingy room, the woman retrieved a jug and a bowl. When she brought them over, Curdac ignored the bowl to seize the jug and gulp from it. As he drank, his mother eyed the sack he had carried and was disappointed by its empty look. After Curdac set the jug down, she asked, "What did ye get?"

"Nothing."

"Nothing? Gone two weeks and nothing? And there's fighting in Lurwic. The roads must be full of folk."

"I went to Lurwic, and there are no folk."

"What?" said the woman, noticing that her son was trembling.

"None on the roads. None anywhere." Curdac reached into his sack and pulled out a child-sized shirt. It was rent with gashes and stiff with dried blood. "This was the most whole thing I found." Curdac's trembling became more violent. "More whole than the boy who wore it. They left nothing. No houses. No crops or cattle. No goods. Just corpses and only bits of them." Curdac took another long draught from the jug. After several more, his hand grew steadier.

Seeing that her son had calmed somewhat, his mother attempted to ease his mood further with conversation. "I sold that cloak to a Sarf."

"A Sarf?" replied Curdac. "What was a Sarf doing *here*?"

The old woman grinned. "Bought himself a strumpet. The cloak was for her."

"Well, the world's gone daft for certain. A Sarf with a whore." Then Curdac shrugged. "Well, why not? Live while ye may. What other news?" He lifted the jug for another draught.

"A bunch of Black Robes passed through town. They were searching . . ."

The sound of the shattering jug interrupted her. The woman glanced at her son with surprise. A look of terror was frozen on his face, and it was a long moment before he could speak. "The Devourer's priests are here?"

"Nay, they found what they wanted and left."

The news did nothing to calm Curdac. "By Karm's tits, that's even worse! Gather up yer things Ma. We must leave by dawn."

"Son, ye're mad. Where will we go?"

"To the Dark Path if we stay. Those priests are an ill sign. They're the crows that fly afore the wolf pack. Those that did bloody work in Lurwic must be headed here!"

As his mother watched openmouthed, Curdac began to dash about the room, stuffing things into his sack. He was too frantic to go about it rationally. Clothing was seized haphazardly and packed with roots, both peeled and unpeeled; dirty dishes; a stolen frock; and various household goods. His behavior inspired fear, and soon his mother was also packing. As she did, her eyes fell again on the child's slashed and bloody shirt. It seemed a token of what would come.

SIXTEEN

IN THE dream, Yim revisited her childhood. She was just old enough to tend goats alone in the high meadows. The new spring grass was lush and felt soft beneath her feet. Clouds filled the valleys, so each peak about her seemed an island in a white sea. The homeward path faded into nothingness and Yim felt she was in a realm of spirits. The clouds rose higher and invaded the meadow. The grass grew pale, as did everything else.

Yim had turned to gather the goats when the mist grew bright and a young woman emerged from it. She was dressed in a simple white robe that fell halfway down her shins. About her bare feet, the grass turned white with frost. She advanced toward Yim, who was unable to flee or even move. The woman's eyes were as dark as her hair. They fixed on Yim, who felt captured by them. The woman gazed at her, taking her measure, but with such a fond look that Yim thought she might be her mother's spirit.

"Mommy?"

The woman smiled but shook her head. "Yim," she said, "tonight when you return to your father, you must tell him to take you to the Wise Woman who lives above your village."

Yim simply nodded, too astounded to ask how the strange woman knew her name.

"When you see the Wise Woman, tell her you met She Who Holds the Balance." Yim noticed for the first time that the woman carried a set of scales. "Do you think you can do that?"

"Yes," replied Yim, "but what if she doesn't believe me?"

"She'll believe you," said the woman. "She's expecting you. Tell her that you're the Chosen."

"The Chosen?"

"The Wise Woman will understand. She'll know what to do."

The mist grew thicker and the woman faded from view. When the air cleared, the meadow was empty except for Yim's goats.

In the dream, Yim was also an observer hovering in the air. She cried out to her younger self, "Don't tell anyone!" Yet, even as she said those words, she knew it would make no difference. Yim had been a dutiful child. She would give her father the message, and he would take her to the dark cottage that smelled of herbs. There, alone with the Wise Woman, Yim would recite the fateful words—"I'm the Chosen." Afterward, her life would be ruined.

At dawn, Yim rose to prepare the morning meal. She lit a fire, then took out the grain sack and noted how little it contained. "I fear we'll go hungry soon," she said.

Honus peered into the sack. "If we eat sparingly, this might last us through Luvein. Then we'll be among folk who'll make us welcome. Meanwhile, we'll supplement our grain by foraging and hunting."

After a meager breakfast, they returned to the road, which descended into a rolling country. The air grew warmer, and though the land was still wild and empty, new foliage softened it. As Karvakken faded in the distance, Yim's heart grew lighter and the way seemed less daunting.

"Master, would you tell me about Theodus?" asked Yim after they had walked awhile.

"Why?" he asked.

"The same burden that sat upon his shoulders now lies on mine. I have kindred feelings toward him, though I can't explain why."

"It's hard for me to speak of him."

"The dead find comfort when the living remember them," said Yim. "At least, that's what they say where I come from."

"I think your people are wise." Honus sighed. "I should talk of him." After a quiet spell, he spoke in a soft voice. "Theodus was my Bearer. He was fond of pointing out that the word 'bear' has many meanings. It means to carry, but also to uphold . . . to announce . . . to give birth . . . to show patience . . . to render witness . . . to be accountable . . . to possess relevance . . . to move steadily . . . and, most importantly, to endure. Theodus encompassed all those meanings."

"How did you meet him?"

"The Seers that chose me for the temple studied all us children. In time, they foretold our destinies. When I was five, I was informed I would become a Sarf. I commenced my training and also began to receive my tattoos."

"The ones on your back or on your face?"

"My face tattoos had to be earned through mastery of the martial arts. Those on my back were divined by the Seers. Only when a child's back is fully tattooed may he or she be paired with a Bearer. The fates of a Sarf and a Bearer are intertwined and the tattoos guide the matching. Theodus chose me when I was seven, though I didn't begin to serve him for nine more years."

"What did he see that made him choose you?"

"Something in my runes. I know not what. Sarfs aren't taught to read, for the portents on their backs are supposed to be mysteries to them."

"I think that would drive me crazy. Aren't you tempted to peek?"

"If I could tell your future right now, would you ask me to do so? Would you really want to dread every adversity before it came to pass and never have a joyous surprise? I think not."

"So you've never seen them?"

"I've glimpsed their reflection a few times, but as I said, I was never taught to read. They're just scribbles to me. Though, when I was young, I was more curious about them. Theodus assured me they must be meditated upon— sometimes for years—before they make sense. He said it was life that gave them meaning."

"Does that mean you could change their meaning by changing your life?"

"I don't know," Honus said. "I've never considered that. Perhaps Theodus did. Before we met, he had meditated for a dozen years."

"So he was much older than you?"

"Yes," replied Honus. "When he chose me, I thought Karm had given me a new father."

"You must have been very fond of him."

Honus's eyes welled with tears, and he strode ahead to hide them. Yim hurried to catch up with him. "You honor Theodus with your feelings. There's no shame in showing them."

Honus let out a sob that seemed to explode from deep within. "Thirteen years I served him! Oh, the tales I could tell! He was wise, but funny, too. People liked him. With him beside me, I was never lonely. Even now, I expect to hear his laugh. My back still feels his hands upon my runes. He consulted them often and said they were his scriptures. I was useful. Now . . ." He gave a hopeless shrug.

Yim was unsurprised when Honus withdrew into silence, and she didn't question him further. But when they paused to rest, she brought up Theodus again. "You said your Bearer was a funny man," she said. "You must have many tales of his jests."

A wan smile crept onto Honus's face. "Yes," he said. "One of my favorites is of the night we stayed with a miser. When a Bearer and his Sarf travel, they rely on charity for their needs. Even if Theodus were given a cart full of provisions, he would have still asked for his supper, for he loved meeting people. He was a good guest, full of tales, but he was also a good listener. He learned a lot that way, and much of his knowledge was useful to his hosts. Once, after helping a man cure his sick cow, he was given a large bag of grain, enough to feed us for days. Nevertheless, he asked for charity the next night at the house of a notorious miser.

"Now, many people fed and housed us solely to honor Karm, but others had different reasons. Some thought it brought them prestige, while others hoped to gain the goddess's favor. The miser who took us in that night was most likely thinking of the latter. It was a well-appointed dwelling, yet the man claimed he was impoverished. He set a pot on the fire and went into his storeroom. When he returned, he brought a small cup of grain to make porridge. It was hardly enough to feed one person, let alone three. 'This is all I have, Karmamatus,' he said, 'but I'm honored to share it.'

"Theodus nodded solemnly and told the man that Karm would repay his generosity. After the man emptied the cup into the pot, Theodus took me aside and told me to secretly refill it with our own grain. This I did when Theodus distracted the man. When the miser discovered the cup was full, he believed at first that he had neglected to pour his grain into the pot. After he discovered that this was not so, Theodus told him that Karm had repaid his generosity. The man declared it was a miracle and added the extra grain to the pot, since it cost him nothing. Theodus slyly signaled me to fill the cup again, which I did at the first opportunity. The miser was delighted to find the cup brimming with grain once more and quickly added it to the pot.

"Although Theodus acted as if it were perfectly natural for the cup to refill itself, the miser became jubilant. He paced gaily about the room, praising Karm. Then a thought came to him, and he rushed to his storeroom. He returned with a bounty of food and drink. There was good red wine, cheese, bread, sausages, pickled vegetables, candied fruit, and more. Everything he brought out was in some kind of container, whether it needed to be or not. We had a merry feast, and the miser was merry with us. Yet I couldn't help noticing that throughout the meal he kept eyeing the containers, waiting for them to be miraculously refilled."

Yim laughed at the tale. "Did Theodus ever tell the man he had been fooled?"

"That wasn't his way," replied Honus. "Besides, he said the miser had fooled himself, so only he could decide what lesson was learned that night."

"It must have been good to travel with such a man," said Yim.

"It was," said Honus wistfully. "Yet it was also trying, especially in the last few years. Theodus was a holy man and a serious one, too. When he became concerned by the worship of the Devourer, he journeyed far to understand it. No hardship daunted him. We came to know Luvein well, and other equally fell places. It was a hard road he traveled, and it came to a hard end."

"What happened to him, Master?"

"I can't bear to speak of it. It's difficult to imagine why Karm would permit such an end to so good a man. Perhaps Theodus could have explained it. I can't."

"It's a great loss," said Yim. "I'm a poor substitute for one so good and wise."

"Yet you're here because of him," replied Honus.

After finishing his frantic packing, Curdac had procured more ale to drown his terror. The result was a hangover that delayed his exodus from Durkin. It was late morning when he departed, fuzzy-headed but fearful, from his mother's home. He emerged into one of the town's narrow and neglected alleyways. Garbage and worse littered the sodden ground between the tightly packed dwellings. His mother followed him, moist-eyed and reluctant. She gazed back at her poor abode longingly, as if she had half a mind to remain there. Nevertheless, she continued onward.

Curdac bore a sack stuffed to the point of bursting. His mother, who possessed but one good arm, had a smaller sack. Curdac had tied it to her back, for she was incapable of carrying it. Thus burdened, the two emerged from the alley onto one of Durkin's unpaved lanes. As usual, people selling goods lined it, their purloined wares set before them on the dirt. That day, there were fewer sellers than normal and no buyers at all. Without the sounds of hawking and haggling, the lane was ominously quiet.

The two hurried as best they could toward the town's entrance, skirting the drunkards that lay in their path and at least one corpse. Curdac quickened his pace upon seeing the gate. It was open and unguarded. He turned and saw that his mother was struggling to keep up. "Come on, Ma. Soon we'll be safe."

"Safe? Homeless in the wild? Most like, wolves will get us." Despite her words, the old woman moved faster. Soon, mother and son were outside the town's dilapidated walls, and the road north stretched before them. It passed between neglected fields before vanishing over the top of a rise. Curdac was just beginning to breathe easy when a dark line appeared on the crest of the rise. He halted and squinted at it.

"Why'd ye stop, Son?"

"There are folk on the road."

As Curdac spoke, the dark line changed shape and flowed down the decline like porridge boiling over the lip of a pot. Within the dark mass, he saw blades flash in the sunlight. Then the edge of the advancing mass seemed to break apart, and he could make out individual men. They were running—running toward the town and him. Curdac grabbed his mother, whose failing eyes had yet to see the danger, and began to pull her from the road. That was when he saw there were men in the fields also. He looked left and right. Death was advancing from all sides.

Curdac tugged his mother toward the gate. "Back to town, Ma!"

"Make up yer mind! Ye said 'twasn't safe."

"Oh Karm preserve us! We left too late."

The woman cackled, still unaware of her peril. "Karm? Since when did ye ever call to the goddess?"

"They're coming!" Curdac jerked his mother's arm, too alarmed to answer fully. Yet the terror in his voice spoke for him, and the old woman finally understood her danger. The pair retreated into Durkin. Curdac threw down his sack and looked about for someone to help him close the gate, but everyone had fled. Then he tried to shut it by himself. Rusty hinges groaned when he pushed the massive timbers, which barely moved.

Curdac glanced down the road. The men were closer. The approaching horde scarcely looked like soldiers. Though some waved swords, others bore hoes or scythes. They advanced with the disorder of a mob, but they did so silently, as men bent on a grim purpose. Beyond this blood-chilling spectacle was something that drew Curdac's attention. At the crest of the rise, there was a figure upon a huge black horse. Wherever the rider advanced, the men reacted like ants goaded from their nest. They grew frenzied and hurried more quickly to attack. There was something about the rider that inspired dread even from a distance. Curdac felt it and was unnerved. He abandoned his effort to close the gate, grabbed his mother, and dragged her deeper into town.

The streets were no longer quiet. News of imminent attack was spreading, and with it came chaos. The town that had thrived on lawlessness seemed intent on expiring the same way. There was no organized defense. Everyone looked out for him or herself. People poured into the streets, some overburdened with possessions while others ran about nearly naked. They jostled one another in their haste and confusion. Some dashed toward the town's only gate. They quickly returned and joined the others fleeing in the opposite direction. Whichever way folk ran within the walled town, there was no exit.

The enemy's entrance was announced by screams and followed by smoke. As time passed, the cries sounded ever closer and the smoke grew thicker. By then, Curdac was wedged in a crowd that tightly packed a lane ending at the town's far wall. There was no place to retreat farther. Those who climbed the wall called down that soldiers were waiting below to slay anyone who jumped. Some men, realizing they were penned like sheep, spurred their courage, drew weapons, and went to meet the attackers.

Curdac joined them. He left his wailing mother and trailed behind a group of burly men who gripped swords. Curdac had only a knife, but he shattered a chair abandoned in the street and took a leg as a club. By then, most of the town was burning, and dense, choking smoke filled the air. Curdac first saw the attackers through this screen. They appeared as pale as wraiths. Only when they came closer did they seem solid. Some were soldiers, but most were ragged men. Though many were ill armed and some were grievously wounded, they all moved with single-minded determination. Each face bore the same expression of fanatical hatred.

A swordsman from the town met the foremost attacker, who was armed only with a club, and stabbed him in the gut. The wounded man rushed toward his assailant, although doing so forced the blade entirely through his body. This allowed him to grab the sword's crosspiece. He held it fast as his fellows assailed the swordsman who, being unable to withdraw his blade, was defenseless and went down quickly. The enemy trampled over his body as well as their slain comrade's to continue the assault. The other swordsmen fell, one hacked to pieces with a hoe.

At the sight of that, Curdac took off and ran until he merged again with the huddled crowd. He gazed about with eyes that stung from smoke, trying to spot his mother. He had abandoned any hope of saving himself or her. His only desire was that they be together when death found them.

It was past noon when Yim and Honus halted by a stream. By then, hunger and the desolate road had taken their toll, and even Honus was weary. Ferns grew nearby, so Yim gathered fiddleheads. These comprised their midday meal, which dulled the rumbling in their stomachs without satisfying it. After they had eaten, they rested a bit. Yim cooled her tired feet in the running water. Honus sat on a rock nearby and gazed at her in a way that awakened her uneasiness. *Last night, he touched my breast,* she thought, repenting her weakness. *Will he touch me again tonight?* The more Yim wondered about it, the more agitated she became.

Honus seemed to notice her change of mood. "What's bothering you?"

"Nothing, Master."

"Speak your mind. I won't have you moping."

Yim summoned her courage. "I was recalling last night and . . . and how you touched me."

"Does the memory disturb you?"

"You took advantage of my frailty."

"You're my slave. Most men would say I did nothing improper."

"Would Theodus?"

Honus didn't answer. Instead, he moved into the shade, sat cross-legged on the ground, and shut his eyes. When his body and face grew rigid, Yim guessed that he was once again searching the Dark Path for pleasant memories. It seemed to her an odd and pathetic habit, and she wondered what would cause a man to seek the joys of the dead. While cool water rippled over her feet, Yim studied Honus's face for some sign of what he found.

SEVENTEEN

AT LAST, Honus ended his trance. "Take up the pack," he said. "We'll walk until the hares come out to feed. Then you can rest while I hunt."

When they encountered a farm, near sunset, two hares hung from the pack. The farm's field was rank with last year's weeds and looked little different from the surrounding wasteland. Only a fresh grave disturbed the ground. Honus halted before it. Beyond the field and near the edge of the forest was a small, rude dwelling made of sod. A wisp of smoke rose from a hole in its top. Honus left the road and approached the hovel.

Yim followed. "We have food, Master. Why stop at this poor place?"

Honus didn't answer, but continued walking until he reached the hovel. It looked more like a mound of dirt than a house. Honus peered down the hole that served as the entrance. A solitary figure cowered inside. He bowed and said, "We're servants of Karm, Mother."

A tremulous voice came from the darkness. "Karm? The goddess?"

"Yes, Mother," said Honus. "Would you share your fire in respect for her?"

"Ah 'ave na food," said the voice.

"We have plenty," replied Honus, "and would gladly share it with you."

"Food? Ya 'ave food?"

"Didn't I say we're servants of Karm? She saw your

need." Honus turned to Yim. "Gather wood while I skin the hares."

Yim went to collect wood, knowing that all that could be easily obtained would have been gathered long ago. It was dark when she brought a heavy armload of branches into the hovel. Its floor had been dug into the earth, so the interior was not quite as cramped as it appeared from the outside. Still, the ceiling was too low to stand. Yim sat down quickly, for the air was less smoky close to the dirt floor. A ragged, frail-looking woman squatted near a tiny fire, regarding Honus apprehensively. He turned to her and said, "This is Yim. She serves Karm also."

Yim bowed her head. "Good evening, Mother." Then, reading the woman's fearful expression, she added, "My master has a fearsome face, but a kind heart. You're safe with him."

The woman's tenseness eased a bit. "Ya ken call me Tabsha," she said.

Yim looked at the emaciated woman. She was dirty, barefoot, and dressed in a filthy shift that was tattered and much mended. Yim tried to guess Tabsha's age. She still had her teeth and her hair was dark, hinting she might be young. Yet her haggard face looked old. Yim gazed into Tabsha's dull eyes and saw a lifetime of hardship.

As if responding to Yim's perusal, Tabsha said, "Ah 'ave na been well since mah 'usband died."

"I'm sorry to hear it," said Yim.

Tabsha merely gazed despondently into the fire.

Yim peered about the tiny room, which made Gan and his mother's dwelling seem grand. There were only two metal tools evident—a worn knife and a mattock. A clay cooking pot, some baskets, a worn deerskin, two wooden buckets, a man's tattered shirt, and an empty cradle seemed to be Tabsha's principal possessions.

"Do you like porridge, Tabsha?" asked Honus.

"Ya 'ave grain?" she asked, showing a spark of animation.

"Yes," replied Honus. "Yim and I don't care for it. Though, if you'd like, we'll gladly make you some."

"Aye. Tha' would be fine."

"Good," said Honus. "We never eat it. I don't know why we brought it along. Perhaps we could leave it here and save the effort of carrying it."

Yim was about to protest when Honus cut her short with a stern, cautionary glance.

"Oh yes, I *loathe* porridge," said Yim.

"Yim, take out the grain," said Honus.

Tabsha's eyes lit up at the sight of the mostly empty grain sack. "Oh, thank ya, sire."

"You should thank Karm, not me," said Honus.

Yim roasted the hares for the three of them and cooked some porridge for Tabsha, who devoured it with particular relish. Lacking utensils, she ate it using her dirty fingers. Yim watched her eat with mixed feelings. It made her glad to see the contentment the porridge brought Tabsha, but she was also aware of the privation Honus's generosity would cause her. She found his actions inexplicable, for they had passed other, equally poor, dwellings without stopping. She knew better than to ask Honus to explain, so she turned her inquiries toward Tabsha.

"Did your husband die recently?" Yim asked.

"Near the end o' winter," said Tabsha.

"And you've been alone since?"

"Aye."

"Were you married long?"

"Ever since Ah comed into womanhood. Eight winters in all."

Yim quickly calculated and was startled to realize that Tabsha was not much older than she. Yim stared at her in appalled wonder. Glancing at the empty cradle, Yim asked, "And you had a child?"

"Five," said Tabsha dully. "Four be dead. One be took."

"Took?"

"Stolen. Ah do na know if she be dead."

Yim wanted to console Tabsha, but felt the woman was beyond comforting. Nevertheless, she clasped Tabsha's dirty hand, which was still sticky with porridge. "I'm sorry."

Tabsha nodded.

Honus sat silently throughout the exchange, his attention fixed on Tabsha. After Yim withdrew her hand, he spoke. "I trance sometimes." Tabsha gave no sign that she understood what he meant. "I can cause my spirit to visit the Dark Path," he said by way of explanation.

Tabsha's eyes widened. "The Dark Path! Why would ya wan' go there?"

"There are things to be discovered, things worth knowing."

"Like wha'?" Tabsha whispered.

"Today I encountered the spirit of the man who is buried in your field."

"Toff?"

"I didn't learn his name, but I learned he was your husband."

"An' 'e spoke with ya?"

"No."

"Toff did na speak much even when 'e beed 'live."

"I cannot converse with spirits, whether they were once talkative or not. But their memories are revealed to me. Those are what I seek. Memory lingers, even after the spirit has departed westward."

Tabsha regarded Honus as if he were a storyteller. Yet, when she peered into his eyes, her disbelief faded.

"I came here," said Honus, "because of Toff's memory of you."

The fire had died to embers. In the dim half-light, it seemed that the Sunless Way had invaded the quiet hovel. Honus's voice sounded distant, almost not his own. "You came from bathing in the brook, wearing only yellow flowers in your hair. He watched you approach, feeling a sense of wonder that was more than passion. Then, his life held only promise. He praised Karm to live in a world that included you. That moment shone throughout his life. Its memory was the treasure he bore to the Dark Path."

Honus spoke as though he was that man, caught in the rapture of love. What his words couldn't express, his eyes told with eloquence beyond the power of speech. Perhaps it was a trick of the light, but it seemed to Yim that Tabsha was transformed. Her face softened and she was no longer drab and worn, but a girl unburdened by tragedies and filled with the hope of youth.

The moment passed. Tabsha didn't move. Her eyes welled with silent tears that made pink trails where they flowed down her grimy cheeks. Yim felt as constrained to silence as an intruder. A sense of emptiness came over her. As she drew up her cloak to lie down and sleep, she saw that Tabsha was looking at her with a questioning expression. Yim ignored her and rolled to face the wall.

Lying in the dark hovel, Yim heard movement and soft whispers. The idea arose that the intimacy she had just witnessed between Honus and Tabsha might soon take a more physical form. The thought disgusted her, yet she found herself straining to hear confirmation of her suspicions. She detected none. Instead, Honus and Tabsha grew quiet. Eventually, Yim turned to face them. They lay motionless beneath Honus's cloak. It was hard for Yim to see, but it appeared that Honus was holding Tabsha, who was sleeping peacefully. As Yim stared at them, she felt alone and forgotten. Despite her exhaustion, it was a long while before she fell asleep.

Yim awoke in the early dawn amid thick smoke. She looked around and saw Tabsha asleep beneath Honus's cloak next to the cold embers of last night's fire. Honus was gone. Yim left the hovel to find him standing, mattock in hand, while the field burned.

"Master, what are you doing?"

"Burning off the weeds to prepare for planting."

"Why?"

"It needs to be done."

Yim sensed it was pointless to question him further. Instead she asked, "Shall I prepare breakfast?"

"You'll have to forage for it first; the grain's for Tabsha alone."

"I don't understand," replied Yim, only partly hiding her irritation. "Didn't you look into her baskets? There were roots and beans in them. She has plenty of food."

"I can tell you're no farmer," replied Honus. "She must plant those for this year's crop. This season often brings a hard choice for the poor—go hungry in the spring or eat the seed stock and surely starve in the winter."

"Oh," said Yim. "Then I'll look for breakfast." As she headed into the tangled wild, she began to hear the rhythmic sound of the mattock striking earth. When Yim could no longer hear the mattock, her spirits lifted. With her master engaged in work, she could take her time and be her own mistress.

Although Yim had been thoroughly taught the uses of wild plants, she found little to eat. This was only partly due to the earliness of the spring; there was a poverty to the land that went beyond the season. Luvein truly seemed the abode of want. After much searching, Yim found some mushrooms and greedily ate them all. *Let Honus find his own food!* she thought. Nevertheless, Yim knew it was unwise to return empty-handed. She continued her search until she encountered swampy ground and spied the first leaves of faerie arrow poking above dark water. She dug in the muck for their tubers until she collected an ample supply. Then, after washing the mud from the tubers and from her hands and feet, she lay back and lazed in the morning sunshine. She stayed as long as she dared before heading back. It was midmorning when she returned to the hovel.

Honus was working steadily in the ashy field. He was drenched in sweat, and before him were long rows of up-turned earth. Tabsha squatted over one of the rows, digging with a stick to plant roots. At the sight of Yim, Honus stopped swinging the mattock. "So, you've returned."

The tone of his voice made Yim defensive. "There were sparse pickings, Master. I found some tubers, but they must be cooked first."

"We're all hungry," Honus said, giving Yim a meaningful look. "You should cook them now."

Yim retreated to the hovel to boil the tubers. She brought them out when they were done. Honus and Tabsha stopped working and joined her to eat. Tabsha nibbled tentatively on a tuber, then wolfed it down. "Where did ya get these?" she asked.

Yim was surprised by the question. "Don't you know about faerie arrow?"

"Nay."

"Then I'll show you how to find it."

"Not today," said Honus. "You're needed to help with planting."

After the meal, they worked steadily until dusk. By then, Honus had turned over almost half the field. Following behind, Yim and Tabsha had planted all the earth he had tilled. Yim was relieved when work halted, for she ached from all the stooping. Looking at her dirty hands and feet, she asked Tabsha if there was someplace where she could wash.

"Aye. Ah'll show ya."

Tabsha led Yim to a small stream about a hundred paces from the hovel. Yim waded into it and began to clean the soil from her arms and legs. Tabsha did the same. "Ah washed more when Toff beed 'live," she said.

Yim, not knowing how to respond, concentrated on her washing.

"Ah be sorry," said Tabsha in a low, shy voice. " 'E . . . 'E made me remember when Toff . . . when Toff . . ." Tabsha's voice trailed off and her face shone as she relived the memory. Then she recalled what she had begun to say and the look faded. "Ah be sorry," she said again. "Ah fergot mah place when Ah slept by yar man."

"My *man*?" said Yim. "He's not my man. You could have tupped him for all I care."

Tabsha stared at Yim, openmouthed.

"I'm his *slave*, Tabsha."

"'Is slave?" said Tabsha. "Ah did na know."

"Well, now you do."

"Toff said they took our girl ta be a slave. Wha' . . . Wha' it be like?"

"I have to do whatever Honus says."

"Then ya be like a wife."

"No, it's not like that. He owns me. He doesn't care about me at all."

"Oh," said Tabsha. "Then it be a 'ard life."

The two women returned to the hovel, hungry and tired. Yim glanced at Tabsha as they made their way through the tangled undergrowth and their eyes briefly met. In that instant, Yim was stung to realize that the poor, broken woman pitied her.

EIGHTEEN

YAUN'S HEAD still throbbed from a hangover as two armed men roughly pushed him into a large chamber. A young-faced man with gray eyes, a deep tan, and a full black beard stood there. He wore a long black robe adorned by a large pendant on an elaborate gold chain.

The pendant was a simple circle made of iron. The bearded man didn't speak, but peered at Yaun as though he were an interesting but disgusting bug.

"Why won't anyone speak to me?" Yaun asked.

Silence.

"I'm not some commoner. I'm due respect!"

The stranger arched an eyebrow as if the assertion amused him.

The look deflated Yaun. "At least untie my hands," he said more humbly. "They took my sword and dagger."

The man drew a dagger from the folds of his robe. "Do you wish to live?"

Yaun grew pale. "Yes."

The stranger moved behind Yaun and pricked his back with the dagger's tip. "I know you're foolish," he said. "Are you also rash?"

"No," Yaun croaked.

The blade plunged downward and sliced Yaun's bindings. Yaun gasped, then realized his hands were free.

"Wait here," said the stranger as he left the room.

Yaun looked about. He was in the main hall of a modest manor house that lay outside the borders of his father's county. Yaun had visited it with the count several years ago. The room had been looted of its furnishings—recently, judging from the fresh bloodstains—but the paneled walls retained their elegance and the windows were unbroken and sealed. Although it was a mild day, a large fire blazed in the fireplace, making the room uncomfortably warm. Yaun wished he had some ale.

No one entered the hall, and Yaun's anxiety increased with the passing time. He paced anxiously and wondered why he had been kidnapped. As the lesser of two sons, he wouldn't be ransomed, and his kidnappers had already taken his money. Then it occurred to Yaun that he might have been seized for revenge. Soon his pounding head filled with frightful scenarios as he recalled friends he had betrayed and women he had abused. The more Yaun thought, the longer his list of potential enemies grew.

"Why did I linger in Durkin?" asked Yaun, his anguished voice echoing in the empty room. The answer was simple, though Yaun would never admit it, even to himself: Afraid to face his father, he had escaped in drink.

When the room began to darken, a door opened. The black-robed man entered, followed by the pair of armed men who had kidnapped Yaun. They seized him from where he had slumped in a corner and brought him forward. "We know everything about you," said the black-robed man. "Though it's your nature to lie, it would be most unwise for you to do so. Is that understood?"

"Yes," said Yaun.

"Yes, *Most Holy*," corrected the man.

"Yes, Most Holy."

"Do you know why you must address me thus?"

"Because you're a priest of the Devourer?"

"Because I'm *holy*!" bellowed the man. "Holiness is power. These men obey my commands. Your life is mine to take. The Devourer has bestowed this upon me, and you can measure my holiness by your fear." The priest grinned malevolently. "You must admit I'm *very* holy."

"What do you want with me, Most Holy?"

"You opposed my lord in battle. That was foolish."

"Lord Bahl?" Yaun whispered.

"Yes. Does that make you afraid?"

Yaun silently nodded.

"It's wise to fear him. Lurwic's duke didn't, and now he's dead. So are his subjects. Your comrades, too. You remain unfinished business."

"Alaric made me fight," whimpered Yaun. "I was his squire. What choice did I have?"

"And what did you gain by your subservience? Glory?

Fortune? You deserve what Alaric received. Would you like to taste his glory?" The priest made a gesture and one of the guards drew his sword.

"No!" cried Yaun, as he fell to his knees. "Please spare me! I beg forgiveness."

"I cannot pardon you," said the priest. "Only one has that power."

Another door opened, and in walked a man dressed in gold and velvet. Yaun scarcely noticed the rich garments, for he who wore them had his full attention. The man appeared neither young nor old, as though years flowed over him without leaving their mark. His unnatural pallor gave him the aspect of a corpse, and his long hair was so blond as to appear white. Despite his cadaverous complexion, he possessed an aura of power. Moving with feline grace, he seemed a man with all softness burned away and in the process transformed, as iron is into steel. Compelling eyes, so pale that only the black pupils were prominent, dominated his face. The man's bloodless lips were drawn into a sardonic smile. Yaun remained on his knees and bowed his head to Lord Bahl.

The lord approached, and the sweat on Yaun's brow chilled as the air turned cold. Yaun looked up and couldn't turn his gaze from the approaching eyes. His entire existence shrank down to the two black pupils fixed on him. Yaun knew his fate was being decided.

"Rise," said Lord Bahl in a low voice that seemed to Yaun both sweet and harsh, like strong drink. It was as equally intoxicating. Upon hearing that single word, Yaun craved to hear more. "So you're the count's son who became squire to a hireling soldier, then servant boy to a Sarf. They found you drunk in Durkin with shit on your sleeves. Can you sink any lower?"

Yaun felt a surge of shame.

"At least the duke paid Alaric," said Lord Bahl. "What did you get? Nothing! The same wages the Sarf paid.

Nothing! The same as your inheritance. Nothing! I see a pattern here."

Lord Bahl produced a dagger. "I believe this is yours." He turned it in his hand, examining it. "The blade's good." He ran his finger along its edge. "Sharp. Do you poison it?"

"No, Lord."

"I find it a useful practice. Yet then, one must decide which venom to employ. There are so many choices—slow and painful . . . paralyzing . . . quick . . . subtle. If you were to poison this blade, which one would you choose? I think the coward's choice—quick."

Bahl waved a hand and the two guards seized Yaun's arms. The priest stepped forward, tore open Yaun's shirt, and pulled it down behind his shoulders to expose his chest and stomach. Bahl grasped the dagger by its hilt. "Do you know how Alaric died?"

Yaun shook his head.

"Of course you wouldn't. You were hiding, weren't you? Well, they gutted him. He died tangled in his own intestines." Bahl's lips formed a mirthless grin. "Do you wonder how that felt?" The point of the dagger poked Yaun's belly. "Be very still now. I have a surprise."

Yaun screamed in pain and fear as the blade moved across his abdomen, parting flesh. Then he fainted. He was revived by an icy hand that forced him to look at his wound. There was a bloody line across his belly, but no entrails spilled from it. The hand released him. "Get up!" commanded Bahl.

Yaun rose shakily to his feet. His cut was painful, but superficial. Blood only trickled from it into his urine-soaked trousers.

"You've partly repaid your debt to me," said Lord Bahl in his hypnotic voice, "and received a gift in return—your life. Moreover, a wound can be a valuable reminder. Henceforward, your flesh will tear more easily there, but if you're obedient, you needn't worry."

Yaun felt a wave of gratitude, followed by the urge to please Lord Bahl and so rise in his estimation.

"Reflect on what you've become," continued Bahl. "How did you end up alone, groping through sewage for coins? Was that what you desired? Was that what you deserved? Think. Who did this to you? How should they be repaid?"

Bahl's words made Yaun recall his brother's good fortune, his father's disappointment, and Honus's scorn. The idea grew that these others were to blame for his woes. Resentment flared into hatred as the thought took hold. *They're responsible! Nothing was my fault! They brought this on me!*

Lord Bahl smiled as if he had read Yaun's thoughts. "I've heard of your brother, so righteous and thin-blooded. I'm told he looks down upon your manly appetites. When he's count, will you still sit at the high table? Will you even be seated in the hall? Perhaps you'll be lucky, and he'll toss you scraps as he does to his dogs, but only if you're meek and beg like them.

"Perhaps you could pray to Karm and beg scraps from her also. You should have kissed that arrogant Sarf's ass while you carried his pack. That was a missed opportunity."

As Yaun listened, each word was a lash driving him to further frenzy.

"Durkin smolders as I speak and none of its folk live. Eastward lies Falsten, your father's county. The Empire is crumbling while I grow mightier. What aid will Falsten receive if I turn on it? It's time to choose sides. I could be harsh or merciful. I might make a treaty and spare Falsten. With which count should I parley? Your father? Your brother? Or you?"

"Me, Lord! Please! Let it be me!"

Bahl held out Yaun's dagger. "Then take what you deserve! The Devourer blesses those who seize their due. Apply your anger! Use this weapon to clear your path." Bahl handed Yaun the dagger and a small vial of liquid. "With this on your blade, the smallest prick will be deadly. When you're count, you'll need a priest. Most Holy Gorm will attend you."

The black-robed priest bowed to Yaun. "Sire, already I perceive the Devourer's power within you. It will be mighty when I see you next, for hate feeds strength."

"Expect His Most Holy in a moon," said Lord Bahl. "All things must be accomplished by then. He will tell you what troops I'll require in satisfaction of our pact."

Lord Bahl held out a hand for Yaun to kiss. When Yaun did so, the fingers' otherworldly coldness stung his lips. Upon receiving that obeisance, Bahl turned and wordlessly left the room. Yaun shivered and was glad for the fire.

"You shall come to cherish that scar," said Gorm. "It will remind you of the day that made you a count. There's a horse waiting for you, but first some servants will tend your wound. Perhaps you would like them to bring ale."

"Yes, Most Holy," said Yaun, his voice reflecting a new-found assurance. "Ale would be good."

From a window, Lord Bahl and Most Holy Gorm watched Yaun gallop off. "What a worm," said the priest.

"That worm will grow into a viper," said Bahl. "When a fool blames others for his faults, he finds much to avenge. Already Yaun seethes with hatred."

"Yet, he's a coward."

"Give him power, and his cowardice will make him all the more cruel," replied Bahl. "Nurture that cruelty, Gorm, but mind how you stir the people. This must be different from Lurwic. Discord will work against our purposes. I want Count Yaun to raise an army. A mob won't do."

"The Devourer is ever hungry, Lord. Restraint will diminish your power."

"I just sacrificed Durkin."

"A thousand souls at most," said the priest. "A pittance."

"Sometimes even a god must fast. Rile Yaun's subjects, but direct their rancor outward. The Rising will come when we have sufficient blades. Then, even Bremven will feel their edges."

Gorm grinned. "A bounty of souls for the Devourer."

"Yes. Karvakken a hundred times over."

NINETEEN

YIM WOKE in the dim light of early dawn to find Honus asleep with Tabsha. Yim lay motionless awhile, but aches from a day spent stooping prevented further rest. Furthermore, the hovel oppressed her. Its closeness, its smell, and most of all, its atmosphere of despair soon drove her to rise. She quietly crawled out the doorway into the chill, dewy morning and paced about to warm herself.

Her labors, along with those of Honus and Tabsha, stretched before her—a patch of upturned dirt. It seemed insignificant. For two days, they had buried roots and beans in that ground, and in the upcoming day, they would finish the job. *Burying all that food in hopes of a harvest. Is it an act of faith or futility?* She thought of the hungry time ahead and doubted Tabsha would reap her crop. It was a dismal thought, and her future seemed equally bleak.

Who will ever take joyous memories of me to the Dark Path? Yim could think of no one. Her mother had died at her birth and she couldn't remember her father's face. All she recalled were his beatings. The Wise Woman who had raised her had not been unkind, but she had been distant. Yim couldn't envision that cold woman mourning her parting. As for her, she had no treasured moment, no instance of bliss to sustain her. *All my life has been for duty, and this is where obedience has led.*

Yim had not cried when she had been captured. Chained in the filthy slave pen, she had been stoic. She had fought tears at every occasion and usually won. But the horror of her latest vision made her fear that Karm had forsaken her. As Yim stood alone in the dank morning, her sorrow burst forth and overwhelmed her. She cried for the loss of hope. She cried for herself. She cried for Tabsha and the ruined land about her. In her despair, she became oblivious of everything. Her sobs racked her until she had to gasp for breath.

Then Yim became aware of another presence and turned to see Honus standing outside the hovel. She had no idea how long he had been watching. The expression beneath his tattoos was inscrutable to her tear-blurred eyes. Yim looked away and struggled to stifle her sobs. She gazed in Honus's direction only after mastering her emotions. By then, he was gone.

Yim walked over to the hovel and called into it with a low voice. "Master, should I gather some breakfast?"

"Take Tabsha with you," said Honus, "and show her where you found the tubers."

Yim heard Tabsha make a sleepy sigh, and she assumed that Honus was waking her. Soon Tabsha emerged carrying an empty basket. She stretched to ease her stiffness, saying, "Plantin' be 'ard work."

"It is," agreed Yim. As she led Tabsha to the swampy spot, she asked, "Don't you collect wild foods?"

"Mah mam be afeared o' the woods, so I larned little from 'er," replied Tabsha. "Toff larned me 'bout settin' snares, but wolves usually empty them. There be some berries in summer. Apples in fall, though they be 'ard an' bitter."

"Well, I can show you faerie arrow and fox sword. Both have tubers even this time of year."

"Tha' would be good. Spring be always 'ard."

Tabsha fell silent while Yim pondered how to help her survive. Those thoughts led to an obvious question, and Yim gave voice to it. "Why do you live alone? Don't you have any family?"

"Nay."

"Then, why not leave and live elsewhere?"

Tabsha seemed surprised by Yim's suggestion, as if it were absurd. "Mah 'usband and mah childs be buried 'ere."

They reached the wet ground where the faerie arrows grew and worked to fill most of the basket before wading out into deeper water for fox sword. Those plants were harder to uproot, and they took only a few of their thick, branching tubers. Afterward, Yim tried to find every edible plant she could and show them to Tabsha. She located only a few after much searching.

When Yim and Tabsha returned, they found signs that Honus had been watering the new plantings. Before they entered the hovel to cook, he emerged from the woods carrying the two buckets filled with water.

"Master," said Yim, "can I have some water for cooking?"

Honus brought over a bucket. While Tabsha started a fire, Yim filled the clay cooking pot with fox sword tubers and water, then returned the bucket to Honus. After joining Tabsha in the hovel, she heard him empty the bucket and trudge off to the stream for more water.

"Do 'e always work so 'ard?" asked Tabsha.

"I don't know," replied Yim. "He's owned me for only a few days."

Tabsha nodded, but made no further conversation. Yim filled the silence with talk of practical matters. "Fox sword tubers have to be boiled until the water turns brown before you can eat them. And never drink the cooking water, it'll pucker your mouth." As Yim cooked, she continued to instruct Tabsha on the storage and preparation of the various plants they had collected. Tabsha listened mutely, as one unaccustomed to talking. Her demeanor discouraged more personal conversation and Yim lapsed into silence upon finishing her instruction. She spoke again only when she heard Honus outside. "I can watch this, if you want to start planting."

Tabsha rose quickly, obviously eager to exchange Yim's company for Honus's. Yim felt more at ease after Tabsha left. Despite her sympathy for Toff's widow, she yearned to leave the dispirited woman and her dismal home.

When the pot finally boiled, Yim stirred the tubers to leach out their astringent juice. When the cooking water turned brown, she used a pair of sticks to place the tubers on a slab of wood that served as Tabsha's only plate. Then she took the meal outside. Honus was away getting more water, so Yim helped Tabsha plant until he arrived. When he did, the two stopped work to eat with him.

"Master, we should finish by noon," said Yim.

Her statement elicited the desired response. "Tabsha," said Honus. "I must resume my journey once the planting's done."

Tabsha nodded without betraying any emotion.

Yim took Tabsha's indifferent response as evidence that she had withdrawn into her shell. That impression made Yim all the more eager to depart. "Will we leave today, Master?" she asked.

"Yes," replied Honus.

After the meal, they resumed work. By early afternoon, the crops were planted and watered. Honus put on his sword and told Yim to get the pack. Then he bowed to Tabsha. "Mother, we must take our leave."

"Thank ya, sire," said Tabsha.

"I'm guided by Karm. If I've helped you, it's her doing. If I haven't, it's my failing. May her peace be upon you." As

Honus bowed again to Tabsha, Yim shouldered the pack. "Come, Yim," said Honus, as he strode away. Yim hurried to keep apace. When she reached the road, she looked back. Tabsha had vanished like a ghost, leaving only the empty field to recall her.

As Yim and Honus walked down the road, Honus looked tired and his gait betrayed the soreness of his muscles. They didn't speak. Yim felt uncomfortable, for after their stay with Tabsha, Honus seemed more baffling.

The Wise Woman had taught Yim several arcane arts. The technique Yim used to call up Mirien's spirit was only one of them. Like Honus, Yim could discern thoughts by gazing into a person's eyes, and she also knew how to shield herself against such an inspection. Both these skills sometimes occurred naturally in people, though to a lesser degree. Thus Yim once had thought that she could probe Honus without arousing his suspicion. She had abandoned the idea. *He suspects too much already,* she thought, regretting her outburst about her visions. That indiscretion made it all the more important to appear ordinary.

Forgoing use of her uncommon powers forced Yim to fall back on observation and conversation to understand Honus. Honus frustrated these, for while he was sometimes talkative, he was always guarded. Yim, accustomed to easy insight into people, keenly felt her uncertainty.

Honus's visit with Tabsha particularly perplexed Yim. She could ascribe a wide range of motives for it, from base to noble. *He might have sought her out for carnal reasons, believing her to be still young and beautiful . . . or, perhaps, he helped her at Karm's direction . . . or to spite me . . . or to atone for something . . . or to honor Toff's devotion.* Yim liked the last idea best, but she had no inkling if it was closest to the truth.

As they walked, Honus seemed to brood. His expression was morose and Yim wasn't tempted to inquire what thoughts troubled him. Yet eventually she asked the question foremost on her mind for three days. "Master, why did we stop at Tabsha's?"

"Do you think we did her good?"

"I don't know. Do you?"

Honus sighed. "I'm no Seer. Yet that's the real question. If we did her good, my reason's unimportant. And if she comes to harm, good intentions matter not."

Yim wanted to press him for a less evasive answer, but his expression discouraged her. Instead she asked, "Will you hunt today?"

"I'm too tired. Tonight, you must forage or fast." He noted how Yim's expression darkened and added, "Surely you don't begrudge her our sack of grain."

"She thanked *you* for *your* generosity," replied Yim, "but I, too, will go hungry."

"I'm certain she was grateful to us both."

"We have a saying back home: 'You thank the goat's herder for the milk, not the goat.' She knew I was your property. In you, she found comfort. In me, she found someone to pity."

"If that's true, then you've given her more comfort than I."

Yim glared at Honus bitterly. "How wonderful for her! She's found someone more miserable than herself!"

Honus replied evenly. "I didn't make you a slave. I haven't asked you to endure more than I."

Yim fought the impulse to throw the pack on the ground. Instead, she said, "It's true. You haven't *asked* me to do anything."

Honus sighed and resumed his brooding. Yim slowed her pace so that she could follow at a distance. They walked this way until Honus eventually stopped and waited for

Yim to catch up. "You must carry my pack because Theodus said it's Karm's will," he said. "But I'll try to make your life easier. I'll hunt this evening. If there's anything else I can do, you need only tell me."

"I want to know who you are," said Yim.

"What?"

"You asked me what you might do, and I've told you. I'd feel more easy if you weren't such a mystery."

Yim smiled at Honus's discomfort, knowing she had trapped him. He would either have to admit the emptiness of his promise or expose himself to her.

"What would you like to know?" asked Honus.

Yim knew exactly what she wished to ask first. "Why do you trance?"

"It's a useful skill," replied Honus.

"That's half an answer at best," said Yim. "It reveals nothing."

A rueful look came to Honus's face, much to Yim's satisfaction. "I've always had the gift for trancing, even as a child."

"It wasn't part of your training as a Sarf?"

"No. Few Sarfs can trance. I was never formally taught the necessary meditations, but picked them up from an older boy."

"Why would a child want to trance?"

"I missed my parents."

"Were they dead?"

"No, but they might as well have been. When one enters the temple, all worldly ties are cut."

Honus's reply made Yim recall her lonely childhood. "But if they were alive, why trance?"

"To find remembrances of mothers and fathers and relive them. I mostly sought out bedtime stories. You'd be surprised how common those memories are. Since then, trancing has become a habit. I find solace in it."

"Did Theodus approve of this habit?"

"Not really. Yet he was indulgent, especially in the last few years, when our road was hard."

"What's it like?"

Honus paused to consider. "The Dark Path is all around us," he said at last. "It mirrors our world, except it's lifeless, worn, and wrapped in mist. One feels one's way with the mind. As spirits travel westward, they leave a trail of reminiscences. When you chance upon one, it briefly becomes your own."

"Do you encounter the spirits themselves?"

"Yes. That is when the memories are most vivid."

"Like Toff's?"

"Yes. Like Toff's. Now are you satisfied?"

"No," said Yim. "Did you expect Tabsha to still be beautiful?"

"She was never beautiful," answered Honus. "Only to Toff."

"Oh."

"To be loved as she was . . ." Honus paused as if overcome by emotion. "Perhaps recalling that gift will sustain her through a trying spring." He gave Yim a knowing look. "I didn't go there for amorous reasons."

Yim blushed. "That never crossed my mind."

A grin formed on Honus's face. "Posing questions is a revealing business. Are there any more you wish to ask?"

Yim's blush deepened. "No, Master. At least, not at present."

Yim and Honus walked until late afternoon, when Honus went out to hunt. Yim rested at the roadside in his absence. He returned empty-handed as sunset approached. In response to Yim's disappointed look, he said, "The woods were empty. I didn't even hear a bird."

"Should I set up camp?"

"We'll walk a bit more. I don't trust a place that animals avoid."

They continued down the road until they reached a

river. All that remained of the bridge that had spanned it were a single stone arch on the far shore and five piers barely jutting above the water. "Unless you care to swim tonight," said Honus, "we must camp here."

"This place is fine with me," said Yim. "I'll gather firewood."

When Yim returned, she found Honus bent over in the river, trying to catch a fish. Yim didn't wish to spoil his chances by talking. Since some daylight remained, she decided to forage in case he had no success. Before she left, an uneasy feeling made her take the knife from the pack. Thus armed, she headed out.

Yim followed the riverbank, thinking it would be a likely place to find something edible. The fallen bridge had forced travelers to look for another place to cross, and there was a crude path heading upstream. Yim hurried along it, knowing there would be little time to find food before nightfall.

Yim was far from the ruined bridge and still empty-handed when she came upon a stone-paved road. It emerged from the forest and entered the river to create a ford to the other bank. *At least I've found a place to cross*. Yim turned toward camp, for it had grown too dark to forage. Then she heard something that made her halt. From up the deserted road came an unmistakable sound—the faint wail of a small and terrified child.

TWENTY

YIM LISTENED carefully, afraid the wail would cease before she could find its source. However, it continued unabated, expressing terror so intense that Yim found herself shaking. She couldn't imagine what horror could provoke such a cry. Remaining passive was unthinkable. Despite the deepening dark, she felt compelled to attempt a rescue.

When Yim sought to locate the child, she discovered that its wail was not a sound that ears could hear. Another of her senses—one honed under the Wise Woman's tutelage—had detected it. *Am I hearing a spirit?* Yet no ghostly voice had ever sounded so immediate. *This is no echo from the Sunless World. It's a scream from this one.*

Yim stopped using her ears and followed her intuition. The cry seemed to be coming from the road that led into the woods. Trees crowded its edges so tightly that in the failing light it resembled a cavern, not a thoroughfare, a place one enters without assurance of return. Nevertheless Yim followed the cry up the tree-shadowed lane. As she slowly advanced, the wail became louder. The sky darkened until Yim was walking nearly blind. She stumbled along the uneven pavement and at last approached a large ruin. All she could see was its silhouette, a huge expanse of blackness against the night sky. Though the structure appeared abandoned, Yim took no comfort from that. She felt the presence of something or someone malign. The impression was as distinct as the scent of a corpse in a dark room. Yim held the knife at the ready and advanced warily.

The night was absolutely still; yet the wail sounded so loudly in Yim's head that she could hardly bear it. Only its piteousness prevented her from fleeing. Just then, the moon peeked over the horizon, and its light revealed more of the structure. It was a castle where vines and trees were completing the destruction wrought by some ancient enemy. Yim could make out a gateless and crumbling gatehouse, breached walls bearing stumps of watchtowers, and a cylindrical keep.

The cry came from the gatehouse. Yim entered it. Between the outer and inner archways was a roofless space littered with rubble. The night sky provided the only illumination, for the moon was too low to shine into the gatehouse's interior. Yim stubbed a toe as she stumbled about in the gloom. While she waited for the pain to subside, she noticed a doorway in one of the walls. It was pitch black, but she could make out a pale object that was suspended in the opening. It was the source of the wail.

Yim carefully felt her way across the rubble-strewn space. She reached the doorway and touched the object. It was a child's skull, dangling from a cord that passed through the eye sockets. Yim's sensitive hands felt the subtle tingling that she recognized as the presence of a spell.

The cries inside Yim's head were agonizing. They conjured images of a toddler trapped in a pitch-black cave, screaming for help that would never arrive. Most appalling was the freshness of the terror. It seemed as if the spirit had just realized its doom and was trapped perpetually in that terrible instant.

Yim cut the cord with the knife and carried the skull to the moonlit road to examine it. There, she saw that the skull was painted with runes. They were the source of the spell her fingers had detected. *This wail I sense may be only a trick, a way to frighten off intruders.* Yim rejected the notion. *It would serve no purpose. Ordinary persons couldn't hear it.* Yim pondered the problem and decided that she should try to contact the spirit within the skull—if there was one. She assumed that the technique for contacting the spirits upon the Dark Path should serve in this instance also. Placing the skull before her, Yim sat on her heels and began the mental rituals that would allow her mind to reach beyond her body.

Yim wasn't prepared for what happened next. Spirits on the Dark Path were distant from the living, but the skull held a spirit that had never left this world. When Yim contacted it, the immediacy of the experience nearly drove her mad. In a confused and horrifying instant, Yim experienced an abduction, a bizarre ritual, a frightening glimpse of a boiling caldron, and a state of perpetual terror. She felt like a swimmer gripped by a drowning person who threatens to sink them both, and it took all her will to break free. When Yim returned to the earthly realm, she was shaking and sobbing.

The skull imprisoned a soul between life and death. Yim couldn't imagine the purpose of such an abomination, but she knew that it must be ended. Picking up the skull again, she felt its magic and realized that destroying it would release the trapped spirit. She took a loose paver from the roadway and used it to smash the skull.

The piercing wail stopped abruptly. Yet Yim wasn't at peace, for it became apparent that the child's cries had drowned out fainter ones. These were no less heartrending. Yim could detect several distinct voices within a cacophony of despair and terror. A woman sobbed. Another screamed. A man moaned piteously. All the cries seemed to come from within the dark castle.

Yim was in a quandary: She was afraid to enter the castle, but she couldn't ignore the tormented spirits. Moreover, she knew Honus would be curious about her absence. *I might convince him I got lost if I return now. That would mean abandoning the spirits.* Yim knew that returning tomorrow would mean revealing her powers—something she had been warned never to do. It was her guardian's strictest injunction, and Yim had taken it to heart. *Should I keep my secret or save these spirits?* Yim felt she would regret whatever choice she made.

A dark figure emerged from the gatehouse while Yim was wrestling with indecision. He moved so silently that she was unaware of his approach until he stepped into the moonlight. Even then, he seemed wrapped in shadow. The dark face over the inky robe appeared featureless, except for two glaring eyes. Yim gave a startled cry and pointed her knife at the advancing stranger. He glanced at the weapon, but didn't slow his pace.

"You've taken something that was mine," he said in a low, hoarse voice. "Now you must replace it."

"Stay back!" said Yim as forcefully as fright permitted. "I'll use this if I need to!"

"So this sneak thief has a sting."

"You're the thief! I know what you did."

The dark man bared his teeth in a grin. "You do? Then you must have powers. Good! Good! That spirit would have sustained me for years, but you're a greater prize." While he talked, the man slowly advanced. His empty hands hung limply. "If you wish to stop me," he said calmly, "you must kill me."

"I will!" shouted Yim, hoping the man couldn't see how her hand shook.

"You lack the courage," replied the man. He stepped in front of Yim, his arms still passively at his side. Yim gritted her teeth and stabbed at his chest. She felt her blade touch flesh; then there was a flash of brilliant blue light. It illuminated a cadaverous face that grinned in triumph. Yim felt a jolt so painful that it seared away her consciousness. She collapsed in spasms on the roadway as the blade, which glowed eerily, was flung from her twitching hand.

Through a fog of drowsiness, Yim thought a goat was licking her stomach. It was a pleasant sensation, and she was inclined to let it lull her back to sleep, despite the fact that the goat was sitting on her thighs. She lay still, enjoying the gentle stroking until a confusing thought came to her—*I no longer herd goats. So where did this goat come from?* Another question arose. *Where am I?* Yim reluctantly decided to open her eyes and find out. When she tried, some force opposed her. As she struggled against it, her initial puzzlement became fear that approached panic. Through intense will, she forced her eyes open. They gazed upon the ceiling of a vast circular chamber. Though a fire cast reddish, flickering light on its stones, the room was shadowy.

The sensations on her stomach were created by a paintbrush. Yim's memory was restored when she saw that the man who had emerged from the gatehouse wielded the brush. He was sitting on her thighs and painting runes upon her naked body. The red-brown paint smelled of herbs, decay, and blood. It tingled slightly as it dried. Already, the man had painted her torso down to the navel. Concentrating on his work, he didn't notice she was watching him.

Too late, Yim recalled the Wise Woman's tales of sorcerers who knew a spell against iron weapons and overcame their foes by enticing them to strike. Such men were said to preserve their lives by use of dark magic. With horror, Yim thought the man upon her might practice such sorcery, for he looked like a sun-dried corpse. His face was formed of human leather that had darkened to grayish brown. Yellowed whites surrounded his gray pupils. Wisps of gray hair surrounded his skull like fibrous fog. The skeletal hand holding the brush was the same shade as the face. Yet, just beneath the sleeves of his black robe, the man's wrists appeared deathly white.

Yim realized her ankles were bound by what felt like a thick, rough rope. Her wrists were tied behind her back. The arm that had held the knife was partly numb. She tried to sit upright and caught a glimpse of a huge brass caldron surrounded by a roaring fire. The man quickly pushed her head back down, slamming it against the stone floor. Through her pain, Yim heard the man's rasping voice. "Move again and you'll regret it." He picked up a large brass needle and pointed it at her face. "I can make you suffer greatly." He made the needle's point wander down Yim's cheek and neck, over her breasts, and down her belly. Yim's flesh stung everywhere the needle scraped. "Next time," said the man, "I'll push down every once in a while. Do you understand?"

"Yes," whispered Yim.

The man took a damp cloth and wiped a spot on Yim's stomach. "You made me smear a rune. That won't do."

"Why are you doing this?"

"Why, why, why?" mimicked the man in a mockingly high voice. "They always ask that. Why does the hawk seize the sparrow? It's natural for the strong to prey upon the weak."

"There's nothing natural about this!"

"It's natural to avoid death. All creatures prolong their lives at others' expense. You're no different. I imagine you've eaten your share of hares."

"Do you intend to eat me?" asked Yim in horror.

"It's your spirit that will sustain me, though I won't waste your meat." In anticipation of Yim's reaction, the man picked up the needle and placed his hand on Yim's throat. "Accept your fate, and you need not suffer until the water boils."

"Why not kill me now and be done with it?"

"For the spell to work, you must be living when you go into the brew."

"This is foul magic," said Yim. "Look what it's done to you!"

"You understand nothing, my young sparrow," said the man. "I've lived over three hundred years. How can you lecture me? I've heard more arguments and pleas than you could possibly imagine. Now shut up and be still if you wish to enjoy what life you have left."

Yim's helplessness made her obey. She lay still and the man returned to his painting. All the while, she thought furiously of how she might escape. No plan came to her. Despite her terror, as the symbols crept down her body, Yim's drowsiness returned. She found it increasingly hard to think, and she became confused. Her eyelids turned heavy and closed.

Suddenly, the man's weight was gone and a sandaled foot was insistently pushing her thigh. Yim heard a voice shouting, "Get up! Get up!" She felt the ropes around her ankles fall away. Someone began gently kicking her. "Yim!" The voice sounded more urgent. "You must get up!"

It required even more effort than before for Yim to open her eyes. When she finally succeeded, she saw Honus standing next to her, his sword drawn. He was not facing her, but the man in the black robe. Yim's mind was foggy, her body felt leaden, and her wrists were still tied. It seemed to take forever to rise. The effort made her dizzy. All the while, the man slowly advanced toward Honus.

"Run, Yim!" yelled Honus, still keeping his eyes on his opponent. "The door behind you leads out of the keep."

Yim saw the doorway and moved toward it with the slowness of a sleepwalker. Her mind was still sluggish and all she could do was stagger. Honus yelled once more. "Run! Run! Run!"

As Yim crossed the room she heard a hoarse voice say, "If you wish to stop me, you must kill me."

Yim passed through the door and a hallway to the keep's entrance. When she stepped into the cold night air, her mind cleared slightly. When it did, terror gripped her. She ran heedlessly across the castle courtyard into the dark gatehouse. There, she tripped over the rubble and went crashing

onto the fallen stones. Yim cried out in surprise and pain.
Her left shin hurt so much that she feared it might be broken. Yet she was able to rise to her feet and make her way
to the road. Once there, she ran down the lane without
pausing to examine her injuries.

Yim didn't stop running until she reached the ford. She
entered the cold water and sat down so it flowed around
her nude body. The river soothed her hurts, but more importantly, it washed away the marks painted on her flesh.
As they dissolved, the spell that clouded Yim's mind eased
its hold, and she was able to think clearly.

Yim left the river to wait for Honus to come and free her
wrists. It took only a short while to realize that he would
never arrive. *He's been ensnared, just like I was.* Yim struggled with her bonds until her wrists were raw, but the knots
wouldn't budge. *I'll need my knife. Perhaps it's still where
I dropped it.*

The last thing Yim wanted to do was return to the castle, but she saw no other choice. Reluctantly, she walked to
the gatehouse to search for the knife. The pavement was
empty. Yim remembered only a jolt of pain between the instant she stabbed at the man and when she awakened in the
keep. Recalling that jolt, she thought she might have jerked
her hand and tossed the knife into the weeds that surrounded the road. Yim began to methodically feel about
them with her bare feet. All the while, she kept a wary eye
on the gatehouse entrance. After a long, anxious search,
her toes touched metal. She squatted down and picked up
the knife. It tingled slightly in her hand.

Yim fled down the dark roadway until she reached the
river. Kneeling down on its bank, Yim began the awkward
business of cutting her bonds. She was unable to see what
she was doing or to hold the knife properly, and it seemed
to take forever. When her hands were finally free, she used
them to scrub the last vestiges of the unholy markings from
her body.

With that done, Yim needed only to flee to obtain her freedom. She could dress in Honus's spare clothes and forage for food until she reached a town. *And who would blame me if I did? No one would even know.* Yet when Yim imagined such a deed weighed on Karm's Balance, she knew she couldn't desert Honus. He had saved her, so despite her fear and her desire for freedom, she would try to save him. It wasn't a rational decision, but it felt like the only right one.

Yim hoped her opponent's sorcery might prove to be his weakness. She reasoned that if she could release the captured spirits that sustained him, the dark man might be gravely weakened or even killed. To accomplish that, she counted on surprise. *Hawks never think a sparrow will attack.* As dawn's first glow appeared in the sky, Yim cut down a stout sapling and made a spear. *His iron spell can only trick me once. When he sees this, he won't say I must kill him!*

At dawn, Yim headed toward the castle carrying a wooden spear and the knife. Though the latter was useless as a weapon, it would be needed to cut down the skulls. Yim's plan was simple—collect all the skulls and destroy them simultaneously. She hoped to do this without alerting the dark man. If she succeeded, she would see what happened next and improvise. Yim had no further strategy other than to use the knife on herself and Honus if things looked hopeless. *That way, at least, our spirits won't be captured.* She wondered what Honus would think of such a haphazard attack. *Not much, I suspect.*

Yim entered the gatehouse and peered about the courtyard. The ancient castle was weathered and crumbling, but no living thing was visible inside its walls. Not a blade of grass grew between the cobblestones. No vine softened the dank keep. Everything was deathly still, but Yim could already sense the torment of the captured spirits. It was evident that the dark man felt no need to hide the skulls, since two were visible from the gatehouse. Yim became aware of three others. If she included the skull that she had already smashed in the pattern, then all the skulls were hung at equal intervals along the castle walls. She cut them down and used their cords as carrying handles.

After Yim collected the five spirits outside the keep, she discerned one more imprisoned inside it. This spirit sounded like a man struggling—and failing—to repress wrenching sobs. Yim worried it might be Honus. With mounting apprehension, Yim entered the keep. When she reached the doorway to the inner hall, she cautiously peered around it.

Honus lay motionless on the floor, bound and naked. Runes covered his body from his neck to his feet, making it look bloody. The fire about the brass caldron had brought the liquid inside it to a boil, and steam billowed into the air. Its putrescent stench nearly gagged Yim. A series of ropes and pulleys spanned the ceiling above the caldron, and the black-robed man was busy with them. He lowered a rope with a brass hook to the floor, grabbed it, pulled it over to Honus, and attached the hook to the bonds around Honus's ankles. It seemed clear that he was preparing to plunge Honus into the caldron.

Yim urgently scanned the room for the final skull. She felt it should be easy to find, since the room was virtually bare, except for the caldron at its center. However, the walls were empty. No skull dangled from a doorway.

The dark man walked over to a rope and began to pull. Wooden pulleys creaked. The rope attached to the hook grew taut. Honus's ankles were lifted up as he was slowly dragged across the stone floor. He came to rest beneath a pulley attached to a rope that spanned the room and passed over the caldron.

The sobs of the spirit imprisoned in the remaining skull echoed within Yim's head. She knew it was close by, but she still couldn't see it. *Think! Think! Spells usually involve patterns. Think about the pattern! A circle of six skulls and a seventh one . . . where?* The answer seemed obvious. *In the center! But what center? Center of the castle? The keep? The room? It must be the room—it's circular. But the caldron's in the room's center.* Yim stared at the boiling caldron, but it seemed impossible for the skull to be there. Her eyes followed the rolling cloud of steam upward and her heart sank. She had found the skull. It dangled from a cord high above the caldron.

TWENTY·ONE

YIM'S EYES left the skull and followed the cord from which it hung upward to the steam-fogged ceiling of the room. There was a tangle of ropes traversing the hall, and most passed over the caldron. The cord that suspended the skull was tied to one of those. Yet try as she might, Yim couldn't distinguish which rope it was. Ultimately, all the ropes passed through pulleys and down to the floor at the far end of the hall. There were over a dozen of them, and Yim knew she would be able to cut only one or two before she would face the dark man again. The prospect left her paralyzed by panic and indecision.

Meanwhile, Honus's bound ankles rose higher from the floor as the man continued to pull the rope. Soon Honus's legs pointed directly upward. Yim continued to agonize over what to do until she heard a woman's calm and authoritative voice, "Throw the skulls into the fire."

Yim turned to see who had spoken, but the hall behind her was empty. Again the voice sounded, more insistent than before. "Burn them now!" The voice was compelling, and Yim obeyed it. She sprinted to the side of the caldron away from the dark man and tossed the skulls into the fire. The man had been facing away, and since Yim's bare feet made little noise, he was unaware of her presence until he spied her dashing toward the ropes. He reacted quickly and released the rope. As Honus's legs dropped to the floor, the dark man darted after Yim.

Yim reached the far end of the hall and grabbed a rope at random. Like the surrounding ropes, it ran from a pulley on the ceiling to a brass ring in the floor. There was no clue whether it was the one that suspended the skull. The sense of purpose that had galvanized Yim only moments before departed as quickly as it arose. It was replaced by desperation as she struggled to cut the thick rope. Before she could sever it, the dark man bounded up. Yim whipped around to face him, dropping the knife so she could grasp her spear with both hands.

The man's pale eyes stood out in his darkened, leathery face. They shone with triumph and malice. He reached into the folds of his black robe and produced a short bronze sword. "Stupid girl," he said in a low, hypnotic tone. "Why would you face me with a stick? Was it for him?" The dark man grinned. "Then you shall watch him die. The steam always wakes them. It makes for quite a show. You'll twist like a pale worm when it's your turn."

Yim kept her spear pointed at the man, but his voice befuddled her. Then the dark man's sword slashed out with what seemed to her to be lightning speed. The spear point she had so carefully whittled became a shower of splinters. Yim was staring stupidly at her spear's blunted end when a second blow shortened it farther. The man was raising his sword for the third blow when he staggered back with a gasp. He swayed as if dizzy or sick. The sword fell from his hand and clattered on the floor. "You!" he croaked out in astonished anger. "You released them!"

The spell that had stupefied Yim lifted as the dark man sank to his hands and knees. His power gone, he looked withered and truly seemed three centuries old. He reached out and grabbed his sword with an unsteady hand that appeared incapable of lifting it.

"Yes," said Yim. "I threw the skulls into the fire." She stood triumphant over her decrepit foe. Her ruined spear still made a stout club. One blow would cave in his skull. Yim fought off the temptation. "I won't kill you," she said. "But I'll free the remaining spirit. If that ends your life, so be it."

"Please," said the man, as he crawled toward her in supplication. "Please."

Yim stood firm. Then with a quickness that seemed beyond his capacity, the man swung his sword at her legs. Yim jumped upward and sustained a slight nick on her foot. She angrily raised her spear like a club. "Why, you snake! I should . . ." Her words were cut short as numbness rapidly traveled up her leg from her tiny wound. The leg lost all feeling and buckled. Yim collapsed to the floor. She tried to pull herself up, but her body was swiftly passing beyond her control. From the waist down, she felt nothing at all. The paralysis traveled up her spine and spread to her arms. All she could do was lower her head to the floor before she became completely helpless.

Through unblinking eyes she watched the man slowly rise. He stepped out of her field of view. She heard him laugh. "Little fool, I still have a few tricks." Then she heard him shuffle away. Yim lay on the floor, made captive by her useless body. Then sensation began to gradually return. She felt the cold stones against her skin. A tingling spread throughout her muscles. She began to twitch and thought that soon she might be able to move again. Before that moment arrived, the dark man returned with ropes to bind her. He rolled her over on her chest and tied her wrists together. Afterward, he bound her ankles. Next, he arched her feet back and poured a liquid into her wound. It stung, and as the stinging spread, Yim's paralysis dissipated.

The man pulled Yim upright so she sat on her heels facing the caldron. Then he wound a rope between the bonds about her ankles and her wrists to insure she would remain in that position. "You shall watch what happens to your friend," he said. His voice sounded frail, but its malice was stronger than ever. "Before I'm through with you, you'll envy him. You hurt me, and you'll pay dearly for that. I require your spirit, so you must go into the caldron alive. Yet you need not go intact. Each day I'll do some cutting—a piece here, a piece there. Before I'm done, you'll beg to be boiled."

Yim shuddered as the man placed his hand on her thigh in the mockery of a caress. "Until that merriment," he said, "there are other games I can play." He took a long brass needle and slowly pushed it deep into Yim's thigh. The needle was coated with venom that mimicked a thousand wasp stings as it passed through her flesh. Despite herself, Yim screamed from the pain. The man grabbed her face and looked into her anguished eyes. "That was just a taste of your suffering." Then, he slowly walked toward the rope attached to Honus.

Yim tried to think despite the searing pain in her thigh. It was nearly impossible. Only a bit of the long needle protruded from her upper leg, which was swelling rapidly. Nevertheless, Yim was aware that she was more clearheaded than she would be once her torment began in earnest. It might be her last opportunity to think rationally.

Yim forced her thoughts upon the voice that prompted her to action. She was convinced it had been Karm's. *Why would she tell me to do such a thing?* Yim couldn't believe that the goddess had not foreseen its outcome. *Perhaps she cared more for the imprisoned souls than for Honus and me.* Yim imagined that five spirits might easily outweigh two upon Karm's Balance. *Now, those five are beyond that man's reach.* A thought arose: *Yet he's not beyond theirs.*

Yim instantly knew what she must do. Just as she had summoned Mirien's spirit to comfort Mam, she could bring the newly freed spirits from the Dark Path to confront their murderer. While her enfeebled captor struggled with the rope, she concentrated all her powers on that task. Anxiety and pain made it difficult to concentrate, and for a while, she feared that she would be unable to summon the ghosts. Yet calmness gradually came to her, and she was able to send her mind toward the Sunless Way. The room before her open eyes seemed to fade and the vaporous forms of agitated spirits became apparent. With her thoughts, Yim beckoned them and led them to the living world.

The air grew frigid as darkness drifted over the stone floor to form a black pool before Yim. Its inky surface appeared stirred by a storm. Waves rose up. When they broke, misty shapes emerged. They sped through the air toward the black-robed man tugging at the rope. The first ghost collided and merged with him. The man gave a startled cry and released the rope. Four more spirits entered him, and he began to scream in an eerie, high-pitched voice. He staggered and jerked as if covered with stinging insects. He dug his nails into his cheeks and began to claw off his flesh. His scream became a series of rasping gasps as he shredded his face. Then, with a final shriek of unmitigated terror, he fell to the floor. His skull made a sickening crunch as it struck the stones.

The air warmed. The only sounds within the hall were the crackling of the fire and the bubbling of the caldron. Inside Yim's head, the sobs of the last imprisoned spirit echoed.

Yim looked around and saw the knife lying on the floor only a few paces away. She began to slide toward it with excruciating slowness. Each time she moved her wounded leg, the needle within it caused fresh spasms of pain. The short journey seemed interminable. Yim wept in agony and frustration, halting until the pain became bearable, only to renew it with fresh movement. Once she reached the knife, she had to pick it up and saw through the ropes that bound her wrists. This proved maddeningly difficult and every motion aggravated her throbbing leg. In her torment, she lost all sense of time. Late-morning sunlight poured through the hall's high windows before her hands were free and she could finally pull the needle from her leg. Trembling, she cut the ropes that bound her ankles. Yim was free at last. She rose unsteadily to her feet and hobbled toward Honus to see if he was still alive.

Honus lay still. His face bore the look of one frozen in a nightmare. Yim pressed her head to his painted chest and was relieved to hear a faint heartbeat. The strain of events finally overwhelmed her, and she began to shake and weep. Yim clung to Honus's inert form as she might to a rock in a stormy sea. Her tears flowed until they smeared the cursed symbols painted on his chest. Throughout this, Honus might as well have been a rock. He was as stiff and silent.

When Yim ceased crying, she felt the calmness that comes from exhaustion. Wearily, she thought of all she must do to hide her powers from Honus. First, she went over to a small pile of clothing and found her tunic. She put it on, then gathered up Honus's garments. Beneath them lay the discarded possessions of the man's previous victims. An infant's smock, simple and tattered, made Yim recall Tabsha's missing child. There was a warrior's rusty chain-mail shirt. Upon a beggar's rags lay a lady's brooch, the kind used for fastening a cloak. It looked old, and its workmanship was exquisite. Each item suggested a tale of a life that ended in unspeakable terror.

Yim felt better when she was clothed, and she turned to freeing the last imprisoned spirit. With time to figure out the tangle of ropes, she determined which one suspended the skull, and cut it. The skull smashed on the floor, and the spirit was at peace.

Yim devised a story to explain what happened to her foe and considered what evidence she might plant to confirm it. With that in mind, she approached the dark man's corpse. As hideous as he was in life, his final moments had rendered him even more gruesome. The man had clawed his face to shreds, exposing bone in places. Yim imagined his final visions were likely the experiences of his victims turned against him.

The man's face told too much about his death, and Yim realized that Honus shouldn't see it. Overcoming her revulsion, she pulled the corpse into a slumped, sitting position, then limped to get Honus's sword. Like her knife, it still faintly tingled from a spell. Yim returned to the dark man. She gripped the sword with both hands, and after much hesitation, swung at the corpse's neck. She shut her eyes before the blade struck and only felt it hit. The sword stopped abruptly.

Yim opened her eyes. The blade was wedged partway through the dead man's neck. When she tried to pull the sword out, he moved. Yim shrieked and jumped back. The dark man fell backward, the blade still in his neck. When Yim saw that the blow had not revived her enemy, she found the nerve to extract the sword from him.

She pulled the corpse into a sitting position again, aimed at the gash in the back of its neck, and swung the sword. This time, she didn't close her eyes. The blade severed the dark man's spine, but not his neck. The result was ghastly. His head flipped forward so his ruined face pressed against his chest. Yim's stomach churned when she realized that she would have to slice through the remaining flesh to remove the head. She was gagging by the time it tumbled to the floor.

Yim pushed the headless corpse over and dropped Honus's sword close by. Picking up the head seemed harder than severing it, for she was loath to touch it. It took time to summon the nerve to grasp the wispy hair. When Yim did, she seized it, limped to the boiling caldron, and tossed the head into it. For a while afterward, all she could do was shudder as she struggled to regain some composure.

When Yim felt able to act, she was still frantic to finish and depart. First she had to wash the painted runes off Honus. She cut his bonds and threw them into the fire. The dark man had a bucket of water and a rag with his painting supplies, and Yim took them to wash Honus. After determining that the runes were painted only on Honus's front, she set to work.

Yim had never seen a naked man before, and as she began to pass the thin rag over Honus's body, she felt both curious and shy. His muscular leanness reminded her of a goat, while his skin's smoothness contrasted with that impression. That smoothness was broken by his scars. Yim was amazed by their quantity. White lines crisscrossed his flesh, forming a chronicle of injury and a testament to his service to Karm. One jagged gash ran from his collarbone down past his navel and looked like it should have been fatal. It was intersected by an angry red scar partially covered with scabs. It was one of several wounds that were only partially healed. Yim washed these especially gently as she slowly cleaned her way downward. When she gingerly washed his manhood, the possibility that he might regain consciousness made her extremely uncomfortable. As soon as she had cleaned Honus's upper body, she dressed him in his shirt before washing his legs and feet.

When the painted runes were removed, Yim finished dressing Honus. Although the magical symbols had been erased, he remained unconscious. She shook him and shouted his name to no effect. He was still under a spell. Yim pondered the situation and concluded the spell had already accomplished its task. Honus's spirit had become ensnared in preparation for his body's destruction. Yet Yim knew that it remained in this world, bound by magic. If

Honus's spirit were to once more animate his body, Yim would have to free it.

The intensity of Yim's encounter with the child's spirit made her wary of contacting Honus's. She knew that she would have to take special precautions if she wanted to hide her powers from him. The Wise Woman had taught her how to obscure her essence when contacting malevolent ghosts, and Yim thought the same skill would be useful in this instance. She sat on her heels before Honus, and ignoring the pain in her thigh, proceeded to meditate. Only when she felt disguised did she venture forth into the nether realm. Yim neither saw nor touched anything, yet these were the closest terms for her experiences. She recognized Honus's presence immediately. He was struggling within a web of confusion, separated from all his senses. Without moving, she drew near him and reached out.

There was no flesh to touch, no barrier between him and her. As soon as Yim contacted Honus, she also entered him. He was naked to her in the most profound sense. The intimacy of their contact made Yim instinctively pull away. Yet even that brief glimpse had been nearly overwhelming. All the contradictory thoughts and feelings that formed his spirit were laid bare to her. It was too much to absorb and far more than she ever wanted to know. As Yim retreated, Honus followed her back to existence. He opened his eyes the same time she did.

Honus looked about with startled confusion, then stared at Yim blankly for a long moment before he spoke. "Yim?"

"Master! You killed him!"

Honus looked puzzled. "Killed who?"

"The man who kidnapped me. You cut off his head."

"I remember only a flash of light . . . and a dream. A very disturbing dream."

"Don't you recall saving me? You told me to run away."

Honus thought awhile. "Yes," he said at last. "I remember. I cut your bonds and turned to face a man in black."

"You must have killed him with your first blow, but you never came back. I waited so long."

"You came back for me?" said Honus with a touch of surprise. "That was brave." The dullness left Honus's eyes, and he began to glance about. "Where's the man's head?"

"I threw it in the pot."

A slight smile came to Honus's face. "Why would you do that?"

"He . . . he frightened me."

"I'd think a severed head would frighten you more."

Yim saw the feebleness of her deception. It was already unraveling, and she realized that she would have to do something fast. Without responding to Honus's remark, she rose and limped over to retrieve his sword. Before she returned, Yim forced herself to sob. "Ma . . . Ma . . . Master, please ta . . . take me a . . . a . . . away from here! I'm so fr . . . frightened!" Yim caused all her fear and pain to well up again and soon she cried in earnest. Although it chagrined her, she clutched Honus like a hysterical child. Between sobs, she pleaded, "Can we go now?"

Honus wrapped his arms around Yim and tried to calm her. "It's all right," he said gently. "There's nothing to fear now." Yim refused to be comforted. Finally, Honus said, "Come. We'll leave this fell place."

Yim's sobs diminished, and she whispered breathily, "Oh thank you, Master." She rose and hobbled from the hall as quickly as her throbbing leg permitted.

Once they were in the castle courtyard, Honus asked, "What's wrong with your leg?"

"The man stuck it with a needle."

"Let me see," said Honus, as he knelt down before her. He raised Yim's tunic to reveal her upper leg. It was so swollen that the skin was stretched tight. A small, black dot marked the needle's entry point. A circle of discolored

skin surrounded it—purple nearest the dot, shading to a
sullen red. He softly touched the mark. Yim winced. "I'm
familiar with such wounds," Honus said. "You shouldn't
be walking."

"Am I poisoned?"

"You needn't worry. This venom is short-lived. Rest
and bathing in cold water will restore your leg. I'll carry
you to our campsite." Honus grasped Yim's uninjured leg
and placed his shoulder against her stomach. Then, he
rose, throwing her upon his shoulder.

"I can walk," protested Yim.

"You're light enough. Besides, I need you to heal
quickly."

As Yim was borne down the path, she reflected how
goatherders similarly carried injured animals. She wavered
between believing Honus bore her solely out of practicality
and supposing he had tender motives. Her brief glimpse
into his spirit hinted at the latter, but she didn't wish to
dwell on it. *His emotions were contradictory,* Yim told herself. *It's impossible to know how he feels. He certainly
doesn't.* She was sure of only one thing: Whatever Honus's
feelings were, they would complicate her life.

TWENTY-TWO

EXCEPT FOR moaning whenever her wounded leg was
jostled, Yim was silent as Honus carried her. Still, her body
spoke to him. He sensed her exhaustion by the way she
slumped over his back. The crusted blood on her cuts and
scrapes, the hotness of her swollen thigh, and the rope

burns on her ankles told of her pain. Honus tried to carry her as gently as possible, though he was still shaky from his own ordeal. He approved of Yim's stoicism, so he respected her silence and didn't ask why she had lied to him.

Honus's own body bore evidence of Yim's deception. His wrists had marks left by bonds. Unless a headless man had bound him, Yim's version of events was false. Honus decided to discover what really had happened before confronting Yim. Until then, he would let her rest.

When Honus reached the campsite, he waded into the river and set Yim upon one of the ruined bridge's stone piers. It was broad enough to lie upon and low enough for her to dangle her leg in the water. "You can rest here," he said. "Bathe your leg. It'll ease the pain and swelling. While you do that, I'll try to find some food."

Yim only nodded and lowered her leg into the river.

Honus returned to the ford and discovered Yim's severed bonds. He also found fresh wood chips close to the stump of a sapling. Trimmed-off branches littered the ground. The evidence indicated that Yim had cut down the sapling and fashioned a spear from it.

When Honus had gleaned all he could from the area around the ford, he walked to the castle. The shattered skull at the gatehouse presented a deeper mystery. Honus picked up a piece of the skull. His hands were unable to detect the remnants of the spell, but the runes on the bone bespoke magic. The broken edges of the shard were unweathered, causing Honus to surmise that the skull had been shattered recently. He suspected that the act might be related to the previous night's events. The latter thought made him uneasy, as did all magic. He felt that the handiwork on the skull was something unnatural and inclined toward evil.

A patch of weeds close to the broken skull had been trampled, and Honus discovered Yim's footprints there. It suggested that the skull and Yim were somehow connected.

Honus entered the ruined gatehouse and spied the cut cord dangling in the doorway. He examined it. The cord was identical to one he found threaded through a shard of the skull. *Whoever cut down that skull probably also smashed it.* Recalling that Yim had the knife when she found him, Honus thought she was the likely one. Still, he couldn't imagine why she would do such a thing.

Honus entered the courtyard seeking answers to his growing list of questions. He found more severed cords dangling in empty doorways, but no more skulls. He entered the keep, which stank of the boiling caldron. The fetid smell evoked Honus's terrifying dream of imprisonment in a lightless void. He tried to push the memory from his mind, but it lingered on the edges of his thoughts as he entered the circular hall.

The dusty floor was marked by a maze of footprints. Honus followed a trail made by Yim's bare feet to a shattered spear fashioned from a sapling. Nearby lay a bronze sword. Honus regarded the remnants of the spear, amazed that Yim would fight a swordsman with such a feeble weapon. His astonishment increased when he examined the sword. Its blade felt slightly sticky. Honus sniffed the bronze and lightly touched his tongue to it. The numbness on his tongue confirmed his suspicion that the blade was poisoned with a paralyzing venom. *There's no way she could have prevailed against this weapon.* He recalled a wound on Yim's foot that might have been a sword cut. Then he spied severed bonds and a long brass needle lying on the floor. These clues suggested a seemingly impossible scenario: After her escape, Yim had cut her bonds, made a spear, and returned to the castle. There, she fought the black-robed man and was defeated. *He tortured her here. Yet somehow she escaped and overcame him.*

Honus turned to the headless corpse for clues to solve the puzzle. One look at its neck confirmed that the beheading was not his handiwork. From experience, Honus knew that when a man was decapitated, his heart still beat briefly afterward. Yet, the floor around the corpse was not sprayed with blood, indicating that the man was dead when his head was severed. In an effort to determine how the man had been killed, Honus searched his strange, unnatural body for wounds. He found none, which increased his puzzlement. He assumed that the missing head told how the man had died and suspected that was why Yim destroyed it. *Was this man slain by magic? Yim's magic? Or did others slay him and free her?*

Though the second possibility seemed more likely, Honus had found only three sets of footprints in the dust—his, the slain man's, and Yim's. Honus's prints told a simple story: He had entered the hall, fallen after he had freed Yim, and had been dragged to where Yim found him. The other prints formed complex trackways that could be read in many ways. The only thing the tracks showed clearly was that Yim had been busy while Honus was unconscious.

The smell of the hall and the unsettling memory it evoked soon drove Honus out into the courtyard. There he pondered whether he should confront Yim with what he had found. Honus doubted she would reveal what had happened. Despite her wound, she had gone to great lengths to conceal the truth from him. He recalled her hysterics when he revived and thought them uncharacteristic. *What's her true character? What did she do here?* The evidence pointed to a brave and selfless deed. Nevertheless, a chill came to Honus when he speculated that she might have overcome their foe using arcane means. His feelings toward Yim were already muddled, and these discoveries only made him more unsettled. *What should I do with her?* Her apparent bravery impressed him. Her deceit worried him. Her presumption that he could be easily fooled made him angry. The possibility that she possessed hidden powers disturbed

him. For all that, she seemed fragile at times and in need of
protection.

Perplexed, Honus keenly felt the loss of Theodus. *He
would have known what to do*. Honus wished he possessed
the calm certainty of his former master. Honus believed
that Karm favored justice and kindness, but that was little
guidance when the choices grew hard and consequences
became unclear. At such times "Karm's will" was an ab-
straction that Honus could not easily grasp. He supposed
that even Theodus's death was Karm's will. If the goddess
was capable of such an inexplicable thing, he despaired of
ever understanding what she wanted. Yet that was precisely what he must do until he found a Bearer. He felt in-
adequate for the task.

Honus decided that he might as well try to catch fish
while he mulled over his predicament. He returned to the
ford and removed his sandals and leggings in preparation
to enter the water. That was when he noticed a faint red
stain on his leg. Honus recognized it as a rune immediately.
Whatever that man was doing to Yim, he did to me! He
found that idea profoundly disturbing, for it meant that he
had been under a spell. Moreover, Honus knew that a spell
could only be overcome by another. As to who could have
worked the second spell, Yim was the only candidate.
Honus became convinced that she was other than what she
seemed.

How could such a woman become enslaved? Honus
could think of only one answer—Karm's will. That reason-
ing quickly led him back to Theodus's admonition that it
was Karm's will that Honus never carry his own burden. It
seemed to Honus that the goddess had ordered events so
Yim would become his slave. *Didn't Yim say as much?
"This is what my visions did to me!" Those were her
words*. This conclusion provided Honus some guidance.
He reasoned that if Karm had made him Yim's master, then

he should remain her master. *At least until we reach Bremven.* There, he could seek counsel from those who understood the divine will better than him. Until then, Honus decided it would be wisest not to alter their relationship. He would keep his conclusions to himself and let Yim think that he had been deceived.

Late in the morning, Honus returned to the campsite carrying three fish. Seeing Yim asleep on the ledge, he found it hard to imagine she possessed disturbing powers. She looked only like a ragged, injured girl, and his heart softened toward her. He knew firsthand how hard a mistress Karm could be. He didn't awaken Yim, but gathered firewood and made a fire. While Yim slept, he attempted to cook the fish by skewering them with sticks and holding them over the flames. When they seemed done, he waded over to Yim and woke her.

"I cooked a meal," he said, presenting her a charred fish.

Yim looked surprised. "I didn't think you could cook." She took a bite of the burnt fish. "And now I know you can't. You should have waked me."

"You looked like you needed sleep."

Yim swung her feet into the river. "I'll come to shore. You needn't stand in the river while I eat."

Honus slipped an arm under her legs. "I'll carry you," he said. Yim looked surprised, but didn't protest when he lifted her above the water and took her to the shore. "How's your leg?" he asked, after he set her down.

"The water helped. It feels better."

Honus picked up a skewered fish that was even more charred than Yim's. It made a dry crunch when he bit into it. He smiled wryly. "There was a reason why Theodus always cooked."

"As you said, he was a wise man."

Despite the quality of Honus's cooking, Yim ate ravenously. When Honus gave her the remaining fish, she devoured that also. After Yim finished the second fish, she limped to the river, took a long drink, and washed the charcoal from her face and hands. Then she returned to where Honus sat. It was past noon, and now that she had eaten, there was nothing to do. Yim noticed Honus watching her with a curiosity that made her feel awkward.

"Master."

"Yes?"

"About last night . . ."

"What about it?"

"Did you think I'd run off?"

"Yes."

"And that's why you searched for me?"

"No."

"No?" said Yim in a puzzled tone.

"I thought it'd serve you right to blunder about in the dark. I intended to get a good night's rest and track you by daylight. It's difficult to hide a trail at night, so I figured it'd be easy work."

"But you came for me in the night."

"I did," said Honus, still gazing intently at Yim. "I woke up and thought I saw you. Then I noticed that the woman before me wore a white robe, not a slave's tunic. Before I could speak, she said, 'Yim is in the castle.' That was all she said, but I knew immediately where the castle lay and that I must go there. I grabbed my sword, and when I turned around, the woman was gone." When Yim didn't respond, Honus asked, "Do you think it was a vision of Karm?"

"How would I know?"

"You said you had visions. You said they ruined your life."

"You'd hardly call them visions. The goddess never spoke to me. I saw insignificant things—the birth of a goat or when the snow would melt. When I bragged about them, people made fun. Their teasing got under my skin. That's why I left with the peddler."

"Do you mean your father?"

"Yes. My father, the peddler. If I hadn't said I had visions, I'd still be safe at home instead of captured and enslaved."

"Then maybe it was a dream, but a lucky one for you," said Honus, his eyes fixed on Yim. "After all, why would Karm care about a slave?"

"You're right," said Yim. "Why would she? It must have been a dream." She rose and limped toward the river. "I'm going to bathe my leg."

"I'll carry you to the pier."

"I can take care of myself."

Yim waded into the water, soaking half her tunic in the process. Honus watched without comment as she struggled to lift herself onto the stone pier. It seemed plain to him that she was avoiding further conversation. *I need not understand her,* Honus told himself. *She seems no threat. All she need do is carry my pack.* Despite it being midday, he found some shade and tried to rest. His nighttime ordeal had left him drained, and soon he drifted toward sleep. His last thoughts were of the enigma who sat on the pier, bathing her wounded leg.

TWENTY-THREE

YAUN WASN'T given to introspection, and as he rode to his father's manor, he didn't ponder why he was so bitter. His thoughts dwelt only on how he had been wronged. His enmity toward his father and elder brother deepened as his journey progressed. By the time he crossed Falsten's borders, it had become pure hatred. Then his hot rage chilled, and like a newly forged sword plunged into water, it grew hard and keen. Yaun turned cold and ruthless—the perfect instrument for Bahl's designs.

Dusk had fallen when Yaun reached the familiar hedgerows of his father's estate and stopped there to prepare for his homecoming. First, he tied his horse securely to a tree. Then he slashed his shirt. Next, he cut his horse and daubed his shirt in the blood. After removing his bandages, he donned the shirt again. As he waited for the blood to dry, Yaun invented a tale of his adventures. It loosely conformed to the facts, but omitted his cowardice during the battle, the trip to Durkin, and any mention of Honus. Naturally, his meeting with Lord Bahl would remain secret. Yaun's only pure fabrication would be an account of an attack by bandits in which he received his wound in a valiant fight and captured his new steed. Satisfied with those fictions, Yaun remounted his horse and rode to the manor.

The manor house sat on a hill surrounded by neat fields. It was large and made of stone, a relic from days when neighboring Luvein was peaceful and prosperous. That prosperity had benefited the count who built the house, just as Luvein's ruin had impoverished his descendants. Although the manor had suffered generations of neglect, in the fading light it still seemed fair. Its three towers looked majestic against the darkening sky, and the windows glowed brightly whether the glass was missing or not.

When Yaun neared the main entrance, a side door opened and a servant emerged. He bore a torch and was accompanied by two armed men. Yaun halted before them. The elderly servant called out in a timorous voice. "Who goes th . . ." He moved the torch closer to Yaun's face and squinted. "Is that you, Master Yaun? I thought you were off with Alaric."

"Yes, it's me, Nug," replied Yaun. "Alaric's slain. I've returned with news." Yaun dismounted and handed the reins to one of the guards. "My horse is wounded. See that it's tended." Then he followed Nug into the manor.

"Your father is at his meat, sire," said Nug. "I'll announce you at once."

"Is my brother there, too?"

"Yes, sire."

"That's good," said Yaun. "Both have been much on my mind."

Owing to the aftereffects of magic, Honus slept through the day and into the next morning. When he awoke, Yim was gone. He wondered if she might have fled, having learned that a trail is best hidden in daylight. Looking at the sun, he judged that she could have a long head start. As Honus considered what to do, Yim emerged from the forest. She was limping slightly, but her face showed no pain. In fact, she looked jubilant.

"Master," she called out. "I've brought breakfast!"

Honus noted that she was carefully carrying a large leaf, folded to make a package. She sat on the ground close to him, and with a bit of drama, opened her makeshift bundle. When Honus saw what it contained, he shrank back in revulsion.

"Wood grubs!" said Yim. "I found a log full of them." She picked up a finger-sized larva from the writhing mass on the leaf. Holding it by its dark round head, she placed its plump white body between her teeth. Then she bit down to burst the skin and suck its contents before discarding the head and limp body.

Honus felt the blood drain from his face.

Yim looked at him in surprise. "Haven't you ever tasted them?" she asked. "They're like mushrooms, only creamy." Yim lifted another from the leaf and held it out. "Here, try one."

As far as Honus was concerned, she might as well have been holding an adder. When he backed away, a look of amusement came to Yim's face. "I thought Sarfs were brave."

"That's disgusting!" exclaimed Honus.

"No, that's breakfast. I take it you're not having any." Yim placed the grub in her mouth and made quick work of it.

"How can you eat *caterpillars*?" asked Honus, as he backed farther away.

"They're wood grubs," Yim replied. "Caterpillars aren't in season."

Honus turned his back to Yim, but he could still hear her eat. He felt she was exaggerating the sucking sounds for his benefit. Then Yim giggled and said, "If I ever have to fight you, I'll know how to arm myself."

Honus didn't reply to her teasing, but walked down to the riverbank and gazed at the water while Yim ate. After a while, he looked in her direction and saw her herding the remaining grubs toward the center of the leaf. Then she wrapped them up, using some grass to tie the bundle. After placing the grubs in the pack, Yim called out, "Shall I forage for something more to your liking?"

"It's not necessary. I'm used to fasting. How's your leg?"

"Much better."

"I saw you limping. Do you feel well enough to travel?"

Yim seemed surprised that Honus had bothered to ask. "I'll be fine," she said. "I'll ready the pack."

For a change, the sky was clear and the weather mild. Honus set a leisurely pace as they traveled toward the ford. When they reached the road that led to the ruined castle, he noted that Yim appeared anxious. Honus suspected that she feared that he had seen through her ruse. "I've been thinking about what happened here," he said. Although he couldn't penetrate Yim's thoughts, he observed that she grew tenser. "In all my travels, I've never encountered anyone like that man in the castle. Surely, he had unnatural powers. Did you learn anything about him before I slew him?"

"No, Master. I was asleep from the moment he surprised me here until you saved me."

"Asleep?"

"It felt like sleep, only with horrible dreams. I'd rather not think about it."

"I had strange dreams myself after I beheaded him. I'm glad you came to wake me."

Honus saw Yim relax. Once again, the idea of confronting her crossed his mind. *What would be the purpose? She won't tell the truth. At least this way she can't hold me in her debt.*

Edmun rode under the same blue sky that spanned Yim and Honus, but unlike them, his heart was untroubled and all his thoughts were cheerful. His aging father was slowing down, and Edmun had assumed many of the count's duties. The afternoon's obligation was a pleasant one—to bless a wedding in a nearby village. As his horse moved through a field flush with spring blossoms, he was happy for the bride and groom. Such a fair day seemed an auspicious time to start a new life.

The sound of a galloping horse interrupted these thoughts. Edmun turned and recognized Yaun. "Brother!" he called. "I'm glad you've come."

Yaun reined his horse alongside Edmun's. "I had to get out of the house."

"You've seen too many grim things," said Edmun. "This festive day will do you good."

"Anything to be away from Father."

"Why do you say that? He was overjoyed at your return."

"Don't play with me, big brother. Last night, I heard rebuke in his every word."

Edmun looked at Yaun in astonishment. "Were we sitting at the same table? I recall no such thing."

"That's because you were unconcerned. Soon you'll have your fortune."

"A falling-down house and a title? My principal inheritance will be a good name."

Yaun sneered. "Am I a fly to be snared with honeyed words?"

"Brother, let's not quarrel. I'm happy you've come home."

"Then my ruin satisfies you. I know you opposed my going."

"My satisfaction lies solely in your safe return. It's true I advised against your leaving. War is gruesome and perilous. You know that now. I feared Alaric had turned your head with his grandiose tales."

"I wanted glory. Shouldn't I have ambition?"

"A warrior's glory is but a trinket—one for which many trade their real treasure. I think Alaric would forsake all his renown to once more feel a spring breeze. Be glad to enjoy what he cannot."

"Well, Father was pleased to be rid of me."

"You seem to forget that joining Alaric was your idea. Remember how you wheedled for days until Father gave his blessing? And when he relented, he spared no expense in outfitting you. He could ill afford that jeweled sword."

"A man must bear a worthy weapon."

"If I had my way, swords would look as ugly as the work they do. To adorn a weapon must affront Karm."

"Oh, spare me your sanctimony. I care not what the goddess thinks."

"I wish you wouldn't talk like that," said Edmun. "She's the source of our good fortune."

"*Your* good fortune. You love her because she smiles on you. To me, she's but a strumpet, tupping with some and denying others."

"My good fortune could be your good fortune," said

Edmun. "When I become count, I'll share everything. You need only settle down and earn true glory, not through bloody deeds, but by good works."

"Those are loving words, brother," said Yaun, "and I repent my hard ones. In truth, my tribulations have opened my eyes. I swear things will be different between us."

Edmun smiled. "You don't know how happy that makes me. You've been dealt a hard blow, but your life will change. I'm sure of it."

Yaun smiled, too. "I'm certain also. Let's take our horses to the river. There, we shall bless our new life." In response to Edmun's puzzled look, Yaun said, "It's a charm I learned in Lurwic. The flowing water washes away the past."

Edmun gladly agreed and they rode to a small river and had their horses wade into it. There, Yaun began his oath. "River, river, wash away the past and receive my blood in promise of a better future. Edmun, draw your dagger and cut my hand."

"I don't wish to draw your blood."

"You need only prick me, a few drops will do."

Edmun reluctantly complied. Then he held out his own hand to Yaun. "Now draw my blood in token of our bond." Yaun drew his dagger and nicked the back of his brother's hand.

Edmun jerked his hand back. "That burns!"

Yaun grinned. "I thought only women were afraid of pricks."

Edmun, oblivious of his brother's coarseness, stared aghast while his fingers curled and stiffened, transforming his hand into a rigid claw. The hand turned numb and gray as the affliction traveled up his arm, which twisted into a grotesque shape. When he looked at Yaun, his eyes were filled with fear. "What have you done to me?"

Yaun abandoned his pretense and laughed. "Why, brother, I'm changing my life."

The poison prevented Edmun from responding with

other than gurgling gasps. His features contorted until only his eyes remained unchanged. As they peered from his graying face, they were filled with disbelief and despair. For an instant, Yaun was horrified by what he had done. He recalled his boyhood and the older brother who always took his side. But those recollections were followed by thoughts of Lord Bahl's venomed words. They washed remorse away, replacing them with maniacal hatred.

Then Yaun exulted in his deed. "Where's Karm now?" he asked, as he kicked his brother's leg from the stirrup and pushed him from his horse. Edmun splashed into the muddy water. Yaun watched him slowly drift away. Then he grabbed the reins of Edmun's steed and led it from the river.

"Oh, Father dear," he said to the empty landscape. "I went riding and found Edmun's horse. I traced its tracks to the river, where I fear my brother has been thrown! Call out the household! We must search for him at once! Oh my! Oh my! They have such dreadful news! That stinking, bloated thing is your sweet, precious Edmun!" Yaun giggled at his little drama. "Oh how you'll weep for your favorite son, the one you always loved best. Poor, poor Father. I'm afraid your grief will poison you."

After Honus and Yim returned to the main road and traveled awhile, Yim's spirits lightened. Her thigh ached, but the pain was not as sharp as before, and she willingly endured it to leave the castle behind. Not only was her ordeal there over, her secret seemed safe. Honus showed no sign of suspecting her. Secrecy had a renewed importance to Yim, for she had come to believe that Karm hadn't forsaken her after all. The goddess had aided her twice during her confrontation with the dark man: First, when she had appeared to Honus and told him that Yim was in the castle. Later, when she had told Yim to throw the skulls into the fire.

Although Yim didn't understand why she had the horrific vision at the pass, she repented her initial reaction to it. She recalled crying "I can't do it!" and "Karm asks too much!" and the memory shamed her. Yim resolved to have more faith in the future. *Perhaps the vision's meaning will be revealed in time,* thought Yim. However, she found that hard to imagine. *What could it have to do with finding the man who's to father my child?*

Honus was another mystery to Yim. The Wise Woman had told her that Karm sent both trials and aid. Honus seemed both. His skill with arms had saved her life, and his desire had jeopardized her quest. Yim's brief encounter with his spirit had exposed a complex and contradictory nature, and she felt leery of trusting him until she understood him better. With that goal in mind, she recalled his promise to be more open and began asking questions. "Master, when we waded that stream, I noticed a scar on your leg. Where did you get it?"

"What scar?"

"It was on your lower calf."

"I forget. I no longer keep track of my scars."

"Scars?" Yim said, feigning surprise. "You have more than one?"

Honus smiled ruefully. "I have a whole collection. More than I'd care to count."

"How's that possible? When you fought those bandits, you looked invincible."

"If you fight often enough, you get wounded. In my early years with Theodus, I fought all the time."

"*That's* what you did for him—fight? I thought he was a holy man."

"He was. You should understand that the emperor's justice is more memory than reality. His authority fades rapidly beyond Bremven. Powerful men make their own rules, and bandits disregard even those. Theodus thought he might use my skills to lend strength to the side of the goddess."

"So you fought for the sake of Karm?"

"Everything from bandits to armies."

"And was the Balance truly served?"

Honus sighed. "It seemed that way, and yet . . ."

"And yet what?"

"It never ended," said Honus. "Theodus came to feel we were seeking to sweep back the tide and despaired of bringing justice to the world. He stopped entering disputes and began to visit Luvein in a search for the root of evil. It was forsaking fighting that led to his death."

"How?"

"He was drawn to study Lord Bahl. He got too close, and I . . . I failed him."

Yim caught the anguish in Honus's eyes, and changed the subject. "Tell me a happy memory. Something from your childhood."

Honus thought a moment. "The garden."

"What garden?"

"The temple in Bremven contains more than a sanctuary. Many live there. I grew up within its walls. In the center of it all, there's a huge garden. It looks like a patch of the world, if the world were perfect. Everything seems natural. Yet each rock, tree, and plant is carefully tended. It was so peaceful. No matter how I felt, it calmed me." Honus's voice grew dreamy. "There was a rock I used to sit upon. It was in a pond, close to the bank. The times I spent there were always tranquil."

Honus smiled slightly. "And you? What memory shines in your childhood?"

"When I was little, I had a goat. Her name was Rosie."

"A goat?" teased Honus. "What of your mother and father?"

A cloud passed over Yim's face. "You said you'd reveal yourself to me. I made no such promise to you."

Honus showed no reaction, but fell into a thoughtful silence. Yim followed suit. As she limped down the road, she

observed the countryside. It was thoroughly desolate. The
few hovels she spied were falling down and appeared long
deserted. The fields about them had reverted to scruffy
woodland choked with thorny vines. Yim wondered if
the absence of people was the dark man's work. Whatever
the cause, it was a disquieting landscape, as if its violent
past had poisoned it. Toadstools and nettles hemmed the
road. They crawled with black spiders. Brambles snagged
her limbs and clothing. Creatures were scarce, as were
wholesome plants. The longer Yim walked, the more her
surroundings affected her. She grew jumpy without knowing why, and when Honus went hunting, she was anxious
for his return.

When Honus appeared, Yim spoke of her unease. "This
place has an unwholesome air," she said. "Do you think it's
the doing of that man in the castle?"

"Theodus would have said both yes and no, as Bearers
are prone to do."

"I don't understand."

"It has to do with the nature of magic. Theodus believed
men and women are incapable of magic without the aid of
a higher power. A Seer's foresight is a gift from Karm, not
the result of learning meditations."

"Surely that man's spells didn't come from Karm!"

"Theodus thought that dark magic arises from another
source, something foul. Furthermore, when invoked for
evil magic, its presence lingers. That is what he believed
haunts Luvein."

Yim recalled her vision at Karvakken Pass and the being
that thrived on slaughter. "So the dark man in the castle is
somehow connected to the first Lord Bahl?"

"Certainly neither man's powers came from Karm,"
replied Honus. "Perhaps that's their only link, perhaps
not."

Yim wondered if the dark man had helped destroy Luvein or had slunk into its ruins only later. Since she couldn't

discuss the matter with Honus without revealing that she had talked with her captor, she asked a different question. "Why did your master visit Luvein?"

"Theodus believed that something happened here that changed the world, something that went beyond the outcome of wars."

"What?"

Honus shrugged. "He was still seeking that answer when he died."

Yim surveyed the blighted landscape around her. "So all this . . ." She paused, groping for a word that expressed the evil she sensed. ". . . all this foulness could be the result of men's deeds? Didn't they realize what they were unleashing?"

"There are those who are mindful only of themselves," replied Honus. "When they act, beware of the consequences."

TWENTY-FOUR

YIM AND Honus journeyed until dusk without encountering another soul. As darkness fell, they set up camp by the huge trunk of a fallen tree. Honus had killed a small squirrel and three sparrows for dinner. The birds were reduced to morsels once they were plucked and roasted. The squirrel was scarcely more substantial. Yim was able to find only a few tough greens to augment their meager meal.

Hunger made Yim grumpy. When Honus asked to see her wound, she looked at him irritably, with more than a hint of suspicion. Nevertheless, she hiked up her tunic to display her discolored thigh. Honus examined it and told her to lie down. Yim reluctantly complied. To her consternation, Honus began to massage her leg. At first, she feared it was another sexual advance. Yet his strong fingers never wandered between her thighs. He seemed intent only upon kneading her sore muscles. Gradually, Yim relaxed. When Honus stopped, her leg no longer throbbed. Afterward, Honus spread his cloak upon the earth, removed his sandals, and lay upon it. Yim settled next to him, throwing her warmer cloak over them both.

Yim and Honus's journey through the remainder of Luvein settled into a wearing routine. Every day, they traveled on a road so neglected that, at times, it was only an overgrown path. They met no other travelers, for the land was virtually empty. Most of the time, they walked silently, for Yim's growing exhaustion made her as taciturn as Honus. Unlike her master, she hadn't trained to endure privation, and it took a greater toll on her.

When the dark man's castle was far behind them, Honus tranced more frequently. Sometimes, his visits to the Dark Path left him tranquil. On those occasions, he shared the memory he had encountered: "The man who planted this tree saw his grandchildren play in its branches." "The child born here was the joy of her parents." "Two brothers forgave each other at this place." More often, the encounters left Honus troubled and morose. Then, he would resist trancing for a while. But he always succumbed to the temptation eventually.

They encountered a few isolated hovels on their journey but stayed at none of them, for the farmers' poverty and the scarcity of the season made Honus loath to ask for charity. Instead, they slept in the open when the weather was fair. When it was not, they found shelter in ruins. Honus disliked such places, for he couldn't trance without reliving their destruction. Yim also sensed the buildings' grim histories. Once, a defaced nursery reduced her to tears. Even when she slept outdoors, Luvein haunted her dreams. Every morning, she awoke feeling vaguely troubled and barely rested.

For food, they survived on the game Honus killed and whatever edible plants Yim could find. It was never enough, and they were always hungry. Starvation exacerbated Yim's fatigue, numbing her emotions and dulling her thinking. She ceased speculating about Honus's intentions and Karm's plans as her existence increasingly centered on the pangs in her empty belly and her tired, aching body. She expended her dwindling energy only on what seemed important—finding food and taking the next step.

In her exhausted state, Yim failed to note the changes in Honus. He gazed at her ever more often. He set an easy pace and let her rest frequently. He gave her more to eat than he took himself, and his voice was gentle, even when he made commands. When he began to massage her back each night, saying that he had done the same for Theodus, she simply accepted his ministrations without questioning his motives. While Honus's growing solicitude made little impression on Yim, she felt more at ease around him. When she thought of their relations at all, it seemed to her that she and Honus were two stones that had rubbed together until they fit.

The days followed one another until they blurred in Yim's mind. Then one morning Honus announced, "If we travel hard today, we'll reach Yorvern Bridge by nightfall. An inn lies there where the goddess is honored."

Yim perked up. "An inn?"

"Yes," said Honus. "There'll be soft beds tonight."

"And food?"

"Bread, cheese, and ale," answered Honus, "followed by a hearty stew."

"It sounds glorious! If I had the strength, I'd run the whole way."

"That won't be necessary," said Honus, smiling at Yim's excitement. "This is our last day in Luvein. Bremven is not so far now."

Happiness faded from Yim's face as she thought of Bremven's slave market. "Oh."

"When we arrive there, I thought I might give you to the temple."

"The temple?"

"Those children chosen by the Seers live there. They need people to care for them."

"And help teach little boys 'the art of killing'?"

"There aren't just boys at the temple. Girls are chosen also, and only some children become Sarfs. Others become Bearers or work in the temple. A few become Seers. And all are needy. It's a hard fate to be taken from your mother and father."

Yim noted Honus's melancholy tone and thought it revealed much about his childhood. Her heart went out to the children and to him also. "Forgive me," she said. "That was an unkind answer to a kindly offer."

"It'd be good work," said Honus. "I think you'd be happy there."

"Thank you. It would suit me."

"Then I'm glad."

The prospect of a stay at an inn sped Yim's and Honus's steps, and at dusk they spied the Yorvern River, a silver ribbon dropped upon a darkening valley. A long stone bridge cut the ribbon with a series of arches.

"I had no idea the river would be so wide," said Yim.

"It's good to see it," said Honus. "It marks the beginning of Vinden, my own land. I've not seen it for three years."

"Do they make good cheese in Vinden?"

Honus laughed. "Why? Does that interest you?"

"I've been thinking of cheese all day."

"And nothing else?"

"Bread, too. And stew. And ale."

"I'm glad your interests are so broad."

"Aren't you hungry, too?"

"I am," admitted Honus. "Roric keeps a good inn. It'll be a pleasant night."

Despite their fatigue, Yim and Honus picked up their pace and reached the bridge as night fell. The structure was a relic from more prosperous times. The roadway between its sides was narrow, designed to slow an advancing army, and its surface was worn by traffic. That traffic and any threat of invasion had long departed, for Luvein lacked both armies and tradesmen. Weeds and saplings grew between the paving stones, and Yim and Honus had the bridge to themselves. On the Luvein side was a ruined gatehouse. On the Vinden side, the gatehouse had been incorporated into a sprawling building of stone and timber. Its windows glowed gaily in the evening. "That's the Bridge Inn," said Honus.

As Yim began to cross the bridge, she thought of her appearance for the first time in days. It shamed her to think of the impression she would make. She was barefoot; her cheap tunic was soiled and frayed; and her cloak bore a large bloodstain. She looked down with dismay at her scratched legs and dirty feet, feeling self-conscious. "Master, they'll think I'm some beggar girl."

"It's true we've traveled hard," said Honus, "but don't worry. Roric is an old friend. We'll be well treated."

"I'd feel better if I could wash before we eat."

"And wait for your cheese? I didn't know you were so dainty."

Yim said nothing, but the look she gave Honus had its effect. "Before we dine," he said, "I'll ask Roric to send a basin to our room."

"Thank you, Master."

They reached the end of the bridge and found a large wooden door barring their way. After Honus rang the bell affixed to it, a peephole opened and a man peered out.

Honus bowed his head politely. "Good evening, Father."

The man turned to speak to someone behind the door. "Better tell Yuv there's a Sarf 'ere."

"Will you open the door?" asked Honus.

The man seemed to hesitate before unbolting a small door within the larger one. Honus and Yim passed through it into a large courtyard flanked on either side by stables. At the opposite end of the courtyard stood a large building that had been altered many times, with the most ancient sections appearing to be the finest. Parts of it were stone, while others were timber, and still others were timber and wattle. The windows were positioned unevenly and varied in shape and size, hinting that the rooms within were mismatched as well. Some windows were glazed with glass, though missing panes had been replaced by wood, while others were covered with oiled parchment. A large passageway tunneled through the center of the inn and terminated at a massive gate.

After spending days alone with Honus, Yim thought the courtyard was a hive of humanity. Soldiers mingled with merchants, farmers, and other travelers while stable hands and porters scurried about. Through the open windows of the inn she could hear the boisterous sounds of the common room and smell the aromas of cooking. Her mouth began to water, and she forgot her disheveled state.

Honus called back to the man who admitted them. "Where will I find Roric?"

"On the Dark Path, like as not. We ran off the outland dog."

"Roric an outlander?" said Honus. "He had this inn for years!"

The man spat. "Grown fat off folk that was borned 'ere. All the more reason to be rid of 'im. We've larned 'ow to take care of our own." He made the sign of the circle. "Yuv's master now. Ye talk to 'im." He pointed to a fat, florid-faced man in a greasy apron who stood by the entrance to the common room. He was flanked by another man, who held an unsheathed sword.

Honus crossed the courtyard and bowed. "You must be Yuv."

"Aye, Karmamatus," replied Yuv, saying the word as if it were an epithet. "I'm master here."

"I trust Karm is still honored at the Bridge Inn."

"We're full up. But there's hay in the stables."

"And food?"

"Aye, I'll feed ye," said Yuv, looking put out by the prospect.

"I'm grateful, and the goddess is honored by your generosity."

Honus turned to Yim and whispered, "I'm sorry about the bath."

"It doesn't matter," she whispered back.

Honus had started toward the entrance, with Yim following, when Yuv yelled out, "No whores in the common room!"

Honus halted and with an icy voice said: "This woman bears my pack and is under my protection."

Yuv shrugged. "Sorry. So she only looks like a whore."

Honus placed a hand on his sword hilt. "You'd best apologize to the lady."

The man with the sword had been snickering, but now he scowled and pointed his blade at Honus. Honus didn't move, but his body had the tense stillness of a snake ready to strike. His gaze never left the swordsman, but he addressed Yuv in a calm, cold voice: "Will your servant be of use if he lacks a sword hand?"

Yuv angrily motioned his man to put away his weapon. Then he bowed curtly toward Yim. "Sorry I mistook ye."

"Come, Yim," said Honus as he entered the common room. She followed him, crimson with humiliation.

The common room was large and paneled with dark

wood. The tables and benches that filled it bore the mark of long and constant use. Most were occupied. The diners and drinkers made the room loud with their talk, and boisterous sounds also poured forth from an adjoining private dining hall. Honus's entrance was noted by a few who inclined their heads and by others who scowled and made the sign of the circle. The rest of the room's occupants ignored the newcomers, being caught up in food, drink, and conversation. Honus found an empty place at a table of merchants, who nodded and muttered "Karmamatus" before resuming their discussion on the price of wool. One of the older merchants, who had his fill of both talk and ale, stared lustfully at Yim. Yim peered about the room and realized that Yuv's interdiction of whores was solely meant to insult her, for several were evident. The drunken man clearly included her among their number.

A waiter with an insolent look brought food and drink to Honus only. The portions were stingy and the quality insulting. The ale's smell betrayed it as spoiled dregs, the bread was a moldy crust, and the cheese looked like a small blue rock. Yim could see that Honus struggled to subdue his outrage. He turned to the waiter, and in a low voice said, "Karm sees the spirit of this gift." The man shrugged and retreated.

Honus broke off a piece of the crust, and then pushed the remainder of his meal toward Yim. "This was meant to insult me," he said. "I hope you don't think I'm insulting you."

"I don't," said Yim. As she looked at her long-anticipated meal, her eyes welled with tears. Listlessly, she picked up the blue lump and crumbled it, hoping to find a small bit that still tasted like cheese.

TWENTY·FIVE

Yim was still picking at the moldy cheese when a man with a military bearing entered the common room from the private dining hall. When he spotted Honus, his face showed surprise, then delight. "Honus?" he yelled over the din. "Can it be you?"

Honus turned at the sound of his name. "It is."

The man bounded across the room, knocking aside several people in the process. He gave Honus a bear hug as he rose to greet him. "Karmamatus, this is a happy chance."

Honus's grim expression softened and broke into a smile. "It's good to see you, General."

"It's just Cronin, now. Back to the highlands for me. I've had my fill of the emperor's court. Where's Theodus?"

"Slain."

Cronin's face fell. "Slain? This is ill news indeed. When did this happen? *How* did it happen? Who's your Bearer now? Have you dined yet?"

"I see you still need to know everything at once," said Honus. "The story of Theodus is a weighty matter and not quickly answered. I have no Bearer, but Yim carries my pack." He gestured toward Yim, who shyly bowed her head. Then Honus waved his hand at the stale crusts, moldy cheese, and sour ale. "And this is our dinner."

Cronin regarded the meal and his face went red. "YUV!" he bellowed, emphasizing his shout by hurtling the ale mug against the wall. By the time the innkeeper emerged from the kitchen, Cronin had drawn his sword and the inn's patrons were scrambling out of his way. "Yuv, you cheap, insolent swine! You're a fool to take a Sarf's humility as license for disrespect. Well, *I'm* na humble!" Cronin swung his sword and split a bench. "You dishonor Karm with this slop!" He threw the moldy cheese at Yuv, hitting him in the belly.

By then, Cronin's comrades had spilled out of the private dining hall. All of them were military men, and hardened veterans by their looks. They seemed to be waiting for a signal to tear the place apart.

Yuv cowered and answered in a quaking voice. "Most honorable sire! Please! There's been a dreadful mistake! I said only the finest for the Sarf and his lady. The waiter must have cheated both him and me. I'll have him whipped and a proper dinner brought at once." He bowed low to Honus. "I humbly beg yer pardon, Karmamatus."

"Bring their meal to the dining hall," said Cronin to Yuv. "They'll dine with us. And bring another round of ale."

"It'll be on the house, sire," said Yuv, bowing again before hurrying off.

Cronin grinned broadly, but Honus looked displeased. "Cronin . . ."

"I know, I know. It takes a strong man to bear an insult. I simply lack your strength, old friend. Besides, there's a lady involved." Cronin bowed politely to Yim, who was disconcerted by his notice.

With the excitement over, the common room's patrons began to settle at their tables, and Cronin's comrades returned to the dining hall. Cronin led Honus and Yim to the head table, where space was made for them. As they entered, waiters arrived with mugs of ale. Cronin seized one and held it high. "Comrades, a toast! To the man who fought beside me against horse raiders in the Eastern Reach . . . the witchriders in Argenor . . . and the warlord of Kambul. To the man who saved my life, na once, but twice. To a faithful servant of the goddess who also happens to be the bravest—and the most modest—man in Vinden. To Honus!"

"To Honus!" shouted the men.

Honus politely acknowledged the toast, but didn't seem to relish the acclaim. Waiters soon brought Honus and Yim a meal that was as ample and delicious as the first one was stingy and unpalatable. It consisted of a rich stew of spiced lamb and vegetables, a hot loaf of bread, three kinds of cheese, pickled onions and beets, dried fruit, and more ale. Yim's eyes shone at the bounty. She waited for Honus to take the first bite, then ate with abandon.

As the waiter served the final dish, Cronin said to him, "Bring your master here."

Soon, Yuv timidly entered the dining hall. "Friend Yuv," said Cronin, "I'm glad you discovered that waiter's misdeed. Now we witness your true generosity. I'm certain the room you've set aside for the Sarf and his lady is as fine as their dinner."

"It . . . It is, sire. They're making it ready as we speak."

"There'll be a tub and hot water, of course."

"Naturally, sire."

Cronin took two coppers from his purse and slapped them on the table. "Here's recompense for your bench. I seemed to have misjudged your piety."

Yuv tried to hide his chagrin as he bowed. "Thank you, sire."

"Send a man to take the Sarf's pack to his room."

"Right away, sire."

Cronin dismissed him with a wave of his hand.

As Yuv retreated, Cronin muttered to Honus, "He'd better kiss my arse. I have two dozen officers staying here and six hundred troops bivouacked outside."

"The goddess isn't honored by coerced charity," said Honus.

"No," admitted Cronin, "but you are. That was my purpose. And your woman deserves a decent meal, even if you're content with Yuv's garbage."

Honus smiled at the sight of Yim relishing some cheese. "Yes, she does."

"I've many questions, old friend," said Cronin, "and news for you as well. Much has happened since you and Theodus left. Your reception at the Bridge Inn foreshadows the mood in Bremven. There's a new emperor now."

"What happened to Theric?"

"A prudent man would say he took ill."

"And you?"

"I grow less prudent the farther I'm from Bremven. I see his brother's hand in his demise."

"Morvus? That coward?"

"Lord Bahl seems to have lent him a spine."

"I see," said Honus. "At what price, I wonder."

"One, I suspect, that shall be more than Morvus will gladly pay. There's a temple to the Devourer in Bremven now. It's already sown much discord."

"I fear Roric was one of its victims," said Honus.

"He was, and countless others. There's madness abroad, and I'm sick of it. I'm going to where folk still respect the Balance."

"I think your ill tidings and mine are pieces of the same cloth. Lord Bahl figures large in both. We should talk privately."

"Yes," said Cronin, "we'll find a place with fewer ears. Then there'll be time enough for grim talk. I'd be a poor host if I did na permit you to enjoy your meal. Moreover, Theodus never approved of wasting food or drink."

"No," said Honus with sadness in his voice, "he did not." He raised his mug to Cronin's. "To Theodus."

At first, Yim had been too engrossed in her food to pay much attention to Honus and Cronin. Yet as her hunger was satisfied, she began to take interest in the man who had so dramatically changed her evening. He appeared slightly younger than Honus, and while it seemed unusual for a man his age to be a general, Cronin fit the part. He had the commanding presence of a natural leader—self-assured, yet not aloof. It was evident that all the men in the room both respected and liked him. He seemed volatile but trustworthy.

Cronin's appearance perfectly reflected his profession. He had a broad chest and muscular arms. His wide face was dominated by lively blue eyes and a quick smile. Brownish blond hair, cropped at the shoulders, framed his tanned complexion, which was marked with a jagged scar. His clothes were cut in the military style—simple, yet finely made. He wore a leather tunic over a short-sleeved shirt and his baggy pants were tucked into calf-high boots.

Yim tried to follow Cronin and Honus's conversation. They were reminiscing about Theodus. Honus alternated between laughter and melancholy as he recounted a long story about his Bearer and an overly proud count. As interested as Yim was in the tale, the din of the room, her fatigue, and the strong ale got the best of her. Before long, her head slumped to the table.

When Cronin noticed that Yim was asleep, he took the opportunity to satisfy his curiosity. Whispering to Honus, he asked, "Who is she?"

"A slave."

"A slave? I've never heard of a Sarf with a slave before."

"When Theodus last read my runes, he said I should never carry my own burden."

"Any of my men would have gladly done so."

"I was in a battle where only one other man survived."

"Was that the same battle where Theodus was slain?" asked Cronin.

"Yes. The survivor was a count's son. At first, he was eager to serve me. Yet he proved unworthy of the task."

"And this slave is?"

"Until I reach the temple, yes."

"Well, I'll say this—she's a pretty thing," said Cronin. "Though I'm sure you've noticed."

When Honus simply grunted, Cronin grinned. "Now that we've agreed on that, what else can you tell me?"

"I bought her in Durkin. She's a peddler's daughter from the Cloud Mountains."

"The Cloud Mountains! That's far away. How did she end up in Durkin?"

"I don't know. I didn't ask."

"Do na give me that, Honus. I know your power to look into eyes and lay bare secrets. I've seen you do it. By now, you understand everything about her."

Honus shook his head. "I don't. In fact, she's a mystery."

"Yet she journeys with you on a perilous road, a girl na older than my little sister." Cronin pulled out a small leather purse and placed it on the table. "Use this to buy her sandals and some proper clothes. Slave or na, you should na treat her like a Sarf. She took na vows of poverty."

Honus looked at the purse without touching it.

"She's a *woman*, Honus. Those rags shame her. She bears your burden, as did Theodus. Allow me to honor his memory with this gift."

Honus took the purse. "You're right, old friend. She deserves better. She's already suffered much on my account."

"And if you're going to Bremven," said Cronin, "she's likely to suffer more."

TWENTY·SIX

ONE OF Cronin's officers gently woke Yim and escorted her to Honus's room. It was in the oldest section of the inn and featured paneled walls, a small fireplace, and glazed windows. In the dim candlelight, it looked elegant. There were two beds, a larger one for a master or mistress and a trundle bed for his or her servant. Both had reasonably clean linens. There was no fire in the fireplace, but as soon as Yim arrived, servants lit one and brought in a copper tub and ewers of hot water. When the tub was filled and the water sprinkled with dried flower petals, they left.

Yim bathed, then washed her tunic. She hung it up to dry and climbed between the sheets of the servant's bed. The lumpy mattress seemed the height of luxury after sleeping on the ground. She fell asleep almost instantly and woke only briefly when Honus entered the room. By then, only embers glowed in the fireplace, and the candle had burned out. She closed her eyes again, and drifted off to sleep as Honus quietly bathed in the cold bath.

Day's first light was shining through the window when a knock woke both Honus and Yim. Honus rose and threw Yim her tunic, then dressed. He opened the door to find a young, blond woman who shared Cronin's good-natured features. "Cara!" he said gladly. "It's good to see you again. How are you?"

Cara formed her face into an imitation frown. "I'm sad, Honus, for my brother has lost his mind."

Honus's lips betrayed a hint of a smile. "Why do you say that?"

"I hear he gave you a purse to purchase clothing for a woman."

"And you deem me unworthy for such a task?"

"Entirely," said Cara, as she held out her palm. "Hand it over."

Honus grinned and brought Cara the purse. She took it and slipped it into the pocket of her short robe. "I'll get Yim outfitted while you and brother waste the day gabbing. Are you hungry, Yim?"

"Yes, Mistress."

"For Karm's sake, call me Cara. The last thing I need is more formality. Come on, let's eat."

With Honus's leave, Yim followed Cara down to the common room, where a waiter brought them porridge. "Zounds," said Cara, "we've been here three weeks outfitting for the trip to Averen. Do you know what that's like? Me being the general's sister?"

"I thought Cronin said he's no longer a general," said Yim.

"Oh, that's what he *says,* but it makes na difference. As soon as we're back in Averen . . ." Cara stopped herself, realizing she was being indiscreet. "Anyway, I have na one to talk to who does na treat me like some . . . some . . . I do na know . . . like some glass flower. Everybody's *far* too polite. Like, if they said something wrong, I'd break. Or more like it, Cronin would break them. He's so protective. But you've been with *Honus*! Zounds, I had such a crush on him. Na that it made the slightest difference. I could have been his baby sister for all he noticed. So, what's it like?"

"He's my master," said Yim.

"I still can na believe Honus has a *slave*! Does he . . . you know . . ."

Yim blushed. "Does he what?"

"All the masters in Bremven sleep with their slaves. I

mean, if they're young and pretty. Why, even if they're plain and old! But maybe I should na ask . . ."

"You shouldn't. Honus is a private man."

Cara grinned excitedly. "I knew it! When I heard that he drew a sword for your honor, and you a slave . . ."

"He didn't draw a sword."

"Well, almost the same thing. Honus never loses his temper. Believe me, I know. But when he threatened Yuv because he insulted you . . . well . . . then it was clear to me and I *knew*."

Yim turned bright red. "Cara!" she whispered. "Knew *what*? Do you think we're . . . we're . . ."

Cara beamed. "Lovers!" she said. "It's *so* romantic!"

"It's not like that at all," said Yim in shocked tones. "I carry his pack and cook for him, nothing more."

"That's *it*?" said Cara, her face falling. "That does na sound like fun."

"It's not."

Cronin and Honus strode along the empty bridge after breakfast, but each seemed loath to bring up what weighed most on his mind. They stopped midspan and quietly gazed at the river and distant mountains before Cronin said at last, "Tell me the manner of Theodus's death."

Honus sighed. "It happened in the duchy of Lurwic a moon ago. The duchy lies northwest of Luvein, beyond the Turmgeist Forest."

"North of Luvein? That's far afield."

"It is. We were there because Theodus met a mercenary named Alaric, whose troop had been hired by the duke. It seemed Lord Bahl was causing unrest."

"I thought Theodus had lost his interest in politics."

"He had. Yet, upon consulting my runes, he thought something was at work in Lurwic, something beyond the contentions of men. The madness of which you spoke last night was abroad there also."

"Men are quick to hate."

"Was it always thus? Theodus wasn't sure."

"Strife and discord have ever been with us. Theodus was wise; he knew that."

"Have you ever traveled through Luvein?"

"Never. What's the point? The roads are bad, and there's naught but ruins."

"Over the past few years, Theodus and I have toured it up and down. Men have always been greedy, but why would a greedy man destroy what he conquers? What profit lies in mindless slaughter? Theodus came to believe that something unnatural occurred in Luvein, something that haunts it to this day. He sought to understand it and its cause. That led him to Lord Bahl."

"Bahl?" said Cronin. "Theodus could have stayed in Vinden. Bahl was here before Theric died."

"At his brother's hand, you suspect."

"I'm sure of it," said Cronin. "After Bahl's visit, Morvus was a changed man. Resentful. Ill-tempered. Theric died soon afterward of an illness that reminded me of a poisoned wound. Emperor Morvus is as tyrannical and reckless as his brother was just and prudent."

"I'm not surprised," said Honus. "All those who took the name of Bahl were able to bring out the worst in men. In the present Lord Bahl, that power is particularly strong."

"I've seen it in action," said Cronin. "When Bahl visited Bremven, most men fawned over him. Too few felt like me and detested him."

"You've met him?"

"Aye, and I'll admit he has a presence. You always knew when he entered a room. I swear, it grew colder."

"I've heard that tale."

" 'Tis true."

"The Empire's still strong in Vinden. You saw Bahl with his powers veiled. In Lurwic, he was not so subtle. He turned it into another Luvein."

"Do you mean he destroyed it?"

"It's a wasteland now. I saw it happen."

"You fought with Bahl?" said Cronin, looking intently at Honus. "This is of particular interest to me."

"So you're not leaving Bremven because you're tired of court."

"The real reason is I fear for Averen."

"To whom have you spoken of this?"

"Na one at court except some trusted fellow clansmen," replied Cronin. "I've spoken to the chieftains in the past, but they remained unconcerned. They claimed the might of the Iron Palace has always waxed and waned. Yet to me, it's like a vine on a ruin. Its leaves may wither each winter, but the vine remains, and season by season, it tears the stones asunder."

"And the vine is in the fullness of its growth," said Honus.

"The chieftains now see wisdom in my warnings," said Cronin. "They've withdrawn the highland regiments to Averen."

"Didn't the emperor object?"

Cronin laughed. "Aye, but if he had the men to stop us, he would na need us in the first place."

"I think the move was wise. It's pointless to look toward Bremven for aid."

"I just hope 'tis na too late. So, how does one fight Bahl?"

"I don't have an answer," replied Honus. "I was one of two survivors after the siege of Lurwic. The other was a coward who hid. Don't ask me how to win such a fight."

"Still, you must have learned something."

"It wasn't like when the horse raiders invaded the Eastern Reach. There was no opposing force until the very end. Mostly, the invasion was like a pestilence."

"I do na understand."

"Folk who lived in peace for generations would suddenly be at one another's throat over some long-forgotten grievance. Men committed atrocities with hoes, pitchforks, and bare hands. And it spread, each crime spurring fresh ones. People fled their homes. Some starved. Others turned brigand and increased the violence."

"How do you know Bahl was behind that?"

"Theodus saw his hand in the growth of the Devourer's following. The two are always linked. Those black-robed priests precede Bahl like crows before a wolf. When the folk of Lurwic began to praise the Devourer, we searched for Bahl. We tramped the countryside, and I tranced to roam the Dark Path. Although we never encountered him, we found the mark of his influence. Everywhere, men's hearts were turning toward hate."

"You speak as though he's more than a man."

"Perhaps he is. How can different men behave the same and possess the same power for generation after generation? Sons seldom mirror the father, except in this line. Theodus wanted to learn why. That quest led to his death."

"How did it happen?"

Honus's face tightened. He was silent for a moment before he took a deep breath and continued his story. "When Lord Bahl finally invaded Lurwic, he used a force that was more like a mob than an army. Most were the duke's own people, turned against him. They came like ants and fought like them also. They were ill armed and unskilled, but they overcame every obstacle with their numbers and recklessness. It's hard to fight men who don't fear death, who'll let you cleave their heads if they can wound you first."

"They sound like monsters."

"They were. Yet they were also ordinary men. Men who kissed their wives and children before they went to slay their neighbors and throw weeping babes into fires. It was madness beyond belief, and it reached its height at the duke's castle. The army approached with Lord Bahl at the rear to drive it on. A traitor opened the castle gates, and the invaders poured in. We slaughtered them until our arms ached, and still they pressed on. They slew the duke. Then they came for Theodus."

Honus halted as his stoicism crumbled under the weight of his memories. When he spoke again, his voice was raw with pain. "I tried to protect him, but it was like fighting a river. They overflowed me."

Honus paused to summon the strength to continue. "They tore him apart! There was no more left of him than what a pack of wolves might leave. Then, his assassins simply stood there—everyday men released from a spell. Yet, when I saw Theodus's blood dripping from their hands, their madness visited me. Karm forgive me, but I murdered them all. They didn't resist. Only when none were standing did I grasp the iniquity of my deed."

Honus's frame wrenched as if racked by sobs, and Cronin put his arm around him. "Do na condemn yourself for avenging Theodus. You were his Sarf. How could you do otherwise?"

"You don't understand," said Honus. "Theodus would've never wanted such revenge. I shamed his memory."

Cronin watched his friend repress his grief and hide it away. After a spell of silence, Honus continued his tale. "Bahl departed right after the battle, leaving a ruined land filled with enmity. I roamed the castle and the town, finding naught but corpses. It wasn't until the next day that I found a drunken squire hiding in a cellar. Before then, I washed the blood from my clothes as best I could. I meditated and purged myself of hate. When my mind was clear, I tranced, seeking Theodus."

"You tranced after a battle?" said Cronin, his voice awed.

"All was chaos. The Dark Path thronged with confused and anguished spirits. Such memories! Such regrets! It tears at you, Cronin. It was a hard thing to do. Yet, even worse,

I couldn't find Theodus's spirit. It was as if it had been consumed."

Cronin shivered as though the warm day had turned chill. "Could the tales of the Devourer be true? Can a man's spirit be destroyed?"

"I don't know," said Honus. "All I know is that darkness is spreading over the world. What good is a sword against the advance of night?"

"I had na expected so dire a tale," said Cronin. "Yet, I fear I shall soon see such things firsthand. Bahl's gaze is on Averen. Already, black-robed ones travel its roads."

"That bodes ill."

"Come with me, Honus. Together, we may defeat Bahl yet."

"I cannot," replied Honus. "I must go to the temple and find a Bearer to guide me. Only then will Karm direct my path again. Perhaps it will take me to Averen."

"I pray that it does."

Honus and Cronin remained on the bridge, engaged in cheerless talk. No traveler overheard them, and the ruins of Luvein lacked living ears. Only when the sun set did they return to the unblighted side of the river. If Cronin brooded that evening, he hid it during dinner. Honus imitated his friend. As the ale flowed and the room grew boisterous, Cronin and Honus acted as if they had idled the day discussing fishing.

Cara entered the dining hall with Yim. "Brother," she announced, "if Yim can eat with the officers, then I should, too. With all these men, she'll need some intelligent conversation." Then, without her brother's leave, she guided Yim to an empty spot at the head table and joined her.

Cronin didn't speak to Cara, but smiled and turned to Honus. "It seems your slave has provided my sister a long-sought opportunity."

Honus didn't reply, for he was struck dumb by Yim's new attire. It was a practical traveling outfit—sturdy sandals, baggy pants resembling a skirt that ended just below the knee, a sleeveless shirt and a long-sleeved overblouse. It wasn't the style of Yim's new clothes that silenced him—it was their color. They were dark blue.

Cara seemed to expect his reaction. "Na a peep about the color, Honus. I paid, so I picked out everything. If Yim's going to travel with you, she ought to blend in. Anyway, it's about time she had something decent. I saw that blood-stained cloak you bought her. Zounds! I'm having it dyed to hide the stain. And yes, it'll be blue also. Dark blue."

Cronin attempted to glare sternly at his audacious sister, but amusement overwhelmed his frown. "By Karm!" he whispered to Honus. "Your slave looks like a Bearer."

Yim grew nervous under Honus's silent gaze. "Master..."

"The color suits you."

TWENTY·SEVEN

CARA KNOCKED on Honus's door early the next morning. When he opened it, she smiled brightly. "Good morning, Honus, I'm here to rescue Yim."

"I didn't know she was in peril."

"She's like to die of boredom. I know brother intends to chatter with you all day."

"It's true that we'll hold counsel."

"And while you chatter, I'll hold counsel with Yim."

"And what grave matters will you discuss?"

"Things beyond your understanding. Come, Yim, I'm starving."

"You talk as if she's your slave, not mine."

"Zounds, Honus, you're na silly enough to believe a man can truly own a woman?" Without waiting for a response, Cara headed down the hallway.

Yim looked at Honus hesitantly. "Master?"

"Go with her," said Honus, smiling good-naturedly. "Just don't believe everything she says."

Yim hurried to join Cara in the dining room. She found her sitting alone at a table, eager to talk. "Did he say anything about your blue clothes?" asked Cara in a conspiratorial tone. "I mean . . . Zounds! The way he stared at you when you came to dinner, *that* was something! I expected . . . well, I do na know what I expected. So tell me—did he say anything to you later, after dinner?"

"He didn't mention it."

"Well, that's Honus, through and through. It's so hard to tell what he's thinking."

"He didn't seem angry," said Yim.

"How could he be angry? I bought them, so he could na blame you. You're a slave. You don't have a say in anything."

"Am I supposed to take comfort in that? Suppose I don't like blue?"

"But you do! Do you na?"

"It's a little late to ask."

For a moment, Cara was silenced.

"It's fine," said Yim. "The clothes suit me."

"Of course they suit you. But you're right, I did na ask, did I? I was just doing it to help you."

"Help me? How?"

"Oh, you'll find out, and—of course—it was a great trick on Honus. I really could na resist."

"How do you dare tease him?" asked Yim. "He has a temper, even if he doesn't show it."

"Oh, Honus is like family. After Mother died, I came to Bremven. I was only nine and grew up around Honus. He was always at our villa. When I was older, I thought he was my dream man for the longest time. It broke my heart when he got married."

"Married!" exclaimed Yim. "I didn't know he's married."

"He's na anymore. Cynetha died of the water fever. She was a Seer, so I guess she knew she was going to die all along. I do na think I could stand that. I mean, how could she get married, knowing she was going to die a moon later?"

"She didn't know she was going to die," said Yim.

"Oh, do na be silly! You had na even heard of her until just now, so how could you possibly know? I mean, zounds, she was a *Seer*!"

"The goddess reveals only what she wants you to see," said Yim. "Visions suit her purposes, not ours. Cynetha wouldn't have known her fate."

"Come on now, Yim, how can you say that? You talk like you've had visions yourself and that's . . . oh holy Karm!" Cara lowered her voice to a whisper. "*Do* you have visions?"

Yim nodded.

"*Zounds!* So what's it like? I mean, does the goddess just pop up from nawhere for a little chat? Boy, the most important person I ever get to talk to is Cronin, and that's only because he's my brother. But you get to speak with *Karm*! How exciting! So, what does she say?"

"I can't talk about it."

Cara let out an exasperated sigh. "You're just like my brother! Nabody tells me anything!"

"Cara . . ."

"Nay, nay, it's all right, I'm used to it." For an awkward spell, both women were silent. Then Cara's mood lifted and she changed the subject. "So, your cloak should be ready this morning and the extra shirt and the pants, too. After we pick them up, I'll take you to my favorite place. Nabody knows about it but me, so do na ask where it is. *I* can have secrets, too." As an afterthought, Cara asked, "Can you swim?"

"Yes."

"Good. Now, that's the only hint you'll get. You'll just have to suffer from suspense until we finish our business in the village."

After breakfast, Cara and Yim walked to the nearby settlement where the principal trade was outfitting travelers. They were escorted by a bodyguard assigned to them by Cronin. The man said nothing, but his presence dampened Cara's exuberance. They went to the tailor, picked up the remaining items of Yim's wardrobe, and returned to the Bridge Inn. There, Cara took Yim to her room and dismissed the bodyguard, saying she and Yim would spend the day there.

Cara waited only a moment before beckoning Yim to the open window. It overlooked a walled garden, so neglected and overgrown that much of the shrubbery was the size of small trees. A vine that grew on the side of the inn obscured much of the view. "Take off your sandals," said Cara. "We must climb down the vine. Come on, I'll show you how." Cara stepped onto the window ledge, grabbed a thick stem nearby, and lowered one foot until her toes felt a hold. Then she quickly descended to the garden below and signaled Yim to follow before disappearing into the shrubbery.

Though Yim climbed down with less assurance, she soon joined Cara beneath the cascading boughs of a large bush. She felt as if they were inside a tent. "Is this your secret place?"

"Oh, it's better than this," replied Cara. "Follow me."

Cara crept through the garden, hidden by its overgrown foliage, until she reached a hole in the ground. There she pulled the end of a thick rope secured to the trunk of a huge boxwood and lowered it down the opening. She slid down the rope and called from the darkness, "Hurry, Yim. It's na far down."

Yim joined Cara in a brick-lined tunnel. When her eyes became accustomed to the dim light, she could see that the tunnel had collapsed close to the inn. In the other direction, wavering light reflected off the walls, suggesting that the tunnel opened on water. "You'll be able to see fine soon," said Cara. "Then, we'll go down to the river. The lower bank is really overgrown, and the sides are so steep nabody comes down there."

"So why are we?"

"You'll see. Just keep out of sight."

When they emerged from the tunnel, Cara led Yim upstream along the bank through a tangle of small trees, undergrowth, and reeds. The way was difficult, and they struggled for a hundred paces before Cara stopped. She parted the dense reeds and pointed to a tiny island a short distance from the shore. "There it is—my secret place." Cara's island was a collection of large boulders and smaller rocks softened by vegetation and a few trees. It was only twenty paces long.

"We have to swim there?" asked Yim.

"The current's na bad. We'll go upstream a bit and swim to the far side of the island. There's nabody on the Luvein shore to see us." Cara led Yim thirty more paces along the bank to where willows overhung the river and screened them from view. "This is the place," Cara said. "The water's deep here." She shed her clothes, stepped into the river, and was already swimming before she reached the dangling leaves. Without waiting to see if Yim followed, she headed toward the island.

Yim hesitated before undressing. When she finally entered the water, she found that it was cold, despite the warm, sunny weather. The current fought her as she struggled to reach the island and threatened to sweep her beyond it. By the time Yim staggered onto the island's far shore, she was exhausted and shivering. Cara was already sunning herself on a large, flat rock. "Is it na wonderful?" she said.

Yim had to catch her breath before replying. "This seems like a lot of effort just to lie on a rock."

"Do you see any bodyguards looking over our shoulders? Zounds, that gets *so* dreary, and it's been like that for *years*. Privacy may na seem important, but try living without it."

"I am," said Yim.

"Then you should understand."

Yim stretched out on a flat boulder and felt its warmth against her chilled skin. "It's very peaceful here," she said after the coldness left her. "Thanks for bringing me."

"When it's sunny, I can spend an entire day here while my brother thinks I'm moping in my room, that is, if he thinks of me at all. Yes, it's a nice place. The only thing missing is someone to talk to, and you've fixed that. It's been lonely at the inn with only Brother, his troops, and a pack of strangers, most of whom are na very friendly. Well, you—for sure—know all about *that*. Na that I miss Bremven. It used to be nice, but now! By Karm, I wish you were na going there. You will na like it. People have turned horrid since they built that temple to the Devourer. I guess they were probably horrid before the temple was built but, *now*— zounds, you can na imagine how nasty they've become! They do na even bother to hide it. I really *did* need a bodyguard in Bremven, as tiresome as that was. Can you na talk Honus out of going?"

"I'm his *slave*, Cara. He doesn't listen to me."

"Do na pay attention to that slave nonsense. I really *do* believe a man can na own a woman; I was na just teasing Honus. It's more the other way around. A lot of slave girls rule their masters, and *that's* na secret."

"It's not that way with Honus and me. It can never be that way."

"Well, I think you're wrong. I *know* you're wrong. Honus would've *never* threatened Yuv if he did na have feelings for you. Maybe you can na read his expressions because of his tattoos, but I can. I see the way he looks at you. Believe me, Yim, he's yours."

"No, he's not. You don't understand."

"Well, I guess so," said Cara. She waited for Yim to explain. When Yim didn't, Cara said, "I did na mean to pry. I'm sorry. Sometimes I talk too much."

"It's all right."

The women fell silent and lay back to gaze into the cloudless sky. The river flowed slowly, making tranquil sounds as it moved around the rocks. The sun dried and warmed their bare bodies and a breeze caressed their skin. The cares of the world grew distant, and for a while, they were both at peace.

Cara stirred first, as if waking from a dream. She stretched and walked toward the downstream end of the island. Peering around a large boulder, she spied Honus and Cronin talking on the bridge. The tranquillity left her face. "I know why they're holding counsel."

"Who?" said Yim sleepily.

"My brother and Honus," said Cara. "They're talking war. Brother will na admit it, but it's coming. I can see it in his face. I hear things, too. Lord Bahl will soon invade Averen. By Karm, I wish I were a soldier! Then, you either win or it's over quick. It's na like staying home, never knowing when they'll smash in the door and . . . and . . . I've heard tales of what Bahl's men do to women, too many to doubt their truth."

Yim sat up, disturbed by her friend's sudden change of mood. "Cara, you don't know what the future holds."

"I can see which way the wind blows, even if the goddess

does na whisper in my ear. Things look grim, all right. Do your visions tell you differently?"

"I don't know the future," said Yim. "My own least of all."

"I've never had a man who truly loved me," said Cara, "and because of this war, it's likely I never will. And you have Honus, or could have, if you wanted him. I do na understand you."

"It's because I'm not free."

"So, you're a slave. That's only a problem if you let it be."

"It has nothing to do with being a slave. It's something else."

"Your visions?" asked Cara. "Does it have something to do with them?"

Yim didn't immediately reply. Instead, she stared intently into Cara's eyes. Unable to break free from that gaze, Cara's hairs rose as Yim probed her. Still locking eyes with Cara, Yim asked, "Will you swear never to repeat this, especially to Honus?"

"I swear," said Cara, arching her thumb across her chest in the Sign of the Balance.

Yim released Cara from her power. "*That* felt strange!" said Cara, looking at Yim with awe. "What did you just do to me?"

"Nothing, really," said Yim, "just a trick I learned."

"Zounds! Some trick! Bremven's full of Seers and Bearers, but none of them knows that one. Why did you do it?"

"I had to know I could trust you."

"Oh, you can! You could tell, could you na?"

Yim nodded. "Cara, I've been dying to talk to someone. This is tearing me apart!"

"Tell me," said Cara eagerly. "I was right, was I na? This has something to do with visions."

"Yes. I'm not free because of them."

"Oh, zounds! You mean Karm really *does* tell you what to do?"

"If only it were that simple. The messages I get seldom make sense."

"Then how can you say you're na free? I mean, if the goddess just babbles nonsense, how can you know what she wants?"

"Because of my first vision. I had it when I was a little girl. The goddess appeared to me and said I should tell the village Wise Woman that I was the Chosen."

"The *Chosen*? Zounds, that sounds grand."

"I'm not special," said Yim, repeating the Wise Woman's favorite phrase, "my task is."

"And what's that?"

"I'm to undo a great evil."

Cara gave Yim a look that combined disbelief with a hint of amusement. "So you're an undoer of evil? You do na look the part, but I guess I do na know any evil-undoers, just evildoers. I know *lots* of those. Bremven's thick with them. So, what are you supposed to do?"

"Bear a child."

"My *mother* did that. Twice! How's having a baby supposed to undo anything?"

"I don't know," said Yim "The Wise Woman said my visions would guide me. So far, they've been little help. Everything's gone wrong. I was on the road only half a moon when my guide was killed and I was enslaved."

"Why go on the road at all? You need na stretch your legs to have a baby, only spread them."

Yim reddened. "Don't make fun of me! There's a lot more to this than getting pregnant. Not any man will do— only one—and I don't know who he is."

"I'm sorry," said Cara. "I did na mean to tease. It's just that . . . well . . . all this seems more than a little far-fetched."

"I know," said Yim with a sigh. "Sometimes, it seems

that way to me. There are days when I fear I've been mis-
led, that I believe I'm the Chosen only because it's been
drummed into my head."

"It *does* sound crazy."

"Yes," replied Yim. "At times I'm convinced I'm just
that—crazy. Then, something happens that seems to show
my visions aren't mere delusions."

"Like what?"

"A vision that made no sense suddenly has meaning.
Months ago, I thought the goddess said, 'Follow the steps
of Theodus.' I had no idea what that meant. Now I know
he was Honus's Bearer."

"But Theodus is dead!" said Cara with alarm.

"Yes," said Yim. "And perhaps my journey will also end
similarly."

"Surely, it does na mean *that*!"

"I don't know what to believe. Mostly, I feel lost. Yet
sometimes I think I see Karm's hand in events. Like when
you chose blue clothes for me."

"Come on, Yim, I did that to tease Honus."

"But you also said it would help me. Can't you see how
you might have been acting for the goddess?"

Cara got a dubious look on her face. "Well . . . maybe. I
do na know. If I was, it was na because Karm told me to.
But what do your visions say about Honus? Maybe it's *his*
baby you're supposed to have."

Yim shook her head.

"How can you be sure?"

"I'm not sure about anything," said Yim, "but I think
I'll know who it is when I'm supposed to."

Cara shrugged. "Well, even if he's na *the* one, he cares
for you. I'm convinced of that. If you do na want to have a
child, well, *that's* easy enough to prevent. So why can na
you . . . you know . . ."

"The goddess said that when I lie with the man I must be
a virgin."

"You're a *virgin*? I've never heard of a slave who was a virgin! I mean . . . na offense . . . I just assumed that . . . that . . ."

"It's unlikely, isn't it?" said Yim.

"Well, I guess if you can chat with Karm, then anything's possible."

"It's our secret," said Yim. "No one else must know. I let Honus think that I'd been raped."

"But did na the men who caught you . . ."

"That's where I see the hand of the goddess most clearly, for it seems miraculous that I've remained untouched. Certainly, the men who captured me had no respect for maidenhood, but they got too drunk to rape me. Nor was I violated in the slave pen—the merchant wasn't able and his guard wasn't interested."

"And Honus?"

"On our first night together, I threatened to kill myself if he forced me to lie with him."

"Would you have really?"

"Yes."

"Zounds!"

"Honus swore he would never use force on me, so I've remained untouched."

"I do na think I could do that," said Cara. "I mean, zounds, you sleep beside him every night!"

"I did have one moment of weakness," said Yim, blushing. "It was after a vision so terrible I felt I couldn't go on. I thought if I were no longer a maiden, I'd be released from my fate. Honus started touching me, and I didn't resist. Yet, just when I thought Honus would tup me, he stopped himself."

"Zounds! Well *that's* a sign, if I ever heard one! I mean, give a man half a chance and . . . well, you know. For him to just stop . . . *that* had to feel strange. Did it?"

"At the time, I was too numb to know how I felt."

"But, later on, did you regret he stopped? It's na

unpleasant, you know." Cara smiled slyly. "I mean, that's what I've *heard*. I do na want to sound cynical, but tupping Honus would seem to solve a lot of your problems."

"What are you saying? I'm with Honus only because he bought me. Even if I ignored the goddess, that's no reason to let him tup me!"

"Custom says it is," said Cara. "The fact that Honus has na pressed that point shows he cares about your feelings."

"I threatened to kill myself, Cara! He knew I meant it, too. He didn't forbear out of kindness."

"Maybe na at first, but later on . . . I think that was different. I believe he's in love with you," replied Cara.

"He lusts for me, that's all. And I don't lust for him, much less love him."

"Look . . . All this stuff about undoing evil and visions and the goddess is way over my head. But I *do* know a thing or two about men, and I've known Honus for years. He *is* kind. He's principled, too. I think it's more than lust. You could do a lot worse. Think about it, and you might change your mind. Take time to decide what you want."

"What difference does it make what I want?" said Yim. "My life has always been in others' hands. The Wise Woman said it's Karm's will."

"*You* have a will also," said Cara. "What do *you* desire?"

"I don't know. It seems pointless to even think about it."

"Maybe you should. When all this is over, Karm may grant you whatever you wish."

A faint look of hope came to Yim's face. "Perhaps."

"Think about Honus, too. Of all the possible masters, you ended up with him. Perhaps that was the goddess's doing. There could be a point to this."

Yim's hopeful look departed. "I'm sure there's a purpose for everything that's happened, just as there was a purpose for what happened to Theodus and Cynetha. Yet, who benefited from their fates? Certainly not them. I'd be foolish to believe the goddess cares about my happiness. She's concerned with greater things."

"Then why obey her?" said Cara. "You need only climb into Honus's bed to thwart Karm. Honus will do the rest."

"Thwart Karm? I couldn't do that!"

"You said yourself that you thought about it."

"I was in shock. It was only a passing weakness. I love Karm."

"*Love* Karm? After what she's done to you?" retorted Cara. "Sure, I'd probably obey her, too. If she tapped me on the shoulder, I'd most likely jump out of my robe and kiss her feet. But I do na think I'd love her for it."

"She's all I have," said Yim. "All I've ever had."

"You have a man who loves you."

"It doesn't matter, even if it were true." Yim threw a stick into the river and watched it swirl as it was swept away. "I'm like that stick, Cara. Can it thwart the current? I'm the Chosen."

TWENTY-EIGHT

COUNT YAUN woke without regrets, though his head throbbed. He had been overly merry at his father's funeral, where his false lamentation had given way to giggles once the drink took hold. Most of the guests had been too wise to comment. Yaun took care to remember those who had. He was still abed when Nug timorously entered the room and pulled the curtains. Afternoon light flooded the chamber. Squinting, Yaun scowled at the elderly servant. "What do you think you're doing?"

"Sire, there's a troop on the road."

"A troop? What manner of troop?"

"Men in black robes and soldiers, too. Some on horse and some afoot."

"Shit! Father just buried, and Gorm already here!"

"Who, sire?"

"None of your business."

"Yes, sire."

"A troop! Shit! He said nothing about a troop."

Nug stood silent, unsure of what to do. Yaun rose and pushed him roughly. "Don't stand there! I need clothes. Clothes befitting a count."

"I'll check your father's wardrobe, sire."

"Check my brother's, too. Now, hurry!"

Yaun nervously paced the room, pausing occasionally to peer out the window. In the distance, a large column of mounted and marching men slowly advanced up the road. The black robes of the Devourer's priests contrasted with the dull shine of the soldiers' armor. Yaun tried to count the armed men, but they were too numerous. "Shit!" he said again.

Nug and two other servants returned with armloads of clothes, which they hurriedly laid out on the bed. Yaun inspected them and frowned at their simplicity. He selected the most expensive-looking garments, ignoring their clashing styles and colors, and ordered his servants to dress him. When they were done, he said to Nug, "I'm going to the great hall. Bring me meat and wine there."

"And when the visitors arrive, sire?"

"Admit the priest called the Most Holy Gorm. Bid the others wait outside."

"Yes, sire," said Nug. He bowed low and departed.

Yaun was on his second bottle of wine when the doors to the great hall were flung open and Gorm strode in unannounced. Following behind him was the entire company that Yaun had spied upon the road. They entered with strict discipline. The only sounds were tramping feet and the clink of mail and weapons. Once the hall was filled to near overflowing, the noises dwindled to an unnerving silence as the soldiers and priests stood perfectly still.

The Most Holy Gorm stood in front of this intimidating assemblage. For a while, he remained as still and silent as the throng behind him. Once he assumed that the proper impression had been made, he bowed low to the quaking figure on the dais. "*Count* Yaun," said Gorm with just a hint of mockery, "I regret I'm late for your father and brother's funerals."

"I think you're early instead. I didn't expect you yet."

"You can never predict Lord Bahl. It's pointless and *most* unwise."

Yaun grew pale and nodded.

"You're a count now," said Gorm loudly. "You need men-at-arms to enforce your commands."

"These are *my* soldiers?" asked Yaun.

"For a while," replied Gorm.

The reply did nothing to lessen Yaun's uneasiness. "And the priests, too?" he asked.

"Your people must be shown the true path. These holy men are here to guide them."

"I . . . I don't deserve such kindness."

A sardonic smile formed on the face of the Most Holy One. "Kindness? These men aren't here out of kindness. They're here out of necessity. You have obligations."

"Obligations?"

"I hope you haven't forgotten Lurwic. Are you not Lord Bahl's servant?"

"Of course," said Yaun meekly.

"Then you will bring an army to Averen. Later, I'll speak more fully of your lord's requirements." Gorm approached Yaun close enough to speak in a low voice. "You're a count now. These men—soldiers and priests alike—will bend the people to your will. And those that won't bend, they'll break. Use them and learn the thrill of power."

Gorm made a signal. A soldier stepped forward and raised his arm in salute. "Count Yaun," he said in a loud voice. "While marching to your manor, we discovered a traitor. This treasonous landholder named you murderer." The ranks in the hall parted, allowing four soldiers to bring forward a young man and woman.

Gorm whispered to Yaun. "This one has a fair estate *and* a fair wife. Didn't she spurn you once?"

Yaun was wondering how Gorm had discovered that information when the soldiers halted. The man they brought before Yaun was well dressed, though a bloodstain marred his shirt. He spoke with difficulty through split and swollen lips. "Yaun, we know each other! What's the cause for this?"

"It's *Count* Yaun now. If you know me, Jon, how could you call me murderer?"

"I merely remarked that your father's corpse looked similar to your brother's. Someone has twisted my meaning."

Yaun barely seemed to listen. His attention was on Jon's wife, Becca. She was a lithe, fair-featured woman with cascades of curly, strawberry hair that reached her waist. Her soft gray eyes were wide with fright. Yaun found her fear so arousing that Gorm had to nudge him to return his attention to her husband.

"So," said Yaun, "you think I'm a murderer." He pointed to a pair of soldiers. "Seize hold of his arms!" He pointed to a third soldier. "Tear open his shirt and expose his belly!" When this was done, Yaun drew his dagger and approached the helpless man. "Do you know how Alaric died?"

Jon looked puzzled. "Who's Alaric?"

Yaun ignored Jon's question. "Well, they gutted him. Ever wonder how that feels?" He touched Jon's stomach with the point of the dagger. "Be still, here's a surprise." He moved the blade across Jon's abdomen, making a thin red line. To his disappointment, Jon didn't cry out. He barely flinched.

Yaun stood in flustered silence for a moment, before recalling what to say next. "So now you've paid me and got a gift in . . ." Yaun halted as Jon's flesh turned gray around the cut. *Shit!* thought Yaun. *The blade's still poisoned!*

Jon gasped and doubled over as his muscles cramped. Falling to the floor, he managed to speak before the poison silenced him. "In this, you treat me like a brother."

Becca screamed and ran weeping to her dying husband. She held him as he twisted into something gray and rigid. Kissing his swollen lips, she inhaled his last breath.

Gorm watched the grief-stricken woman dispassionately. Then he whispered to Yaun, "When you kill a dog, you must see to his bitch as well."

A gleam came to Yaun's eyes. "Seize the woman!"

Two soldiers struggled to haul Becca away from her husband, succeeding only after she had bloodied their faces with her nails. Her struggles increased Yaun's excitement, but he didn't approach Becca until her hands were bound and she grew subdued.

"So, Becca, you made two mistakes. You spurned a count, and you married a traitor."

"You weren't a count when you tried to kiss me last. Now, you are." Becca pursed her lips and lifted her chin. Yaun grinned and moved to take the offered kiss. When he drew close, Becca spit in his face.

Yaun slapped her hard. He drew his dagger, but stopped himself when he saw the triumph in Becca's eyes. Realizing her ploy, Yaun sheathed his weapon and spoke to the soldiers grasping Becca's arms. "Lock her in the north tower. The servants can show you where it is. Then bring the key to me."

"Yes, sire," said the soldiers as they moved to obey.

"And one more thing," said Yaun, his eyes on Becca. "Before you lock her up, strip her naked." He found her look of horror and revulsion satisfying. It made him think of the greater satisfactions to come. Yet, as Becca was taken away, she assumed a dignity that diminished his pleasure.

Yaun regarded the twisted corpse on the floor. "Cut off his head and display it where she can see it from the tower window."

Gorm nodded with approval. "Your sternness will be a lesson to your people. It's good to be feared."

Yaun recalled Becca's look of horror and savored the memory. "Yes," he said in a distant voice. "It's very good indeed."

The officers' dinner at the Bridge Inn was subdued. Late in the afternoon, Cronin had briefed his staff on the substance of his and Honus's discussions. Thus the news was out that the journey to Averen wouldn't be a homecoming but the beginning of a desperate defense. Though younger soldiers might have been eager for battle, all the men on Cronin's staff had seen combat in the Eastern Reach and many had fought with him in earlier campaigns. As seasoned veterans, they had few illusions about what lay ahead, and their mood that evening reflected their knowledge. Honus preferred the solemn atmosphere, for it matched his own musings.

Throughout the meal, Yim and Cara talked together at a far table. Though Honus had long given up trying to perceive Yim's thoughts, he watched her closely, trying to read her expression as an ordinary man might. She seemed sad, but she often seemed sad. Cara caught Honus gazing at Yim and whispered something to her. Honus quickly averted his eyes. When he glanced again toward Yim, Cara was watching and gave him a knowing look.

In a low voice, Honus said to Cronin, "I'm beginning to see why you banned your sister from the table."

Cronin chuckled. "Does she make you uneasy?"

"I don't know what you're talking about."

"Then ask Cara," said Cronin. "She misses little. If she were a man, she'd make an excellent adjutant."

Honus grunted by way of an answer, which made Cronin grin. "You would na be the first man who fell in love with his slave."

"Is that what Cara told you?"

"She's na the only one with eyes. It's been a long time since Cynetha died."

"Your sister's a romantic. It seems to run in the family," said Honus. "Though it may disappoint you both, I'm giving Yim to the temple."

"The temple is na the haven it once was," said Cronin, "You may na be doing her a favor."

"I'm mindful of what you said today, but the temple's protected by the goddess. How can it not be safe?"

"I'm a soldier, na a Seer," said Cronin. "Yet it seems to me that more than men are contending in these struggles. There are two temples in Bremven now, that of Karm and that of the Devourer. I fear even Karm's sanctuary may be in peril."

"That's all the more reason for me to go there."

"So I can na persuade you to linger?"

"No. I'm resolved to leave tomorrow. I must find a Bearer."

"When you do, may Karm send you our way."

When the meal was finished, Cronin and his officers stayed to drink more ale. Honus abstained, and departed soon after Yim. When he entered his room, he found Yim already in her bed, wearing her old tunic as a nightgown.

"Did you have a pleasant time with Cara?"

"She's good company, but the future weighs heavily on her. She's worried about the approaching war."

"War's her brother's concern. I would've hoped a woman's thoughts would dwell on gentler things."

"If Bahl takes Averen, Cara feels a soldier's lot will be easier than a woman's."

Honus sighed. "I wish such talk hadn't darkened your day. It would ease my heart if you were content." Honus prepared for bed and blew out the candle. When he climbed between his sheets, he said, "Come lie beside me."

"Why? The room's warm enough."

"Do you think I'd violate my oath?"

"No."

"Then why do you sound uneasy?"

"I cannot say."

"Can not or will not?"

"That's an unfair question. Must I bare my thoughts to you?"

"When have you ever done that?"

"What do you want of me?" asked Yim, adding as an afterthought the word "Master."

Honus shrank from putting his feelings into words. Instead, he replied, "I'll pose your own question—what do you want of me?"

"To be left alone."

"I ask but this little thing," said Honus quietly. Then, he hardened his voice to hide his longing. "It's my right. Come."

Yim let out an exasperated sigh and crawled into Honus's bed. Once beneath the sheet, she turned her back to him.

Yaun ascended the tower alone, holding a lantern to light the winding stairs. He had spent a tedious afternoon and evening with Gorm learning the extent of Lord Bahl's "requirements." They were likely to impoverish him or—more accurately—his subjects. Yaun pushed all that from his mind, replacing it with exquisite anticipation. He had even drunk less than usual so as not to dull his pleasure. His hand trembled with excitement, and he had difficulty inserting the key into the lock. When he finally succeeded, Yaun kicked open the door. "If you please me," he said, "I might let you live."

There was no reply.

Yaun swung the lantern around, expecting to find Becca cowering in a corner. The bare stone room had no place to hide, but there was no sign of Becca. Yaun immediately suspected treachery, though he had the only key. He was pondering the mystery of Becca's disappearance when his eyes fell upon the room's single window. It lacked glass or bars, but it was so tiny that Yaun couldn't imagine anyone squeezing through it. He inspected the window with his lantern and found blood on its rough stone edges.

Peering beyond the opening, Yaun spied the pale form of Becca's body sprawled on the ground below. He cursed. She had spurned him yet again to join her husband on the Dark Path.

Yaun descended the tower in a foul mood. Going for some wine, he encountered Gorm. "Done with your sport already?" asked the priest. "I thought such things were best drawn out."

"She was already dead," replied Yaun crossly. "She jumped out the window."

Gorm shrugged. "Put bars on it. You're a count now. There'll be others."

TWENTY-NINE

WITH FIRST light, there was a knocking on the door. "Honus, are you awake?"

Honus remained in bed, reluctant to leave it. "I am now, Cara."

"Brother said you're leaving today, and we never had a chance to talk. I mean, we talked, but na *really*. If I'd known you came here just to rush away again . . . well . . . Are you going to open the door?"

"Let me dress," replied Honus, rising and pulling on his pants. Yim merely pulled the sheets over her head. Honus opened the door and said, "Couldn't this have waited?"

Cara peered around Honus's shoulder and smiled when she saw Yim's form under his sheets. "Nay. I know all about good-byes, for Brother has left often enough. If you wait to the last moment, you never say what needs to be said and you end up babbling some pointless thing like 'until next greeting' or something like it when the *real* truth is you do na know if you'll ever see that person again or . . . or . . ." Cara lost her composure and appeared to be on the verge of crying.

"Come in, Cara," said Honus in a gentle voice. "There's still time to say good-bye properly."

Yim emerged from under the sheets and shook her head violently at Cara's quizzical look. Honus caught Cara's end of the unspoken communication. "To whom," he asked, "have you come to bid farewell?"

"Why, to you and Yim both. You're like a second brother, Honus, one that's never cross with me. And Yim . . . well, she's special. I hope you know that, Honus. I'll be disappointed if you do na. She's na a slave, you know. Na really, she's . . ."

"Cara!" exclaimed Yim in an anxious tone.

"She's stolen goods," continued Cara, disregarding Yim's outburst. "She's been stolen from herself and paying ten coppers to the thieves who did it does na mean you own her. I would hope you'd know that; you're na as silly as most men."

Honus smiled. "And when did you acquire such an understanding of men? Isn't Cronin strict with you?"

"I've been living in *Bremven,* for Karm's sake! While you've been wandering all over who-knows-where, I've learned a thing or two. And do na think I've been leading a wild life. If we'd had a proper talk you'd know I was really quite respectable, which does na mean I walked around with my eyes shut. After all, one does na have to roll in mud to understand pigs. Na that you're a pig, Honus. Far from it. You're so . . . so *special*. I hope that Yim . . ." Cara cut herself short and embraced Honus tightly. "I wish you were na leaving. Everything is . . . is so . . ." She started mingling sobs with her words. ". . . so . . . Oh, I can na bear to talk about it! Later this morning, I'll be the general's brave sister. I will na cry then. Take care of Yim." She released Honus to embrace Yim. "Take care of Honus," she whispered, then kissed Yim's cheek. Cara was still crying as she ran from the room.

"I've never seen her like that," said Honus.

"She believes she's going to her doom," said Yim, "and she suspects we are likewise."

Honus sighed by way of response. "As long as we're up," he said, "we should prepare for our departure."

True to her word, Cara was clear-eyed and outwardly cheerful as Honus and Yim left the Bridge Inn. She waved and called out "Until next greeting!" as Yim and Honus headed down the road. Cronin waved also. "If you journey to Averen, Honus," he called, "you know where to find me." Yim turned to wave as the pack, made heavier by provisions and her extra clothing, settled on her shoulders. Her heart was heavy, and she didn't speak.

When the inn was out of sight, Honus broke the silence. "Cara is overly fond of the sound of her voice, but she's wise beyond her years. She's also clever and more than a little mischievous. You *do* realize what she's done?"

Yim pretended she did not. "No."

"She has sent us on our journey having dressed you as my Bearer."

"Your Bearer?"

"Yes," replied Honus, "and our journey will go easier if you behave like one."

"And how can I do that? I've never even met a Bearer."

"Would you rather be seen as a slave?"

"No," replied Yim, "I would not. What must I do, Master?"

"First, your must never use that word for me. You will address me as Honus. When you speak of me to others, you should call me your Sarf."

Yim smiled slightly. "*My* Sarf. I like the sound of that."

"Don't be overbearing about it. Remember, a Bearer is always a humble master."

"Yes, Honus," said Yim, clearly pleased to answer him by name.

Though he tried to hide it, a faint smile came to Honus's lips. "You will be the one," he continued, "who will ask for food and shelter in Karm's name. When people say 'Karmamatus,' it's you—not me—they're addressing, and you must be the one who answers."

"What should I say?" asked Yim.

"Theodus used to say, 'If you want to sound profound, say little.' Let that be your guide. When you must speak, be calm and gracious. That's all that's necessary."

Yim looked at Honus dubiously. "You make it sound simple."

"Most people will care little what you say. A Bearer's concerns are not those of ordinary people. Usually, if you nod and make the Sign of the Balance, that will be sufficient."

"Is there anything else I must do?"

"You must still carry my pack and cook when cooking needs to be done."

"That's easy enough," said Yim. "May I also study your runes?"

"No," said Honus quickly. "The runes are not for your eyes. You're only pretending to be my Bearer."

"I understand, Honus." Yim smiled again.

"You must learn to call me that with a solemn face."

"Then I'll need practice, Honus."

As Yim walked down the road, she silently thanked Cara again and again. Cara had obviously understood Honus better than she did. It had never occurred to Yim that Honus would actually treat her as a Bearer. She was still amazed that he did. *How can he treat me like his beloved Theodus?* Yim couldn't understand it, and Honus's explanation was unconvincing. *He's never cared before whether our journey was easy or not. He could have made me wear my slave's tunic. Why didn't he?* Yim pondered that question. *Did he take Cara's assertion that I'm "stolen goods" to heart? Or was Cara right in saying that he cares for me? Is this the proof?* Yim hoped it wasn't, but she couldn't see Honus's expression to make a guess. He solemnly preceded her, assuming the traditional position for a Sarf walking with his Bearer.

The road they traveled followed the river awhile, then turned south into a countryside of gently rolling hills. There were no weeds on the highway, for its paving stones were kept clear by traffic. Soon the surrounding woods gave way to orderly fields, vineyards, and orchards. Vinden was an ancient land, but unlike Luvein, history had been kind to it. The pleasant countryside reflected the caring husbandry of generations.

Yim had never seen anywhere like it. Her mountain homeland was harsh and flinty. Only the lowest hollows supported crops, and even there, cold alpine winds made farming a chancy business. In contrast, the earth of Vinden was rich. Although the cottages she saw were not large, they seemed homey and comfortable. In the yards of many, spring flowers blossomed. The folk she saw appeared well fed and content. A few nodded toward her and made the Sign of the Balance. Yim inclined her head and returned the sign.

"How could you ever bear to leave here, Honus?"

"Whether I wished to leave or not was of no consequence," he replied. "Karm directed my Bearer elsewhere, and I followed him. Yet I'll admit I'm glad to see these hills again."

"It looks so peaceful," said Yim. "I find it hard to believe Cara's tales. She claims many here now follow the Devourer."

"That's also what Cronin said."

"I can understand why someone like Gan might turn to the Devourer. He had nothing, and craved vengeance when none could be had. But why would folk in this fair place take up such worship?"

"That question puzzled Theodus also," said Honus. "If the answer eluded him, what hope have I of learning it?"

Yim had no reply. Instead, she turned her attention to the sights around her. The sunny landscape, awash in the colors and scents of spring, soon banished her dark musings. The manner of the people they passed on the road matched the warmth of the day. Most were friendly, and everyone was courteous. All salutations were directed to her, not Honus. After some initial surprise, Yim grew accustomed to others' deference. For the first time since her capture, she had regained her dignity. It made her optimistic about the future. Soon she would be living in Karm's temple. *What could be a better home for the Chosen?* she thought. *Perhaps I need only to bear a child who will undo evil. My fate could be a peaceful one.* Yim fancied that her trial was over, and hope invigorated her steps.

Yim and Honus walked until noon, then stopped on a stretch of the road that was lined by trees. Beneath the shade of a huge sycamore, they ate a lunch of fresh bread, well-aged cheese, and spicy sausage. Yim dined with relish.

Afterward, she lazed upon the soft grass. Honus was less lighthearted. He watched Yim wistfully before lying back to gaze skyward.

Yim turned on her side and studied his pensive features. "Honus, did it hurt when they tattooed your face?"

"Yes."

"Why did they do it?"

"To mark my mastery of the martial arts."

"But why do it at all? They don't tattoo Bearers."

"A face such as mine is useful in combat. It's hard to see at night. During the day, it's fearsome and difficult to read. However, the Seer who made these marks gave me another reason."

"What?"

"He said my face reflects Karm's wrath."

"Her wrath? Do you think Karm's wrathful?"

"That's a question you should ask at the temple. I'm only a Sarf."

"*Only* a Sarf! How can you say 'only'? You do Karm's work."

"I'm her tool. Does a hammer understand the carpenter?"

"Don't be silly. Why call yourself a hammer?"

"You're right," said Honus. "As you once said, I'm a sword. I build nothing."

Honus's answer surprised Yim, and she didn't know how to respond.

"I'm fit only for killing," said Honus. "Karm must be wrathful indeed to have need for one such as I. No wonder you shrink from me."

Honus's despondency tugged at Yim's compassion. Almost without thinking, she gently stroked his blue-lined cheek. "No," she said. "The Seer was wrong. Yours is not the face of wrath."

Honus froze at Yim's touch. She withdrew her hand and realized her fingertips were wet. Gazing into Honus's eyes,

she saw they glistened within their pools of permanent
shadow. Yim was reminded of when she contacted Honus's
spirit in the dark man's castle. This time she needed no special powers to see his torment. She had caught hints of it
before, but had never felt its full force. *He's consumed by
self-doubt.* Yim looked away, rubbing her moistened fingers. *These tears are his confession.*

Yim felt that she had mistaken Honus's intentions on the
previous night. *He wasn't spurred by lust, but by loneliness.* A loneliness that seemed like hers. Then Yim wished
that she hadn't judged his need for closeness so harshly and
could unsay the words she spoke that night. An urge to
comfort Honus seized her. Yet, even as she thought to fling
her arms around him, she remembered Karm. Yim saw her
impulse as yet another test, perhaps the most severe of all.
She recalled Cara's words—"*You need only climb into
Honus's bed to thwart Karm. Honus will do the rest.*" Yim
stifled her feelings.

Only when Yim regained her composure did she look at
Honus. By then he had wiped his eyes and formed his expression into one of calmness. Yim studied his tattoos. The
angry visage they created was hard and implacable. *Such a
face must be difficult to bear.* The marks seemed callous
treatment for a lifetime of devotion. In that way, it reminded Yim of her own fate. *Perhaps the Seer understood
Karm after all.*

Honus remained silent, and so did Yim, for she was unsure what to say. She felt awkward, and she imagined
Honus felt the same. It was a relief when he asked her if she
was ready to resume their journey. Yim replied that she was
and put on the pack. They headed out with Honus in front,
his face hidden from Yim.

As the day wore on, Yim began to encounter hostility.
No one dared abuse Honus; all the ill will was directed
toward her. Sometimes it was only a baleful glance. Once,

she was forced from the road when a cart suddenly swerved. She heard muttered curses, but not all the curses were muttered. After passing a particularly foul-tongued man, Honus turned and caught Yim's shaken expression. "I'm sorry, Yim. I hadn't foreseen this."

"Aren't Bearers supposed to forgive abuse?"

"You're not a Bearer."

Yim held her head up. "I can act like one."

Later, they came upon a burnt cottage. About the blackened structure were signs its destruction had not been accidental. Fences had been knocked down. A pair of dogs had been hacked apart and bits of them were strewn about. Grathti was painted on the smoke-stained walls. The derelict house looked so out of place in the peaceful countryside that Honus left the road to investigate it. Yim followed him, but he stopped her at the doorway. A sweet, sickening smell issued from the interior. "There's no need to look inside."

"What happened here?" asked Yim.

Honus didn't immediately reply, but moved a short way from the cottage and sat down to trance. Soon he opened his eyes. "This farmer's grandfather came from Averen. That was enough to condemn him in his neighbors' eyes."

"They killed him for that?"

"Him and his family. Cara's and Cronin's tales were true. Vinden has changed since I was here last."

"Why?"

"The answer is hidden from me. One thing is plain, though: The Devourer's followers did this."

Yim looked about and saw the land in a different light. "Was Luvein once as fair as Vinden?"

"Tales say it was even fairer," replied Honus.

By late afternoon, the small cottages had given way to large estates. Broad fields and orchards surrounded the manor houses and their outbuildings. When evening approached, they spied such a house. It lay far from the road at the end of a lane flanked by newly plowed fields. The house was built of stone, and except for some of the ruins in Luvein, it was the largest Yim had ever seen. Honus said, "It's time to ask for food and lodging."

Yim's experiences in the afternoon heightened her trepidation as she approached the manor and knocked on its door. A man dressed in a long gray robe opened it shortly afterward. An elaborate brass medallion hung from a chain about his neck, and his face bore a haughty look. He fixed his eyes on Yim.

Yim bowed her head. "Father, we're servants of Karm. We request shelter and food in respect for the goddess."

The man didn't return Yim's bow. Instead, he replied, "My master decides who receives hospitality. I'll speak with him." Then, he closed the door.

Honus said nothing, but Yim thought he looked surprised. It seemed a long time before the servant emerged from the house and shut the door behind him. "Follow me," he said. Then he led Yim and Honus around the manor house to a long, low hut in its rear. Built of wood and constructed like a shack, it provided seasonal housing for the field-workers. Since it was early spring, its single, narrow room was mostly empty. "Find a bed to your liking," said the man as he pointed to the row of straw-covered wooden pallets. "Then, I'll show you to dinner."

Yim laid the pack on an empty pallet and looked around for a place to wash. There was a basin near the door. She washed her face and hands in it, though the cloudy water obviously hadn't been changed recently. When Honus had done the same, the gray-robed man led them to the rear of the manor. A door there opened on a room with a long table where three dozen servants and field hands were eating their evening meal. A rotund woman with a good-natured face rose when Honus and Yim entered. Their escort addressed her. "Our master bids these two be fed." Then he left.

"Karmamatus," said the woman to Yim, "I am Emjah,

the cook and mistress of this meal. I'd be honored if you and your Sarf sat by me."

Yim bowed her head. "The honor is ours."

Some of the diners slid down the bench to make a place for Yim and Honus. A little girl brought out bowls of thick porridge, wooden spoons, and empty ale bowls for the new arrivals. Upon the table were loaves of coarse, brown bread, ale flagons, a large chunk of cheese, and a crock of shredded cabbage preserved in brine. These were passed toward Yim and Honus when they sat down. According to custom, Yim served her Sarf before helping herself.

Emjah appeared eager to talk, but she first let Yim take the edge off her hunger. When Yim finished her porridge, Emjah smiled and said, "Would you like some more, Karmamatus?"

"No, thank you, Mother," replied Yim as she broke off another piece of cheese.

"Please call me Emjah, Karmamatus."

"Then you must call me Yim."

Emjah smiled at Yim in a maternal way. "Yim, you look so young to be a Bearer."

"All must be young once."

"And where have you been traveling?"

"In Luvein."

"Luvein!" said Emjah with amazement. "Such a fell place! Your tender looks are deceiving; you must be made of stern stuff."

A man laughed harshly. "Our old hen has found a new chick."

Yim looked at the man who had laughed. He was burly and coarse-looking, with a bushy beard and a dark tangle of greasy hair. There was dirt beneath the nails of his large hands, and his rough clothes were thoroughly soiled. Two similar men flanked him. He stared contemptuously at Yim. "So, girly," he said. "Me and my mates plowed from sunrise. What did you do to deserve supper?"

The room hushed. Honus remained silent, but Yim saw from the corner of her eye that he flushed red beneath his tattoos.

"Who can tell what a person deserves?" replied Yim evenly.

"So you're fond of riddles," said the plowman. He leaned across the table to snatch the cheese in front of Yim. "Well, I'll answer yours. A man deserves what he has strength to take."

"So you follow the path of the Devourer?"

The plowman tugged at a cord around his neck to produce a circular pendant. "Times are changing, girly. When the Devourer's priests visit, they dine with the master."

"Those black crows!" said Emjah. "They're honored only out of fear."

"You should learn our master's lesson," said the plowman. "The world honors power. 'Tis the sign of the Devourer's grace. Is that not so, girly? You've traveled. In every land, isn't the strong man respected? Dare you deny that he deserves whatever his might wins him?"

Everyone's eyes were on Yim, and she knew that she must respond. "I've heard that speech before," she said. "It reminds me of a certain village north of Luvein built on the shore of a large lake. The market town lies on the opposite shore and the route around the lake is a hard one. To make matters worse, a nobleman exacts a toll on all who pass that way. Some years ago, an enterprising fellow built a boat to ferry the villagers to market. The trip was easy and short. The fare was less than the nobleman's toll."

"Speak to the point!" said the plowman.

"I am," replied Yim. "The nobleman sent men abroad who spoke very much like you. They would go into the taverns and say, 'How can you abide that boatman? When the wind blows, one side of the boat gets wet with spray. Yet that overbearing lout makes everyone stay in place. Why must a strong man tolerate such treatment? He should do what's best for him and sit away from the wind. If someone is in that place, then let them move aside." Yim looked at the plowman. "Isn't that your message?"

" 'Tis."

"In time, many on the ferry came to agree with you," said Yim. "One day, a hard wind blew up. The largest men aboard the boat, thinking only for their own comfort, crowded to the drier side. And who could stop them? They were strong." Yim addressed the plowman. "Wasn't it their right?"

"Aye," said the man. "By the Devourer, 'twas."

"Thus the boat was unbalanced," said Yim. "It tipped over. All aboard were drowned. And the nobleman? He increased his toll."

The plowman scowled and looked away.

Emjah laughed. "Yim's got you there!" The cook glanced around the table and saw she expressed the general opinion.

"It seems to me," said an elderly man, "that Karmamatus deserves more respect than *some* would give her." He gazed balefully at the plowman. "Perhaps if her Sarf lopped off a head or two, she'd get it."

"You mistake the working of the Balance," said Yim, "if you think chopping heads would be a remedy. Karm's scales don't favor such deeds. Only goodness counterweights evil."

"I can see why you're a Bearer," said the elderly man. He turned to the plowman. "You should be thankful Karm chose so wisely."

The plowman's face darkened. He and his fellows quickly downed their ale and left the room. Yim concentrated on the last of her meal, modestly avoiding the glances of her audience. She didn't notice how Honus regarded her, nor did the other diners, who avoided the eyes of the fierce-faced man. Thus, none noted his wonderment. When Yim eventually looked his way, his expression was bland again. Seeing that he had finished his meal, Yim spoke. "Emjah, my Sarf and I have journeyed far and must rest." With that, she rose and bowed her head. "Karm sees your master's hospitality and your graciousness as well."

Honus led the way back to the workers' hut. There was no lamp or fire in the long, tunnel-like room. The only illumination was the twilight entering through unglazed windows. Within the dim room, Yim could see the plowman and his two comrades seated on a pallet. Somehow, they had obtained a large jug of ale and were passing it back and forth. When they noted Honus's aggressive carriage, they moved to the far end of the building.

"Will we be sleeping with them?" Yim whispered.

Honus nodded. "It wasn't my place to speak at dinner," he whispered, "but as your Sarf, I'll protect you. Sleep untroubled."

Yim removed her sandals and sank down into the straw. She quickly sat upright. "Phew! This bedding stinks! I'd almost rather sleep outside."

"You'll get used to it. Be glad it's spring. The winter has killed the lice."

Yim leaned toward Honus and whispered, "I thought a Bearer's life would be less trying."

"It's seldom easy."

"I learned that at dinner," replied Yim.

"That plowman gave you a hard time, but you acquitted yourself well."

"Now I understand why Bearers have Sarfs. I would have feared to speak without you by my side."

"That parable you told . . . I've never heard it."

"I made it up. Was that wrong?"

"No. It was a tale worthy of Theodus. More importantly, it spoke wisdom. Now get some sleep. I'll watch over you."

Yim lay down and tried to ignore the smell of old straw, dirt, and stale sweat. Her exhaustion aided the effort. As she drifted off to sleep, she saw Honus sitting upright, keeping watch in the darkening room.

THIRTY

YIM WOKE to the sound of the plowman and his comrades, the worse for their night of drinking, moaning and cursing the dawn. She glanced toward Honus and found him in the same position as when she fell asleep. Yim wondered if he had slept at all. "Is it already time for breakfast?" she asked sleepily.

"Most estates don't feed the servants until midmorning," replied Honus. "We should be gone by then."

Yim stretched and put on her sandals. "Then let's leave now."

Honus readied himself while Yim washed her face. They were heading for the road when Emjah emerged from the manor house. "Yim! Wait!" She hurried over and handed Yim a loaf of bread. "For your journey, Karmamatus. Have your Sarf keep a keen eye. These are dark times." Emjah bowed and dashed back into the house before Yim could thank her.

Yim broke off a piece of the still-warm loaf and handed it to Honus. Then she took a piece for herself. The bread was white and flavored with honey and dried fruit. Its rich flavor contrasted with the coarse brown bread they had eaten at dinner.

"I think this was baked for the master's table," said Yim.

"It's not servants' fare," agreed Honus.

Yim and Honus walked as they dined, for the morning was still too cold to sit comfortably. When the sun rose higher, the air warmed. Soon the road began to fill with traffic. Those travelers who worshipped Karm were courteous. The Devourer's followers were rude. Others averted their eyes, seemingly afraid to reveal their convictions. Thus, by the way she was greeted on the road, Yim could discern the beliefs of the surrounding countryside. As the day advanced, hostility predominated.

In the afternoon, a young man spit on Yim as he passed. Honus whirled at the sound, his hand upon his sword hilt. He found Yim calmly using her sleeve to wipe the spittle from her cheek. Her placidity set the example, and Honus released his sword. Only when he faced forward did Yim permit herself a shudder. She didn't want to arouse Honus's concern, for she wished to continue acting as his Bearer. Yim found the hate of Karm's enemies easier to endure when she recalled her former status. As a slave, her feelings were irrelevant. At the inn, men had been bold with their glances and free with their hands whenever Honus was absent. Even Cara had made demeaning assumptions. Spit was less painful than such treatment and easier to wipe away.

When dusk approached, Yim and Honus were traveling a stretch of road that was thick with the adherents of the Devourer. Thus Yim was uneasy as she approached a manor house to ask for food and lodging. Its construction was typical of the region. The outer walls of the house and the farm buildings were linked together to form a single compound.

As they walked up to the building, Honus commented, "They're behind in their plowing."

Like its fields, the manor house looked neglected. Though a light shone in an upper-story window, the first-story ones were boarded up. "It seems this estate has fallen on hard times," Yim said. "Perhaps we should ask elsewhere for charity."

"It grows late," replied Honus, "and we've already traveled far. Our modest needs should be no burden."

When they reached the manor's entrance, the door opened before Yim could knock. A woman who was younger than Yim stood in the doorway. "Come in quickly, Karmamatus." The urgency in her voice made Yim and Honus hurry inside. The woman anxiously scanned the darkening countryside before shutting and bolting the door. Only then did she bow toward Yim. "Welcome, servants of Karm."

Yim returned her bow. "We request shelter and food in respect for the goddess."

"We're honored by your request. I'll tell my parents."

The woman left Yim and Honus standing in the entrance hall while she went to announce their arrival. As Yim waited, she thought the woman's appearance confirmed her impression that the estate's fortunes had declined. Her once-fine clothes were worn and soiled, and though she seemed to be the master's daughter, her hands were rough and she performed the duties of a servant.

There was a grand stone stairway with black marble treads that led to the upper apartments. Yim looked up it, expecting the master and mistress of the house to appear at its head. They did not. Instead, a middle-aged man and woman entered from a side door. In soiled clothes, they looked as if they had been interrupted in the midst of some menial task. The man bowed gracefully to Yim. "Welcome to my home, Karmamatus. I'm Yorn and this is my wife, Karyen. You've already met my daughter, Wenda. Your presence graces us, and I pray you'll dine and stay the night."

Yim returned Yorn's bow. "Karm sees your generosity, and we're grateful for your hospitality."

Yim regarded their hosts and found them genteel, despite their worn clothes. Yorn had the olive complexion and the dark hair and eyes common to the people of the region. His wife was blue-eyed, with reddish blond hair and sunburnt skin that appeared to have once been very fair. Wenda favored her mother in looks, except for her dark eyes.

"You must be tired from your journey," said Yorn. "Wenda will show you to your rooms, so you may refresh yourselves before dinner."

Wenda bowed toward Yim. "Karmamatus, shall I take your pack?"

"No, thank you, Wenda. It's mine to carry."

Wenda bowed again, then led Yim and Honus past the stone stairs and through a doorway. The old house was an elegant structure, but it looked bare. They passed through several empty halls to a long corridor with doors on one side. Wenda opened one to reveal a bedroom.

"This is your chamber, Karmamatus. I'll show your Sarf his room and bring water for you to wash."

"Let him help you, Wenda. And please call me Yim."

Yim set down her pack as Honus and Wenda left. She examined her room with interest. Whatever the household's current fortunes, the chamber seemed luxurious. It featured a colorful tile floor, albeit a dusty one, and painted plaster walls. A large walnut bed had not only sheets and covers, but also a feather mattress. It was the first Yim had ever touched, and it seemed marvelously soft. Though the room was large, the bed was its only furnishing. There were hooks for wall hangings, but all that remained of these were darker rectangles on the faded paint. A glazed window looked out to a large courtyard, which contained the remnants of a formal garden. Part of it had gone to weed, and a vegetable patch had replaced the rest.

Yim sat in her room for a long while before Wenda and Honus returned. Honus bore two large ewers of warm water, and Wenda carried a large, empty basin with a washing cloth and towel. "I'm sorry it took so long to heat the water," said Wenda. "But you'll have time to wash and rest. I'll come when dinner's ready."

After Wenda left, Yim grinned at Honus. "Is your room as nice as this?"

"They gave you the finest room, but mine is more than adequate."

"Did you see the rest of the house? What's going on here?"

"I saw the kitchen and the rooms between here and here. I'd say they've sold off most of their possessions. I think the only servant is an elderly cook. Wenda treats her like family."

"The land looks rich, and these people seem respectable," said Yim. "What has befallen them?"

"I'm not sure," replied Honus. "Maybe we'll find out at dinner." He turned to go, then stopped. "Would you tell me when you've bathed?"

"Don't you want to wash first?"

"No, this water is for you."

"I'll be quick," Yim said.

"Don't hurry. I'll fetch the basin when you're done." Then Honus departed.

Yim stared at the steaming bath. It was but the latest example of Honus's new solicitude. He seemed almost another person ever since they had left the inn. Yim thought she should find the change pleasant. Instead, it was disconcerting. She feared that Cara had been right and Honus's behavior was a sign of love.

Love was something Yim knew little about. She never encountered it growing up. Her mother had died upon Yim's birth, and her father had not been loving. Nor had her guardian. Sensing Yim's otherness, the boys and girls in the village avoided her, denying her even gossip of love. Since the Wise Woman was a midwife, Yim had learned the facts of lovemaking, but the passions that spurred it remained a mystery. She had only a vague idea about them. Sometimes Yim doubted she was capable of such feelings, or if she was, capable of recognizing them. *I wish Cara*

were here. She could tell me what's going on. Yim had no
confidence in her own impressions on the matter and wondered if she might be misreading Honus.

Despite Honus's parting words, Yim washed hurriedly,
so the bathwater was still warm when Honus carried out
the basin. She thought he looked at her with fresh interest,
as though they had not walked the entire day together. It
was unsettling. Yim opened her window to let in the evening air and flopped down on the bed. As Yim attempted to
banish thoughts of Honus, she heard a young man's voice
in the courtyard. ". . . was a foolhardy risk, Wenda."

"I looked. I didn't see anybody."

"Still, they could have been watching. There are lots of
places to hide."

"I'm tired of being afraid."

"Then maybe you should . . ." The young man's voice
was cut off by the sound of a closing door, leaving Yim to
wonder what frightened Wenda.

Dinner was served late. Wenda led Honus and Yim to
the dining hall where Yorn and Karyen greeted them. They
were dressed in worn but elegant clothes, as were Wenda
and the three young men who sat at the table. These
proved to be Wenda's older brothers. They had names
that, in accordance to local custom, sounded like their father's. Yim immediately confused Vorn, Thorn, and Dorn,
but she recognized the youngest brother's voice as the one
she had heard in the courtyard. A meal of roots, porridge,
and cabbage was already on the table, but an elderly
woman brought out a scrawny roast chicken after Yim
was seated.

Yorn asked the woman who brought the chicken to take
a seat at the table, but she shook her head and whispered,
"Nay, sire. 'Twill na do." Then she quickly retreated.

"Karmamatus," said Yorn as he passed her the chicken,

"we have no one to serve you this poor fare, so you must help yourself."

Yim guessed the tiny chicken was a late addition to the menu and one that was dear to her hosts. "Please call me Yim and make no apology for this fine meal. Your kindness lends it extra savor."

The meal, though plain, was as ample as any Yim had eaten, and her hosts were scrupulously polite. She sensed no insincerity in their good manners, but thought they masked an underlying tension. The dinner conversation was bland and conventional until Yim decided to ignore Honus's advice about saying little to seem wise. "When I journeyed through Luvein, I slept on the ground and ate things that made even my Sarf grow pale. I don't travel for pleasure. A Bearer's task is to take on burdens." She looked directly at Wenda. "Why were you so frightened at the door?"

Wenda looked hesitantly at her father, afraid to speak.

Yorn spoke for her. "Wenda is a nervous girl. She worries needlessly about . . ."

"She's afraid of our neighbors," interrupted the youngest son. "We all are."

"Vorn!" said his father angrily.

"Why not tell her? After all, her visit may provoke them further."

"I won't be governed by fear!"

Vorn snorted at the statement. "What choice do you have? Look around, Father. Where are our farmhands and servants? Remember what happened to our crops? Who of us dares to walk alone?"

Yim looked at Yorn. "Your plight is all too common these days. Would you tell me your story?"

Yorn sighed as a man setting down a heavy load. "My family has lived here for generations, but Karyen is from Averen. Within the past few years, my neighbors have come to take offense at that."

"Take *offense*!" said Wenda. "They turned on us! People who we thought were our friends."

"Most do it out of fear," said Yorn. "You must forgive them."

"I detect the shadow of the Devourer," said Yim.

"You're right," said Yorn. "Our troubles started with the arrival of his priests. They stirred up resentment and encouraged hatred. At first, only dregs and malcontents were attracted to them. But as time wore on, they gained more respectable converts. Now they have the sanction of the emperor. Who can say why someone embraces hate? Fear? Greed? Envy? Power? Perhaps it's different for each person. Our neighbors began to call us 'outlanders' and worse. My son spoke true. We're surrounded by hostility, and all our friends have fallen away."

"An odious man comes and barters for our things," said Wenda. "A tiny bag of seed for a silver candlestick."

"What choice do we have, Wenda?" asked her mother. "We have to eat and na one else will deal with us."

"I say he works for the priests," said Vorn. "They're looting us for themselves before they loose the mob."

"Don't upset your sister," said Yorn.

"We think," said Karyen, "that Wenda should go stay with my sister in Lurwic."

"No!" said Honus so sharply that everyone was startled. Yim realized it was the first word he had uttered at the table. He bowed his head toward her. "Forgive me, Karmamatus."

Yim guessed the proper reply. "You may speak."

"Lord Bahl has overrun Lurwic," said Honus. "It offers no refuge."

This news came as a blow to the already dispirited family. Karyen began to weep softly. The food in Yim's stomach turned leaden as she became aware the entire family was looking to her. Yorn spoke for all of them. "Karmamatus, what should we do?"

Honus's eyes were also fixed on Yim. In the silent room, her quiet voice seemed loud. "I cannot tell you what to do. I can only give this advice—think upon what you love most."

For a long while, no one ate, drank, or spoke. Everyone sat frozen in reflection—even Honus, whose eyes remained on Yim. At last, Yorn broke the stillness by gazing at each member of his family in turn. Then he spoke. "A house is but a pile of stones. We'll leave it and go to Averen."

After dinner, Yorn plied Honus with questions on how to effect his family's escape, and they spoke at length. Although Honus's long absence prevented him from advising on the state of the road, he knew much about traveling unnoticed. When he had imparted all he could, Yim rose from the table. Honus rose also and took a rush candle to light Yim's way to her room.

"Honus," said Yim when they reached her door, "are you angry with me?"

"Why should I be angry?"

"I took my pretense too far. Look what I've done! These people are leaving because of me."

"As I recall, you said they should think upon what they loved most. That's good advice for anyone."

"But . . ."

"This house was a stone around their necks. It would've dragged them to their deaths. I've seen it before."

"I'm glad you're not angry. Well, good night."

Yim entered her room and changed into her old tunic before blowing out the candle. Moonlight streamed in the window as she crawled into bed. As Yim sunk into the feather mattress, she tried to imagine how it would feel to abandon such comfort. *How sad for them to trade all this for the hard ground and an uncertain fate.* The family's plight stirred thoughts of Luvein's ruin. *Is this how it began?*

Will someday folk like Gan and his mother live in the shell of this house?

At first, it was a dream. Cara was sobbing and bleeding while Yim tried to aid her. Yim woke, but the sobs persisted. A woman was weeping in the courtyard. Yim thought she must be Wenda, and with a pang of conscience, wondered if her advice was the cause of her sorrow. Yim lay in bed and waited to hear another's voice offering solace. It seemed impossible that the girl's parents had not heard the lamentation; it resounded so clearly.

Time passed, and the only sound Yim heard was weeping. It conveyed a depth of sorrow that seemed beyond the capacity of one so young. The sound became unbearable, and Yim felt compelled to act. She left her bed and went to the window. In the moonlight, she made out a white-robed figure upon a bench at the far side of the courtyard. The window was low to the ground, and Yim easily stepped over its sill. Once outside, she made her way to the sobbing figure. The setting moon cast a dim light, and only when Yim drew near could she tell that the woman was not a member of the household. Regardless, she approached the slumped figure, whose face was buried in her hands. The ground turned icy beneath Yim's feet. Even before the woman looked up, Yim knew she was no mortal.

Yim recognized Karm immediately, though the goddess seldom appeared to her. The deity on the bench looked the same as always—except for one thing. Blood stained her white robe and dripped down her bare limbs. *Is it her blood?* The idea was alarming. *Can the goddess bleed?*

Karm gazed at Yim, her wet eyes glistening in the last of the moonlight. She appeared so grief stricken that Yim pitied her. Then the goddess's expression changed into one even more unsettling. Karm regarded Yim in tearful supplication. Then the pleading goddess dissolved, and Yim was alone in the dark courtyard.

Yim shivered violently, chilled to her very bones. Immediately, the disorientation that followed every vision overwhelmed her. Staring at the empty bench, Yim wondered if she was slipping into madness. This vision was the most bizarre and incomprehensible yet. *How could Karm be helpless?* The very idea ran counter to divinity. *What am I supposed to do?* Karm had always given directions, even if Yim failed to understand them. This disturbing visitation told her nothing.

Insecurity gripped Yim and grew into panic. She felt abandoned, alone without guidance. The shadowy world seemed full of menace—a place where even the goddess was beyond comfort. Yim made her way back to her room, but she didn't return to bed. Its emptiness felt too forbidding. Instead, she went to Honus's chamber and shook him. He bolted upright, and Yim saw the gleam of his partly drawn sword before he froze. "Yim?"

Yim didn't respond, but climbed under the covers and pressed her frigid body against his. "Hold me," she whispered.

THIRTY-ONE

HONUS STIRRED and Yim woke. The soft mattress made a valley that pressed them together. She felt his breath and the damp warmness where their bodies touched. Night was giving way to dawn, and with the growing light, the terror that drove her to Honus faded. Yim felt his arm around her, and all she could think was *What have I done?*

Yim tried to slip out of bed, but Honus gently pulled her closer and whispered in her ear, "Good morning."

"I must leave."

"There's no hurry."

Yim pulled away and sat up with her back to Honus. "What if we're found together? They'd think we'd been tupping."

"It wouldn't matter," said Honus. "It's not uncommon for Karm's servants to make lives together."

"I know. Cara said you married a Seer."

"So, she spilled that to you?"

"She spilled more than that. She said you loved me."

"I told you Cara was wise. Yim, I . . ."

"Don't say it! You can't love me!"

"Why not?"

"Because you mustn't. It's . . . it's impossible." Yim felt Honus touch her shoulder, but she dared not face him.

"Yim, you're shaking."

"Don't touch me! You've mistook my feelings."

Honus withdrew his hand. "Then why did you come to me?"

"I was cold, that's all."

"The night was warm," said Honus. "I was wed to a Seer, so I understand your chill. What vision drove you to me?"

"I cannot say."

"Yim, look at me!"

There was an edge to Honus's voice, and Yim knew she should obey. She rose and turned to face him. "Yes, *Master*."

Honus winced at the word, but his voice was mild. "At the temple there are people who understand such things. Speak with them before you say how I must feel."

"All right," Yim replied. "Maybe they can make sense of this." Despite her words she felt dubious.

"You should change," Honus said. "We'll want an early start."

Yim headed for the door, then stopped with her hand on the latch. "Honus, I'm sorry."

To the north, in Falsten, the planting season was well under way. Dawn found Hendric in harness pulling a plow. His wife, eight moons pregnant, guided it over their plot. As the peasant strained against the plow's resistance, he worried. The plot was small, but well manured, for sheep had grazed on the stubble of last year's harvest. With Karm's grace, the rains would come and there'd be enough grain for the winter and to pay the count's portion. It was the new count that worried Hendric. Count Taun was demanding more than grain. If he pressed his claim, Hendric's small family would likely starve, rains or no.

For his wife's sake, Hendric had kept his worries to himself. But when he saw some of his neighbors marching down the road, he feared she'd soon learn what troubled him. He was surprised that the men had returned so soon. This time they had a black-robed stranger with them. Hendric assumed he was one of the new priests that folk were talking about. Slipping out of the harness, Hendric walked over to his field's boundary to meet the procession. His wife left the plow to join him.

With exception of the priest, Hendric had known the approaching men all his life. Yet when they halted before him, their faces had an unfamiliar cast. It was mostly their eyes that made them seem different. Some looked horrified. Others glared at him with rabid intensity. That look made Hendric's hair rise. Moreover, the men carried scythes, pitchforks, and hoes. They held them not like farm implements but like weapons. Hendric was alarmed to note that some of the tools were bloody.

One of those with a rabid look was a burly man carrying a bloodstained pitchfork. He stepped forward. "Hendric, we've talked with ye afore. Our count needs men to fight the Averen folk."

Hendric recalled that the man had always groused about the old count, and thought his younger son a useless wastrel. Thus he hoped to reason with him, despite his changed demeanor. "When we spoke last eve," said Hendric, "I said my plight's like that of Thom down the way. My wife's with child and my sons be only babes. They cannot bring a harvest in."

The man only grinned in a disturbing way and motioned to one of his fellows, who dumped the contents of a sack on the ground. As the bloody bits tumbled out, he spoke. "We fixed Thom's problem. We can fix yers, too."

Hendric stared aghast at the horrendous sight, his breakfast rising in his throat. From what seemed far away, his wife screamed. He felt someone's hand grip his shoulder. It was the priest's. Hendric gazed into the man's face.

The priest had the sandy hair of someone from foreign parts. His deeply tanned face made his pale gray eyes stand out. They were fanatical and seemed somehow older than the priest's young face. "Averen is our foe," said the priest, "and those that won't fight are its friends. On whose side do you stand? Ours?" He pointed to the carnage on the ground. "Or theirs?"

"I'll join ye and fight."

"Husband, the crop!"

Hearing his wife's despairing tone tore at Hendric's heart, but he forced his voice to sound hard. "Hush, woman," he said. "To the hut. Ye have our babes to tend. The crop be only grain." Then he took up a mattock and reluctantly joined the men.

Morning found Honus and Yim on the road to Bremven, having left Yorn's house shortly after dawn. Honus had said little before their departure and nothing since. Because he led the way, his face was hidden, and Yim could only guess his mood.

Yim was also quiet. Her latest vision, not Honus, was

foremost in her thoughts. She remained shaken by the previous night's visitation. Throughout her lonely life, the goddess had been her sole comfort. Recollections of Karm's first appearance and her loving look had sustained Yim through many trials. Yet in her latest visitation, the goddess hadn't offered comfort. Instead, she seemed to need it.

It was an unsettling reversal of roles, and Yim struggled to make sense of it. As she ruminated, she recalled that the Wise Woman had said Karm worked her will through the deeds of believers. Thinking upon her own inadequacies, Yim considered people fallible tools at best. She imagined Karm witnessing the evils in the world without being able to directly intervene. That seemed a form of torment not unlike Yim's ordeal at Karvakken Pass. *Is that what Karm experiences? Does she feel people's agony as if she's drowning in their blood?* Somehow, Yim knew it was so. Then she understood the cause of Karm's sobbing. Moreover, she thought she knew why the goddess was pleading. *Karm needs me to do what she cannot.*

The idea of Karm's torment roused Yim's compassion. It also made her ashamed. She felt that by taking refuge with Honus, she had rejected Karm. Yim repented her weakness and resolved to be stronger in the future. Yet, for all her resolution, she had no idea how she would help Karm. Yim knew she must bear a child, but she needed guidance to find the father. Yim had always assumed that Karm would lead her to him, but after her last vision, she was no longer certain.

That uncertainty bedeviled Yim. For a while, she felt as lost as she had in the courtyard after the goddess vanished. Then she thought of the temple's holy sages, and hoped that not all of them would be as remote as the Wise Woman or as closemouthed as the Seer who had played the peddler. *Someone might offer me guidance.* But to get to the temple, she needed Honus.

Yim regarded the Sarf striding ahead of her. Despite the

pretense that she was his Bearer, she remained his slave. *He still controls my fate.* Yim wondered if Honus, having been spurned, would still give her to the temple. Thwarted men often acted spitefully, and Yim feared that she might be sold in Bremven. *I could end up on a treadmill or tupping patrons in a pleasure garden!*

Those dire possibilities caused Yim to consider reneging on her pledge to never flee again. She rationalized that she'd be doing it for the goddess's sake, so Karm would forgive her oath breaking. But whether the goddess approved or not, Yim realized that fleeing would be a desperate move, one with a small chance of success. Even if she evaded Honus, she'd be a lone woman far from home. *Without Honus, I can't pose as a Bearer. I'll be seen for what I am—a slave without an owner.* An honest man would try to restore her to Honus, and a dishonest one would keep her for himself. When Yim pondered her options, she thought she might probe Honus as she had Cara. By that means she could learn his intentions. Revealing her talent seemed less drastic than running away, but still imprudent. Thus Yim hesitated before finally calling Honus's name.

When Honus turned his face toward Yim, she needed no special skill to perceive the tenderness in his gaze. The look didn't seem entirely new, though it was more pronounced. Yim wondered how long it had been there. *Why have I just recognized it?* She felt naive for not having seen it sooner. Upon reflection, Yim came up with two possible explanations for her error: Either the look had grown so slowly that the change hadn't been noticeable or she hadn't wanted to see it. In one way, Honus's affection was reassuring. It seemed to promise that he would do nothing to harm her. Yet Yim was also disquieted, for the gaze expressed a need she could never fulfill.

THIRTY-TWO

"HONUS, DID you have to kill the dog?" The sun had set, and Yim's voice betrayed her weariness.

"I had no choice. It would've ripped your throat."

Yim shuddered. "I suppose you're right." She trudged silently awhile, mulling over the encounter. "We'd already turned back. Why did they loose a dog on me?"

"For the sake of malice."

Yim sighed. "I thought the goddess was honored in Vinden."

"She was when I was here last," replied Honus. After a quiet spell, he said, "Perhaps it would be better if you dressed in your old tunic."

"No!"

When Honus didn't press his suggestion further, Yim took his silence for acquiescence. It was, and she was unsurprised. Throughout the course of the day, she had come to understand that the balance of power had shifted between them. Though she was still Honus's slave, she had gained a hold on him. *Cara said a lot of slave girls rule their masters,* thought Yim. She didn't believe that she ruled Honus, but she suspected that she could sway him. To test her power, Yim had begun to assert herself. She had called rest breaks rather than waiting for Honus to do so, and each time Honus halted. She had decided when to eat the midday meal.

"We'll camp tonight," said Yim in yet another test "It

seems futile to seek hospitality. We've been refused five times this evening."

"There's a wood beyond the next hill where we could spend the night," replied Honus. "However, camping means no dinner."

"I don't care," replied Yim. "I won't knock on another door." She gazed at the hill, a black hump against the dark sky. Already footsore, she was disheartened by its distance.

The moon had not yet risen by the time they rounded the hill. The forest beyond it seemed a vaporous shadow. Within the blackness burned a single campfire. It winked in and out as Yim and Honus passed among the trees. Mindful of their previous receptions, they neared it cautiously until they could make out two figures seated near the blaze. Behind them was a wood-sided wagon. "I know that style of wagon," whispered Honus. "Those travelers should be from Averen. Shall we try for hospitality one last time?"

Yim thought of Cara and Cronin. "Yes."

Honus approached the fire first. The travelers proved to be a man and a woman. Upon hearing footsteps, the man sprang up and drew a knife. His partner darted into the darkness. Brandishing his weapon, he called out, "Who's there?" When Honus stepped into the firelight, the alarm left the man's face, and he sheathed his blade. Honus motioned to Yim, and she stepped forward. Before she could utter a word, the man bowed and spoke. "Karmamatus, will you join us? 'Twould be an honor."

Yim was relieved to be welcomed. She smiled as she returned the bow. "Karm sees your generosity, and we're grateful."

"Hommy," called the man. " 'Tis safe. 'Tis a holy one and her Sarf."

A short woman, plump and pregnant, emerged from the darkness. She had the blond hair common among Averen folk. Her expression was warm and friendly as she bowed toward Yim. "Welcome, Karmamatus."

Yim bowed in return. "Please call me Yim."

"I'm Hamin," said the man, "and my wife is Hommy. We're taking wool to sell in Bremven."

Yim regarded their host, who seemed relieved to see Honus and her. His craggy, weather-beaten face made him appear much older than his spouse.

"Pet," said Hamin to his wife, "throw more roots in the stew and make tea for our guests. Come, Yim, rest by the fire."

As Hommy scurried into the wagon, Yim sat on a log and removed the sandals from her tired feet. Honus remained standing. "My Bearer and I haven't traveled this road for several years," he said. "We'd welcome any news of the way."

Hamin shook his head. "If I'd known aforehand, I'd have never brought Hommy. This trip is our wedding journey, and a sorry journey 'tis been."

"So this road's new to you?" asked Honus.

"Nay, I've traveled it each spring since I was a lad," replied Hamin, "and nary a problem, until last year. But now, by Karm, 'tis a different path. We're branded 'outlanders' and treated worse than dogs."

"Everywhere?" asked Yim.

"In truth, nay," said Hamin. "It just seems that way. But the closer we get to Bremven, the worse it gets."

"This counters reason," said Honus. "Karm's holy temple is there."

"So now is the Devourer's black pile. They razed a whole district to build it across from the emperor's palace. I've heard 'tis covered with gold inside, though I would na venture a look."

"There was no such thing in Bremven when I left," said Honus. "They certainly built it quickly."

"Lord Bahl sent three thousand slaves to speed the work. He said 'twas a gift to the new emperor."

Hommy came out of the wagon to augment the stew simmering in a kettle on the campfire. Then she set a small pot of water in the flames. "Karmat . . . er . . . Yim, is mint tea all right?"

"It'd be wonderful," said Yim, smiling at Hommy. "We've had a trying day. Your kindness is our single joy."

"Have you traveled far?" asked Hommy.

"We've journeyed through Luvein," replied Yim.

"Luvein!" said Hommy. "Is it haunted as they say?"

Yim thought of the ghostly battle at Karvakken Pass. "Yes," she replied quietly. "I'd rather not speak of it." Then, in a heartier voice, she said, "So this is your wedding journey."

Hommy beamed. "Aye," she said. "Hamin and I have been married but eight moons." She proudly patted her rounded belly. "This will be our first child. Will you bless it?"

Yim placed her hands on Hommy's womb. "May Karm bless your daughter and guide her steps."

" 'Tis a girl?" asked Hommy.

Honus glanced at Yim, but said nothing.

Yim caught Honus's look and regretted her slip. "Yes," she replied. "You'll have a daughter."

"How can you tell?" asked Hommy.

"Such skill is not uncommon at the temple," injected Honus, as he gave Yim a knowing look. "A Seer I knew was famous for it."

"A girl!" said Hommy happily. "Hamin, we're going to have a girl!"

"There's a saying in Averen," said Hamin to Yim, "that a firstborn girl brings Karm's blessing."

"And now that she has yours, Karmamatus," said Hommy, "she'll be doubly blessed."

Yim smiled at Hommy's remark, but her thoughts were still on Honus's knowing look. It was not the first time he appeared to have seen through her. She wondered how much he had surmised. *Quite a lot,* she decided. That led to the next question. *Does it matter?* She concluded that it wouldn't once they reached the temple. There, Karm's Seers would readily discern that she was the Chosen. *Then all this secrecy will be unnecessary.* Yim took comfort in the idea that she would soon unburden herself and gain guidance from wiser heads.

While Yim thought, the tea water began to boil. Hommy poked a stick through the pot's handle to lift it from the flames, produced some leaves from her apron pocket, mixed them in the hot water, and went to the wagon for some cups. When the tea was brewed, Hommy grasped the hot, sooty pot with her apron to fill the cups, burning a finger in the process.

Hamin watched his wife and shook his head. "I meant to stay in inns along the way. Hommy deserves better than to cook on campfires."

"It's fine, pet," replied his bride. "The people were so horrid, I'd rather camp."

"I'll tell you plain," said Hamin to Yim. "I was over-joyed to see your Sarf. I'm hoping you'll ride with us to Bremven."

"That's very kind, but . . ."

"Please, Karmamatus," said Hamin. "It would ease Hommy's mind to have a Sarf with us."

Hommy looked at Yim with hopeful eyes that also be-trayed fear. "The wagon's big," she said. "You've never slept on anything as soft as a pile of wool."

Yim knew the decision would be hers. Yim bowed her head toward Hamin. "You honor Karm and us with your kindness."

Hamin grinned. "No, the honor's ours."

As soon as Yim accepted Hamin's offer, she was glad that she did. Traveling with the wagon would simplify her dealings with Honus, for she was certain that Hamin's and Hommy's presence would subdue his feelings, or at least cause him to hide them.

After dinner, Hamin and Hommy bedded in the wagon and Yim joined them. Honus lingered by the fire awhile, giving Yim the hope that he'd keep watch outside. But eventually, he climbed into the wagon. It seemed crowded with four inside, but Hommy was right about sleeping on wool. It was as soft as a feather bed. For Yim, it had the added benefit of smelling like sheep. The Wise Woman occasionally received lambs for her services, and as a child, Yim had cuddled with them, seeking the affection her guardian withheld. The smell evoked pacifying memories that lulled her to sleep.

The following morning, the travelers headed out. Honus rode next to Hamin at the front of the wagon. Yim stayed in the rear with Hommy, who lazed quietly upon the soft cargo. Hommy's silence suited Yim, for there was little she could speak about truthfully, and she would rather not lie. When Yim grew restless, she left to stroll behind the wagon.

Though walking without the pack felt leisurely and the weather was pleasant, Yim's stroll wasn't entirely peaceful. When she passed others on the road, she often encountered hostility. The unpleasantry waxed and waned. There were stretches of road where it was absent.

On one such stretch, Hommy left the wagon to join Yim. "It's nice to have protection," said Hommy. "You must feel safe traveling with a Sarf."

"I do," replied Yim.

"And he's so fond of you."

Yim blushed. "What makes you say that?"

"Any woman could tell," said Hommy. "It's the way he looks at you."

Is it so obvious? Yim wondered, disappointed to have

her conclusion confirmed. Again, she felt foolish for not seeing it earlier.

"Mayhap," said Hommy, giving Yim an earthy look, "you'd like the wagon to yourselves tonight."

"No," said Yim a little too quickly. "I wouldn't dream of inconveniencing you."

"'Tis na problem. Really."

"No," said Yim in a tone she hoped conveyed finality. "I wouldn't think of it. You're with child, and you've been kind enough already."

"You can always change your mind."

"Will this be your first trip to Bremven?" asked Yim, eager to change the subject.

"Aye. I can hardly wait to see it."

"I, too," said Yim. "I'm eager to visit the temple."

"What's it like?"

"Peaceful," replied Yim. "There's a garden in its center with a pond and a rock near the shore. That rock's my favorite place. It's very calming there." Yim acted wistful, as if Honus's memory were her own.

"Tell me more about Bremven."

"I won't spoil its surprises," said Yim. "It's more fun to discover them yourself."

"Hamin says we'll be there in two days," said Hommy excitedly. "There's a whole quarter filled with Averen folk, with a large, fine inn where we'll be welcome. Hamin says they'll treat me like a princess."

"You certainly deserve it."

Hommy beamed. "That's what Hamin says, too."

The two women continued to walk behind the wagon while Yim plied Hommy with questions about Averen. Her curiosity was genuine, and the subject was a safe one. From Hommy's answers, Yim began to envision a rugged highland not unlike her own homeland, folded by many low mountains and populated by hardy, independent folk. Hommy spoke of lakes hidden within steep-sided valleys;

of fierce, snowy winters and brief summers painted with wildflowers; of snug huts tucked among the trees of isolated hollows. Yim perceived Averen's mark on Hommy and Hamin, as she had on Cara and Cronin—a reserve of inner warmth to counter the harshness of the land.

Hommy and Yim talked pleasantly until they approached a small village. There, the enmity that Yim had sensed earlier returned with renewed force. Hostile stares and scornful words soon drove them to the refuge of the wagon. Hommy sat stiffly on the wool, her face anxious and troubled. Yim hugged her and felt her tremble. "It's all right," she cooed. "You're safe. My Sarf is here."

Sitting with Hamin at the front of the wagon, Honus noted the villagers' hostility. He turned to his host and said in a low voice, "When we camp tonight, it should be far from here." Hamin nodded in agreement.

The wagon rolled on through the village. Once Yim and Hommy were hidden from view, the onlookers became silent. None had the courage to harangue a Sarf. Instead, they stared balefully. At the far edge of the settlement stood a tavern. Three rough-looking men sat outside, taking their ale in the afternoon sun. They followed the wagon with hard eyes, and as it passed, they muttered angrily among themselves. They continued their discussion until the travelers were out of sight. Then they gathered their weapons and trailed the wagon.

THIRTY-THREE

HAMIN DROVE his horses for as long as he could, but was forced to stop when evening approached. It would be a dark night. Thick clouds filled the sky, and he knew his team could not find their way on a moonless road. While light still remained, he guided them into a small wood between two large estates. There, he set up camp.

Honus helped tend the horses while Yim and Hommy prepared dinner. Though Hommy wanted Yim to behave as a guest, Yim wouldn't hear of it. After a brief battle of wills, Hommy relented and admitted she was glad for the help. Yim gathered firewood and wild herbs. Afterward, the two women cooked while discussing the merits of various plants for flavoring. Hamin smiled as he watched them. "Somehow," he said to Honus, "I expected a holy person to be different. More distant, perhaps a little cold."

Honus gazed at Yim and smiled also. "A caring heart best serves the goddess."

"I see that now," replied Hamin.

The men joined the women at the campfire. A stew was simmering in the kettle while Hommy stirred it. Yim placed another branch in the fire, then rose. "I think I'll get more wood while there's still light."

The clearing where the wagon stood was surrounded by trees that further dimmed the twilight. As Yim tramped through the undergrowth, she found it increasingly hard to see. Then she heard a furtive noise. Yim stopped and listened. The darkening woods were silent. *Just a squirrel,* she thought. She waited a long moment, but the sound didn't return. Yim hurriedly collected a few more branches and headed for the fire, for the sun had long set and the woods had grown gloomy.

Returning to the circle of light, she found Hamin telling Hommy about the marvels of Bremven. ". . . and wine," he said. "You've never tasted such wine."

"I've never tasted *any* wine," said Hommy.

"Well, soon you will," replied Hamin lovingly. "There is a special kind with bubbles in it. We'll get some at the inn."

"Bubbles in wine!" said Hommy. "Is it sorcery?"

"I do na know," replied Hamin. "Perhaps. If so, it's pleasant magic."

Honus turned to his host. "When you go to Bremven, perhaps you might deal with Commodus on the Street of Looms. He's an old friend of mine."

"I know of him," said Hamin. "He has a name for honest dealing, but he buys cloth, na raw wool."

"Well, that shows how much a Sarf knows about trade," said Honus. "Commodus is a good man. I thought he might help you."

"He may yet," said Hamin. "Hommy is gifted at the loom. Perhaps, next year, I'll have cloth to sell." He beamed at his wife. "A few bolts of her plaids would be worth more than a wagonload of wool—and far easier to carry."

"You'll have me work my fingers numb," teased Hommy.

Hamin seized her hand and kissed her fingertips with clumsy earnestness. "Never, Dearest. You're my true treasure. Besides," he said with a gleam in his eye, "our daughter will help you soon enough."

Yim watched Hommy basking in Hamin's love and envied her uncomplicated life. *Soon she'll be drinking wine with bubbles, while I . . .* An inexplicable chill came over Yim. She fought to dispel it, concentrating on the present.

The warmth of the fire, the aroma of the stew, and her hosts' good natures gradually calmed her. Yim's fears for the future faded, leaving only an echo of unease.

Dinner was festive and relaxed. Honus and Hamin regaled Hommy with tales of Bremven's wonders until the young woman's eyes shone with excitement and expectation. Yim listened with equal wonder, though she tried to hide it. Eventually, the fire burned to embers and the soft wool beckoned. Everyone entered the wagon and dropped off to sleep.

Something struck the wagon's wooden side, disturbing Yim's sleep, but it was Honus's reaction that waked her. He leapt from the wagon, drew his sword, and disappeared into the night. Yim sat up and peered about. A pale, flickering light illuminated the campsite for a moment, then suddenly went out. She heard movement through the undergrowth around the camp. Yim cautiously poked her head out the back of the wagon to peer into the darkness. She could see nothing. Behind her, she heard Hommy and Hamin stirring.

A flame arched out of the woods like a tiny comet. It struck the side of the wagon and remained there. Yim saw it was an arrow with its shaft wrapped in a burning rag. "Someone's trying to set us on fire!" she exclaimed. "Quick! Hand me the water skin!" Yim felt the water skin being thrust into her hands. She grabbed it and descended to the ground.

The arrow was too high to reach. Yim thought she might climb to the wagon's roof and douse the flames from above. As she looked for a means to ascend, she heard other arrows—unlit and invisible—strike the ground and wagon. Then someone crashed into her, sent her sprawling, and landed atop her back. Yim was knocked breathless, and as she gasped for air, the person seized her and rolled until they both lay beneath the wagon. Then Yim heard

Honus's urgent whisper, "Stay in the shadow. Don't move
The flaming arrows are for lighting targets." Before Yin
could respond, Honus rolled from safety and sprang to his
feet.

Honus severed the burning arrow's shaft with his sword
caught it midair, and threw it into the dark. The flame died
out, but not before it illuminated the figure of a man
among the horses. Honus sped in his direction. He
crouched low as he advanced, for it was so dark that only
things silhouetted against the night sky were visible. There
was the sound of stamping hooves and the uneasy neighing
of the skittish steeds. Honus advanced toward the sound
He saw the dark shapes of the two horses and also a
smaller shape in front of them. He stabbed at it and felt the
resistance of flesh. Someone moaned and struggled at the
end of his blade. The struggling ceased, and what had been
a man became only a dead weight. Honus pulled his sword
free. There was a soft thud. Honus groped for the body in
the darkness. He touched a leg and quickly felt his way up
to the neck. He hacked it, just to be sure.

As quickly as that was done, he scanned about for the
flame that had lit the arrow. He knew a covered lantern hid
the fire. Such lanterns were not entirely invisible; they required air holes to feed the flame. Honus saw a row of faint
red points in the darkness. They weren't close. Cautiously
he advanced toward the tiny lights. Both he and the
archer—or archers—were blind in the dark. That meant
the people around the wagon were safe. Honus listened
He could hear no sounds of retreat. That foretold another
attack.

As Honus quietly approached the dull glow, it blossomed into a yellow flame as the lantern was opened and
an arrow lit. Its light revealed two men. They stood in thick
undergrowth. The burning arrow arched into the campsite
and the enemy was cloaked again in darkness. Honus had

ixed the men's position in his mind and charged toward it. He could hear bowstrings twang in the night. Then, Honus was upon his quarry, slashing at shadows. He groped as much as he attacked with his blade. It was fighting blindly—clumsy and desperate. Honus crouched near the ground and swung his sword like a scythe. He felt weeds and saplings part against his blade before it struck something more substantial. A man screamed, and Honus swung in the direction of the sound. The sword struck flesh and bone. A second cry resounded, one that mingled fear with pain. Another blow cut the scream short. It was followed by the noise of the second man blundering off into the darkness.

Retreat was Honus's safest option, but he had Hommy and Hamin to consider. He doubted they would abandon their wagonload of goods. But if they remained, they would be vulnerable to the surviving archer. He need only kill their horses to render them immobile. Then, at the very least, they would suffer ruin. Honus realized he had to track down the last attacker.

He moved toward the sound of the fleeing man as quietly as he could, feeling the way with his bare feet as well as his hands. As he feared, his foe soon stopped moving. Honus stopped also and strained to hear any noise that might betray his enemy's position. Ahead, he detected the metallic sound of a sword being slipped from its scabbard. He moved in its direction.

From the campsite came a cry of despair that set Honus's heart pounding. For a moment, he was torn between rushing to the campsite and continuing his hunt. Then his training asserted itself, and he concentrated on his quarry. Honus heard snickering in the dark and thought of a ploy to flush out his foe.

"If the Devourer loves power," Honus said, "then he loves me. I've slain two of you." As soon as he spoke, Honus quietly changed his position.

"I've bagged prizes also," said a voice. Honus moved toward the sound.

"That was no real fighting."

"I'm not done yet. The bitches were only target practice."

Honus's heart froze, and he found himself straining to hear Yim's voice coming from the campsite. All he could hear were Hamin's sobs. Honus struggled with his despair and fury. He took a deep breath, suppressed all emotion, and focused on the task at hand.

"Women are always easy prey," said Honus.

"That doesn't diminish the fun," returned the voice.

With the last reply, Honus gained a general notion of where his opponent was. He painstakingly moved in that direction by an indirect route, taking care to be silent. His toes touched a short, stout branch. Honus picked it up and continued his slow advance. As time passed, Honus's silence began to unnerve his foe. "Did you care for one of the whores?" he asked. Honus didn't reply. "Was it the fat one or the slender one? Not that it matters. I got them both."

Honus closed in on the taunting voice. He tossed the branch so it crashed into the undergrowth behind where he thought the man hid. The invisible man slashed the bushes where the branch had landed. Quickly and lethally, Honus attacked. It was over in two blows.

Once the man was dead, Honus rushed to the campsite and was greeted by a stark scene. Hamin sat upon the ground, illuminated by a burning arrow. His face was a mask of disbelief and sorrow. Hommy lay before him, an arrow sprouting from her chest like an evil weed. She bore an expression of surprise as she stared blankly at the starless sky.

Yim knelt close by, facing away from Honus. A broad bloodstain was spreading over the back of her tunic. She seemed oblivious of it and everything else except the dead woman before her.

"Yim!" cried Honus.

Hamin seemed barely aware of Honus's arrival, but Yim turned at the sound of her name. Her grief nearly matched Hamin's. In a flat voice she said, "She left the wagon. Before I could warn her to get down, she was . . . was . . ." Yim began to sob.

"Do you know you're wounded?"

Yim appeared confused. "I am?"

Honus pulled up her tunic to reveal where an arrowhead had grazed her, leaving a long, ugly gash beneath her shoulder blade. Honus lowered the tunic. "I'll need to take care of that."

"Why?"

"So it'll heal."

"No," said Yim. "Why Hommy?"

Honus stood mute, but the mention of Hommy's name roused Hamin like a slap across the face. He stared at Yim with such intensity that she shrank from his gaze. "You blessed my child!" he said. "Is this how Karm shows her favor?"

THIRTY-FOUR

Only Yim's sobbing broke the awkward silence following Hamin's outburst. In the stillness, Honus ministered to the living with the sangfroid of one accustomed to violent death. First, he rekindled the campfire. From his pack he took a leather pouch and his small brass pot. He filled the pot with water and set it on the fire. Then he turned to Yim. "When this boils, I'll make medicines to tend your wound." Yim simply nodded.

Then Honus sat beside Hamin, who had ceased glaring at Yim. "Hamin, I'm truly sorry. The men who did this are slain."

"It will na bring her back."

"No, it won't." Honus paused. "Shall I pull the arrow from her?"

"That would be good of you. I can na bear to do it."

Honus drew his dagger. "You should look away." The arrow had pierced Hommy's sternum and he feared its head would have to be cut out. This was necessary because Averen folk believed that spirits could not travel westward while iron remained in the body. Honus made quick work of the gruesome task and tossed the arrow into the flames.

"Hommy will rest on wool," said Hamin. "She liked that. I'll get her blanket. Then could you help me lift her into the wagon?"

"Aren't you going to bury her?" asked Honus.

"Nay. I said I'd take her to Bremven, and that I'll do. The coins that would have bought her wine will pay for her funeral instead." Hamin went into the wagon and returned with a plaid blanket to be his wife's shroud. Even by firelight, Honus could tell it was skillfully woven, and he wondered if it was Hommy's work. Hamin closed his wife's eyes, tenderly kissed her, and began to weep again. Then, with Honus's help, he wrapped her body and placed it in the wagon.

Honus returned from the wagon alone, carrying a blanket and two cups. He found Yim staring at the fire with a distraught expression, tears freely flowing down her face. She seemed almost as hurt by Hamin's outburst as by her wound. But with Honus's arrival, her injury seized her attention. "Blood's flowing down my back," she said in a frightened voice.

Knowing that being unable to see her injury fed Yim's fears, Honus replied as calmly as possible. "It's a graze, not a gaping hole." Then, as Hamin's sobs broke the night's stillness, Honus spread the blanket on the ground near the fire. "Take off your tunic and lie so your back's lit by the fire," said Honus. "I'll need light to tend your wound."

Yim complied, and Honus covered her with the blanket so only her back was exposed. Yim lay quietly, but clearly apprehensive, while Honus set to work. From the leather pouch, he took two vials. One contained dried herbs and the other a dark powder. He put some herbs in one cup and a pinch of the powder in the other, then filled both with boiling water. He cut a strip of cloth from the hem of Yim's tunic and put it in the pot, which he refilled with water and set back on the fire. "After this boils," he said, "I'll clean your wound."

"Is . . . is it bad?" asked Yim.

"No, but it'll need stitches."

"Stitches!"

"Calm yourself," said Honus. "I was taught more skills than killing. I've sewn many a wound, even some of my own." He gently rubbed Yim's back, keeping well away from the oozing gash. "The herbs make a drink to ease the pain. It'll be ready soon."

Honus continued to touch Yim, as much to calm himself as her. When the cloth had boiled awhile, he fished it out of the pot with his dagger and let it cool. Then he cleaned around the gash. Yim tensed and her breathing came in short gasps, but she said nothing. Honus peered at the wound. It was still bleeding, but more slowly. He could see no bone. "You're lucky," he said.

"I don't feel lucky."

Honus took the cup that contained the leaves. "Drink this."

Yim raised herself on one elbow, wincing as she moved, and quickly gulped down the brew. Then she lay down and Honus wiped away a fresh flow of blood. "That tasted terrible," she said.

"Hope that you taste it only once."

Yim lay quietly awhile before saying, "The ground . . . it's moving."

"That's the brew working," said Honus. "Stay still."

A short while later, Yim moaned. "Honus," she said thickly, "I don't feel so good."

Honus rubbed her back again to calm her. "It'll pass," he said. "Then you'll feel drunk."

"Drunk!" Yim started to laugh, but winced instead. "Drunk! I've never been drunk in my life. Wha' ya mean . . . uh . . ." Yim paused as if she'd forgotten what she was saying. "I'm . . . I'm not . . ." She gasped. "I can't feel my feet!" Yim started to turn around, but Honus gently, yet firmly, pressed her down.

"Lie still."

"All right, I won't move." Yim began to giggle. "Why . . . I . . . I can't move! I'm all numb! Like when he cut me."

"Like when *who* cut you?"

"Oh, you know, silly. That man in the castle."

"Oh, him," replied Honus, hiding his interest. "I remember now. Why did he do that?"

"Wanted my soul," replied Yim in a slurred voice. "Wanted yers, too."

"But you saved me."

"Yeah," said Yim groggily.

"How?"

Yim mumbled something incomprehensible and passed out.

I made that brew too strong, thought Honus. But when he dabbed the solution made from the powder into Yim's wound, he was glad she was unconscious, for she moaned as the liquid foamed up pink from the gash. Honus washed a curved needle and a strand of gut in the same liquid. He closed the wound with a series of neat stitches and washed it once more with the cleansing solution. Carefully and tenderly, Honus wrapped the blanket more securely around Yim. As he bent to lift her into the wagon, he kissed her

cheek. When he placed her upon the wool, he noticed
Hamin. He had ceased sobbing and was sitting upright,
watching over Hommy in the dark.

"You should try to rest," said Honus.

" 'Tis na possible. I doubt I'll ever rest again."

Thinking of Theodus, Honus replied, "I know it feels
that way, but you will. Hommy would want it so."

Honus stood watch for the rest of the night, though all
their assailants were dead. His guard would not bring
Hommy back, nor erase Yim's pain or prevent her scar.
Honus kept watch as penance, for he saw the night's disas-
ter as his fault. The familiarity of his homeland and his desire to sleep close to Yim had caused him to ignore signs of
danger. He felt certain that the attack would have failed if
he'd been on guard. Honus resolved never to make that
mistake again.

In the darkness, his thoughts turned to Yim's revelations. Most were not surprises. Honus had already surmised that Yim had rescued him from the dark man and
that she had received a paralyzing wound in the process.
Still, he hadn't expected to hear his deductions confirmed
by her own lips. Her statement that the man was after their
souls was news. Honus wished he could have learned
more, but that opportunity was gone. Yim would not remember what she had said, and Honus decided not to
bring the matter up until she was settled at the temple. Until then, he wouldn't pry into her mysteries.

At first light, Hamin left the wagon to tend the horses.
Honus went over to help. By the dull look in Hamin's eyes,
Honus guessed he had not slept. "I want to get far from
here," Hamin said. "We'll eat on the road."

"Before we leave, I should hide the slain men," said
Honus.

While Hamin hitched the horses to the wagon, Honus
found the three corpses, dragged them far from the road,

and hastily covered them. Yim was still asleep when they headed out, but woke when they reached the paved road and the wagon wheels rumbled on its stones. She rose, pale and bleary-eyed, and made her way to the front of the wagon, still wrapped in the blanket. "Are we traveling already?"

"Hamin is anxious to leave," said Honus. "How does your back feel?"

Yim withdrew one hand inside the blanket to touch her wound. "You sew neatly," she said. "It's sore, but I guess that's to be expected."

"I'd like to look at it."

Yim turned her back toward him and lowered the blanket. Honus couldn't help noting how lovely she looked, wound and all. Then he examined the gash and was pleased by what he saw. "It's mending well."

"My first scar," said Yim. "Though I suppose you're unimpressed. You've lost count of yours."

"So have you," replied Honus. "Have you forgotten the sword cut on your foot?"

Yim acted as though she hadn't heard him. "I should get dressed. Will you look away?"

Honus withdrew and joined Hamin at the front of the wagon while Yim dressed. When he glanced back at her, she was asleep again. Neither Honus nor Hamin had slept since the attack. Honus was trained for privation and remained alert. Hamin seemed to have spent all his strength hitching the horses. He stared at the road with vacant eyes, silent and withdrawn. When Honus took the reins from him, Hamin didn't seem to notice. Honus perceived an emptiness in his companion that went beyond exhaustion. It was as if Hamin's spirit were seeking Hommy's on the Dark Path.

They traveled until noon without any incidents on the road. Honus's chief concern was Hamin. He refused to rest, though he was incapable of guiding the team. Honus had the self-discipline to stay awake, but he realized he was losing his edge. Even a Sarf needed sleep. If he were to keep watch through the night, he would have to get some. When they stopped to rest the horses, Yim was awake, and Honus asked her to drive the team in the afternoon. She reacted with an uneasy look. "Will you show me how, first?"

"You're a peddler's daughter," said Honus. "Surely your father had a wagon."

"He did, but I never drove it. I was his princess."

"So you've claimed," replied Honus. "Still, I'd think you'd have picked up the skill by watching."

"I didn't."

Honus regarded Yim skeptically, but shrugged. "Well, it's easy enough to learn."

Hamin wouldn't leave his seat at the front of the wagon, so when Yim took the reins, Honus had to crouch behind her to give instructions. These were simple, since the horses virtually guided themselves. Honus retreated to the rear for a nap, leaving Yim alone with Hamin. She, like Honus, readily perceived Hamin's surrender to despair. He didn't respond to Yim's attempts at conversation, and after a while, she gave up.

The region Yim drove through became more populated. Villages gave way to ancient-looking towns, and the land between them was thick with small holdings. Traffic increased. Although most of the folk she passed were not overtly hostile, Yim was able to see beneath appearances. She often sensed hatred directed toward her and Hamin. The fact that people took care to hide it made her especially wary.

Yim didn't waken Honus until the sun neared the horizon. Then he took the reins and drove until he found a suitable place to camp. Though it was swampy, no settlement lay close by, which was what he wanted. Honus drove the horses over sodden, reedy ground until the road was out of sight. He halted in a copse of willows on the shore of a stagnant pond. Dead trees stood in the dark water, and while Honus unhitched and fed the horses, Yim removed her sandals and waded out to break off branches. The effort proved far more painful than she anticipated, but she returned with enough wood for a small fire. Honus met her when she returned to camp, wet and muddy to the knees.

"Why did you do that?" he asked in a scolding tone. "You're injured."

"I thought a fire and warm food might raise Hamin's spirits."

"Yim . . ."

"I'm worried about him, Honus."

Honus lowered his voice. "I am, too. He doesn't wish to live."

"He'll get Hommy to Bremven. I'm sure of it."

"Yes," agreed Honus. "And after her funeral, he'll get himself killed. He'll pick a fight he cannot win or do something equally rash. I've seen it before."

Yim shook her head sorrowfully, certain that Honus was right.

Yim cooked a meal, which she forced Hamin to eat. He ate mechanically before entering the wagon. There he succumbed to exhaustion and fell into a fitful sleep. Yim and Honus remained by the fire, where Yim busied herself with brushing the dried mud from her feet.

Whenever Yim looked up, she saw Honus watching her. His expression was different and Yim suspected that her brush with death had given his feelings greater urgency. Whatever the cause, the intensity in Honus's gaze flustered her. It seemed as raw as Hamin's grief. Yim found little

comfort in Honus's look. His ardor felt like another burden upon her journey.

"When . . . when do you think we'll reach Bremven?"
Yim asked in an attempt at casual conversation.

"The day after tomorrow, I think. We may even see a
sign of the temple next evening. There's a flame upon its
mount that can be viewed from afar."

"The temple," said Yim in a distant voice. "Now that
we're so close, I feel nervous. I can't imagine how I'll fit
in."

"You were meant for the place. You'll soon feel at
home."

"Will . . . will you be there, too?"

"For a while. The matching of Bearer and Sarf can't be
hurried. My Bearer may not even be grown yet."

"You might choose a child?"

Honus smiled at the question. "I'll choose no one. My
Bearer will choose me."

"But how?"

"Karm acts through the Seers to guide the selection. The
process can take years."

Yim could tell that Honus was waiting for her reaction.
Though not knowing whether she was disappointed or
pleased by the news, she chose the polite reply. "I'm glad
you won't leave soon."

"I also."

They shared another awkward silence. Yim resumed
rubbing the dirt from her feet, avoiding Honus's gaze.
When she was done, she rose to retreat into the wagon. "I
know I've rested most of the day, but I'm tired."

"You have a wound," replied Honus. "Pain exhausts the
body." He rose also, but didn't move toward the wagon.
"Sleep well. I'll keep watch."

"You aren't going to sleep?"

"I will a bit. But lightly, so no foe can surprise us." With
that, Honus stepped from the circle of light and blended

into the shadows. Yim entered the wagon where two bodies lay, one at peace and the other in torment.

Honus sat motionless against a tree. Wrapped in his
cloak, he was a shadow within shadows. The night was
clear and lit by the moon. From where Honus sat, he could
both peer beneath the wagon and see through its rear to the
sky beyond its open front. No one could enter it unde-
tected.

As Honus sat alone in the darkness, he thought of Yim.
He had sensed her unease that evening, but he had been unable to take his eyes away. Shyly rubbing her soiled feet,
Yim had looked younger than her years—a mere girl.
Honus tried to reconcile that vision with his conviction
that Yim was a woman of power and holiness. He found
that he couldn't. The discrepancy made Yim more endear-
ing.

The night was old when Honus spied movement. Yim
peered from the wagon and glanced about before retreat-
ing into its interior. There Honus could discern the silhouette of her upright form. She appeared to be sitting on her
heels. Honus was curious, but not alarmed. He remained
still and watched. Yim remained still also.

Nothing happened for a long while, and despite his best
efforts, Honus grew drowsy. Then it seemed that a second
form arose next to Yim. Honus was uncertain what he saw,
for it was nebulous—more like black vapor than anything
solid. Honus rubbed his eyes to clear his vision, and after
he did, he briefly glimpsed a luminous form. It resembled
Hommy, nude with a tiny infant in her arms.

Honus rubbed his eyes again. Peering into the wagon, he
saw nothing unnatural and suspected that he had been
dreaming. As he watched, Yim knelt down to embrace
Hamin. Then Honus heard a quiet voice. It was too faint
for him to make out what was being said, but the words
sounded soothing. He heard Hamin's voice next. At first, it

was raw with pain, but it gradually softened and became weeping. Yim continued to hold Hamin. She rocked him slowly, as if comforting a child. Eventually there were no sounds at all.

The moon was setting when Yim lowered Hamin down upon the wool and lay down herself. Honus didn't stir. Instead, he sat and wondered what had transpired.

THIRTY-FIVE

WHEN HAMIN rose at dawn, Honus discerned by his vigor that he had undergone a change. It made Honus curious to discover its nature. He approached Hamin, who was tending the horses. Hamin appeared somber, but his vacant look was gone.

"Were you able to rest?" asked Honus.

"Aye," replied Hamin. "Far better than I expected." After a pause, he added, "I had a dream."

"A dream?"

"Aye. I saw Hommy. Our child also. They seemed as real to me as you do now."

"Really?"

"Hommy spoke and asked me to honor her by living. She said time passes differently in the Dark Realm. Even if I come to her as an old man, it'll be a short wait for her. How can that be?"

"I'm not one to answer such a question."

"While I do na understand it, I know she spoke true," said Hamin. "My Dearest feared I might do something rash."

"Will you?"

"Nay. Na now."

"I think she loved you greatly to visit you like that."

" 'Twas Karm's doing," said Hamin. "I take back my hard words. She's the goddess of compassion."

"You speak truly."

Hamin nodded. "I wish to make an early start. When we reach a village, I'll buy bread for our breakfast."

Honus helped hitch up the horses. As soon as they were on the road, he went to rest in the wagon's rear. There he found Yim in a deep sleep. She was shivering and deathly pale. He touched her hand, and it felt icy. The discovery made Honus question whether he had merely dreamed that Yim invoked Hommy's spirit. Judging from Yim's appearance, he suspected that he had not and she had undergone some ordeal. Honus wondered what toll it had exacted and concluded it had been a heavy one. Before he lay down, he wrapped his cloak around Yim.

Honus's thoughts returned to the previous night. He had heard tales of Seers who could invoke the dead, and he knew all Seers were taught the necessary meditations. Despite that learning, no living Seer had accomplished the feat. The ability was a gift that required more than knowledge. Some said it was a blessing from the goddess, while others claimed it was a curse. Looking at Yim's face, haggard even in sleep, he suspected it was both. *Did she do for Mam what she has done for Hamin? If so, I have cause for regret.* The recollection of his righteous anger and of Yim shivering on the moldy hay disturbed him, making it difficult to fall asleep.

Honus woke from his nap when Hamin stopped to buy bread. Yim still slept, but some color had returned to her face. Honus rose and moved to the front of the wagon. He was sitting there when Hamin returned, bearing a large loaf of bread.

"Has Yim arisen yet?" asked Hamin.

"She sleeps still."

Hamin climbed onto the wagon and turned to look at Yim. "She seems too frail to carry your burden," he said. "I imagined a Bearer would be tougher."

"If you think she's weak, then you're deceived," replied Honus. "She's more powerful than I."

Hamin grinned, assuming Honus was jesting with him. When he saw that Honus was earnest, he turned serious. "Such things are beyond my understanding."

"Mine also," replied Honus.

It was nearly noon when Yim finally awoke. When she sat up, Honus silently handed her part of a loaf. Yim was glad that he didn't ask why she slept so late or why her hands trembled, for she was too tired to come up with a convincing story. Both were consequences of raising Hommy's spirit, which being only recently deceased, had clung to Yim overlong. The results had been devastating. Immediately after Hommy's departure, Yim was nearly overwhelmed by the effort of living. Beating her heart was exhausting and every breath wore at her. When Yim was finally accustomed again to life, she still suffered from other aftereffects. The Dark Path's coldness lingered in her flesh, and the memories of the dead troubled her thoughts. These were extremely disturbing, for only the most recent and the most traumatic surfaced. They flitted into her mind— moments of anguish or terror—and departed before she fully comprehended what she had experienced. Yim had lain awake, buffeted by frightening perceptions, until they grew fainter and more sporadic. Only then was she able to fall into a deathlike sleep.

Yim ate silently, focusing on basic sensations—the taste of the bread, the softness of the wool, and the warmth of the air. Through that means, she kept the disturbing intrusions at bay. When she had finished eating, Honus said to her, "I'd like to see your wound."

Without replying, Yim lay facedown upon the wool. Honus climbed down from the front seat, knelt beside her, and pulled up her shirt to expose her back. "This is healing well," he said. "More quickly than I imagined. When you get to the temple, a healer should remove the stitches."

Honus didn't immediately cover Yim's back, but softly rested one hand upon it. Yim's whole attention went to his touch. It felt warm and exquisitely delicate, a sensation purely of the living world. Slowly, Honus's fingertips moved up and down her back, tracing a line parallel to her spine. When he lifted his hand, Yim lay perfectly still, hoping his fingers would return. They did not. Honus pulled down her shirt and left. Yim remained prone upon the wool awhile and realized that Honus's touch had banished the intruding memories.

Yim put on her sandals and climbed from the wagon to walk. It felt good to move about, and the air was free of the faint odor emanating from Hommy's shroud. Since the highway was busy with traffic, Yim stayed behind the wagon to keep out of its way. She had never seen such a densely populated land, nor one that bore the look of centuries of habitation. To her eyes, the old buildings and the ancient towns were marvels. As she gazed at them, she felt provincial. Yet her glimpses of the dead's memories had given her another view of the surrounding land. She had seen its unrest. Malice moved among the people, and the ancient stone walls hid—but didn't restrain—its spreading poison.

After Yim had walked awhile, Honus alighted from the wagon and approached her. He didn't assume the customary position of a Sarf. Instead, he walked beside her. It reminded Yim that their roles of Sarf and Bearer were only pretense and the pretense would end soon.

"Did you sleep well?' asked Honus.

"I slept long, but poorly."

"It's not restful to sleep with a ripening corpse."

"No, it isn't."

"Hamin should move Hommy off the wool. Otherwise, his goods might get spoiled."

"He doesn't care," said Yim. "This is his last trip to Bremven."

"He told me he'd do nothing rash."

"He won't be rash," replied Yim. "He has sworn to take Hommy's ashes back to Averen and call upon her mother and sister."

"This is news to me," said Honus. "When did he tell you this?"

"He talks in his sleep."

"I see," replied Honus, sounding unconvinced. They walked awhile in silence before he said, "You don't trust me."

Yim glanced his way and saw Honus studying her. She averted her eyes. "Honus, you *bought* me. I'm here through compulsion, not trust."

"I've kept my oath to you."

"You have."

"Therefore, don't I deserve your trust? Look at me, Yim."

Yim turned to face Honus and made her eyes impenetrable. "I don't know what you're talking about."

"I think you do."

"Trust goes both ways, Honus. Do you trust me? Would you set me free without conditions?" She waited for an answer and got none. "I thought not."

Toward day's end, the road climbed a rise, and Bremven was visible in the distance. It lay beyond the Yorvern River, covering five hills with stone buildings. To Yim, it was an awe-inspiring sight. Before darkness obscured the view, they approached close enough for Honus to point out some landmarks—the emperor's palace, the residential and commercial districts, the riverfront harbor, and upon the highest hill, Karm's temple.

"I see no temple," said Yim, "only a bare, rocky cliff."

"It harmonizes with its surroundings," replied Honus. "See that cleft in the rock? That's the temple entrance. Within that cleft are huge bronze doors, green with age."

Yim peered at the hilltop, trying to discern human handiwork, but couldn't. "I expected something grander."

"I think you'll find it grand," said Honus. "Remember, Karm's the Goddess of the Balance. Her temple celebrates nature rather than seeking to dominate it."

"What's that huge black building near the palace, the one with all the sharp-pointed spires?"

"That one's new to me. It must be the Devourer's temple that Hamin spoke of."

Yim gazed at the structure and was dismayed by how it dominated the city. "It looks hideous, almost cruel."

"Then it's fittingly constructed."

Hamin drove his horses until they reached an open field on the outskirts of the city. Scattered about it were numerous wagons and carts with cooking fires burning between them. Yim and Honus, who had continued to travel on foot, watched a man emerge from a small shack and approach Hamin. They talked briefly before Hamin handed him some coins. The man called out, and two more men exited the shack. One led Hamin to an empty spot in the field. The other followed with a wheelbarrow filled with firewood and fodder.

Honus and Hamin tended the horses while Yim lit a fire. She was heading to the wagon for provisions when Hamin called out, "You'll na cook tonight, Yim." As if on cue, a woman appeared with a handcart laden with food and drink. Hamin went over to her and purchased three large, flat loaves, upon which the woman piled an aromatic mixture of cubed meat and vegetables. Hamin also bought a large bottle of wine. He handed loaves to Honus and Yim while the woman opened the wine. When she departed,

Hamin said, "Tonight we'll feast in honor of Hommy and Honus."

"Hommy deserves honor," said Honus. "I don't."

"You avenged her murder," said Hamin. "Without you, I'd be slain, too."

"If I had more foresight," said Honus, "she'd still be alive."

"True," replied Hamin, "but na man has foresight. It's said na one may know his or her fate, na even Seers."

"That's true," said Honus after seeming to reflect a moment. "Karm hides those things that concern each person most."

"Then do na blame yourself, Honus. You did your best, and I'm grateful." Hamin went to the wagon, brought out three bowls, and filled them with wine. He raised his high and said, "To Hommy and Honus."

Yim took a sip and made a face. She had never tasted wine before, and it was not what she expected. She looked over her bowl to see Honus grinning at her.

"Did you think it'd taste like grapes?" he asked.

"Yes," she said, taking a second, tentative sip. "But it's not bad, once you appreciate it for itself."

"Understanding a thing's true nature is the key to appreciation," replied Honus. "That goes for persons, too." He gave her a meaningful look.

Yim sighed. *Not again*, she thought. *I'm tired of his innuendoes*. She turned her attention to the food instead.

The meal was delicious, and it quickly occupied everyone's attention. Hamin paused from eating only to refill the bowls with wine. After her initial disappointment, Yim discovered that she liked the wine. Hamin was a diligent host, and he made sure her bowl was never empty. Soon, she felt relaxed and happy. The night was clear and the lights of Bremven blazed in competition with the stars. Yim gazed at the scene in tipsy ecstasy. "Oh! It's so . . . so *pretty*!"

Honus glanced toward the city and nodded. He had drunk but a sip from his bowl. "It is."

Yim continued to stare at Bremven. "But where's the light you said . . . you know . . . the one on the temple? I don't see it."

Honus peered into the darkness and looked puzzled. "I don't see it either."

"Probably something's blocking our view," said Hamin. "But what's one missing light? 'Tis a grand sight. I only wish Hommy . . ."

Yim's loud sob interrupted him. Both Hamin and Honus turned to see tears welling in eyes that only moments before had shone with delight. "Oh Hommy," Yim whimpered before dissolving into racking sobs. She tried to say something else, but her bawling made it unintelligible.

Honus wrapped an arm around Yim, and she leaned to bury her face in his chest. Her hands clutched his shirt as she dampened it with tears. "I fear," said Honus to Hamin over Yim's sobbing, "that you were overgenerous in your pouring. She's unaccustomed to drink."

"Drunk or na," replied Hamin, "she honors Hommy with her tears." His own voice had turned husky with grief and his eyes glistened in the firelight. "I should be to bed. There's much to do tomorrow." He rose and entered the wagon.

Yim's sobbing gradually subsided and, as it did, her embarrassment grew. *I've upset Hamin,* she thought with dismay. She was also chagrined that, once again, she had sought refuge in Honus's arms. Yim pulled away and wiped her face with her sleeve. "You must think I'm a fool."

"No. You've shown a kind heart."

Yim didn't reply, and Honus dropped the subject. He yawned and said, "They post guards here, so I'll sleep easier tonight." Then he crawled under the wagon and wrapped himself in his cloak.

Yim walked over to where Honus lay and knelt down. "Aren't you going to sleep in the wagon?" she whispered.

"I'd rather not sleep next to a ripening corpse."

Yim remained kneeling, undecided where to sleep. Her feelings toward Honus pulled her in opposite directions. His love was unsettling and inconvenient. On the other hand, he offered protection and eased her loneliness. Sometimes Honus seemed safe, and sometimes he seemed the opposite. *Which is he?* Yim wondered. She was in no state to decide. Nevertheless, she took off her sandals and crawled beside him.

THIRTY·SIX

YIM OPENED her eyes to see a pair of bare feet on frost-covered ground. They were spattered with gore. She looked from under the wagon and saw Karm, her white robe still dark with blood. The goddess stepped back and made a beckoning gesture with a red-stained hand. Then she turned and walked away. Yim left the warmth of the cloak she shared with Honus and followed. Although the sun had not yet risen, people were already stirring. None seemed to notice Karm or her.

Karm reached the empty road and turned to face Yim, who immediately knelt before her. Yim gazed up at the sad-faced goddess and waited for her to speak. Karm said nothing, but there was something in her expression that encouraged Yim to ask the question that had troubled her ever since the last vision.

"Goddess," whispered Yim, "whose blood is this?"

"Yours."

"Mine?" said Yim in alarm.

"Mingled with the blood of countless others."

"But why is it upon you?"

"Because you've gained the wisdom to see it."

Yim was perplexed by this response, but dared not say so. Instead, she humbly bowed her head. "What do you wish me to do?"

"What's necessary."

"Do you mean bear a child?"

"Not yet."

"Then, what?"

"You already know."

"I don't," cried Yim. "I truly don't!"

"Don't what?" asked Honus as he gently shook Yim. "Why are you shouting?"

Yim lay beneath the wagon, next to Honus. She was surprised to find herself there, and for a moment, she looked at him in confusion. "I . . . I had a dream," she replied, "but I've already forgotten it."

The wagon above them creaked as Hamin rose and climbed down. "Since everyone's up, we might as well head out. Bremven's gate opens at dawn."

Most of the other travelers were preparing to leave also. Hamin hitched the horses and went to find the woman who sold food and drink. He returned with a loaf of bread and an earthenware jug filled with hot, spiced tea. Yim drank the tea gratefully, for she was chilled to the bone. The drink brought a bit of warmth and eased her headache from the wine, but she still ached from the cold. Her discomfort seemed proof that her conversation with the goddess hadn't been a dream. Yim wished that it had been. *It made as little sense as a dream,* she thought. *Why can't Karm speak plainly?*

"You look glum," said Hamin, "for someone returning home."

"I'm not glum," she replied, "just tired."

"Would you like to ride beside me?" asked Hamin. "It'll be your last chance."

"Thank you, I would."

When Hamin came back from returning the tea jug, he found Yim sitting in the wagon's front, shivering beneath her cloak. Taking the reins, Hamin sat beside her. Then he spoke to Honus, who was sitting in the rear. "Would you hand Yim a blanket? It's a chill morning."

Honus passed a blanket forward and Yim wrapped herself in it. Hamin flicked the reins and they were off. Fog had risen from the river, obscuring the city. The highway disappeared into a gray void. After they traveled in the dank mist awhile, shapes materialized ahead. At first, Yim thought they were trees flanking the road, yet as they came nearer, Yim saw that she had been mistaken. What had appeared to be tree trunks were stout poles. They were not crowned with leaves, but with hanging corpses. There were men, women, and even children—so many that they formed thick layers. Yim closed her eyes in horror. "What is this ghastly thing?"

"Emperor Morvus's idea of justice," replied Hamin.

Yim kept her eyes squeezed tight. "Tell me when we're past them." Although she couldn't see the dead, the damp air was heavy with their odor and the call of crows assaulted her ears. She felt colder than ever.

Hamin wrapped an arm around her quaking shoulders. "I forgot this sight is new to you. Theric was emperor when you were last here."

When Yim heard the sounds of water, Hamin said, "We're past them now." Yim opened her eyes and saw that they were on a bridge. It was broader than the one at the Bridge Inn and could easily accommodate two passing wagons. Soon, the high walls of the city and the tall arch of the gateway loomed out of the fog. They drove past two sleepy soldiers who barely seemed to glance at them.

Yim peered about in wide-eyed amazement. Everything seemed gigantic, beginning with the huge, ironclad gate. She had to remind herself that she was pretending to be returning home and must hide her wonder. Yim didn't have to keep up the charade for long, because Honus soon grabbed the pack and alighted from the wagon. "Our paths diverge here," he said to Hamin. Yim climbed down to the road and the three said their good-byes.

As Yim watched Hamin drive away, Honus started to shoulder the pack. "Don't," said Yim. "That's my job."

"Your wound . . ."

"It won't bother me."

"You say that without a pack resting on it."

"It's important that I carry it. Didn't Theodus say it was Karm's will?"

Honus gave Yim a dubious look, but he handed her the pack. Yim shouldered it, forcing herself not to wince as she did so.

Honus watched her carefully. "Are you sure you can do this?"

"Yes, if we walk slowly."

Honus assumed the customary position of a Sarf and began to walk up the street. Yim couldn't see his face, but he moved with a lighthearted step. Her own feelings were more complicated; she was excited, nervous, curious, and fearful all at once. Coloring everything was her awe of the city. Because of the early hour, its lanes were largely deserted, which made them seem mysterious.

Honus turned up a narrow street flanked by stone residences three or four stories high. At street level, there were only stout doors and blank walls; windows were reserved for the higher floors. From the onset, the road sloped upward. "Is this the temple's hill?" asked Yim.

"No, Temple Mount lies beyond this hill. How's your back?"

"It doesn't hurt at all," lied Yim.

"Good," said Honus in a tone reflecting skepticism.

After walking awhile, they reached the crest of the hill. The road twisted, and as it began to descend, Yim caught a brief glimpse of Karm's temple. It crowned the small mountain that dominated the skyline. The rising sun made the mountaintop glow. From her closer perspective, Yim could see that walls built by human hands blended with natural rock formations to enhance their beauty. Glorious in dawn's light, the mountaintop seemed a fitting home for the goddess.

When buildings hid the temple again, Yim turned her attention to the street, which was slowly filling with people who moved with the purposeful pace of persons on important business. As Yim observed the other pedestrians, she had the impression they were avoiding Honus. They attempted to do it casually by crossing to the other side of the street before he drew near or by subtly gazing elsewhere. Yet it soon became obvious that Honus's approach cleared a pathway, and no one looked him in the eye.

"Honus, do people here fear Sarfs?"

"No, I've many friends in Bremven. At least, I did once."

"Then why do people seem uneasy?"

"I don't know."

"But you've noticed it, too?"

"I have."

After a while, the road sloped upward again, more steeply than before. As Yim climbed higher, the homes grew larger and grander. Except for ornate doors and doorways, the structures remained plain at street level, but the stonework of the windows and facades of the upper stories were elegantly crafted. Most homes featured walls enclosing trees with blooms that were visible from the road.

"Rich merchants live here," Honus said.

"It must be pleasant to gaze upon such gardens."

"A friend of mine lives near the river in such a house. Indeed, the world looks comely from his windows."

The road grew steeper. Soon it hugged the mountainside, and there were no buildings to obscure the view. Bremven stretched below, bathed in the soft light of dawn. The sounds of a waking city rose with a breeze that carried the smell of wood smoke, spice, and abundant humanity. By then Yim's wound throbbed, and she feared that it might reopen. Still, she said nothing. *Perhaps, bearing the pack is all that's necessary,* thought Yim, but she suspected the notion was wishful thinking.

Honus was aware of Yim's pain, and he walked slowly despite his impatience to reach the temple. He thought he understood her desire to bear the pack to the end of their journey, and he was sympathetic to it. It was the kind of thing he would do.

The road switched back and forth to climb the hill. The cleft that held the great bronze doors was visible and soon the doors would be also. Honus recalled how they had fascinated him as a child. He could almost feel the intricate reliefs on their surfaces, the green giving way to gold where they had been polished by the touch of countless hands. For him, the doors reflected the enduring grace of the temple, and he was eager for Yim to see them.

Finally, the road turned one last time and the entrance to Karm's sanctuary lay in front of them. Honus froze, shocked into immobility by the sight before him. The doors lay shattered upon the ground. The instant passed. Honus drew his sword as he raced into the ravaged temple, leaving Yim alone and forgotten on the roadway.

THIRTY-SEVEN

AT FIRST, Yim was too stunned and confounded to do anything but stay put. She knew only two things: A calamity had befallen the temple, and her life had taken another unexpected turn. She felt as she had on the night she was enslaved; in an instant, both her hopes and fears had been rendered irrelevant by a new and unknown destiny. Yim could see nothing encouraging about it. When Honus failed to return, her foreboding grew.

Yim felt conspicuous on the empty road. With trepidation, she entered the cleft to rest and wait for Honus. She removed the pack and sat on one of the fallen doors. The pain from her wound added to her fatigue from climbing the steep road. As she rested, she looked about. The shattered doors were huge and made of oak sheathed in bronze. Evidently, great effort had been needed to destroy them. One had been reduced to little more than splintered wood and jagged metal. Yim sat on the more intact door of the pair. Its bronze decoration had been marred by many blows, but parts still retained their loveliness. Leaves and curling vines stood out in high relief. It was exquisite work, a flattering mirror to nature where every leaf and tendril was perfect. Yim discovered bronze butterflies and beetles in the foliage, each a miniature masterpiece.

Beyond the doors lay the first courtyard of the temple. It was eerily silent. The only sign of its occupants was their dried blood. The outlines of broad, red-brown pools stained the stones. When Yim gazed upon them, echoes of atrocities arose in her mind. She looked away and recalled Karm weeping in Yorn's courtyard.

"So this is my journey's end," Yim said. Yet, even as she uttered those words, she knew it wasn't so. The temple was no longer a meaningful destination. She was still a slave, a slave in a strange city. It was likely a hostile one, a place where her dark blue clothes would attract danger, not respect. Her future remained in Honus's hands, and there was no sign of him.

The silence of the temple and the stillness of the road made time drag. As Yim waited, her mood changed from anxious to impatient to irritated. Eventually, she decided to venture into the temple and find Honus. She removed the knife from the pack and put it in the waist pocket of her overshirt. Then Yim hid the pack and entered the courtyard.

Her immediate impressions were contradictory. One was of peacefulness. There was a studied tranquillity to the temple. Nothing appeared grandiose in the irregularly curving courtyard, yet every stone seemed shaped and placed with care. The effect was simple, elegant, and beautiful. The idyllic setting strengthened the opposing impression of appalling violence. The stain of butchery was everywhere. It was plain that many had died on the perfectly laid pavement. The air smelled of blood, and swarms of flies darkened the discolored stones. A bloody trail marked where bodies had been dragged deeper into the temple. Yim followed that trail in hope that Honus had done the same.

At the far end of the courtyard was a large, curved structure with an arched doorway. The trails led to it. Yim entered the building and found herself in a circular room that was sixty paces in diameter. It was made of irregular stones that had been fitted together with such precision they required no mortar. The walls rose to a domed ceiling that was open in the center. A thin stream of water arched from a spout at the opening's edge to fall into a huge circular basin carved from a single block of black basalt. The stone vessel had been shattered and water spilled from it to form pools on the floor. These were tinted red. Yim didn't know the purpose of the room, but she thought it might be a place for refreshment or cleansing.

There were adjoining rooms, but the trail Yim followed didn't lead to them. It traced a path through the room to a doorway opposite the one she had entered. Skirting the ruined basin and the bloody pools, Yim followed it to yet another courtyard. This one was deeper than the previous one, and in addition to paved portions, it contained natural features. A small waterfall fed a brook that meandered across the open space. Trees had flanked its course, but they had been chopped down. Except for the gruesome trail, there still was no sign of the temple's occupants. The bloody trace was broader and clearer, having been fed by many tributaries. The gore sickened Yim, and she feared where it would lead. Nevertheless, she continued onward.

There was no bridge across the brook that traversed the courtyard. Yim approached the waterway's edge and saw its bed was cut into stone. It was impossible to tell whether this had been done naturally or artificially, but the shallow waterway was no obstacle. Yim removed her sandals and easily waded across. When she reached the other side, she paused to let her feet dry and to gather her resolve. Yim peered about and thought she discerned a pattern to the temple's buildings and courtyards. The complex seemed to be laid out like growth rings of a tree, and the trail she followed seemed to be leading to its heart.

Yim put on her sandals and entered the building at the far side of the courtyard. There was no doorway to this structure, just a broad colonnade. The huge stone columns were carved to resemble tree trunks, and like natural trees, they were irregularly spaced. The effect was similar to peering into a forest. Yim could see into the hall, but the columns prevented her from glimpsing its end. She couldn't help but marvel at the sight. Her wonder and admiration increased when she entered the structure. It seemed endless and imbued with the same solemnity as its natural counterpart.

The farther Yim walked into the hall, the more shadowy it became. A cold sweat moistened her body, and she felt the same dread she had experienced on the road to Karvakken Pass. There was a malevolent presence that either arose from the recent horrors or was drawn by them. It was attempting to discourage her from proceeding. Yim struggled against its influence, and owing to her strength—or its weakness—she succeeded. Yim picked up her pace and was deep in the hall when a faint sound startled her.

It was tapping. Yim paused to listen. The sound seemed distant. Thinking it might be a signal from Honus or a survivor of the massacre, she strained to determine its origin. The irregularly placed columns played tricks with the acoustics, and for a while, Yim's efforts were frustrated. She walked a few paces, listened, walked some more, and listened again. By slow degrees, she advanced so the sound became louder. It led her down the dim interior of the hall.

Yim was beginning to think the structure was endless when its columns became thinner and more widely spaced. The light around her grew brighter, and she could discern a large arch in the distance. It was the source of the light. She had the sensation of approaching a sunlit glade after wandering in a forest. Not only did light come from the opening, but the tapping sound did also.

Yim was advancing toward it when she noticed something on the floor. It looked like a lost glove, but it was a woman's hand, severed at the wrist. The palm was upward and the delicate fingers were slightly curled in a final plea for mercy or perhaps in warning. Yim skirted the hand and proceeded more cautiously than before.

The arch was the entrance to a large room where sunlight streamed through an open ceiling. A rock outcropping stood in its center like a miniature mountain. A huge mosaic depicting Karm standing on that rock covered the far wall. It reminded Yim of her childhood vision. The goddess was barefoot and wore a white, sleeveless robe that reached halfway down her shins. In one hand she held a balance, and she extended the other in a beckoning gesture. Her walnut-colored hair looked windblown and her dark eyes appeared serene. The look calmed Yim and gave her the courage to enter the room.

The tapping came from behind the outcropping. Yim moved toward the sound, clutching the knife in her pocket. She peered around the rock. A ragged, elderly man was pounding a knife with a cobblestone to chisel tiles from the mosaic. When one popped loose, he followed its trajectory and caught sight of Yim. His face turned pale as he brandished his knife. "You a ghost?"

"No," replied Yim.

The man's expression became belligerent. "Then leave me be if you don't want to become one."

Yim withdrew her hand from her pocket, leaving the knife inside it. "I'm no threat."

Keeping a suspicious eye on Yim, the man bent over to retrieve the fallen tile. "Keep away! I found them first."

"I will."

"Good. The blue ones might fetch a few coppers. There's no one here to miss them."

"Can you tell me what happened?"

"Don't you know?"

"I just arrived this morning."

"A mob, that's what happened."

"I don't understand."

"There's nothing to understand. Five nights ago, they swarmed up here. The rest you've seen for yourself."

"Why did they do it?"

"What's reason to a mob? Those in the Black Temple

stirred them up. Called it 'righteous anger,' but it seemed more like madness to me. Madness, pure and simple."

"Didn't the emperor do anything to stop them?"

"Oh, his men gathered some stragglers to hang from the poles, but they bided their time doing it."

"And the victims? What happened to them?"

"Burnt. You could smell the stink for days. Some folk say that not all of them were dead when they went into the pyre."

Yim's eyes widened. "Can that be true?"

The man grinned at Yim's shocked expression, then shrugged. "Who can tell? Not me. It's not my business."

"But stealing is?"

"This isn't stealing. No one's coming back. The place is cursed."

"So that's why it's empty."

"Aye. Folk are afraid of it."

"But not you?"

"What's the goddess to me?" replied the man with bravado. He gazed up at the mosaic image. "A mere bare-foot girl." He turned his gaze toward Yim. "For all her power, she could be you. You look enough alike." The idea caught his fancy, and he bowed to Yim. "Goddess," he said with mocking obsequiousness, "pray spare a poor man a few stones. It's a small gift, considering you gave your servants to the mob."

Yim reddened. "Take them!" she shouted. Then, spinning on her heels, she ran from the room. The man's laughter followed her.

Yim ran until she encountered the broad smear of dried blood that had guided her into the hall. Then she let it guide her out. The light grew brighter, and soon she could see another open space with low buildings at its far side. This space was too broad to be a courtyard, and only the area closest to the hall was paved. The rest resembled a natural landscape, except the plants were trampled and all the trees had been cut down. They apparently had been burned, for the pavement contained the remnants of a great fire. The bloody trail ended there, and Yim knew she had found the pyre the man had described.

The air of malice had grown more oppressive, and Yim feared the onset of some horrific vision. None came, nor was any necessary to reveal the magnitude of the slaughter. The sight before her was sufficient. A mound of charred bone rose waist-high and spread over forty paces. Winds had blown the ashes, which stained the surrounding ground. Even as Yim watched, a breeze raised a sooty cloud.

Honus sat cross-legged and still before the mound, and Yim realized he was trancing. She had an inkling of how perilous it must be to seek the memories of those so recently and savagely slain. It seemed extremely foolhardy. Yim walked over to where Honus tranced to await his return to the living realm. She sat down and watched his ash-blown face for signs of revival. Tears flowed from his closed eyes and disturbing expressions crossed his face like shadows of clouds traversing a landscape. These were the only hints of the horrors he was experiencing.

Yim and Honus remained motionless and silent for a long while. Then, without warning, Honus's eyes flew open. They glared at Yim without recognizing her, and his expression was terrifying. The Seer's tattoos only faintly foreshadowed the fury that dominated his features. Honus had become the embodiment of wrath. In a sudden, fluid motion, he leapt to his feet and drew his sword. He stared at Yim with a look of blind rage. She cowered, too terrified to speak. Honus raised his blade with the grim ceremony of an executioner, and Yim feared he would hack her to pieces in his madness. Then awareness came to his eyes. Alarm followed. Sheathing his sword, Honus dropped to his knees and embraced Yim. Holding her with fierce tightness, he uttered, "Oh Yim!"

THIRTY-EIGHT

TERRIFIED, YIM submitted silently to Honus's embrace. Passivity seemed the only prudent course. Honus trembled when he first held Yim, but gradually stopped. When Honus finally released her, his face was calm. Yim found that calmness unnerving. It seemed unnatural, and she was certain that his wrath was only hidden, not subdued. It made her wary, and she waited for him to speak first.

"Come, Yim," he said presently. "There's nothing for us here."

Yim silently followed, her mind spinning. Honus didn't speak again until they reached the shattered gates and Yim took the pack from its hiding place. "Put it back," he said. "It can stay here awhile." Yim complied, but looked puzzled. Honus responded to her confusion. "You've borne it to the temple. Your task is done."

"Then you intend to sell me?"

"No."

"Then what's to become of me?"

"Didn't you say your father was a peddler?"

"Yes."

"I'm taking you to a friend who's a merchant. He may be able to help you."

"How?"

"That remains to be seen. Whatever happens, you'll no longer be a slave."

"You're setting me free?"

"Yes."

Yim's eyes welled with tears. "Thank you, Honus. I've yearned to be free again."

"Then I'm glad," replied Honus, not looking glad at all.

Honus led the way down into the city. The streets had grown crowded, but his grim face and aggressive carriage caused people to avoid him. The route he took soon confused Yim, though she had the impression they were returning to the riverfront. As she trailed behind Honus, her joy at her emancipation subsided when she realized that her fate still remained in Honus's hands. She knew no one in the city and had no idea where she was headed.

At last, Honus stopped in front of an impressively large stone building. A deep colonnaded arcade ran across its front, sheltering tables that displayed cloth samples. Shoppers and vendors were busily bargaining there. When an agreement was struck, the vendors dispatched a stock boy to procure the order. Honus took the same route as the stock boy and led Yim through a doorway in the center of the arcade. Once inside, they found themselves in a large storeroom, crowded with shelves stacked high with cloth and bustling with activity. The room grew quiet as soon as Honus entered. Speaking to no one in particular, he asked, "Is Commodus in residence?"

A young man nervously approached and bowed. "He is, Karmamatus."

"Tell him Honus is here."

"I will at once." The young man bowed again and sped away, clearly relieved to depart. The activity in the room slowly resumed. A short while later, the young man returned with an older one. By the deference shown to him, Yim guessed the second man was Commodus. He appeared to be in his fifties and his short, dark beard was streaked with gray. His large eyes and broad forehead gave him an intelligent look, while his red, fleshy nose and wide mouth befitted a common tradesman. Apparently aware of the latter impression, he was dressed in a manner to contradict it. He wore a colorful and elaborately pleated robe of gold-embroidered cloth.

Commodus appeared glad to see Honus, but uncertain how to act. He took on the reserved manner of someone greeting a friend at a funeral. Commodus seemed puzzled by Yim, but it was to her that he bowed. "Welcome to my house, Karmamatus. May I offer you and your Sarf some refreshment?"

Yim returned the bow, glad that she could fall back on formality. "Karm sees your generosity. We'd be grateful for some refreshment."

"Then I'll show you the way," replied Commodus. He led them through a doorway in the rear of the storeroom. Beyond it was a corridor that ended with stairs. Commodus led his guests up them into the private apartments on the second floor. There, the utilitarian furnishings gave way to sumptuous ones. Evidently, Commodus was a successful merchant and an extremely wealthy one. He waved off everyone who approached and took Yim and Honus into a richly furnished room with a window overlooking the river. After closing the door, Commodus dropped his formality and embraced Honus. "I never thought I'd see you again, dear, dear friend. Such times! Such dreadful times!"

"It's good to see you once more," said Honus, returning the hug.

"Tell me of Theodus."

"I've sad tidings," said Honus. "He was slain in Lurwic."

"Each day brings yet another blow! When I saw you had a new Bearer, I feared the worst."

"This is Yim, and though she's dressed as a Bearer, she's not one."

Commodus regarded Yim with undisguised curiosity.

"It suited my needs to garb her so," continued Honus. "She has served me faithfully and borne my pack through many perils. She's the reason I'm here. I've come to ask a favor."

"Anything is yours," replied Commodus.

"Take Yim under your protection and teach her your trade. I'm certain she'll prove an asset to your household, for she's resourceful and has a fine character. Sheltering her would also honor Theodus, whose burden she carried."

As Commodus listened to Honus, he watched his eyes carefully, causing Yim to suspect that he had the skill to perceive much that was unsaid. When he regarded her again, it was with new appreciation. Then he smiled, and his shrewd eyes turned warm. "You must be worthy indeed, for Honus is never generous with praise. Have you no kin?"

"I'm alone."

"Then, if it would please you, I'll become your kin. It would honor me to be your guardian."

"The honor would be all mine," replied Yim.

"Then, it's done," said Commodus. "Honus, have you just arrived in Bremven? How did you get past the guards?"

"We rode in a wagon and weren't troubled. Why do you ask? Are Karm's devotees now unwelcome here?"

"Sarfs make Morvus nervous after . . . You *do* know what has happened?"

"I've visited the temple and tranced there," said Honus.

"Tranced? *There?*"

"Yes," replied Honus in a cold, hard voice. "I know all." For just an instant, his face betrayed the wrath that Yim had witnessed at the temple.

Commodus caught the look and grew pale. "What will you do?" he asked in a hushed voice.

Honus glanced toward Yim. "Yim carried my pack up Temple Mount this morning despite an injury. I'm sure she's tired. We shouldn't neglect her needs while we talk."

Commodus caught the hint. "Where are my manners?" he said to Yim. "You're weary and I'm gabbing. You must think poorly of my hospitality."

"Of course not, sire."

"Oh, no 'sire' for me. 'Commodus' will do just fine. You're family now." He rang a bell, and a servant entered from a side door. "Jev, this is Yim. She's my new ward. Treat her as my daughter. She's tired from her journey and in need of rest. Give her the garden bedroom and have Gurdy tend her."

Yim knew she was being sent away, however graciously. "Honus . . ."

He turned to gaze at her. Though he fought to keep his expression neutral, Yim could see turmoil in his eyes. Sensing his inner struggle, she was tempted to probe him and discover its nature. However, she decided not to try in front of Commodus.

Honus approached Yim and delicately stroked her cheek, which was still gritty with ash. "After all you've been through, you deserve some peace." He bent toward her, and for a moment, Yim thought he would kiss her. Instead, he abruptly turned away.

"Are you ready, Mistress?" asked Jev.

"I guess so."

Still, Yim hesitated, feeling she should say something to Honus. He had walked over to the window and was staring out of it, his back to her. She had the impression that he had just said farewell, yet she was at a loss as to how to reply. The presence of strangers made it all the more difficult. In the end, she simply followed Jev from the room.

As Jev led the way down a long corridor, Yim was conscious of the curiosity behind his formality. She knew she was being judged, though she had little idea by what standards. The corridor turned and led to a row of beautifully carved doors. Jev opened one to reveal a large room with a window that overlooked a walled garden. It reminded Yim of her room at Yorn's manor, though it was far more opulent.

"Perhaps Mistress would care for refreshments and a bath."

Yim looked down at her legs and sandaled feet. They were blackened from sitting near the pyre. "Just a bath," she said, somewhat embarrassed. "I've already eaten."

"I'll see that Gurdy attends to it."

"Thank you."

Jev bowed and departed. Left alone, Yim explored the room with wonder. By the window were several walnut chairs featuring delicately carved birds and flowers. A huge bed with a soft feather mattress was carved in the same manner. Upon the bed was a fluffy comforter beneath an embroidered coverlet. Yim walked over to the window to admire its view of the garden, still lovely despite the spring bloom having peaked. The walls of the room were covered with tapestries that depicted the same garden in different seasons. Yim was examining a huge bureau inlaid with mother-of-pearl when someone knocked on the door.

"Mistress," said a woman's voice, "your bath is ready. Shall I bring it in?"

"Please."

The door opened and a young woman entered lugging a big copper tub. She was followed by five men bearing large ewers filled with steaming water. The woman set the tub down and removed some articles from it before the men filled it with water. The men departed, but the woman remained. She bowed toward Yim. "I'm Gurdy, Mistress. I'll attend you." She was neatly dressed in a tan tunic that ended just above her knees. Gurdy appeared about Yim's age and her plain, but pleasant face featured the light complexion, blue eyes, and sandy hair more common among folk from Averen than Bremven.

Gurdy dropped flower petals into the bathwater and stirred them with her hand. The rising steam carried their fragrance throughout the room. After drying her hand on her tunic, she knelt before Yim and began to unfasten her sandals.

"What are you doing?" asked Yim.

"Undressing you for your bath, Mistress."

"I can do that myself."

"Yes, Mistress." Gurdy rose and stepped back, but didn't leave the room.

"Why are you still here?"

"To bathe you, Mistress."

"Bathe me? I'll bathe myself. You can go."

Gurdy started to leave, then stopped, obviously distressed. When she spoke, she stared nervously at the floor. "Have I done something wrong? Are you displeased with me?"

"No, why?"

"If you're not displeased with me, why don't you want me?"

Yim looked at the distraught woman and had an unsettling realization. "You're a slave, aren't you?"

"I'm *your* slave, Mistress."

"I don't want a slave. I was a . . . a . . . I'm unaccustomed to being served."

"But all fine ladies have slaves," said Gurdy. "*Please*, give me a chance."

"You *want* to be my slave?"

"I've always wanted to be a lady's slave. Even though I'm a house slave, I know about serving a mistress. I've helped attend ladies before. Just try me, Mistress. Please."

Gurdy's plea left Yim perplexed and uncomfortable. *If I don't accept her, she'll still be a slave. I'll be doing her no favor by sending her away.* Yet the thought of having a slave went against Yim's grain. Meanwhile, the cause of her quandary had assumed an expression of abject humility as she silently awaited her answer. "I'm not a lady," Yim said at last.

"But you are! Jev said you're Master's ward and we're to treat you like Lady Jobella, Master's own daughter."

Yim looked Gurdy in the eye and quickly read her earnestness. She sighed. "So serving me would make you happy?"

Gurdy's face brightened. "Oh yes, Mistress."

"Then you may, but you must call me Yim."

"Oh, I couldn't do *that*! People would think me rude. They'd be angry with me and think less of you."

Yim sighed again. "There seems to be a lot of rules about being a lady."

"You're new to Bremven, but I can help you, Mistress."

"I'd be grateful if you did," said Yim. She undressed and stepped into the warm, scented water.

"Would you like me to wash your back?" asked Gurdy.

"Sure, that would be fine."

Gurdy grabbed some soap and a washing cloth as Yim leaned forward. Gurdy gasped when she saw Yim's back. "Mistress! You're injured!"

"Didn't you know I traveled with a Sarf? Our journey was hard and dangerous. An arrow did that."

Gurdy gently washed around the stitched-up wound. "Then, surely the goddess has rewarded your suffering by making you a fine lady."

Yim didn't respond, for she was struggling not to cry. The day's traumatic events had finally overwhelmed her. She was distraught without fully understanding why. In her heart, Yim didn't believe the goddess had rewarded her. Instead, she feared that she was about to face another trial.

Gurdy sensed Yim's distress and began to massage her soapy back. "You'll be happy here, Mistress, I know it. Master Commodus is a good man. Everyone is kind, and you'll lack for nothing. Don't worry about your wound. I'll fetch a healer. You needn't worry at all. I'll take care of everything."

"And what do you get in return? How can serving me make you happy?"

"I'll get to live your life. I'll attend you at feasts and eat fine foods. I'll accompany you on travels and see the sights.

I'll sleep in the comfort of your room. Don't worry about me, Mistress. I'm happier washing your back than scrubbing floors."

"Don't be so certain that living my life will be pleasant. I haven't found it so."

"But your life has changed."

"I hope you're right."

In her despondency, Yim became passive. She submitted to Gurdy's ministrations and allowed the girl to wash her and to dry her also. Afterward, Gurdy tucked her into bed while she went to get clean clothes. Yim lay upon the soft mattress, convinced that she couldn't possibly rest, and quickly fell asleep.

THIRTY-NINE

YIM WOKE in the early afternoon, and for a moment she was unsure where she was. Then she remembered that her journey was over. The luxurious bed she lay upon was her bed, and the young woman sitting by the window was happy to serve her. Sleep had revived her spirits, and the future no longer seemed so bleak. Her vision at Karvakken Pass had steeled her against sights of slaughter, so while the events at the ravaged temple saddened her, she wasn't shaken to the core. Already, their terror had faded, making Gurdy's comforting words seem more probable. *Perhaps the goddess has rewarded me, and in this peaceful place I'll fulfill my destiny.*

Yim envisioned what that destiny might be, imagining the child that she would bear restoring the temple and guiding people back to harmony. The more Yim thought upon this version of the future, the more she believed it. Everything fit neatly. *That's why I was Honus's slave, so he could bring me here to safety.* Having fulfilled his function, Honus had freed her. Soon he would depart. Yim regretted not having said something when she left him with Commodus. She planned to make amends at dinner.

Gurdy rose as soon as she saw Yim was awake. "Mistress, I have clean clothes. They're Lady Jobella's, but you'll soon have your own." She laid a selection of robes upon the bed. Yim had never seen such rich fabrics. They seemed too fine for everyday wear, and she wondered about Gurdy's judgment. Yim selected the plainest garment of the lot—a simple, white sleeveless robe. Even this garment was made of some marvelously smooth and supple material.

As Yim put it on, she asked Gurdy, "What cloth is this?"

"It's spun from moth cocoons, Mistress. It comes from far away."

"And Lady Jobella wears things like this for everyday?"

"Master is a cloth merchant. All his family wear the finest clothes. He says it's good for business. When I serve you at feasts, even I will wear a fine robe," said Gurdy with evident delight.

Yim was disconcerted by how the robe clung to her body. "You don't think it's too revealing?"

Gurdy smiled. "I can see you're new to Bremven, Mistress. If you wore such a robe to a feast, you'd be called prudish." She tied a white silk girdle around Yim's waist and then brought Yim's sandals, which had been cleaned and oiled. "Master Dommus wanted to know when you wakened, Mistress. Should I tell him?"

"Master Dommus? Who's he?"

"Why, Master Commodus's son. He wishes to welcome you. Will you see him?"

"Yes," said Yim. "Of course."

After Gurdy departed, Yim regarded her attire with growing embarrassment. The length of the robe was modest enough; it reached halfway down her shins. The square neckline was decorous also. However, her nipples plainly showed through the clingy fabric. Yim thought of changing, but a rapid examination of the other robes affirmed that she was wearing the most modest garment of the lot. *How will I ever get used to such a life?* She was still pondering that question when she heard a knock.

"Yim, may I come in?" asked a masculine voice.

"Yes, please."

A man in his late twenties opened the door and smiled pleasantly as he bowed. Dommus's dark features were more finely formed than his father's, but he had the same broad forehead and large, intelligent eyes. It was a handsome face. "Welcome to our family," he said.

Yim returned Dommus's bow. "Thank you."

"So much has happened, you must feel dizzy."

Yim flashed a wry smile. "This day's been most confusing."

"It's brought surprises to us all," said Dommus. He smiled again. "For me, you're the most pleasant one."

Yim blushed as Dommus's eyes passed boldly over her body. "I'm glad," she replied a little stiffly.

Dommus appeared amused by her embarrassment. "I know you're new to Bremven, but not much more. Father told me little, other than you traveled with Honus. Were you with him long?"

"Ever since we met at Durkin." Yim noted that surprise briefly crossed Dommus's face. "We journeyed through Luvein to get here."

"That's no easy road. Nor do I imagine Honus was an easy traveling companion."

"He's not altogether what he seems."

"Neither are you, I suspect."

"And what do you suspect?"

Dommus laughed. "A forthright question."

"Which you're evading."

"You're lovely, but I suspect you're much tougher than you look. You're certainly direct."

"I don't mean to be ill-mannered."

"Don't worry. We're merchants here, not courtiers. Plain speaking is the rule in this house."

"I'm glad to hear it. I've a friend who said that's not the case in Bremven."

"I fear your friend's right, but that's not true within these walls."

"Then Honus has brought me to a haven."

"He has. If you'd like, I'll show it to you."

"I'd like that very much. If I'm to follow your trade, I've much to learn. I want to be useful."

"You will," said Dommus. "We all work here. My sister's away on a buying trip, and I've recently returned with a caravan. If you don't wish to travel, there's much to do right here."

"I certainly hope I'll be suited for something."

"Father said you're a peddler's daughter, so trading must run in your blood."

"I'm afraid I learned little about selling and buying. I spent most of my time gathering herbs and herding goats."

"You'll do fine. Father's a patient teacher, and I'd be pleased to instruct you also."

"Your kindness is more than I merit."

"Father would disagree. He was devoted to Theodus, and Honus was like Theodus's son. Father would do anything for him."

"So I've done nothing to earn my good fortune."

"That's untrue," replied Dommus. "You earned Honus's respect. I heard you even saved his life."

"Honus said that?"

"That's what Father told me. You seem surprised."

"I thought Honus didn't know."

Dommus looked puzzled. "Why would you conceal your bravery?"

"I had my reasons. I thought you were going to show me around."

Dommus bowed, though a smile fought with his formality. "I'd be most honored."

Yim's tour began in the building's lower level, where she discovered that Commodus and his household lived above a bustling commercial compound as large as any manor. There were stables to accommodate animals for caravans, a shop for housing and maintaining wagons, a garrison of guards, a countinghouse, and numerous storerooms. As Dommus led Yim around, it became apparent that he was on easy terms with everyone who worked there. The workers seemed like part of a close-knit family, and whenever Yim was introduced, they already knew about her arrival.

Dommus lingered longest in the storerooms, for he clearly loved the merchandise he sold. He communicated some of that passion to Yim as he pulled bolt after bolt of material from the shelves for her to touch and admire. After showing her a room full of exquisite brocades, he ended his tour in a huge room piled high with bales of dingy white cloth. "I don't want you to think we only deal in luxury goods," he said. "We clothe everyone. Most of the field slaves in Vinden wear tunics made from our cloth."

Yim fingered the coarse, flimsy fabric and recalled the tunic in which she had been sold. "This seems hardly fit for clothing."

"It's poor stuff, but it sells. It's cheap, and that's what they want."

"You mean the slave owners."

"They're the customers."

Yim reflected a moment. "When I work here, will I have money of my own?"

Dommus grinned. "I can see you're a merchant's daughter after all."

"Well, will I? Money that I earn myself?"

"Why is that important?"

"I want to free Gurdy and pay her to serve me."

"That seems a roundabout way of doing things. She already serves you."

"But she's not free."

"So? Jev says she's overjoyed to serve you."

"Suppose it's a hot day and she wishes to swim in the river, she'd have to ask my permission."

"And I imagine you'd give it."

"But she'd have to *ask*," said Yim, "and that makes all the difference."

"Maybe it did to you, but Gurdy doesn't mind being a slave."

Yim looked at Dommus sharply. "What do you mean by that? What did your father tell you?"

"He said nothing about your slavery. You revealed that yourself by saying you met Honus in Durkin. There, women are either thieves or slaves, and I'm sure you're not a thief."

Yim flushed red. "Now that you know, am I still welcome in your family? Perhaps it would be better if I merely worked for you."

"It makes no difference that you were a slave," said Dommus. "Slavery can befall anyone. There's no shame in it."

"Tell that to a slave!"

"Yim, most of the people here are slaves. Don't look so shocked. We treat them well. You've seen that for yourself. If we hadn't bought Gurdy as a child, she might be laboring on a treadmill or bedding her master against her will. Slavery's a fact of life, whether you like it or not."

"That doesn't make it right."

"You've been around a Sarf too long. Such people see the world in black and white."

"And you disapprove of that?"

"It's not a question of approval or disapproval, it's one of practicality. For centuries, Karm's devotees prayed and labored in the temple. Yet did they save the world? They couldn't even save themselves. Holiness achieves little. The things we do here may seem less grand, but they make a difference in everyday lives. We deal honestly and provide goods people need. We treat our slaves so they're content with their lot."

Yim didn't want to argue her point further. Indeed, she feared that she had already said too much and glanced at Dommus to see if he was offended. She found only an indulgent expression and something else that surprised her. His gaze betrayed desire. *We've just met! How could he have such feelings?*

"Yim, you look upset."

"I . . . I was just thinking that . . . that I've no right to criticize. You must think me ungrateful."

"I don't," said Dommus. "Idealism is fine, but there's no need to imitate a Sarf. You can live well and still honor Karm. Before you give Gurdy her freedom, find out if she truly wants it. Be sure you're not confusing your desires with hers."

"I'm not sure what I desire," said Yim. "Since my desires never mattered, it seemed pointless to consider them."

"They matter now," said Dommus.

"As I said before, this day's been most confusing."

"I understand. You don't have to figure out everything at once."

They left the room by wandering through a maze of cloth bales. Dommus took Yim's hand to lead the way. He still held it as he guided her into the walled garden she had seen beneath her window. It was quiet and empty. Spent blossoms colored the ground in pastel shades and a fountain filled the air with soft sounds. They sat upon a stone bench, where Dommus reluctantly let go of Yim's hand. They said nothing, but it wasn't an uncomfortable silence. Yim looked at the tranquil beauty around her and hoped Dommus was right—that it was possible to live well and still obey the goddess.

Yim turned to Dommus and met his eyes. She saw ex- citement in his gaze—the look of a man who had happened upon a treasure. Unbidden, a thought came to her: *Could this be the man who will father my child?* Almost as if he were responding to that idea, Dommus placed a hand on her shoulder. Before Yim could react, his fingers traveled down her back and raked across her wound. Yim cried out, exaggerating the pain she felt.

Dommus instantly withdrew his hand. "What did I do?" he asked, his voice conveying alarmed concern.

"You touched a wound that's only partly healed."

"I'm sorry, truly sorry, I didn't know. Should I get a healer?"

"Is it bleeding?"

Dommus looked at the back of Yim's robe. "It doesn't seem to be."

"Then I don't think I need a healer. I'll just have Gurdy look at it."

"I'll walk you to your room."

Dommus escorted Yim to her door and left, saying he'd see her at dinner. As soon as Yim entered the room, Gurdy said in an anxious voice, "Why did you cry out, Mistress? Are you all right?"

Yim realized that Gurdy had been watching from the window and wondered how many others had also ob- served her and Dommus in the garden. *Had Honus?* The question made her feel oddly guilty. "Dommus touched my wound," said Yim. "Would you look at it?"

"Of course, Mistress." Gurdy untied the girdle and raised the robe until Yim's back was exposed. "It looks fine," she said. "Maybe a little red." She let the robe fall back down. "What did you think of Master Dommus?"

"I'm not sure," said Yim. "He seems pleasant, but rather forward. What do you know of him?"

"It's not my place to say, Mistress."

"I'm new to this house and know nothing of the people

here," said Yim. "I need your help, so I'll ask again—what do you know of him?"

Gurdy looked at Yim and was immediately trapped by her gaze. She seemed to realize that her mistress would see the truth, and goose bumps rose on her arms. "He's . . . he's kind," said Gurdy. "He truly is."

"And fond of women?"

"Yes. I'm sure he's fond of you."

"Should I be wary of him?"

"Oh no!" said Gurdy. "He's so nice you'll want to . . ."

Gurdy flushed red, and Yim saw that she was one of Dommus's conquests. While Yim understood the woman's discomfort, she didn't relent. "Were I to refuse him, what might he do?"

"You'd refuse him?" asked Gurdy, as if the possibility had never occurred to her.

"Yes," said Yim. "I need more from a man than a moment's passion."

"I don't know what he'd do," said Gurdy. "He's not used to that. When he wants a woman, he must have her." Gurdy's face lit up. "He might marry you! He truly might!" She became enthusiastic. "Master Commodus wants Dommus to settle down and produce an heir. Maybe you'll be the one! Then what a grand lady you'd be!"

Yim released Gurdy, who avoided looking at her for a long while. When she finally did, she asked in a timid voice, "Did the Sarf teach you how to force truth from people?"

"I learned that skill long before I met him," said Yim. "I'm sorry if I frightened you." She walked over to Gurdy and gave her a reassuring hug. "You've a good heart. I saw that."

"Thank you, Mistress."

"If you can't bring yourself to call me Yim when we're alone, at least don't call me 'Mistress.' It saddens me that you feel I own you."

"But you do."

"Up to this very morning," said Yim quietly, "I was a slave myself."

Gurdy's only response was a look of surprised disbelief.

"It's true," said Yim. "Dommus has already found out, and I suspect the news will soon spread."

"Then the goddess has truly blessed you to have raised you up so high."

"Yet when I think of my own servitude, I feel guilty being your mistress."

"Don't," said Gurdy. "I was given to you. It's all right. I really don't mind."

Yim looked at Gurdy and saw she spoke the truth. *That's the greatest pity of all,* she thought. Yim sat on her bed to think. She would have liked to be alone, but she was hesitant to send Gurdy away. Yim knew the girl would have a hard time keeping secrets.

While Gurdy gazed serenely out the window, Yim reviewed the day's events, seeking some sign of the path she should take. Gurdy's speculations about Dommus offered the only hint. *Perhaps we're destined to marry. A son by him would possess the power riches bring.* Yim wondered if wealth could overcome evil. *If so, must I marry Dommus? Is that what the goddess wants? Is that what's necessary?* Yim was unconvinced, and the optimism she had felt earlier that afternoon seemed wishful thinking.

As Yim further pondered her destiny, she questioned whether logic could guide her at all. Little that had happened since her first childhood vision could be described as logical. Circumstances had pushed her one way and then another. Whatever purpose she perceived could easily be her imagining, no more substantial than shapes in clouds. *And now I'm considering marrying a man I've just met!* Yim decided it was foolish to act when she was so uncertain. *The proper action should be compelling. It should feel urgent, even inevitable.* At the moment, having a child—whether by Dommus or anyone else—did not. *Perhaps it will.* Waiting for some clearer sign seemed the only prudent course.

Yim remained in her room until Jev arrived to escort her to dinner. It was served in a banquet hall large enough to seat dozens. Only Commodus and Dommus were there, their voices muted by the opulent emptiness around them. Rich tapestries hung on the walls and the soft light of dusk suffused through high windows. A slave was already lighting candles. Both father and son ceased talking and rose when Yim entered. By the way they looked at her, Yim suspected that she had been the subject of their conversation.

"Welcome, Yim," said Commodus warmly.

"Thank you," replied Yim. "You've shown me so much kindness."

"I only hope you find this home a haven," said Commodus as Yim was seated. "Honus told me you've suffered many trials, including one this very morning."

"Where is he?" asked Yim. "I thought I'd see him here."

Commodus's eyes became sad, then evasive. "He's fasting."

"Here?"

"Elsewhere."

"He left without a word for me?"

Dommus laughed. "That's a Sarf for you."

Commodus shot his son an angry glance before turning to Yim. "Of course he left a message. He said to thank you for all your help and that he'd see you soon."

Yim was certain that Commodus was lying, but felt it was neither the place nor time to say so. "I shouldn't be surprised he forgot to say good-bye," she said. "He's a man of few words."

"He was," said Commodus, his voice mournful. His reply sent a chill through Yim, for it seemed to her that Commodus spoke as if Honus were already dead—or soon would be.

FORTY

COMMODUS SAT in his bedchamber sipping a nightcap of hot spiced wine, for the night was chilly despite the season. *It's been a strange day,* he thought, *and it ended with a strange dinner.* Throughout the meal, Yim had been polite, but edgy and withdrawn. Something about her made him uneasy, though he couldn't precisely say what. Commodus wondered if he would regret his impulse to make Yim his ward. It had been uncharacteristic of him to act without calculation. *I had to do it for Honus,* he reminded himself. *He needed that bit of solace.* Recalling the heartbreak in Honus's eyes made Commodus grieve anew. *The way of the goddess is hard; Theodus taught me that. Whatever trouble Yim brings, I'll not repent what I did.*

Commodus could foresee one trouble already: Yim infatuated Dommus. Easily turned by a pretty face, he was already considering marriage. Commodus thought that premature at best and wondered how much his son knew about Yim. *Does he know Honus loved her?* Commodus decided not, for Dommus lacked the ability to read people's eyes. *Yim has that skill.* Honus had hinted at others. Whatever they were, Commodus felt certain they'd make Yim a difficult bride. He doubted Dommus could handle her.

Knocks on the door interrupted Commodus's thoughts. "Yes," he said. "Who is it?"

"It's Yim," replied a muffled voice. "We have to talk."

"We can talk tomorrow."

"We have to talk now."

So much for courtesy, thought Commodus. *I hope this doesn't foreshadow our relations.* "Come in," he said testily.

Yim entered the door and closed it behind her. She was still dressed in the white robe she had worn at dinner. "I'm sorry to disturb you."

"Couldn't this have waited?"

"I'm afraid not."

Commodus caught Yim staring at him and made an irritated gesture, as if brushing a cobweb from his face. Then he looked away. "Don't try that trick on me, young lady. I know how to defeat that glance. So, what do you want?"

"I need to know Honus's plans."

"I've already told you. He's fasting."

"He doesn't intend to return. Why?"

How did she discover that? wondered Commodus. "I can't tell you. I swore not to." He glanced at Yim again and was annoyed to find that she was still staring at him. Commodus tried to turn his head, but this time he couldn't. He felt as helpless as a mouse in the jaws of a cat. His world quickly contracted until it consisted only of Yim's dark eyes. When she spoke again, it seemed that her words came from inside his head.

"What does Honus intend to do?"

Commodus heard his voice answer. "Fulfill his destiny."

"How?"

"Tomorrow at dawn, he'll enter the Devourer's temple. There, he'll embody the wrath of Karm."

"He'll kill," said Yim, her voice heavy and discouraged.

"He'll slay all he can until he's slain himself."

"Where is he now?"

"I don't know." Commodus felt Yim's hold on him relax, and he found himself once again within his bedroom. He stared at the woman halfway across the room with a mixture of awe and fear.

"He doesn't understand!" said Yim.

"Doesn't understand what?"

"It's not Karm's will."

Commodus summoned his courage and replied, "Don't you think one raised in Karm's service would best understand her will? After all, a Seer tattooed his face to show Karm's wrath."

"You're wrong," said Yim. "He mustn't do this!"

"And how . . ." Commodus was cut short as Yim dashed from the room. He could hear her running down the hallway. For a moment, Commodus thought of having the house guards stop her. He decided against it. "This matter's beyond my ken," he said to himself. Instead of calling the guards, he gulped down his wine and rang for his slave to bring more.

Yim sped past a startled guard into the deserted street. Her thin robe provided scant protection against the night's chill, and the shock of cold air cleared her head. She grew calmer, but her sense of urgency remained. *Honus must be stopped! How can he believe that slaughter will please Karm?* Yim was angry with him for even conceiving the idea. It also made her sad, for it seemed the only thing he could think to do. For the first time, she realized how helpless Honus was without Theodus. *Despite his skill and valor, he's but a tool without a hand to guide him.*

Yim had no idea how she could prevent Honus from carrying out his attack, but she knew she had to try. She couldn't bear the idea of him throwing his life away in an act that would grieve the goddess. Yim's visions had never revealed a wrathful deity. Karm had wept—not raged—in Yorn's courtyard, and Yim was convinced that further deaths would bring Karm only further sorrow. She wondered why Honus couldn't see that another round of slaughter would feed hatred. Yim recalled her horrific vision at Karvakken Pass and the malevolent entity that thrived on death. *I felt its presence at the temple today!* She grew frightened and even more desperate to stop Honus.

Where would Honus choose to spend his last night? Yim concluded it would be at the pond in the temple garden, the one place where he had found peace. High upon its mount, Karm's temple was the sole place in Bremven that Yim had any hope of finding. *If it's Karm's will, Honus will be there.* Yim shivered from the cold and briefly thought of returning for her cloak. Instead, she ran to warm herself and reach the temple quicker.

Honus wore his chain-mail shirt as he sat upon the rock in the temple pond and gazed at the moon's reflection on the water. The surrounding garden had been ruined; only the pond remained unchanged. He concentrated on it, meditating to bring calmness. Yet peace wouldn't come.

Honus didn't fear dying; neither did he welcome death. He saw dying as a duty, one foretold when his face had been tattooed. When the sun rose, Honus would do his utmost to embody the wrath that the Seer had envisioned. He wondered if he would succeed. At the moment, he didn't feel wrathful, only weary and sad. Leaving Yim had been painful. It was the hardest thing he had ever done—his ultimate sacrifice to the goddess. Dying would be easier. *Yim's better off without me,* he told himself. *She's free and safe. She won't miss me.* Honus had tranced too often to believe that he wouldn't miss her. The departed shed their memories slowly upon the Dark Path. Death wouldn't quickly ease his longing.

Running down twisting streets, Yim worked up a sweat before she caught sight of the temple through a gap in the buildings. It wasn't where she expected. Reorienting herself, she hurried off again. The narrow lanes soon confused her, and when she next spotted the temple, it was no closer than before. Tired, Yim slowed to a rapid walk. When she did, her sweat-soaked robe chilled her.

A voice came from the dark. "What's the hurry, pretty?"

Yim froze, unsure where the voice came from. "I need to find the temple."

A rough looking man stepped out from a shadow. He was close enough for Yim to smell the wine on his breath. "It's 'cross from the palace. Yer goin' the wrong way."

"Not that temple," said Yim, backing away. "Karm's temple."

"It's cursed. No one goes there now," said the man, who grinned as he ogled Yim's body. "That's a skimpy robe fer a cold night. Let's go someplace cozy. I'll warm ye." He lunged at her.

Yim leapt out of reach and began to run. She heard the man chase after her, cursing as he went. "Slut! Think yer too good fer me?" Yim ran until her sides ached, her wound throbbed, and her breath came in ragged gasps. She stopped and could hear nothing except her own panting. When she caught her breath, she started to walk again.

Proceeding more warily, Yim blundered about until she eventually found the road Honus and she had climbed that morning. Long after she left Commodus's home, she reached the temple's entrance and groped beneath a shattered door for the pack. It was still in its hiding place. When Yim searched inside it, her heart sank; the chain-mail shirt had been removed. Fearful that Honus had already departed, she hurried into the first courtyard.

In the pale moonlight, the bloodstained pavement looked black and the ruined temple seemed sinister. It was more than the appearance wrought by nightfall; the place had changed. The ominous presence Yim had sensed in the morning was stronger. As at Karvakken Pass, slaughter had worn thin the boundary between the living world and the Dark Path. Yim could feel the nearness of an evil presence, a thing from the Sunless Way that was eager to break through. It was close enough for Yim to perceive how it both hated and hungered for the living. It craved blood, and Honus was about to feed it.

The unseen malevolence became aware of Yim. Suddenly, her limbs felt so heavy that a single step was an effort. Soon she stood rooted as a wave of despair passed through her. The bloodstained pavement turned wet, and a viscous stream flowed toward her. Ghostly figures formed. Unspeakable acts took place before her eyes.

Yim cried out. "This time, I'll not succumb. You can't surprise me twice." From deep inside, she found a source of strength. Yim fought the presence that was trying to invade her mind. Though she stood perfectly still, it seemed to her that she wrestled with a huge, shadowy eel. It was slippery and kept twisting in unexpected ways. Yet she held it fast until the thing faded. As it did, Yim's heart lightened and the gathering ghosts dissipated. Yim was able to move forward. The bloodstains were dry again.

Yim passed through the building with the shattered basin and crossed the second courtyard. When she approached the colonnaded building, she felt a sense of foreboding. Nevertheless, she entered it. It was dark inside the building, and as she moved among its columns, the darkness deepened. Soon it was pitch black, and she had to grope about to avoid walking into a column. Yim stepped into liquid. Then, with the suddenness of an unexpected blow, the malevolence returned even stronger than before.

Ear-piercing screams echoed throughout the hall, and there was the sound of running feet accompanied by the sickening noise of butchery. Yim felt the air move as blades passed close to her face in the dark. Warm, sticky liquid spattered her until she felt drenched. Then eerie light, like that of flickering flames, illuminated the horrors she was hearing. Slaughter was taking place all around her. Yim not only saw the victims die, she felt their terror and their pain. Yim fought against it, and was buffeted from every direction. Wrenched one way and then another, she felt like a hare seized by a pack of dogs. Her mind was being torn part. In her agony and horror, Yim perceived that was her enemy's intention.

Then Yim did the one thing her opponent could not expect. She embraced the suffering about her. As she had with Mirien and Hommy, but without any preparatory meditations, Yim embodied the anguished spirits about her. She became them all to share their burdens of terror and pain. She was a young woman with a severed hand, fleeing in panic as she bled to death. She was an elderly man, standing defiant and still while the mob approached. She felt the blows from their cudgels before she became a wailing infant being swung into a stone pillar.

Yim died countless times, experiencing each terrible moment. Yet because she was driven by love, each time she took on a spirit's suffering she helped that soul transcend it. The encounters were overwhelming—sad, but so profoundly intense that they had a kind of beauty. Yim felt simultaneously drained and uplifted. The sounds in the hall diminished into silence and the light faded. When all was peaceful, Yim stood alone and shaking in the dark. For a long while, she was too spent to move. Then strength from the departed spirits flowed into her. Yim took a deep breath and resumed groping through the hall.

Soon the darkness was no longer absolute. Moonlight filtered between the columns ahead. Yim walked with more assurance. When the tread of her sandals upon the stone floor disturbed her, she removed them to advance barefoot. Eventually she emerged on the other side of the building. Before her was the dark stain of the pyre, and beyond that, the ravaged garden. In the distance, she spotted the glint of moonlight on water. She strained to see Honus, but couldn't. Still, Yim headed toward the pond, skirting the circle of ashes in her way.

Focused on his meditations, Honus didn't see Yim approach until she was quite close. The moon was at her back, so she was almost a silhouette. All he could make out was a dark-haired woman, barefoot and wearing a white robe. In one hand she appeared to be clutching a set of scales. Awe made his voice a whisper. "Karm?"

The advancing figure didn't speak until she reached the pond. "Honus?"

"Yim?" said Honus with surprise. Then his voice turned harsh, almost angry. "What are you doing here?"

"I know what you intend to do."

There was a tense silence before Honus spoke. "So Commodus betrayed me."

"Don't blame him," said Yim. "I forced the truth from him. I have that power."

"I guess I shouldn't be surprised. I've caught you doing stranger things. But why are you here?"

"I've come to stop you."

"Stop me?" said Honus incredulously. "Then you've wasted your time. Go back to Commodus. This matter doesn't concern you."

"It does," said Yim.

"Tomorrow I must obey the goddess and fulfill my destiny."

"Killing won't please Karm. Blood defiles her! Theodus would've never allowed such madness."

"Theodus is dead," said Honus, his voice hardened by despair. "I must take my own counsel."

"You're only a Sarf."

"And you were only a slave until this morning," replied Honus. "Am I to regret giving you your freedom?"

"I was your Bearer."

"Don't profane Theodus with that lie! You bore my pack because I forced you!"

"No. I bore it because it was Karm's will. Even you must understand that."

Honus stared at Yim with growing agitation. "Cease tormenting me! You won't sway me from the goddess's path."

"I'll lead you to it instead."

Honus laughed mirthlessly. "You're deluded. What do ou know?"

Yim hesitated before she answered. "Karm speaks to ne. She came to me this morning. I'm doing what's necessary."

"You're only saying that to save me. Why? You don't ove me."

"I can't. I can only love the goddess. My life is dedicated to her."

"Nonsense!" said Honus. "What Seer chose you?"

"None. Karm did herself. I'm the Chosen."

"People like you came to the temple all the time. Silly girls with grandiose delusions. The Seers read their thoughts and sent them packing."

"I've the power to shield my thoughts from your eyes," said Yim. "I'll drop that guard and let you see the truth."

Honus, torn by indecision, took a long moment before he sighed and said, "I'll do so only if you agree to return to Commodus afterward."

"I agree."

Honus rose from the rock and leapt to the shore. "Turn to face the moonlight." Yim obeyed, and Honus moved until he was a hand's length from her. "You seem afraid of what I'll see."

"I am," said Yim.

Honus stared into Yim's eyes, using his fullest powers to probe the mind behind them. At first, he saw nothing more than a tired and sad expression. Then veils fell away and Yim's pupils seemed like twin abysses. Honus's being plunged into their depths. Then he saw light brighter than sunlight and sublimely beautiful. It illuminated and filled him as if he were made of glass. The experience was beyond comprehension, something so intense and holy as to be unbearable.

Honus shut his eyes, and when he opened them again,

he was standing in the moonlight peering at Yim's face. Amazement spread over his features. When he looked away, his eyes were filled with tears. Honus sank to the ground and began to sob at Yim's feet. "Forgive me, Karmamatus," he said. "Please forgive me."

FORTY·ONE

YIM WATCHED with consternation as Honus wept. She had been free of him, but by doing what was necessary she had drawn him back. Yim hadn't anticipated that consequence and feared it couldn't be undone. For a while, she was unsure what to do. Then she followed her instincts and sought to comfort Honus. Kneeling down, Yim stroked his wet cheek. "There's nothing to forgive," she said. "Everything happened for a purpose." Yim embraced Honus and held him. As she did, she felt some of the pieces of her life fall into place. The events of her journey had been more than trials; they had been opportunities to make choices. *And those choices have brought me to this moment,* she thought. She had survived the journey south and she was free again, but she felt another choice had yet to be made.

Yim held Honus until he grew peaceful. Then she released him and put on her sandals. "Let's leave this place," she said. "It's no longer holy."

"Yes, Karmamatus," said Honus. He rose. "What's our destination?"

Yim had no idea. She considered the question while Honus passively waited. Her experience that night had shaken her. The menace lurking in the temple seemed formidable. Yim felt certain it would strike back, and Bremven was unsafe. She wondered if there was any refuge from such a foe. At last she said, "I don't know where to go."

"You might ponder that question in the house of Commodus."

"I'm not sure he'll want me back."

"With your leave, I could explain what's happened."

"What *has* happened, Honus? What did you see?"

"What I should've seen before. That the goddess shines within you."

"Is that all?" asked Yim, wondering if he was aware of her obligation to bear a child.

"You're guided by Karm. That's all I know. That's all I need to know."

"I'm not sure 'guided' is the proper word. I know what I must do, but the path's unclear."

"Whatever path you take would be easier with a Sarf," said Honus. "If you choose me, I pledge my protection and my obedience. Will you, Karmamatus?"

For the first time, Yim thought she understood Karm's instruction to "follow Theodus's footsteps." It seemed that she had been destined to take his place. Resuming Theodus's quest gave her a destination of sorts, and upon that journey she might find the man who would father her child. Moreover, she'd be in charge. Already, Honus saw her as his Bearer; all that was needed was her assent to make it so.

Yim gazed into Honus's pleading eyes and knew his devotion was absolute. He was hers to command, whether she wished it or not. She could keep him or order him away, and he would obey without question. Though Yim considered sending Honus away, she knew she couldn't. She needed him as much as he needed her. He would not make an easy companion, but he would do his utmost to serve her. A pensive smile came to Yim's face. "Yes, you may be my Sarf."

Honus bowed deeply. "Thank you, Karmamatus."

"Oh, Honus, you'll tire my ears if you keep calling me that."

"Yes, Mistress."

"That's even worse!"

A hint of a smile crossed Honus's lips. "Yes, Yim."

The two passed through the dark temple, with Honus leading the way. He was oblivious of the evil presence, but Yim could detect it. She had thwarted its hunger; no blood would flow tomorrow morning. Frustration had heightened its malice, and Yim knew that malice was directed at her. Thus she was relieved when they finally reached the temple's entrance. Honus removed his chain-mail shirt and placed it in the pack. When that was done, Yim shouldered the burden and told Honus to lead the way to Commodus's. Once they were on the road, the oppression Yim felt faded until it was a mere echo of an echo, but it never wholly disappeared.

The woman in Yaun's tent began to scream, waking the Most Holy One. Gorm encouraged the count's perversions, but he was annoyed when their commotion interrupted his sleep. Nevertheless, Gorm was loath to interrupt Yaun's sport. Instead, he rose and threw on a cloak to take a walk. If the count stayed true to form, the screaming would persist awhile.

Exiting his tent into the moonlit night, Gorm gazed about the army's encampment. It occupied a broad field. Already thousands of booted feet had reduced it to hard-packed dirt, and more were arriving every day. Everywhere about him were makeshift tents or men sleeping on the ground, sheltered only by their cloaks. The soldiers were raw recruits, but their numbers were impressive. Count Yaun's domain was poor but populous, and he was emptying it of males—from boys to graybeards—to meet Lord Bahl's demands. Gorm had watched them drill. Conscripted by force, they trained halfheartedly. That didn't concern Gorm. Neither did the fact that the soldiers drilled with sticks, not swords.

It was necessary only for them to learn the killing strokes. After Lord Bahl armed them and goaded them to hatred, they would become invincible.

The massacre at Karm's temple had heightened Bahl's ability to inflame minds, and the forthcoming slaughters would increase that power. Gorm had learned from his previous mistakes, and this Lord Bahl would succeed where his predecessors had failed. The source of Bahl's power was growing ever stronger. Soon, it would overwhelm him and assume his flesh. Then Gorm's god would walk among the living and rule them, bestowing authority and eternal life upon his most faithful servant.

When the screams issuing from Count Yaun's tent suddenly ceased, the Most Holy One returned to his own pavilion. Its shadowy interior was deathly cold, alerting Gorm to his unearthly master's presence. Within the dark, a deeper blackness moved, and Gorm felt emotions other than his own. He experienced unbridled malice, gnawing hunger, and something new. His master was disturbed.

Since the Devourer lacked a voice, Gorm would have to perform sorcery to learn what unsettled it. He left his tent to obtain a necessary item. Glancing about the training field, he spotted the form of a sleeping boy. He strode over to wake the lad with a kick. "Get up," he said. "I have a job for you."

The boy sat up and began to put on his boots.

"Don't bother with those. Just come."

Clutching his cloak about him, the boy obeyed. He was glad for the cloak when he entered the Most Holy One's pavilion, for its interior was icy. Inside the enclosure was a second tent made of heavy black cloth. Gorm entered it and lit an oil lamp that gave forth a pungent scent. Then he bade the boy enter. The lad complied and discovered the black tent's interior was colder yet.

Gorm closed the flap. "Kneel," he said. When the boy did so, the high priest set a large iron bowl before the lad's knees. Then with practiced quickness, he grabbed the boy's hair and slit his throat. His victim stared at him in shocked surprise, mouthed some soundless words, and died. Still holding the boy's hair, Gorm bent him over to fill the bowl with blood. It steamed in the icy tent. With that accomplished, Gorm pushed the corpse aside, took up a brush, and carefully painted a wide circle on the tent's dirt floor. He had performed this ritual for centuries, but knowing the consequences of carelessness, he took pains to insure the circle had not even the slightest gap.

When Gorm was satisfied with his handiwork, he took a black bag from a chest and stepped into the circle. The bag's surface was stitched with spells written in a language even more ancient than the bag itself. Without ceremony, Gorm spilled its contents outside the circle. They were human bones. Gorm had boiled the flesh from them over two centuries ago. Yellowed by age and handling, each was carved with runes.

Gorm studied the positions of the bones and their shadows to augur what disturbed his master. As always, the signs were vague. Only in special places, such as Karvakken Pass, was the Devourer's will easy to perceive. Nevertheless, long practice had made Gorm skilled at reading subtle signs. He discovered several: Mountain. Temple. Foe. Weakness. The shadows of "weakness" and "foe" touched, indicating that the foe was weak. Gorm assumed that the foe had triumphed, thus infuriating his master. Gorm found no further signs, for the Devourer still perceived the living world imperfectly. The foe might be a man or a woman, an individual or a group. Until the Rising, Gorm must strive to serve as the Devourer's eyes, ears, and tongue. That, and do its bidding. Gorm was certain what his master wanted. The foe must die. And die soon.

Gorm blew out the lamp and waited for the darkness to warm before venturing from the circle's protection. As he sat, he thought. There was only one temple on a mount and that was Karm's temple in Bremven. That puzzled Gorm, for six nights ago the bones had told him that it had been destroyed. *Yet something's happened there to upset my master.* He couldn't imagine what. The impending campaign needed Gorm's full attention, but the matter in Bremven required action also. *I must send someone clever and ruthless, a man who'll command the Black Temple's obedience.* A name quickly came to mind.

A slave bearing a lantern woke Commodus. "Sire, the Sarf has returned with your ward. Shall the guard admit them?"

"At once," said Commodus as he rubbed his eyes. "I'll see them in the little hall."

Soon afterward, Commodus entered the room where Yim and Honus waited. "I see you brought her back," he said to Honus.

"It was I," said Yim, "who brought Honus back."

"It's true, old friend," said Honus in response to Commodus's quizzical look. "Yim has saved me once again. This time, from profaning the goddess. I'm guided by Yim's wisdom now."

"What do you mean?" asked Commodus.

"Yim's my Bearer."

"Your *Bearer*! How can that be? She's an untrained girl, your former slave."

"That's all true," said Honus. "Yet it doesn't alter Karm's will. A holy one graces your home." He bowed low to Yim.

Commodus glanced back and forth from Honus's tranquil but radiant face to Yim's tired and solemn one. He sensed that Yim's power—the power he had experienced in his bedroom—was hidden again. Yet he saw it reflected in Honus's eyes, and it filled him with awe and joy. Commodus felt certain that he was in the presence of someone extraordinary. He bowed to Yim. "I'm only a cloth merchant, and such matters are beyond my ken. I'll help any way I can. What may I do?"

"Shelter us," said Yim, "until I'm fully healed and ready to travel."

"Travel? You've just arrived! Where will you go?"

"Evil now haunts Temple Mount. I've encountered it before. Like Theodus, I'll seek its source."

"Where?"

"I'm not yet sure," said Yim. "Averen, I think."

"Averen?" said Commodus. "I've been there. It's a fair place. What dark thing do you expect to find?"

"Lord Bahl," said Yim.

"Bahl? The very man who caused Theodus's death? Why seek *him* out?"

"To resume Theodus's quest. I must follow his footsteps."

"Even if they lead to the Dark Path?"

"All journeys eventually end there," replied Yim. "Why should mine be any different?" Then she smiled at Commodus, and his heart lightened. "Yet that's no reason to forsake hope. So far, Karm has guided me through peril and given me a devoted servant. These seem signs that I may yet fulfill my destiny."

Commodus bowed to Yim even lower than before. "And what's that, Karmamatus?"

"The way of the goddess seldom runs straight," replied Yim. "I can't foresee where it will take me. Though I was chosen for this path, tonight I take it for myself. It is *my* path from now on, and I will follow it to the end."

END OF BOOK ONE
The story will continue in the sequel to
A Woman Worth Ten Coppers.

ACKNOWLEDGMENTS

WRITING A book is a journey best undertaken with companionship, and I would like to thank those people who helped me on my way. Richard Curtis was with me from the very beginning with advice and encouragement when the undertaking seemed hopeless. Betsy Mitchell provided insight and guidance when I needed it most. Gerald Burnsteel, Carol Hubbell, Justin Hubbell, and Nathaniel Hubbell provided the all-important perspective that comes from thoughtful readers.